The Cooking School
At Z

BY DANIEL KENNEDY

THE COOKING SCHOOL AT Z

Copyright 2005 by Daniel Kennedy

This is a work of fiction. Names, characters, places and incidents either are the product of the author's imagination or are used fictitiously, and any resemblance to actual persons, living or dead, events or locales is entirely coincidental.

Second printing, spring, 2005

Cover illustrations by Jane Kennedy
Book design by Jeff Byrd

ACKNOWLEDGMENTS

"The Cooking School at Z" required support from many quarters.

My wife, Diane, is both my first love and my insightful first reader. Our daughter, Jane, contributed fine illustrations and continuing support, along with brothers John and Brian. In Zihuatanejo, invaluable assistance was provided by David and Rene Ferguson. Aid with background, local colloquialisms, and other insight was provided by Josefina Sanchez Marciel, Virginia Marciel Villegas, and Paula Erica Islas Gonzalez, to whom I am very grateful. Any errors are surely the author's. Book design and production were capably assisted by Jeff Byrd and Melanie Saeck.

Development of the story was aided by Daphne Gawthrop's tireless energy; initial insights from Laurel White and Linda Williams; and patient critiques from Karen Joy Fowler and the merry band of other writers who patiently helped shape this manuscript at Karen's house, sentence by sentence. A debt of gratitude is owed to Gunter Stannius, a chef and hotelier par excellence, who introduced me to serious cooking years ago.

Rene Ferguson passed away in late 2003, after a long and heroic battle for life. She left her mark on people who knew her. In her memory, a foundation has been created, which will allow gifted young women from Zihuatanejo in financial need to undertake tertiary studies not otherwise available to them, comparable to community college education in the U.S. Part of the proceeds from book sales are underwriting scholarships, with the first young scholar already funded for September, 2005.

The website, www.cookingschoolatz.com, contains a full range of information about the author, the foundation, where to buy the book in Mexico or the U.S., and other FAQ.

"The Cooking School at Z" is an ideal read for book clubs, with books at a discount. Within Northern California, the author and group sales will often be available to aid non-profit food, wine, or cooking fundraisers. Speaking engagements can be arranged.

"The Cooking School at Z" is entirely a work of the imagination. No actual individuals are depicted herein.

1

I don't think Doctor Irma Shafter knew we were stalling.

She'd arrived punctually, so to kill time, Mia and I showed her some of our Mexican pottery. Then we discussed local restaurants. When we couldn't delay any longer, we migrated to our terrace with its new cooking island, which was adorned with gold matte helium balloons and vases of lilies in honor of our grand opening. The Cooking School at Z, now in business, in a manner of speaking. We'd badly miscalculated what was needed for a successful launch, and today we were paying the price.

"Oh my God, this view," Irma said. She immediately moved to the large clay pots of bougainvillea along the terrace edge.

Our guest, who ran an emergency room at a Philadelphia hospital, then looked down the hill at the roof tops of either dried palm or clay tiles, floating in a sea of green foliage on coconut, sea almond and mango trees. The celebrated white sands of *Playa La Ropa* was just beyond, only five minutes away on foot. The calm waters of Zihuatanejo Bay opened into the Pacific Ocean at the distant headlands.

We knew very well the first experience of our view. You wonder, Why on earth am I living where I do, and not here?

Exotic fragrances moved subtly on this early December morning. The African tulip tree overhanging much of the terrace has partylike red-orange petals, and a mysterious vine weaves among the branches. Its humongous white blossoms drop without warning, like orchids from heaven. One fell by Irma, who was in its shade.

"I could stay all day in this exact spot," Irma said, picking up the flower for examination. "I may never leave. Philadelphia got four inches of snow yesterday. I'd have to be crazy."

She was a fast-talking, slight, and very professional woman in her early forties. It was easy to imagine her receiving and dispensing bursts of information a thousand times a day. Her frizzy hair was held back in a scrungy that matched the acrylic colors of her dress -- the kind of outfit that would shortly go into the back of her closet.

"I know the feeling," said Mia, now at her side. My wife was wearing a sleeveless natural linen dress with a silver necklace. "Sometimes I still have to pinch myself. When are you flying back?"

"Tomorrow. Thank God you opened today."

I glanced at my watch one last time. All our promotion said reservations were necessary, but we'd been praying for walk-ups. Apparently there would be none. I caught Mia's eye, and we surrendered to the inevitable.

Mia guided Irma to our cooking island. Bouquets of herbs were in water. Fruits and vegetables were arrayed in bowls and on the work surface. I filled three flutes with chilled, sparkling rouge de noire from a Sonoma vineyard, not too far from where Mia and I had once lived and raised our children. Mia had come down for good in August. I'd come in October, just two months ago, after selling our house in San Jose, California and tying up loose ends. We'd visualized our grand opening so many times, laughing and imagining a crowd -- not the single patron we had today.

"How many people are coming?" asked Irma, who perhaps had noticed the lack of additional stemware.

"Actually, you'll be our guest today," I said.

"I thought I'd be part of a group," Irma answered. Her eyes

grew large, seeking an explanation. Her disappointment showed.

"We'd hoped for that too," I said. "There was one other couple, but they canceled last night."

We'd make one mistake after the other leading to this moment. We'd hurried the opening, had relied too much on word of mouth, and with the very high price we had to charge for such exclusivity -- half a day, great ingredients, no more than six people at a time -- hadn't factored in what a hurdle that might be, with no established reputation as yet. Never mind that this was Zihuatanejo, with so few tourists and so much competition for the food entertainment dollar.

"Half the fun would be meeting new people," Irma went on. A true Philadelphian, what she was thinking just came right out. But as someone who dealt with trauma on a daily basis, she seemed to pick up how difficult this moment was for us. Her expression softened.

I cleared my throat. "We need a toast," I said.

"Here's to your success," Irma said, graciously extending her glass. "To the Cooking School at Z."

"Thank you."

We all clinked glasses in this awkward moment.

"And to us," Mia said, turning my way for a kiss. Just lips, given our guest.

"Jeff wanted to delay another week," Mia then said, "but I didn't want to wait any more. We postponed the opening twice because of construction delays. The range and oven came six weeks late from Mexico City. Then our tile man had a crisis that took him to Oaxaca. If we waited, who knows what the next delay would have been. So welcome." She clinked Irma's glass a second time, in that disarming and engaging way my wife has, which puts people at ease.

"Actually, I'm alright with you not doing the cooking school today," said Irma, "if you just want to not have it. I understand."

But she wasn't eager for that to happen -- that was evident in her tone.

Personally, I could have taken her up on that offer, although I'm not sure how I would have phrased it.

"Absolutely not," Mia said. "Let's get started. And it's more champagne for us anyway."

"The silver lining," said Irma.

"I want this to be a memorable day," Mia declared. She touched Irma's forearm, making her at home.

Then Mia squeezed my hand to give reassurance. My wife believed in optimism, and in living in the moment. She knew from our worried discussion last night that I was interpreting our lack of reservations as a terrible omen. We'd been promoting our cooking program for a month. Not only was today a sorry turnout, but future reservations were very weak. Perhaps we never should have done this. We were a couple with very little financial cushion. This first year had to go well. And the high season, when we'd have to earn enough money to tide us over to next year, was just around the corner.

— • —

Mia donned one of our festive red aprons created by a local seamstress, with embroidery that read *Cooking School at Z*. I tied Irma's apron behind her back. The two women established themselves at the cooking island. The grouting on the tile sides had just been sealed yesterday, and I was worried it might pick up stains.

I fetched the flat of spiny *langostas* I'd ordered at considerable expense from a fishing village north of Troncones, about an hour's drive up the rugged Pacific coast. Zihuatanejo lies southwest of Mexico City, in the dicey State of Guerrero, a region where the southern Sierra Madre foothills often come right up to the ocean.

I'd kept the small lobsters nestled in seaweed, covered by a moist towel in the refrigerator. Grilled quickly, brushed lightly with butter and lime, their sweet briny taste would stand out in Mia's new appetizer. I'd pre-ordered enough *langostas* for the couple who had canceled last evening, and then some, hoping against hope that more patrons would materialize.

When I drew back the towel to show off the lobsters, Irma winced with embarrassment.

"I'm allergic," she whispered, hating to say the words. "Forgive me. I can't eat shellfish. Last spring there was shrimp in a soup base and I was sitting on a dais at a medical conference, wearing strapless, and I had to rush out of there. I'm so sorry."

I kept a pleasant face. Of course it wasn't her fault, but it was deflating. Mia actually laughed, however.

"You're being punished for sins in a former life," my wife speculated.

"That must be it."

"I hope you enjoyed yourself, whoever he was. Missing out on lobster and shrimp in Mexico is a big price to pay."

"I wish I could remember," Irma said. "I remember a hairy chest, but I can't recall the name." We all laughed.

Mia moved on to a course using dorado, or mahi-mahi in the States. The two women set to work on a lime and cilantro *mojo*. I heated the grill. I rubbed the fish very lightly with oil so it would pick up the grill marks.

"Speaking of hairy chests, my first husband had the hairiest chest in Pennsylvania, but it wouldn't have been him," Irma said. "God, he was no fun. I'd be talking to him and he'd keep walking around the apartment. You'd feel like you were talking to yourself. 'I can do two things at once,' he'd say if I gave him a bad time. 'I heard everything you said.' He'd repeat my last sentence verbatim. I think a refill is in order, to expunge the memory. What a prick. Forgive me for being honest."

I refilled her glass for the third and final time, as the bottle was empty. Mia started Irma on prepping several tomatoes and an orange habanero pepper to be grilled for another *mojo.*

"And my second husband, he was almost hairless. I realized he was just a boy. Now I'm done with men. How did we get on this subject?"

Mia winked my way. "Jeff has wonderful chest hair," she said, "but I'm starting to see grays."

I opened a button of my tropical shirt and glanced within. "I see no gray. I'm as virile as ever," I told Irma.

"Honey, I'm not the one you have to convince," the doctor answered.

— • —

Our patron from Philadelphia was no novice in the kitchen.

"Cooking is what I do to relax when I have the time, which is almost never," Irma explained.

"You should make the time," Mia insisted.

Irma sampled the hibiscus flower water that I'd just poured for her. A slightly tart drink with a red hue, Mia had made it with unrefined brown sugar, the traditional way. Irma was unimpressed, and went back to her rouge de noire.

"Now how are you going to cook the fish?" she asked.

"Well, Jeff got it from the fishermen this morning," Mia said, both hands on the counter while she spoke. "I don't think it's been out of the ocean more than eight hours. So we'll just sear it the way you would ahi, but with the skin on." Irma put the fish on the hot grill.

For today's grand opening, we were serving on seventy-five-year-old Talavera ceramics, which were hand-painted with fanciful scenes featuring Mexican birds. I brought three of them to the cooking island.

"Where did you get these?" Irma cooed. "They're marvelous."

Mia explained how this tin-glazed style of crockery began hundreds of years ago, when it was first painted by the artisans of Talavera only in two colors, white with blue.

As the sun rose in the sky, we sampled the fish with the *mojo* sauces. "Nothing like this exists in Philadelphia," said Irma. Then she and Mia moved on to the next item on the tasting menu: grilled pork loin.

At that point I cleared the dirty dishes and made myself scarce, as Mia and I had planned -- my presence would be in a secondary role, especially if the patrons were all women. I checked upstairs to see if there were any messages for reservations, as I'd set the phone not to ring. No luck.

I had things to do, but I let myself observe the two women. I felt so emotional watching Mia at work on our terrace, finally running the Cooking School at Z. I knew how happy it made her. Beyond happy. Some other realm of joy, where you've finally found your destiny.

— • —

A loving husband shouldn't be asked to describe his wife. Objectivity goes right out the window. I'll always think of Mia as a beautiful actress, wearing a torn dress in one of those classic movies set in post-war Italy. She is the character who pushes her dark hair off her forehead as she gamely barters her cherished silk stockings (but not the shapely legs in them) for food for the children. My wife is indeed largely Italian, blessed with an olive complexion that shows no pores and probably never will. I see French tracings in my wife's face as well -- the aquiline nose and broad cheekbones of her grandfather, who grew up on the streets of Nice.

Mia has added a pound or two -- far fewer than I have -- since leaving behind her spinning classes in California. She has a full, softening figure, one that's held up well for a woman in her late forties. Now she wears her auburn hair short. It's easy to keep and shows a natural wave. Her brown eyes are expressive and engaging, inviting people to open up about their lives. After an hour, people regard her as a best friend. I've seen it happen all our married life.

But of course Mia is not a European actress -- far from it. She was born in northern New Jersey (although she lost that accent long ago, thank God). Her features, when they compress in a smile, have lines of maturity that weren't in the movie. We go back, me and Mia. The two of us dropped out of college after she became pregnant early in our sophomore years -- hers at the Fashion Institute of Technology, where she had a notion of going into fashion, and mine at New York University nearby, where my fantasy about becoming a filmmaker had already collapsed.

— • —

I returned as Irma was painting a grilled pork loin with a heated papaya barbecue sauce that contained molasses, cumin, garlic, and a half-dozen other ingredients. Irma tasted the sauce with her finger.

"Oh God, I'm weak in the knees." She feigned grabbing the counter to steady herself. "So tell me how the two of you decided to do this. I need to know everything."

"First we need to move to the table for lunch," Mia said. "Everyone take something."

We took the pork and some flash-grilled baby squash from our garden, rubbed with a savory paste of roast garlic, all on a black ceramic platter. Irma opted for a *cerveza* when I ran through the drink possibilities. Mia made it two. I brought *Sol* all around, a light beer for midday.

"How did we get here? Well, our children are all out of the house," Mia began. "That's the first thing."

"Okay," said Irma. "Stop and tell me about them."

"Notes for your charts?"

"I need patient history and family information."

Mia ran through the basics. Our youngest and the artistic one, Daphne, was in her sixth and hopefully final year of college in New York City. With her, you always crossed your fingers. Our oldest, Lauren, lived outside Chicago. She had a business degree and worked for an international consulting firm that kept her on the road too much. She'd been fighting unsuccessfully to keep her wedding plans out of the clutches of her future mother-in-law, so a March destination wedding in Zihuatanejo was beginning to look like an option. And we described our son, Rowan, a cut-up as a child, and now a script writer having a measure of success in Los Angeles.

"Have any of them been down here?" Irma asked.

"They're all coming during the next few months."

"And Lauren, your oldest daughter, is how old?"

"Twenty-seven."

"You don't look old enough to have a daughter that age."

"Actually, we had our first child when I was twenty," Mia explained. "Jeff and I married young. Don't ask."

"But the marriage obviously took."

"We were lucky," Mia said.

"So how did the two of you end up here?" Irma asked.

"We'd been coming to Zihuatanejo on vacation," Mia explained. "We found an efficiency unit we liked the very first year, and we just inhaled the place. It always killed us to go home. Then when we were here last February, we learned this house was available. We hadn't been thinking seriously about coming here at all, but suddenly this was on the market."

"'House?'" Irma interrupted. "This isn't a house. A house is what I live in. This is beyond house. I don't know what it is."

"Thank you." We'd promised her a tour later.

Irma was an intent listener. It was easy to imagine her with patients and staff in the emergency room. She'd forgotten about eating her food, so I gestured and she resumed.

"We'd already realized there's not much for people to do who come on vacation from the States," I said. "Not a lot of women go charter fishing with their husbands."

"Lying in the sun, reading books, eating," Irma said. "That's all I did this week."

"Exactly," Mia said. "A half-day cooking school experience seemed like a natural. We'd talked about it, the way you fantasize. Then we suddenly had this decision to make about whether to try it."

"Opportunity comes when you're ready for it," said Irma, cutting her pork.

"Not in this case," Mia said. "We definitely were not ready. But we did it."

"Now the challenge is getting customers," I said. "We may have approached this wrong."

"Things will pick up once the word gets out," Irma said.

Mia and I smiled appreciatively. Mia then excused herself to check on a dessert that she and Irma had stuck in the oven earlier-- a *camote*, a baked sweet squash. Mia brought it to the table and drenched it with fresh cream. I got another set of small plates and served. Irma groaned in ecstasy.

"Your skills as a chef...," she said, seeing no need to finish the sentence.

"Thank you," Mia acknowledged. "But I'm not a real chef by any stretch of the imagination."

"She's being modest," I said.

"So tell me where you learned to cook like this."

"It could be a long story."

"Do I look like I'm eager to go somewhere?"

Mia reflected a moment. "I'll get something then," she said, excusing herself.

I was left alone with Irma.

"Have you stumbled across what 'Zihuatanejo' means?" I asked. She hadn't.

"It's Indian, meaning 'a place for women.' I first heard of Zihuatanejo in that movie, The Shawshank Redemption. Tim Robbins dreamed of coming here if he could escape prison, and then Morgan Freeman came at the end."

"Well, we'll let men be here, as long as you're good."

— • —

Mia brought to the table a black-and-white snapshot, faded with age. It showed a young adult couple in another era, standing with a little girl. I knew the photograph well, and precisely where it came from -- a hand-tooled leather binder, with sturdy stitching, which Mia had purchased in Florence several years ago. It was one of many photos and memorabilia from her mother's side.

Our guest examined it carefully.

"Do you mind if we go sit on the side of your pool, and I soak my ankle. I turned it on a rock when I was hiking out to *Playa Las Gatas*. I'm sorry to ask. I am completely without class, but it's throbbing."

"Of course," said Mia.

The infinity pool on our lower terrace has walls of small, royal blue tiles, with the water running over the edge on three sides. At the south end the tiles run higher, so one can sit with feet on a ledge. Irma sighed with pleasure as she stepped in, and arranged her skirt just above her knobby knees as she sat. Mia joined her. I pulled up a chair.

"Back to the photo," Irma insisted, taking it from me for a second look.

Mia explained, "The couple is Anna and Gerard, my

11

grandparents. Behind them you can make out the name of the Trattoria Monteveglio on the wall. The place has been in the family since the 1800s. It's in a little town called Bonassola, on the Bay of Genoa. Are you familiar with Italy?"

"Once I was in Rome for a week with a girlfriend twenty years ago. That hardly qualifies. And the young men I met didn't have hairy chests, believe me."

"The trattoria's still there. The town is like Zihuatanejo in some ways -- a gorgeous beach, but smaller. Mountains all around, steeper than these. When you swim at midday, the sunlight is like razors flashing down into the depths. My grandfather used that image with visitors. He had a French phrase for it, something I don't remember. The water is a pure aquamarine."

Irma returned the photo.

"When I was a teen," Mia continued, "my mother used to fly me over to Italy for the summer. I worked there with my cousins and the family. The cousins were glad to see me, because I'd bring them clothes, whatever the kids were wearing in America. The idea was to keep me out of trouble."

"I had to work in my father's office," Irma said. "He was a podiatrist. I don't think you and I had the same experience."

"I was a difficult teenager," Mia said, "maybe because I was an only child. In Italy I had no say. Since my Italian wasn't that good, the relatives stuck me in the kitchen instead of inflicting me on the wealthy Milanese who vacation there."

"And who was the little girl in the picture?" Irma asked.

"The little girl is Anna and Gerard's daughter, Emma. She became my mother. And the trattoria actually wasn't my grandparents' place, which is another whole story."

"Which you're going to tell me," Irma said, dismissing a bee.

The ends of Mia's hair danced in the light breeze. I realized she would have to get used to telling such stories.

"Then here it is. Emma was actually born to my grandmother

12

you see in the picture and her first husband, not Gerard, the one shown here. He was an Italian boy from town who died in a fishing accident shortly after Emma was born. Five years after his death, a French shipping clerk from Nice comes into the trattoria with two other young men, all of them on holiday. Anna, still a widow, serves the Frenchmen their lunch. To hear her tell it, she knew right then that Gerard was meant for her. What confirmed it was that he ordered the *trofie* with pesto, her own favorite dish. He'd been sent by God 'to end her sorrows,' as she put it. Her exact words."

"Why do women let themselves think that?" Irma asked.

"His friends moved on, but the young Frenchman stayed, only for her. Gerard, the one in the picture. He came to the trattoria every day. They quickly fell in love, and forgot about returning to Nice. But it was all too sudden, in the eyes of the older people. And, he was French. That made two strikes against them, in a town where one strike was too many. My grandmother's exact phrase."

"Gerard towers over your grandmother," said Irma.

"He was a gangly man, with a big adam's apple. Fortunately he was Catholic," Mia continued, "so my great-grandparents relented. They let their daughter marry him. I don't know how much choice they really had."

"This was before the war," I noted. I knew the story.

"It was a troubled time in Italy," Mia continued. "Mussolini had a stranglehold on people's lives. If Gerard had returned to France, he would probably have ended up in the French army. I've always wondered how much that was a factor in him staying and marrying an Italian girl. People faced difficult choices."

"Difficult choices are something I know," said Irma.

"But my grandfather was never fully accepted into the town, or by some in the family. I think he was a little arrogant, a real Frenchman. So one winter night -- they'd been married less than two years -- my grandparents Anna and Gerard, with their daughter Emma, set out from the town without telling anyone. And despite the war, they managed to reach America."

— • —

Mia had me bring out the iced coffee.

"My grandmother Anna found work in an Italian restaurant on the Lower East Side," Mia said, "and my grandfather worked in the warehouses in what's now Tribeca. My grandmother took over the restaurant kitchen when the original cook died from spoiled blood sausage. That's the legend, anyway. My mother grew up in that restaurant and moved on to get married and had me, and she had a very small restaurant in New Jersey that never was very successful. We had our issues, but my mother and I ended up very close. She died six years ago."

"You must have had a restaurant too," Irma said, swinging her feet back over the side. She gestured for a towel, and I gave her one.

"Not with three children. God no. We moved to California and I did a little catering."

"She's being modest," I said.

"I cooked dinner parties for executives in their homes. I was personal chef for some clients. I also had a cheesecake business, supplying restaurants out of my kitchen, until the health department caught up with me with all their regulations."

"And she taught cooking classes at a store like a William Sonoma, with a demonstration kitchen," I said.

"The owners were friends of ours. I put away most of the money for the kids' college. But no, I never had a restaurant."

— • —

When the radio-despatched cab arrived for Irma -- an old white Volkswagen with the Utaaz emblem on the driver's door -- I gave the driver instructions in my cursory Spanish.

"E-mail me that you got home okay," said Mia.

"We'll stay in touch, and thank you again." Irma waved as the cab pulled away.

Once our guest was gone, Mia and I stepped back inside. Some gold and white balloons, tied to the outside light, breezed in with us. I reopened the door and kicked them back out, like cats.

"You survived," Mia said, putting her arm around my waist.

"She's the kind of person we want to have. We just want it to be plural, not singular."

"I kept thinking," Mia said, "how wonderful it would have been to have other people. It hit me when we were grilling the pork loin. I almost started crying."

— • —

For now we would only be open three days a week. Looking ahead, we had one couple reserved for Wednesday, which was tomorrow, and another for Friday. Not a soul was signed beyond that point. A month ago we were so confident in our new venture, we'd joked (only to ourselves, thank God) that we might need a bouncer outside in a chef's jacket, to keep people away.

When Mia and I had started promoting in early November, we thought we covered enough bases. We'd held a midafternoon tasting for the hotel and bed and breakfast management in the area, such as it is. The few who came courteously praised the food, but we realized that no business would follow. They had kitchens to support or lucrative referral arrangements with restaurants. And we were breaking from the local custom of offering them commissions, confident we could make it on our own.

As for the restaurant owners, only two chefs and one partner had RSVP'ed for a special reception we ultimately canceled, rather than embarrass ourselves. We were hearing that they saw the

Cooking School at Z as competition in a tight market.

Another weekend we'd laid on spectacular hors d'oeuvres for a smattering of the expatriate community, hoping to build word of mouth. We made a sad discovery. Those who could afford the Cooking School at Z had their Mexican cooks, of course, but they didn't care about fine cuisine. If it were the Drinking School at Z, it clearly would have been another story, judging by what was consumed at our reception.

It was clear. Our fate would rely on *Norte Americanos* down on vacation.

We selectively distributed elegant printed cards for the Cooking School at Z, bearing our names and a phone number. We felt a minimalist approach would create an aura of such exclusivity that guests would feel they'd learned about a secret, and so they wouldn't balk at the high cost, specified in very small type. "Limited to eight guests," it also read, hinting at the finest service. When the high season began in several weeks, we would operate every day but Sunday.

We'd thought through the food aspect with great care. The American and Commonwealth and E.U. visitors didn't seem to want higher-end Mexican food in Zihuatanejo, and the best restaurants didn't serve it. Why is a mystery, but not ours to question. We'd decided not to offer a three-hour primer on tamales or the marvels of *Nuevo Latino*, especially since Mia had little experience with such dishes. What we wanted was flexibility to suit our patrons' wishes. So Mia illustrated a few staples of Provençal and California cooking on our cards, with just a *soupcon* of Mexican influence -- a small pepper that was as whimsical as the other vegetables.

"That looks like a half-erect penis," I told Mia when she first showed me the drawing. We were out on the terrace, we'd drunk too much, and the cooking island several feet away was a half-built mess on that October evening, with an astringent powdery smell from the cement.

"I wonder what inspired me," Mia said. "Certainly not you."

"Definitely not me."

We left the pepper. People could think what they wanted. This was Mexico, and they were on vacation.

Not until late October did we go public with the true explanation for the construction on our terrace. Our delay was strategic. We didn't want anyone stealing our idea, because the Cooking School at Z was such a sure thing.

— • —

Now that Irma was gone, I followed Mia back down the stone steps to our terrace. Neither of us found it necessary to speak. It is held as scientific fact by our children that their parents share just one brain, although we see many things differently.

I immediately shifted the grand opening flowers from the terrace to inside the house, where we wouldn't have to be reminded of our failure. Then I set to work on the dirty dishes. Mia took her chef's knife and pop, pop, pop, assassinated three fancy balloons, in a way that showed her frustration. Then she crouched to clean up the finely chopped onions that Irma had accidentally brushed off the island counter and mashed into the Mexican pavers with her sandals.

I know what was on my mind. Apparently it was on Mia's as well. She put it in words as she came up from her hands and knees.

"Tell me this isn't just a big mistake," Mia said.

"It isn't," I said, simply because one of us needed to say it.

2

We first came to Zihuatanejo the year that our youngest went off to college. It was Mia's idea, a reward to ourselves for having survived three teenagers.

No television or newspapers, no schedules, no calls to action. At night we could see the lights of the fishermen heading out from the *Playa Municipal*, the town beach, in their open *pangas.* In the morning we bought their catch along the *Paseo del Pescador*, or through the stalls at the *Mercado Centro*, where Mia could easily lose two hours among the vanilla lady, the herb vendors, and the *pollo* cubicles, where the long necks and heads of the scalded birds hung over the counter edge. Routines arose that we loved: lingering endlessly over coffee in the morning, walking the beaches, chatting with familiar faces.

In Zihuatanejo, the world stops in mid-afternoon. Trade and the slow-moving affairs of state, such as they are, go on hold during siesta. The weather is in the eighties almost year round, ideal for living from November through mid-April, less so during the buggier, more humid summer season with its rains. Our precious days moved in slow motion, letting us feel again. After superior lovemaking at night we slept soundly, knowing the Mexican Navy maintained a small garrison in Zihuatanejo, the country's oldest port city. Its gunboats stand ready to fend off the galleons of any late-arriving Spanish conquistadors -- that was our standing joke.

Each morning the roosters and the barking dogs would summon our bones out of bed.

— • —

This February past, we were having drinks in a beachfront cantina with a Santa Fe couple who'd been coming to Zihuatanejo for two decades. They mentioned, as a point of interest, that a particular house might be on the market. Its official mailing address was *Carretera Escencia a la Playa La Ropa S/N,* short for *sin numero,* meaning no number necessary. It was simply known as *Casa Rosalinda.* In a beautiful script that name was painted on lemon-colored ceramic tiles set into its roadside wall, which was a vibrant blue and scribbled with vines.

"We've been in it," Mia said. Then we explained.

The year prior, an English couple who lived year-round in Zihuatanejo invited us to tag along to a reception. The owner of *Casa Rosalinda,* a Señor Izturis, whom everyone called "Izzy," was introduced to us before he had to leave the gathering on some important business. He was there only briefly. He simply was letting his house be used for evening cocktails to honor supporters of a bilingual school program that taught Spanish to Nahuatl Indian children.

The organizers were skittish without the owner there because of his precious collection of Mexican pottery and ceramics, so tours of the house were not permitted. We couldn't even nose around through the time-honored trick of hunting for a bathroom, because one was right at hand at the terrace level. But what little we saw, and the gorgeous two-tiered terrace itself, had taken our breath away. Back in California, we gushed about *Casa Rosalinda* to our neighbors. We even brought some of its landscaping touches to our backyard.

After drinks with the Santa Fe people, Mia and I strolled along

Playa La Ropa. Casa Rosalinda was clearly visible on the steep hillside above our beach. I was an inveterate checker of real estate sections and home prices wherever we traveled, and Mia loved seeing how homes were decorated.

"Maybe we can talk our way in to see it," Mia said.

"What's to lose."

The owner couldn't know that Mia and Jeff Farrell were just faking it.

— • —

We were able to set up an afternoon appointment the next day with Izzy, an octogenarian widower. He was a Peruvian national with a leathery tan who clearly enjoyed my wife, and probably women in general -- that was Mia's read. He professed to remember her from the party long ago because of her beauty. He was like the cock of the walk, strutting around bare-chested with his little belly, clad only in a red Speedo and worn sandals. Mia was wearing a saffron scoop-necked dress of crushed cotton, with a cord belt, and he ogled her more than once. Mia would later say that Izzy physically reminded her of Picasso in his later years, when he became a slightly ridiculous old goat putting it on for the women.

"Come, I'll show you everything," Izzy said.

As he led us around, Izzy alluded to his mining interests, a home in Peru, and a restored castle in Portugal where he seemed to spend the most time. Though he loved *Casa Rosalinda*, he explained that he had only been in Mexico for three weeks this year. Moreover, his schedule would only worsen. Worldwide prices for whatever came out of his mines had been depressed. Thus he was selling. He wanted to find a buyer soon, and was about to list it with a real estate representative, who would charge the obligatory commission.

"It's a shame to give it up," Mia said, "but if you can't be here to enjoy it...."

Izzy shrugged haplessly. Such was life. He was an old man, and he had learned. And my wife, already admired for her beauty, could now be acknowledged for her insight.

— • —

Casa Rosalinda had been designed somewhat like an inn, but it had only four bedrooms. Izzy said he'd originally planned to rent *Casa Rosalinda* at times, but in fact he never did. He had made one brilliant move, however. He let his niece, an architect in Mexico City and a fan of the famed Luis Barragan, design *Casa Rosalinda* -- named after a wife of Izzy's who'd died long ago -- in a sculpted, concrete style that featured accent walls of pistachio, violet, and pumpkin.

Even from the outside *Casa Rosalinda* hints at the spectacular. A cobbled entrance way goes to the carved wooden door of four-inch thick mahogany with Spanish brass ornamentation. We had high expectations, from our glimpse last February. Still, we were blown away.

Izzy started us on the landing of hand-chiseled stone inside the front door. He then toured us through the uppermost level, which included an open-air sitting area with a magnificent view of the bay. Further along on that level, the two large bedrooms each had a spacious tile shower in the bathroom.

"I don't believe this place," I whispered to Mia. She squeezed my hand as she kept up her running dialogue with Izzy.

Stone steps cascaded down to the two lower levels, the stairs turning all the while like a castle keep. It was stunning the way the living spaces were open to the elements. Rooms had only a thigh-high wall of stucco facing west to the Pacific Ocean, topped by a hardwood log rail of polished *bocote* wood. The Bay of Zihuatanejo and and beyond were simply there, with nothing intervening. The

21

rising *palapa* roof work, with its large dried fronds arranged tightly over log supports, let the air circulate freely.

"What do you do in the rainy season?" Mia asked.

"We have the winds two, three times, but not so bad. You see how the roof extends, which keeps out the rains."

Standing in one of the bedrooms, we inhaled the light sea breeze. I slipped my arm around Mia's waist. I was born for this. Mia had a look in her eye too. Living in *Casa Rosalinda* would bring us the ambient sounds of Mexico day and night. The insects and lizards, smells of the sea, the sounds of the waves, even the yellow-winged, crowlike cacique on a nearby flood lamp. Had the bird flown in to say, You only live once?

Down in the second-level great room, Izzy turned into a curator. He spoke in great detail about the striking ceramics and other pottery on the shelves. We'd also seen pieces set into colorfully painted *nichos*, niches for display, a feature of Mexican architecture. That these feather-light ceramics from Mata Ortiz in Chihuahua were made entirely by hand, with such intricate designs, was beyond anything I could imagine.

"I could see myself reading here every day," Mia was saying.

"Absolutely. This would be the central living area."

"I do my work here," Izzy said. "It is like being in nature."

"I think I'd prefer to have the bedroom on this floor, not upstairs," Mia said, keeping up the fantasy. "It wouldn't be so much up and down."

"I like to move, move, move," said Izzy. "Up and down. But maybe not everyone." He touched her arm and guided us along. Touching her arm, touching her back -- he was the most caring guide. Moments earlier he'd planted his hand on her lower back, escorting Mia to a shelf.

After the tour, a Mexican woman brought refreshments, setting the tray on a leather footrest. We were all seated. Izzy got down to business.

"Tell me are you interested in buying *Casa Rosalinda?*" our host asked.

"I think we need to discuss it," I said, playing along. Mia agreed. There was no way, really, that we could buy this.

But I couldn't resist asking, "Did you have a figure in mind?" Izzy gave us one.

It was high, yes. But not as high as I might have expected.

What Señor Izturis was asking for *Casa Rosalinda* was basically equal to the equity in our forty-two-year-old house, with its single-paned windows and four small bedrooms, but on an unusually large lot. Our home just happened to be located in Willow Glen, a neighborhood in San Jose, where values had skyrocketed over the years, and stayed high, even though the stock market had collapsed and other housing prices had fallen off. Places like ours, called "scrapers" in the local parlance, were bought and bulldozed by the new rich. It was our one and only asset.

"We'll get back to you," Mia said, not meaning it.

"I'm giving you this chance, just for you. But you understand. I want to sell. The price is good. No commission."

— • —

For the next few hours we had great fun, imagining life at *Casa Rosalinda*. But eventually Mia asked, "Why shouldn't we consider it?"

Hadn't we conjectured on last year's trip that some sort of half-day cooking school concept would do wonderfully in Zihuatanejo? We could establish it at *Casa Rosalinda*, right there on the terrace.

"I would give up ten years of my life to live here," I said.

"We'd probably live longer. I look at this, then I think of the way we're living in California...." She didn't need to say more. Our lives were in a rut, and we'd talked about it, about needing a big change the way we'd come West years ago.

Into the wee hours, and again in the morning, we weighed

it from every angle. Part of the problem was that we couldn't imagine ourselves falling into something so extraordinary. Amazing opportunities only happened to friends, or their friends, or people you read about.

Calling the jobs I'd had for nearly a quarter of a century a "career" would be a serious overstatement. When I was young, I'd wanted to make films, or be a screen writer, or an author, but I took my communications skills into sales. I was married, we had a baby, then two more children. Bills needed paying.

Our one and only ship came in after I started a free shopper magazine that listed Silicon Valley homes for sale. It began as a part-time endeavor, and swelled into a cash machine once the housing market took off. The only entrepreneurial venture in my life, I'd sold it for a good price several years earlier.

Then I'd invested our new nest egg in a startup company, because I knew the founders and sort of understood their complicated transistorized invention. It seemed to make sense. And everyone was investing and getting rich at the time. Mia was dead set against it, but I wore her down. Neither of us would have to work another day in our lives when this company went public some day. People all around us -- even receptionists -- were scoring left and right. Why not us?

The company failed. We lost all that money. I deserved her wrath, but Mia was angry at herself too, for relenting. Luck had brought us our nest egg, and recklessness had taken it away. If I hadn't been such a fool, this decision about *Casa Rosalinda* would have been an easy one.

— • —

"Actually, I think there's only one question," I told Mia as we walked the beach, twenty-four hours after seeing the house. "How do we live with ourselves if we pass it up?"

"That's what I was thinking." She brought up a friend of hers who'd had breast cancer and died not long before. Before the friend was diagnosed, she was always talking about moving to Washington State and getting a teaching credential.

We'd gotten serious. We'd already concluded that unless we said yes in person, in the next forty-eight hours, we'd never get it. A decision had to be made, here in Mexico. Otherwise Izzy would put the word out, and our ability to compete from afar wouldn't carry the day, not with a unique property like *Casa Rosalinda*.

"I don't see how a cooking school could fail," Mia said. "And I know it's not relevant, but we'd see the children more in Mexico and than we do now. They'd love to come for vacations. I say we do it."

"Do you realize the risks?"

"Do you know how happy we'll be when this works?"

Our steps were making deep indents in the sand as we trod on.

Mia finally stopped, taking my hand. "How do we want to live the rest of our lives?" She looked into my eyes and wouldn't look away.

"I think we know that answer," she concluded .

— • —

"We want it," we told our Peruvian friend.

Izzy and I shook hands. The truth is, I thought it was a great deal for Mia and me. My wife was beaming. When the old buzzard wanted to hug, she donated her breasts to whatever pressure he sought.

Mia and I whooped it up over dinner that evening, drawing looks with our boisterous, champagne-fueled behavior at *La Hacienda Que Susurra*, the priciest, most elegant spot around, with its broad view of Zihuatanejo's bay and the harbor lights.

"I can't remember feeling like this," Mia said by candlelight. She glowed from drinking too much wine. "Not even when the kids were born. I wish my mother were alive to share this."

"Shit, who can believe we're doing it." My words were perhaps a little slurred. "I can't. It's not real. It hasn't sunk in."

One minute I was exhilarated, the next I was terrified.

"This is better than getting our own restaurant," Mia said. Opening a very little restaurant in California had been one of the ideas for change that we'd considered.

"Absolutely. No irksome staff, no eighty-hour weeks, no toilets overflowing in the restrooms." The alcohol was flushing out my eloquence.

"I'm not a real chef anyway. Let's not kid anyone."

"But it doesn't call for a chef. What do you need line experience for? People aren't coming to you for that. They'll want to learn some things about cooking...."

"True." Mia nodded sagely, having reached the point where stringing words together was challenging.

"They'll want to eat wonderful food while they're there...."

"True again." She was nodding in such vigorous agreement, the honeymooners at the next table were watching.

"And, that other thing...."

"Great conversation."

"Exactly." We'd said all this before, but it seemed important to keep saying it.

Mia leaned close. "We still don't have a name. I want to have the name before we go back. We can't leave it named for his dead wife." Under the table, she must have shed her sandals, because I suddenly felt her bare toes in my crotch. She winked. I love you, she mouthed.

We named The Cooking School at Z that night.

As for renaming the house itself, Izzy had explained to us that *azul*, blue, was considered good luck in Mexico. This was new to us. Striking shades of blue appeared throughout the house, including a pair of Talavera ginger jars with zigzag patterns in blue and white that we wanted to buy from him.

"Americans won't know what it means if we call it *Casa Azul*," Mia said. We were in bed at this point, talking softly, touching preliminarily.

"Maybe the Blue House?" I suggested huskily.

"Sounds like the White House. Casa Blue," she decided. And because we abandoned the conversation at that point, the name stuck.

— • —

What didn't stand up was the price, during intense, long-distance negotiations that followed.

Even over the phone I could tell that Izzy was enjoying the dance, being back in the game once again, using tactics that had built his fortune. Every day the old goat had second thoughts, or factored in a new condition to the sale. I easily imagined his dealmaking face.

"We settled the price," I argued early on.

"No, no, no, no, no," he countered, breathing excitedly.

"Izzy," Mia said with honey in her voice, "you promised. You named your figure and we agreed."

"A price to begin with. Nothing more."

We hung up, crestfallen.

"That little shit," Mia said.

Izzy tried to persuade us that another buyer had emerged who was willing to pay more. We suspected this wasn't true, but certainly he would get added suitors if he spread the word. We couldn't bring ourselves to walk away, even though he was demanding an extra seventy-five-thousand dollars.

"I looked into the value," Izzy said. "I had not done that. You came to my door, the next day I showed you my house to be hospitable. I was not ready."

"We can't afford another seventy-five-thousand dollars," Mia pleaded.

"I know your country, and where you live. I am an old man from Peru with holes in the ground that are losing me money."

"A deal is a deal," I said.

"With respect, we have no deal. You could tell me now you are no longer interested, and what do I have? I have nothing."

Mia fumed; I wheedled. In the end, we agreed to bump up our offer by sixty-five-thousand dollars. This was going to seriously crimp our available cash for getting the cooking school launched and profitable.

I said, in a sobering moment, "Maybe we just say fuck it."

"Jeff, if we get this, it completely changes our life. It's just money we're talking about. Money comes and goes. It's paper. You certainly taught us that with your investment." Then she teased, "I already have *Casa Blue* redecorated. Do you remember the floor in that big room?"

"Actually, no."

"It has that flower design set in the stained concrete. Were you listening when he explained how it was made with inlays from crosscut mangrove branches?"

"I don't think I was."

"God, it has so many beautiful touches. Jeff, this place is meant for us."

Mia described how the grand room would one day look, with rattan sitting pieces, white duck cushions and a large sisal rug. She would introduce a three-foot-high, zanily painted rooster we'd seen in a local artisan's work shed. Several of her dad's watercolor paintings would get places of honor.

During my dickering on the phone with Izzy, Mia would soundlessly mouth advice from close range, to "Stay calm," or "You can do it," or "Stay positive." When she took her shots with Izzy, I massaged her neck and shoulders, putting my head near hers and listening in. Certain fees and legal costs -- Izzy said he was learning about these, and regretted having to add them to the cost.

Next it was the pottery collection. "My niece has no place. She will take only a few pieces. I've decided I am selling my collection with the *casa*. They are part of the spirit." So off we went again for the next thirty-six hours, with the price kicking up another seventeen thousand dollars by the time we were through.

We hung in there until the end, which didn't take that many days -- it just seemed that way. I calculated we would barely have cash to do necessary construction. On the shaded terrace, Mia needed to install a large island work area, with gorgeous tile work; two commercial sinks; and a six-burner range with a double oven and separate broiler. This showpiece would become the heart and gathering place for the guests of the Cooking School at Z, which had to be five star. But now we would need the Cooking School at Z to be successful its first year. A big gamble. How firmly did we believe in ourselves?

More than once during those negotiations I closed my eyes and motivated myself by visualizing the two-tiered terrace, my favorite aspect of Casa Blue. The lower level featured the infinity pool we loved so much. Fresh water gushed from substantial Mayan-style fish heads that protrude from the stone wall supporting the upper terrace, which requires a climb of eleven steps. The *casa* had a full kitchen on that level within a cavelike opening in the house, and we would come to call it The Inferno. With the western sun, no windows, and the heat of the stoves, it could be hell in there. Two walls in the Inferno were painted the true *azul anil*, a deep ultramarine color believed to ward off evil spirits, the same mission as the string of garlic. The tiling was the bright yellow accent so often used as a companion color, as on our front wall.

Izzy deflected every attempt by Mia to inject her wiles into the financial negotiations. For this woman of great beauty and her feckless husband, the price went up yet again, another six thousand dollars, ostensibly to help pay fees and taxes that were unclear to me. Before we could object, he said he had already overnighted a preliminary sales agreement to us with the final figure.

The brief document arrived two days later via DHL. It had Izzy's signature. That didn't mean we had to sign it. So it sat on the dresser, torturing us for a day. This agreement would lead to the formal documents of a *Fideicomiso*, a fifty-year renewable trust for use of the property, arranged through a bank, which must pledge -- it's in the documents -- that the land is not being used for military purposes. Mexico doesn't allow foreigners to own property outright within fifty kilometers of its coastline, lest Americans secretly build a beachhead and invade. I'd done my reading.

We needed an outside review. I ran it past Ken Hewitt, an attorney friend. The preliminary agreement was what it was, with no land mines. We signed at his office, and his paralegal notarized.

"Would you like a glass of water?" the young woman asked.

"All the blood's drained out of your face," Mia said to me, amused. She seemed at great peace, now that it was over. Then she stepped into the corridor to take a call about a large dinner party she was doing that night, which was in crisis.

"The old buzzard picked you clean," Ken chuckled when we had him and his wife over to dinner some days later. He was legendary for being too blunt. "You wanted something too badly and you let it show, and he made you pay."

"But now it's ours," Mia said, "and I am one happy girl."

— • —

Not until the end of the negotiations did Mia and I let the kids in on our secret. Our eldest, Lauren, the one with the business head, didn't take us seriously until we assured her there was an actual signed agreement.

"You're doing this?" she said on her cell phone, incredulous at this turn of events.

"Lauren, when you're our age you'll see things differently," I said. "This is perfect for your mother and me."

Our son, Rowan, thought it was cool. "You guys will like it," he said right off. For him we were a direct flight south from Los Angeles International near his apartment.

With Daphne, our youngest, it was more complex. She and Mia spoke cross-country on the phone several times a week, not to mention nearly daily e-mails. Daphne thought it sounded exciting. But clearly she felt she was losing her mother, and me to a lesser extent.

"We can still e-mail," Mia assured her. "And you're not planning to come back to California after college anyway."

"It's so far," Daphne said. That became her refrain.

We staged our own farewell party at our house two weekends after the deal closed. It was more a fiesta than a farewell, because I would have to stay on and work into the autumn to bring in every last penny. Mia would go to Mexico before that.

We'd already flown down for the elaborate signing ritual with the *notario*, Señor Echeverria, who drafted and recorded the documents. We listed the children as secondary trustees. They had no rights as long as either of us were alive, so they didn't have to be present. Izzy had received his payment in full, as mortgages are all but unheard of on Mexican real estate.

Our California house had sold in a snap. We'd found a buyer who was a general contractor. He'd raze it to build a mansion for his own family, and was willing to wait the additional time because a large lot was so difficult to find.

"You have to come visit," we told people at the party, and they did through late October, when we put an end to it.

Starting on November first, which happened to be the Day of the Dead, we would be all business.

3

During the initial hour of darkness in Zihuatanejo, the air takes on a texture that Mia likens to satin, or the cooling taste on the tongue of Chinese bitter melon eaten in summer.

Distinct sounds stand out, few in number after the day's hubbub: a familiar melody played on a squeeze box in the small camper park down the hill; a dog aarfing in the distance; a parent's yelled instruction for a child to come in, usually in Spanish. Smells of meals being prepared, of the palm trees and parched earth and the salt tang in the air -- it all drifts to our terrace above the *Bahia de Zihuatanejo* with the nonchalance of a clock reaching the hour, indifferent to whether anyone's paying attention.

"I can't imagine not living here," Mia said quietly. Our first day of the cooking school was almost behind us.

Mia was nursing the remains of a drink. She pushed her hair back, but one side wouldn't stay. Her spirits had declined as the hours passed.

"Stop blowing this out of proportion," I said. "Today was our first day. "

"Now you're optimistic?"

"One of us has to stay upbeat."

"I think I'm just tired. Thank God we're only open three days a week to start," she said caustically.

The phone had rung once in the afternoon. We'd pounced on it in hopes of a reservation, only to be disappointed.

"How did Irma pay?" I asked.

"With a check," Mia said.

That was something to be discouraged, but now wasn't the time to bring that up. There could be great delays in depositing personal checks in Mexico, drawn on U.S. banks. The World Monetary Fund moves cash more quickly. And if one bounced, what then?

"We should frame it," I said. "She was our first customer."

Mia gave me a baleful look. "Why don't you start cooking. Do something with those lobsters. We can't save them."

"Is this how you're going to be?" I asked.

She pondered my question, her chin propped in her hand. "I'm counting on you to keep me up sometimes. I'll be alright. I was just sitting here thinking of the kids, and everything we left for this."

"Excuse me, but do I know you? You wanted to hurry and get the cooking school going, and everything would work out. Suddenly I'm talking to a different woman."

"I never worried about whether we'd have people coming. I don't know why I just presumed we would. "

"Usually you can rise above things."

"Well, shoot me then. Right now I can't."

I'd brought a big pot of water to a boil. Now I added the *langostas* — far too many for us, so some would have to reappear in a salad. I flashed through a side of squash and jalapenos. I opened a chilled bottle of a Chilean sauvignon blanc that had become our house wine.

We were just sitting to dinner when the door bell rang. I'd replaced Izzy's brass knocker so patrons would hear a melodious sound the very first moment they arrived.

"I thought she wasn't coming until later," Mia said.

"So did I."

"You go get it, and I'll put out another plate. I'm sure she'll want to eat."

— • —

I'd read somewhere that later in life, a woman's body begins to produce more than trace amounts of testosterone. This would seem to explain why Philomena Drisopoulos, a woman of a certain age, so strongly resembles a particular ex-President of Mexico, right down to her incipient mustache. To assert femininity, Phil favors long-sleeved billowy dresses of boldly printed fabrics. She is never without a striking necklace from her collection, which must have its own closet. This evening was no exception. On the north our property abuts an undeveloped hillside of scraggly brush; on the south, Philomena's place is right next to Casa Blue, which authorizes visits at any hour, especially dinnertime.

"Jeffy," she said, smooching on the landing. "How did your first day go? I'm so excited for you both."

"We're just sitting for dinner. Have something with us."

"Oh, I'm going to make an egg at home."

"We can do better than that."

Our stone stairs would make for a nasty fall, so I stayed a step below to help Phil descend, one hand on the rail, the other on my shoulder. A big woman, she struggles with an uncooperative knee. Between her and Irma, only the lame were coming today. On the second flight of steps Phil began to mumble to herself like Julia Child, and had to take a breather. Eventually she was ensconced in a chair at our table. Mia had quickly set three portions of the tomato salad. I poured wine all around.

A *doyen* among the ex-pat Americans who lived in Zihuat, Phil had adopted us. But then, she had adopted dozens. She did have a husband, Angelo, who presided over a network of warehouses and shipping companies on three continents, which kept him overseas for months at a time. He was rarely in Mexico. Phil was free to do what she'd been born for. She had a knack for getting people to spill their life secrets, their worries, their family machinations. Working like an archaeologist with whatever fragments she unearthed, she spun tales about everyone. By embellishing their lives, she embellished her own. She could be counted on to violate every confidence sooner or later, in a kindly, forgivable way. The key was to regulate what you revealed.

In our case, the relationship had another dimension. Phil's meager family life -- the absent, disinterested husband, and a grown son in London who refused to have much to do with Phil -- brought empathy from Mia. She allowed Phil to take on a protective, nearly maternal role with us, letting our family be a proxy for hers.

"So was everything wonderful?" Phil asked Mia.

Mia's first instinct is to be candid. I nudged her under the table, a way to remind her that whatever she said would reach Guadalajara by sunrise.

"It was incredible," said Mia.

"Won-der-ful," Phil approved.

"Everything was perfect. Except, we only had one person."

Phil's fork paused in midair. Finally she willed it into her mouth. She chewed very slowly, then put her napkin to her lips to buy more time.

"Oh dear. I know you were expecting more. Did people cancel?"

"The one couple that had made a reservation."

"It was the first day," I said. I tried in vain to catch Mia's eye, so she wouldn't mention future reservations.

"Our guest was wonderful. A doctor. Just the kind of person we want to have. Now we have to see about the rest of the week. We have four people signed up, total. Next week has nobody yet."

At this news, Phil stopped eating altogether. She knew our expectations, and what had to happen financially. Phil could let no bad turn in life go without her intervention. As she listened to additional details from Mia, she thought about how she could come to the rescue -- the inner workings of Phil's mind were that transparent.

"You know, the Shillings are down, visiting my friend Harriet -- and I was telling them what you were doing, and Pam Shilling was so interested. Thursday would have been perfect, but you're not open. He has some very important job in the State Department. She's likes to cook, and he cooks too -- he barbecues, actually, but he wasn't against coming. I'll call Harriet for you."

"Please don't do that," Mia said firmly.

Phil would portray us as an object of pity.

"The husband can be difficult," Phil went on, as if she hadn't heard, "but it would be two people for you."

"Phil," I said, in a deep register that caught her attention. "Promise you're not going to do that. Do not call Harriet."

Surprised at my tone, Phil raised her hand in submission. If that was what we wanted, alright then.

"This is a wonderful salad. Tell me what's in this," Phil asked.

"Tomatoes, balsamic vinegar, basil, sea salt and pepper," Mia said. "Toss it, let it sit several hours, and it's ready. The key is not to refrigerate it. Fresh tomatoes shouldn't be refrigerated, ever."

"Of course. Although why do I care? I never cook."

Phil theatrically took in her last mouthful. "It's heavenly. But then, so is your view. Look at that." In the new darkness, we still had a muted panorama of the bay, the headlands, and the Pacific Ocean beyond. The moon, I noticed, was a risen pearl.

"Your view is so much better than mine," Phil continued. "I have those two trees in the way on that other man's property, and that unfinished building with the roof I've had to look at for the past ten years. Angelo offered to buy it, but the owner lives in Mexico City and wants a ridiculous sum."

She told us the amount, and yes, it was ridiculously high, though the price we'd paid for *Casa Rosalinda* was even more egregious. This had been pointed out to us in recent months by any number of people who spoke English and lived in Zihua. The price seemed to be common knowledge. Phil had confided that Izzy bragged to someone about gouging the rich American couple from Sillycone Valley.

"The building that blocks my view," Phil went on, "has had a dead bird on it for a month now, at the edge of the roof. I'm having to watch it actually shrivel up and decompose. Tavo had the hose out again just this morning. He was up on a ladder on our patio, trying to reach it with a jet of water to wash it off, but the water pressure is so bad."

"A dead bird on the window sill is a bad omen," Mia said. "I think that's Chinese. Jeff and I had friends who were showing their house in Redwood City. A rich couple from Taiwan was going to pay cash for it, a lot more than the asking price. They came back with the wife's sister for a final look and saw a dead pigeon just visible in the rain gutter. I guess the bird's head was lolling over the gutter." Mia cocked her head for an instant and mimicked the dead bird, her tongue hanging out, and we laughed. She still had her sense of humor. "Our friends had never noticed it. The buyers turned around and left. No deal."

"More wine?" I asked. If so, I would need to open another bottle. Mia said please. Phil's silence always meant yes.

— • —

"So how is your father doing?" Phil asked Mia. We were well along on the new bottle. "Are you two still having a big battle?"

"Nothing's changed," Mia said. "He's getting around. He has his friends, and he says he's taking his medication. He doesn't want to move down with us, but I think he's getting reconciled to it. His doctor's very much on our side. But with dad you never know."

This new development had come about after her father's

most recent seizure, which happened in late September. Mia had immediately flown to New York to see him, and had visited him again in late October, further depleting our bank account. But family was family. We both understood that it was necessary.

"Are you going again?" Phil inquired.

"I'm hoping not to," Mia said. "Daphne lives in Brooklyn, and dad doesn't really have much to bring down here. My plan is she'll help him go through his things and take him to the airport, and they'll fly down here together. Some of his old pals and their wives are helping out with getting rid of all the junk he's accumulated."

"He's very well read," I told Phil. "And he paints watercolors. He's actually pretty accomplished. I think he'll like it well enough once we can get him here."

Stanley was generally healthy for his age, but he'd had two additional seizures since the original one nearly two years ago. He wouldn't, couldn't, or forgot to take his medication. A doctor friend of ours in Zihuatanejo, who was going to look in on him once he came, had shocked us with the news that sixty percent of people who received kidney transplants wouldn't religiously take their medications, so they died or ended up in dialysis. Stanley's condition wasn't that dire -- episodic cardiac arrhythmia, a late-onset epilepsy -- but he could choke and die, or September might repeat itself, when he'd collapsed and banged his head on a table edge rather severely. Fortunately one of his poker buddies found him, lying in a pool of blood from a head wound.

The phone rang. Mia went to get it. She wasn't long.

"That was Lauren," she said, "calling to see how today went. My daughter has the kind of cell phone where she can call from anywhere on earth," she explained to Phil.

"What did you tell her?"

"I said it went great. She asked how many people we had, and I managed to not answer. I don't want her worrying about us."

— • —

Early the next morning, Mia accompanied me to our dusty mini-van.

I made a mental note, yet again, to change our California plates, which would further cut the tie to our former life. We needed to have our new allegiance stamped in metal. But it required a ninety-minute drive to the town of Lazaro, and I'd been told the clerks in the *Banjercito* office spoke no English and extensive documentation was required, originals of everything and duplicates. I'd also been told that our vehicle had to be naturalized before we could register it, through a sort of amnesty for foreign cars that Mexico had last authorized a few years back. Some day I'd get to the bottom of it. Meanwhile I was driving with a long-expired California sticker.

"Don't forget the shrimp," Mia said.

"Why would I forget?"

"Because you forget everything."

She leaned in the window and we kissed. Today was a new beginning. We had a couple from Seattle coming.

Casa Blue sits on a two-lane road halfway up the hillside, with an abundance of pronounced, winding curves. Speed is king, however. Mexican drivers in flatbed trucks chase the vehicle in front, and taxis flee the devil. In unexpected places, a steep driveway will dangerously veer up the hillside to an expensive home. On the downhill side of the road, a battered cyclone fencing keeps pedestrians from stumbling over the edge to their deaths. Concrete structures rise perilously from stilts or massive foundations -- a restaurant here, a tiny open-air bodega or other business there, everything in *concreto*. People were out in number. Mexicans were heading to jobs, often carrying a plastic shopping bag with a change of clothing or other footwear. I narrowly avoided a threesome of young Caucasian women, in racerback T-shirts with bobbing pony tails as they got their run in before the heat of the day.

After about a mile the roadbed descends toward *Centro*. At the chaos of the Plaza Kioto roundabout, I hung a turn down the *paseo* that parallels a long concrete drainage canal. Then it changed into Juan N. Alvarez, an *avenida* lined with concrete buildings that are brightly painted in some instances, but more often faded and chipped, none higher than four stories, the height limit. I parked in the small lot by the *Sector Naval*. Then a short walk down the *Paseo del Pescador* brought me to the early morning fish market, which was bustling under the diminutive palm trees on the beach.

The fishermen had drawn their wooden or fiberglass *pangas* up on the sands of the *Playa Municipal*. Whatever catch they hadn't wholesaled to the central market was available here at lower prices, either on oilcloths spread on the sand or on scarred wooden work stations or tables.

I'd come for a half dozen *huachinango*, a delicate red snapper, far superior to the varieties of snapper available in the states. Each was slightly under a pound, and one was still weakly slapping its tail. These were insurance, in case the Seattle couple we were expecting for this Wednesday class was supplemented by other last-minute patrons. I exchanged pleasantries with the fisherman, Hidalgo Martinez, a wiry man with rheumy eyes who gutted them for me. His wife, Ivelisse, gestured to the good-sized dorado that her husband had also caught.

"You buy?" she asked. "*Estar dorado es muy bien.*"

"Not today," I said.

She said with a big grin, "*Puede pagor con dinero viejo.*"

We both laughed. Once I'd tried to pay with worthless coins that had been retired from the currency system, believing that outdated Mexican money still had value. For the joke of it, she made a great show of examining my currency.

"Tomorrow?" she asked, as the dorado were running.

"*Nos vemos el Viernes*," I replied. Friday. I knew my seven days.

I moved to several tables run by many generations of a single family and purchased pink shrimp caught in the night at *Laguna de Potosi*, ten miles south of Zihuatanejo, where the family's shrimp farm was in fact just a wall of nets on poles set in the water. I declined their offer to remove the heads, knowing Mia would want to serve our guests from the Pacific Northwest an authentic-looking scampi.

We still had produce from yesterday, so there was no need to visit the downtown marketplace. I returned to the minivan and drove back to Casa Blue.

— • —

The look on Mia's face immediately told me that something was wrong.

"I had two calls while you were gone," she said. "Which bad news do you want first?"

The first was from an innkeeper for the Seattle couple. It seemed the woman "wasn't feeling quite up to par," and they would have to cancel. It was a repeat of yesterday.

"What was I going to say?" Mia said.

Then the famous Harriet rang us up on behalf of her house guests, the Shillings. Phil had in fact called Harriet. After consultations, Harriet's guests from the States thought they might enjoy something different today, or at least the wife would, and so they would be coming to the Cooking School at Z. "'I *know* it's short notice,'" Mia mimicked word for word, "'but Phil was saying it's your first week and you don't have people....'"

"I thought Phil promised not to talk to Harriet."

"'He does barbecue,'" Mia continued. "'Perhaps you can do something.'"

41

As she poured olive oil into a ceramic cruet, Mia returned to her own voice. "Of course, Harriet. We'll roast a goddam Hawaiian pig, maybe he'd like that. Digging the hole, heating the rocks. An overnighter. We'll get right on it."

"You didn't say that."

"I could have."

"We could be having nobody," I said.

"Which would be *better* than having these two people coming as an act of mercy. I know exactly how Phil portrayed us. She made us sound pathetic. Harriet even asked if we wouldn't give them a special price."

"She didn't."

"Yes, I'm not lying. I was too stunned to say anything. And they'll be here" -- she checked her watch -- "in exactly eighteen minutes."

4

"We're so sorry," Pamela Shilling said at the door. "I hope it wasn't too much trouble, adding us at the last minute."

"Not at all," Mia said.

We escorted the Shillings down to the terrace, where they discovered they were the only guests. Pamela tried unsuccessfully not to look disappointed.

"We have Casa Blue martinis to start with," I said brightly. "Something a little different."

The Shillings took their seats in our cushioned teak chairs. I figured them for their mid-fifties. Pamela was a short, hippy woman with big Texan hair, and she liked to talk. Her loud, infectious laugh brought others in. Ned was bald, and carrying a lot of weight. He seemed easy not to like, and didn't smile, except at things he had to say. Phil had said he was getting underfoot for everyone at Harriet's.

"Delicious," Pamela declared. "It's like gazpacho, but it has a shrimp taste too ... and these are actually avocados?"

"You scoop the avocado with a melon baller, and put them on the toothpick," Mia said. They resembled olives.

Ned said, "I don't taste the vodka."

"It has no alcohol," I said. "It's just a fresh taste to wake up the palate."

Ned put his glass down. I suggested a bloody mary, and he took me up on the offer.

We heard about their trip to Zihuatanejo thus far, and about their daughter, a pharmacist. Apparently they'd seen the world during the years he was overseas with the State Department. Pamela sat with one leg crossed over, her foot moving constantly in an open-toed gold sandal.

— • —

"You can decide which of three cuisines you prefer," Mia said at the cooking island. "We can do French, Thai, or Italian, using what was available in the market this morning."

We were doing this to learn our customers' preferences. For the Thai, the red snapper and shrimp would be prepared using the fish sauce, frozen kaffir leaves, lemon grass and the spices we'd special ordered from Superkise, our Japanese Mexican distributor in Mexico City -- we'd send a fax, and two days later anything Asian arrived on a bus via *Estafeta*, a national delivery service. We had local coconut milk. The French or Italian would be straightforward enough.

"From what part of Italy?" asked Ned the Barbecuer.

"What region would you like?" Mia countered.

"Actually, I *loved* the tastes we had when we visited Venice," Pamela gushed.

"*Venezia*," Ned corrected.

Pamela touched her husband's arm. I sensed that he'd violated some agreement they had about correcting her in public.

"Surprise us," Pamela said. "You choose."

"In that case, we'll do Liguria," Mia said. "I have relatives with a restaurant there. It's where I started in the kitchen. And Liguria is the birthplace of pesto."

"What was the name of that restaurant we ate at when we went there?" Pamela asked her husband.

"All I remember is you liked the anchovies."

"The anchovies! So fresh from the sea, drizzled in lemon juice and olive oil. I thought I'd died and gone to heaven. That was Levanto."

Mia asked a few questions to get some sense of the Shillings' cooking skills. Pamela seemed to have experience.

"You just have to keep her away from meat," her husband remarked.

"Ned does the *best* New York steaks on the barbecue you have ever had," Pamela said. "He special orders prime beef from the butcher."

"Aged," he said. "Dry-rubbed."

"Everybody thinks it's incredible," Pamela said.

"So you're not doing Mexican in Mexico," Ned said.

"A lot of Americans, for whatever reason, don't look for Mexican food in Zihuatanejo," I said. "So we don't buy for it."

— • —

Mia explained how we would prepare and taste as we went, taking our time.

"There's absolutely no hurry," she said. "And if you don't want to do something, don't. I'll take care of it. This is Mexico. You're on vacation."

Pamela, Mia and I put on our Cooking School at Z red aprons. Ned declined.

"There are a few keys to Ligurian pesto," Mia explained, professionally dividing her enthusiasm between Ned and Pamela. "One is to crush the basil with a mortar and pestle to release all the flavor, a little at a time. It shouldn't touch steel. It takes a little more time the Ligurian way, but you can taste the difference."

Ned looked skeptical.

"This basil is from our garden. There is a variety of basil grown in Mexico called *albahaca*, but it's not right for this."

Mia lifted big stems of our fresh-cut garden basil from a ceramic pitcher and put them in front of Ned, along with a mortar and pestle. "Here's where a husband comes in handy," Mia told Pamela, woman to woman. "You and I will make *trofie*. Did you have those when you were in Italy?"

"They're the twisty pasta?"

"They look like plaster nails," I said. Ned and I were picking basil leaves from the stems.

"They're made only in Liguria," Mia said. "When I was a girl, I must have rolled a million of them during my summers there." She lightly floured the work surface, then put out a small mound of flour, adding a little salt. She formed a well and poured more than a cup of water within it. With floured hands, Pamela followed Mia's lead, working the dough. "If you do it at home, let the dough sit for thirty minutes. We'll cheat and cook the *trofie* right away."

As the two women kneaded, Pamela happily recounted her favorite meals from Italy. Ned seemed indifferent as he ground his basil, then crushed the pine nuts, garlic and salt into the mortar, per Mia's instructions. Soon Mia was demonstrating how to roll very small pieces of dough out, then back at an angle, all in one motion, to form the *trofie*. A pot of water was boiling.

"When we put these in," Mia explained, "you know they're ready when they float to the top. And before we drain them, we'll mix a little of the starchy water into the pesto. Do you remember how the pesto you had in Liguria was pale green and very silky?"

"I remember, yes," said Pamela.

"The cooking water from the *trofie* is part of that. After this we'll put a Ligurian lemon cake into the oven for dessert. Then we'll make a few crostini, for fun. After that, we'll do scampi-style shrimp for lunch. It won't all be Ligurian."

"How could life get better," Pamela exclaimed.

46

— • —

As the two women rolled *trofie*, they brought up their mothers' cooking. Ned had no interest, and wanted to get the weight off his feet. We established ourselves in chaise lounges, where we could watch the women.

"So when did you go to Italy?" I asked, needing a topic.

Just then Pamela's laugh broke free in a high register. The two women staggered in amusement at whatever had been said.

"We were there two years ago, on a seven-day cruise." He glanced harshly at his wife. I gathered he didn't care for her laugh. "Six months after, we got separated. Then we got back together this past summer. 'Give it another try.'"

He picked absently at something in or around the entrance to his far nostril and tried to flick it away, succeeding with a second effort.

"But it's not working," Ned said. "She's got someone she's seeing. A man knows something like that. She won't say. She denies it."

Why was he telling me?

Earlier I'd noticed a stale odor of tobacco on the man. "We sell Cuban cigars," I mentioned.

That got Ned's interest. We went to my display case with the glass top, containing four cigar boxes, with a prominent card specifying the prices. The Corona Especial with the little pigtail, which he chose, cost me eighteen U.S. dollars. I'd only marked it up three dollars. Ned made a production of the ritual -- examining his cigar carefully, cutting off the end, lighting it with a rolling action over a steady flame.

"Top drawer," he announced, an odd expression for an American.

"Do you know the story behind those?" I asked. To keep him company, I'd lit up an inexpensive panatela from the Dominican.

He was stretched out again, like a dictator, and I was in a chair.

"I heard it somewhere."

Well, he was going to hear it again, because we needed a subject that was light years distant from his marriage. I gave a leisurely lecture about how a member of Castro's security force in the Sixties was smoking these cigars, crafted by a local artisan. How Fidel tried one and liked it so much, he established the cigar maker in an Italianate mansion and opened a company for the cigars, branded Cohiba. How Fidel provided access to the best leaves in the top ten *vegas* in the preferred *Vualta Abejo*, and the leaves themselves were given a unique third fermentation to remove any surviving harshness.

"For fourteen years they were only for diplomatic and government use," I went on.

"A lot of what they sell as Cuban down here is fake," Ned said. His lower lip protruded when he stated facts.

"There's a distributor in Mexico City who gets them from the Cuban government. That's where your cigar came from. It's the real thing."

The women came over with forks, napkins and little plates of *trofie* for us. I let my cigar go out. Ned stayed with his cigar and didn't try the food, even after his wife encouraged him.

I was curious what this man had done overseas. Given his diplomacy, some foreign governments might be plotting against the United States out of simple revenge.

"What's your specialty in the State Department?" I asked.

"Facilities manager. Six countries before we moved back to D.C. You know what the problem is down here, don't you?" For added wisdom, he drew on his cigar.

"It's economic to start with. Half the adults in Mexico don't have jobs. The half that do, the median wage is under ten dollars a day. A college graduate earns four hundred a month U.S. in Mexico City. Look it up." He cleared his throat.

"We roll in here, we put more money on our credit cards in a week than your average Mexican makes in a year. You ever wonder what they're thinking? Behind their eyes, I'm talking about." He puffed, exhaling on an upward trajectory.

"We're going to start an eyeglass program next year," I said. "People who bring prescription glasses they're not using, we'll do something with them. An hour from here you have people with no access to glasses. How about another beer?"

Indeed yes. I put the next *cerveza* in Ned's hands, suggesting that we join the women. They were just putting a Ligurian lemon cake into the oven.

"I'm good right here," Ned said.

Soon he fell asleep. The cigar went out in his fingers. He was holding onto it, as a child sleeps with a favored toy. When I brought out the dishes, Pamela advised us to set only three places at the table.

"He doesn't enjoy food like this," she said quietly. "He'll have something later. I'll take some cake for him when we leave. This shrimp looks wonderful."

Afterward, Pamela let Ned sleep while she got a tour of the house. I prepared the bill, a simple handwritten number in U.S. currency, always to be rounded in five-dollar increments, never with change or a decimal. The charge came on a little note bearing a pre-written, personal expression of thanks. I wrote in the guests' names. The bottom read Mia & Jeff, signed in the same fountain pen. Never before in our lives had we thought ahead as tactically, as minutely, as we had in creating the rituals for the Cooking School at Z.

When the two women returned, Pamela awoke her husband with a birdy little voice. She gently prodded his shoulder, then tenderly ran her hand along his head. I doubted Pamela was cheating on the bastard.

Ned hacked and hawed as he returned from the netherworld.

He finally struggled to his feet, then put the unlit cigar in his mouth. After he examined the bill, he took the cigar from his mouth so he could speak.

"You're charging for the Cuban?" he asked.

"Yes."

"*Ned*," said his wife, blushing.

"What about the beers?"

"My pleasure." Indeed. "I only charged for one person for the program."

"I thought the Cuban was on the house," said Ned.

"It's your only charge," I said, in case he hadn't understood.

Mia looked incredulous. Her mouth hung agape. Pamela stepped in.

"*Ned*," she hissed once more. "They're being more than generous."

I had to go upstairs to run his credit card, first converting the charge to pesos. I brought down the credit slip and a gold Cross pen. Ned was arguing with his wife off to the side. It looked like he wasn't having any of what she was saying. Mia was angrily clanging pots and silverware as she cleaned up in silence, biting her tongue.

When I handed Ned the credit slip, he examined it with suspicion. "What exchange rate are you charging?"

That did it. Mia came over, making a statement with her presence.

"Just pay the people," Pamela said sternly.

"So you deducted the cigar," Ned said.

"Your experience was entirely on us."

"Ned, pay the man," his wife insisted.

"It's the least I can do to thank you for your service to our country," I said.

He removed his cigar from his mouth, to let me know he'd caught the sarcasm. "It never should have been on there," he said, jabbing a finger at the slip of paper.

Pamela told Mia, "I had a *lovely* time."

"And I enjoyed having you." She touched Pamela's arm while her husband finally signed the merchant copy.

"The pen," Mia reminded him.

Perhaps not meaning to, he'd been about to pocket it. He rolled the pen on the table.

Mia was unable to hold it in any longer. "Do you think you're being cheated? Is that it?" She had her hands on her hips.

"I don't see...."

"Just shut up, Ned," Pamela said. "Don't say one more word."

Marching Ned toward the stairs, Pamela made an apologetic wave in Mia's direction, one woman to another. I followed the Shillings upstairs and closed the door behind them, putting day two to an end. Cursed by God, I went back to the terrace.

"What did you say to him when he got the cigar?" Mia asked angrily.

"I specifically said we sold Cubans. He picked one. The prices were right there. He had to know."

"I can't believe you gave in and comped him on everything."

"It wasn't worth arguing. I wanted him gone."

"He got this whole morning for free. And he was such a dickhead."

"Well, we can't have dickheads going around Zihuatanejo saying the Cooking School at Z ripped him off."

Mia removed her apron. She threw it on a chair like a dirty towel. She moved to the edge of the terrace to compose herself. Her head was shaking back and forth, in disbelief at the way things were going. I knew the feeling.

5

After two weeks, it was clear that the Cooking School at Z was going nowhere. We couldn't kid ourselves that it was just a slow start because of the construction snafus and the sudden opening. Ahead lay Christmas, with the high season coming right on its heels -- a dozen weeks during which we had to make serious money.

Irma had come on the opening Tuesday, the Shillings on Wednesday, and on our first Friday, our patrons were three Canadians who clearly expected something else. An elderly grandmother from Alberta was treating her daughter and college-age granddaughter to a Mexican holiday. The latter was on her curling team at college and normally existed on microwaved mac and cheese in her dorm room. Like any girl that age, she had no real interest in how food was made.

"Oh good Lord," said the grandmother, covering her mouth as we told her that the bill was in dollars, not pesos, a roughly tenfold differential. Everyone was embarrassed. We reached an accommodation. I'm sure they were just being polite when they insisted they truly wanted a half dozen of our Chinese recipes, including one for lotus-root soup, which featured papery white discs floating in an anise-scented broth.

Tuesday during our second week we hosted a young chef from Santa Fe and his new bride. She clung to him like fat on a lamb chop. The chef grilled Mia, probing to see if our concept had any viability back home, deciding it didn't. They excused themselves early. The next day the Cooking School at Z recorded its first goose egg. And that Friday delivered a Mormon couple from Provo, Utah to the door. They let us know their five-bean salad back home was better than anything we'd offered. A single came as well that day, a woman in her forties who'd come down to work on a book, and she valued everything we did. We needed more people like her, and like Dr. Irma. That made a total of five people for our second week, down one from the week before.

Why was this happening?

— • —

"Americans vacationing down here won't use the phones," Phil said over coffee that Saturday morning. "They can't even dial an operator, because the operator speaks Spanish. So they need help. The call has to come through the place where they're staying, and those people aren't promoting you."

Mia and I had been agonizing over every possibility. Maybe it was Phil's phone reason. Or not offering commissions to the hotels. Were we too low profile, with just the name in tiles on the front wall? Perhaps the minimalist cards that were supposed to be so elite didn't send the right message, or weren't getting into people's hands where we'd placed them. Not enough buzz?

"If you weren't on this road, you could put out a sandwich board," Phil suggested. "But they're not allowed. It would be confiscated."

Was the Cooking School at Z too expensive? A serious possibility, but we couldn't back down on price. We were learning that operating Casa Blue was more costly than we'd imagined. Electricity bills were higher than California, even without heat or air-conditioning. Water was precious, costly, and unsafe to drink. The pipe that ran along the hillside road actually pumped water only three hours or so every night, to replenish our cistern. Once, in November, after a three-day interruption due to a breakage in the line, we'd called in a water truck, which provided less expensive water -- but it was forbidden to call the truck for cheaper water except in an emergency. Mexico wasn't a free market economy. Sewage, garbage, taxes. Propane cost a fortune. Our accountant in Centro had alerted us to stay on top of these costs. It was demoralizing, to say the least.

More than once I awoke in the darkness, shaken by a nightmare that we were broke and had sold Casa Blue at a big loss. And on program days during that second week, I noticed a change in Mia. By the time I awoke, she was already busying herself downstairs, as if getting up earlier and trying harder could bring more people.

— • —

For Mia, the Cooking School at Z was just the half of it. Increasingly there was also her father to deal with. Stanley was becoming defiant, despite his doctor's assertion that he could no longer live by himself. He was saying that he wasn't leaving Brooklyn.

Mia was calling him almost every day, using an ingenious service we'd been tipped to. She'd call a computer in Florida, let it ring once, then hang up. Within thirty seconds the computer called back, and an artificial voice asked for the requested number. The computer placed the call, then patched her in. Thus it became a call originating in Florida, not Mexico, cutting the cost significantly.

"How does this doctor think I get along now?" Stanley ranted on this Saturday afternoon, with me listening on the extension. "I can take the pills. How hard is that? I shop for myself. I travel the subway."

"Even if you take your pills, you might have another setback,"

Mia countered. "You need testing to monitor how much anti-convulsant medicine you have in your bloodstream. You haven't been going in for that. And when you have your next seizure, who's there to take care of you?"

"That's my problem."

"No, it's my problem. I'm your daughter. And we're past the decision point. Way past. You agreed to move down here."

"Well now I'm changing your mind."

"You're not changing your mind. Jeff and I have a wonderful room for you, the weather's beautiful, and you have to get here. Don't make me come up there to get you. I have a business to run. I can't pick up and leave. And if I have to buy a ticket now, it's too expensive. This is the holidays."

"And this is my life you're talking about, or does anybody think about that."

Mia reiterated that everything had been arranged -- the airline ticket purchased, his flat subleased, new filings accomplished with his bank, Social Security, the Mexican Consulate.

Stanley then launched into his ridiculous furniture issue. He had a mahogany chair with a needlepoint seat that had been his mother's, which he wanted to ship down to Mexico, along with a side table that had a marble surface. These fit in Casa Blue the way an iguana belonged in Brooklyn. But Mia relented, and promised to have the pieces shipped.

The next day, her dad informed us that one of his oldest friends and his wife, despite their diabetes and heart troubles and other afflictions of age, were inviting him to come live with them in Queens. They had an empty bedroom.

"They also have two children and five grandchildren who live on their street," Mia argued. She had an incredible memory for names, birthdays, the minutia of families. "You can't be underfoot in their house. What happens if you need care? You can't put that on them. If you're not doing well, it's too late to move you here.

You need to come now."

Exasperated after that call, even Mia's eyelids were quivering. She looked ready to scream. "When I get old," she said, "promise me you'll put a pillow over my head."

Had Stanley needed to live with us back at the beginning of the year, when we were still in California, I doubt we would have bought *Casa Rosalinda*. Under the circumstances, I was less than thrilled to have him, but I felt I had to support my wife on this. Fate determines these things, and family must step up. So I told myself. Yet Stanley had never had much use for me, the young man who interrupted his only daughter's college days, got her pregnant, then married her and took her to live on the other side of the country, with the crazy people in California.

"Let's go walk on the beach," I strongly suggested.

— • —

Playa La Ropa, Zihuatanejo's finest beach, is not for everyone.

A mile long and rather wide, with beautiful white sand and easygoing waves of warm water, it nevertheless lacks the laundered appeal of certain resort destinations in Hawaii or the Caribbean. Here, the incoming tide regularly spits out the odd fish carcass. Intent Mexican teenagers play soccer matches near the water's edge and must be skirted. Mexican families far outnumber the *Anglos,* bringing discomfort to those tourists who wish to see only their kind. At low tide, men in the shallows root around for sand crabs, while others work with throw nets, drawing them back in hopes of catching small fish. Dogs without collars trot along, fully capable of sniffing a foreign crotch.

And strange things happen. Sometimes large spotted eels surf ashore in February, especially on incoming tides. Their snakelike writhing frightens some people. At the southern end of *Playa La Ropa,* where a sleepy creek comes down to the beach, a sign in

Spanish warns not to wade into the heavy inland foliage, where large *crocodilios* do indeed lurk in the creek. Occasionally a pair of Mexican marines, dressed in white and armed with rifles, traipse down the beach for no apparent reason.

For all that, the natural beauty of *Playa La Ropa* is stupendous, especially looking out toward the headlands, which pinch the mouth of the bay. Walking the sand under the clear sky, breathing in warm Pacific air that's just reaching land, it's easy to see the big picture in life.

"Dad could die the next time he has a seizure," Mia was saying. "This is really serious. He doesn't understand that."

"It's a hard thing to accept."

"My father *is coming* to Mexico. I have to get that across to him." We waded into the bay. Mia raised her arms as a wave rushed past at thigh level. Then the waters settled into a sandy turquoise color marbled with foam. We continued farther out. "I remember so many wonderful times we had, in his little garden in the backyard ... he always had me do the picking ... and he'd go painting somewhere, and I'd tag along. Where do those times go? Why did mom have to die?"

I reached out with empathy, but she wanted none of that. Mia ducked under a wave, then headed off on a swim. I stayed and rode the occasional wave, but they weren't a good size today.

After her swim, Mia settled beside me on the beach. She reached for my hand and resumed our conversation. "I'm counting on you," she said. "I can't do this alone with the cooking school and my dad."

"You don't have to do it alone," I said. "But let me say this. Maybe it's not a good idea to have him here. I know it's late in the game, but I have to say it. If the worst happens with the cooking school, and we have to return to the States and pick up again somehow, he becomes part of the equation."

"If the cooking school doesn't make it?" she said incredulously.

For even raising that dark possibility, I got a look that could have left grill marks on my face.

"I hate to say that. I don't want to put the curse on. But maybe the status quo would be better with your father until we know one way or the other how this is going to play out."

"I'm done talking about it for now," Mia said abruptly. "Not one thing is turning out the way we thought it would, but this is going to work."

"I can't believe we're so naive, we can't do this."

"We're doing something wrong. Or not doing something."

"C'mon," I said, "we'll get a massage. My treat."

— • —

Two women had set up a white tent for massages in front of an undeveloped area with coconut trees, leftovers from the plantation that had been on this beach many years ago. We signed up. A poor photocopy of some sort of certificate attested to their competence -- the International School of Beach Massage, something on that order. The Polizia Turistica would clear them out soon enough. The two big inns along the waterfront each had *masaje* service available at far higher cost, and wouldn't tolerate low-cost competitors to undercut them.

I drew a rail-thin Mexican girl of indeterminate age, and Mia's table was tended by the mother. Neither spoke English. The girl spent fifteen minutes on my feet, back and neck, then had me turn over. Clearly she was an amateur. She surprised me when she pulled my suit down perilously low in the front so she could knead my stomach muscles, a maneuver that seemed designed to end constipation -- I couldn't imagine what else it accomplished. Then she massaged my legs, kneading them up and down, sometimes brushing the white netting inside my suit with the back of her hands. I was an old man to her, but nevertheless. A sluggish erection with a mind of its own took shape. At least I'd worn my standard-issue, baggy bathing trunks. I opened my eyes just enough to squint at her covertly, to see if she realized. She seemed indifferent, but then said something I missed, and her mother glanced my way and seemed amused.

Afterward we went to Erica's, a beach bar that has umbrellas and resin tables. Mia ordered a Sol, I had a Victoria, and we shared chips and salsa.

"We can't spend every day talking about how many reservations we have, and wondering who's going to show up," Mia said. "And analyzing whether somebody liked a goddam roasted carrot, or the way the shrimp was prepared. When did we become these people, always worried and straining?"

I would have spoken, but Mia wasn't done.

"We didn't move to Mexico to have this kind of life, Jeff. We haven't even had sex in two weeks. I don't know whether you realize. Who's ever in the mood?"

"Yes I realize." Moments ago it had just been brought up to me.

"All we do is obsess about the cooking school. I can't keep doing that."

"We have to care," I contended. "That's what our business is. Pleasing people, building word of mouth."

"What word of mouth? I don't see any."

"I know, I know. And Christmas week should be big." But as we both knew only too well, the reservations hadn't picked up.

"I think we have to go to commissions," I said.

Mia closed her eyes in pain. I'd uttered the unthinkable.

"Nobody who's come said they were recommended by the place where they're staying," I said.

"So now we're going to suck up to these managers, and offer them a cut to get them to recommend us? What happened to" -- she searched for a word -- "neighborliness?"

— • —

We took turns washing sand off our feet in the tile trough near the front door, where water runs constantly from a fish head spigot. We situated ourselves on our terrace with two gin and tonics, facing the bay and our future.

"We'll make all this work," I assured her.

Sunset was coming. The horizon had chalky tones of maroon and marigold. Wires of iridescence outlined the low-hanging clouds. The sun was molten orange. Down on the *Playa La Ropa*, the pale young couples having their first night of vacation would be baptizing their feet in the sinful cool of the sand, certain that sex would come later. The contrast with where these couples had been yesterday -- driving in a snowstorm in Denver, talking to an irascible client in New York -- only heightened their pleasure. We had been those people once.

"Do we still love each other?" I asked.

"Of course we do," Mia said.

"In what way?"

She gave me an uncertain look.

"In every way," she said. "As long as we keep you away from money decisions."

The jab was meant to lighten the moment, but it smarted.

"I was being funny," Mia said. She reached for my hand. She brought it to her lips. "Don't be hurt." She slid one of my fingers into her mouth and bit the fingertip, looking at me all the while.

"Let's go inside," I said huskily.

Mia arose.

"Over here," she said, moving instead to a chaise lounge that was somewhat exposed on the terrace. She efficiently peeled off her bathing suit right in the open air. She stepped up and kissed me. My suit came off as well, aided by four hands.

"You have sand on your butt," she said as we embraced.

"Your skin is sticky. And if anybody's looking...," I said. I'd always been the one concerned about propriety. Certain terraces and windows had a clear enough view, though they were distant. And darkness hadn't fully lowered its veil.

Mia whispered in my ear, "I thought you wanted buzz?"

6

We had this other issue to worry about -- Mia's father, who was being a complete pain in the ass with his on-again, off-again rhetoric about whether he'd actually cooperate and fly down right after the New Year.

If Stanley was going to live with us, he would need a companion at all times, at least in the beginning. Hadn't we made a big fuss that he was by himself in Brooklyn when he'd had his two seizures? Mia wanted someone lined up before he arrived.

"Isabel's the answer," Mia concluded over dinner. "She's perfect if she'll do it."

Mia and I had stayed in the same small efficiency unit in Zihuatanejo from the beginning, prior to buying Casa Blue, and it was there that we'd met Isabel, the new daytime concierge starting the winter before last. Mia liked to cook in Zihuatanejo. She tried her hand at some Mexican dishes -- fabulous meals some evenings, like *mole negro oaxaqueño* with chicken, which called for small amounts of twenty different herbs and vegetables. Recipes like that necessitated shopping at the *Mercado Centro*, where Mia could linger for hours.

Isabel, a young mother of two, became Mia's consort on where to find what couldn't be found in the *mercado*. Her English skills were far better than most of the young Mexicans in Zihuatanejo. Knowing Isabel's love of sewing and fashion, Mia brought her yards of material that couldn't be found at Zihuatanejo's big fabric store on *Benito Juarez* when she'd moved down several months ago.

Isabel had quit her position last May, to try her hand at designing and selling clothes as a business. She'd sounded very resolute about it. But in the class system of Zihuatanejo, her chances of establishing a successful business were probably slim to none, although that wasn't for us to say. Isabel had lived in Los Angeles for two years with her husband and their babies before the age of twenty, and she'd been touched by the American dream, even as she labored in a sweat shop near Maple Avenue. She'd left her husband after she discovered he had a girlfriend. She'd fled by herself with the two children and somehow returned to Zihuatanejo.

We knew that Isabel's inspiration was her mother, the woman who made our embroidered Cooking School at Z aprons and side towels. Isabel, and her mother, Reyna, and the two children were living together in hard circumstances. When Isabel stopped by Casa Blue in November to see us, she explained that her mother's diabetes was necessitating visits to private doctors that cost twenty or thirty dollars U.S., because they didn't have the national healthcare for the entire family that automatically comes with a regular full-time employment in Mexico. Isabel spoke of this burden with a hint of resentment. The mother, the children ... yes, she loved them, but it was hard. She seemed to need a job once again.

— • —

Mia got word to Isabel through a third party. The diminutive, energetic young woman in her early twenties, still with something of a figure, came by the next day. She was wearing tight jeans, a Calvin Klein T-shirt, and immaculate white running shoes -- always white footwear, always immaculate. Her lustrous dark hair, which

63

had been long, now was cut stylishly short in a North American style. On the sliding scale of who is "white" and who is not, a matter of some significance, Isabel's complexion is on the dark side, a negative in class-conscious Zihuatanejo.

"So how is your business going?" Mia asked Isabel. The three of us were having iced tea.

"It's okay," she said. "Only not so much. And my mother, you know, with the doctors."

With her command of English, Isabel could probably earn four hundred U.S. a month at a hotel, more than twice the wage paid to ordinary Mexican resort staff. Mia and I had already determined that we would make an offer far better than the going rates, which seemed almost immoral. It would be an extra expense, but in the end, it wasn't going to break us. The Cooking School at Z would catch on or it wouldn't.

But would Isabel do it? Taking my cue, I excused myself at the appropriate time so the two women could talk.

Mia briefed me after Isabel left. "She's going to talk to her mother about it. Her mother would have to assume responsibility for the two children during the day. I'm not sure how they're working it now."

But taking care of Isabel's children proved to be only one issue with Reyna, the mother -- this was the update we received two days later. What also mattered was the propriety of her daughter being a living assistant for this unknown man. Reyna had never even met us.

As a sign of respect, Mia suggested we visit Reyna in her home.

"I get the feeling this is a delicate matter," I said to Mia.

"Listen, it's not the greatest job in the world for this girl, but the money's good. Dad will be wonderful with her. It's us he fights with."

I must have looked skeptical.

"Trust me, the worst thing he might do is talk her ear off. And

Isabel would have a ton of flexibility with her schedule, which she might want. She wouldn't have that anywhere else." The upper-class Mexican households in Zihuatanejo were notorious for being hard on their help, and certainly hotel managers weren't going to offer flextime the way we could.

— • —

Three days later, Mia and I headed north through Zihuatanejo, past Ixtapa, and on to the inland village of Barrio Viejo. We rode a *microbus*, a bread truck sized vehicle that we'd transferred to in *Centro*, where Isabel had come to meet us. Isabel would have to make this hour-long trip each way, but that would be true for any job she found in *Playa La Ropa*. We wanted to see exactly what this trip was like.

Once off the bus, the three of us walked down a dirt lane past several one-story dwellings. Pigs and chickens went about their lives. Trees grew in the nearby foothills, but here on the flat, dry land, only brush grew outside the yards.

We went through the dilapidated wooden gate to the dwelling that Isabel and her family now called home. Isabel had spent her own money, she'd once explained, fixing up their last place. But their landlord had refused to reimburse her as promised for the paint and other materials, so they'd moved out as a matter of principle.

Their yard was hard-packed dirt, with one each of certain plants and trees: papaya, banana, lime and guava trees, and herbs such as *epazote*, mint and *albahaca* grown close to their two-room shelter of rough masonry. The walls were gray. Wooden logs supported the shed-style fiberglass roof. A pile of worn truck tires next to the house was not supposed to be there, Isabel explained, but the landlord hadn't come for them. An extension cord brought one light bulb into each room, hanging unadorned from a rafter.

Isabel introduced her girls, Griselda and her younger sister, Lucy, who got hoisted into her mother's arms to meet us. They were all eyes.

Reyna was a short woman, in her fifties, dressed in a white blouse and a red skirt for this important occasion. She wore an apron and large hoop earrings. Her hair was in a bun. She spoke no English, and our Spanish was inadequate, so Isabel translated.

"My mother says she remembers you bringing me fabric, and how beautiful it was," Isabel said after the initial introductions.

"It was our pleasure," Mia responded for translation, "for all the help you gave us. And the aprons are very, very popular. We need to order more, because people will want to buy them to take back to the States." We'd cautiously held back on investing in inventory.

The kitchen and eating area were a narrow strip across the front of the dwelling, beneath a roof extension, with a concrete slab below. Isabel and her mother insisted that we sit at a pitted table with a formica top.

Reyna began to slit the shells and clean out the veins of the shrimp. She removed the innards from the heads of the shrimp, but left the heads on. She accomplished this laborious task in a sink area that did not have running water -- she had buckets to work with, drawn from the only available source, the spigot on the side of the house. Isabel's children played nearby, always watching us. Lucy finally let Mia hold her in her lap. As we discussed their history in embroidery and sewing, Isabel chopped tomatoes, onions, and garlic, worked ground cloves, cumin, salt and pepper with a stone mortar and pestle.

Reyna's concern about her daughter caring for Stanley needed to be addressed obliquely, so Mia eventually spoke about our family, including her father. Isabel translated. Reyna nodded a great deal and smiled at times, seemingly unconcerned. No one ever peeled shrimp more slowly. All mentions of Stanley -- how he sold shoes much of his career, the beautiful watercolors he painted, his reassuring ways with Mia growing up -- were currency that both women no doubt understood.

Isabel took down a twelve-inch skillet hanging from a nail. She heated a little vegetable oil on their propane stove, adding all her ingredients. Then she wiped her hands and brought out some of her creations -- embroidered pantaloons, aprons, skirts and dresses. Next came some of Reyna's tablecloths, napkins, and clothing. They were simple, which was their charm. Reyna did much of Isabel's embroidery, sitting beside a lime tree in the yard.

"It's all very beautiful," Mia said. "Regardless of whether you come to be with us," she continued, "we should have some of these things available for our guests to buy at the cooking school, in addition to the aprons and towels with our name on them."

Isabel translated, which clearly pleased Reyna.

"You have a lovely name," Mia said to the mother.

After Reyna proudly listened to the translation of that remark, Isabel explained that it meant "queen," and had been given to her because she'd been born on January Sixth, a more significant date in Zihuatanejo than Christmas Day.

I'd noticed from the moment we'd arrived a plastic bag of chicken parts sitting in the sun against the wall, and Isabel took it now for preparation. It might turn our fragile stomachs into clenching, heaving organs of misery for a whole week, or it would be fine. How could we know?

"That's not for us, is it?" I said. "Too much food, Isabel. We won't be able to move."

"No?"

"No, please," Mia added. "You're so gracious, but we can't eat that much. Save it."

And save us from an embarrassing moment.

— • —

The shrimp, cleaned in their shells, went into a large saucepan with all the other ingredients and water and were left to simmer. A pot of water was put on to boil for maize. Reyna finally joined us at the table.

"My mother would like to tell you about El Arracadas and her own life," Isabel said.

Reyna nodded and began to speak with soft-spoken dignity, using her hands occasionally, allowing her daughter to translate.

"El Arracadas was very handsome, with a mustache and one earring. He and his friend with white hair who was from elsewhere in Mexico were holding meetings, because they wanted better lives for the people.

"They had no guns," Isabel went on with the translation, the mother and Isabel alternately talking. "They were like Don Quixote and his friend, something like that. My mother was sixteen. This was not here, but in a little village near Pantla which is not so far. The government heard about this, and soldiers came and they shot the people at the meetings, and they shot the Indians. They came with lists and pulled people from the villages and killed them. She was running in the hills with no shoes, my mother is saying. When she stopped at Pantla, she saw many people carrying the bodies."

"When was this?" Mia asked.

"Maybe forty years ago," Isabel said, not needing to ask her mother.

For a moment I'd thought it was in more recent times. Little dolls of Zapatistas were sold for a few dollars in several stores in *Centro,* holding stick guns and dressed in black. Guerrero was a tough, impoverished state.

"I had been forced to marry a man and have his babies," Isabel said, now speaking in the first person for her mother. "One day I was making tortillas, and the government soldiers came through the bushes. They were looking for my husband. I told them where he was, in a meeting."

"She told the soldiers?" I asked, to make sure I'd heard right.
"*Si.*"

Isabel injected her own low opinion of her father and his evil mother, Isabel's grandmother, now long dead, whose home on a coconut plantation was a shelter for drug sellers. Her father was very bad to her mother, and beat her. Reyna looked on, nodding. She understood some of what was being said in English. She had wanted him dead, and hoped the soldiers would kill him. But he escaped and lived.

After the movement was squelched, the young Reyna was forced to bear four more children under the watchful eye of the grandmother, who did not want her taking herbs to prevent the births. "She lived like a Cinderella," Isabel translated in a voice as soft as her mother's. But when she was thirty-two, pregnant with Isabel, she escaped with the two youngest girls to Mexico City. There they made a better life. At this juncture, Isabel went inside for snapshots that showed a nice house, enabled by one of her mother's employers -- she worked several jobs -- a man who owned an automobile parts company and had a good family.

We were served the shrimp in its sauce. We peeled them as we went -- the shells were left on to add flavor, Reyna said -- and we ate with spoons and spoke of other things. I had the sense that El Arracadas was the love of Reyna's life, her Don Quixote. He'd been shot by the soldiers, and his white-haired Pancho had been hung from a tree, so long ago.

Isabel at one point broke into song with the words from a *corrida*, a folk song about El Arracadas, to demonstrate how popular he'd been. Soon after, she excused herself to dress. She was filling in tonight as hostess on a dining terrace at a small hotel, for a friend who was sick. We conversed with Reyna -- the language barrier kept it limited -- complimenting her, asking her to identify all her herbs in the yard. The girls stuck with us as we looked at plants, Griselda casually holding hands with Mia, the littler one engaged with a cat.

"Isabel," Reyna said, patting her heart. "*Ella es mi princesa.*"

Finally Isabel emerged from the darkness of a room. She'd showered under the hose, and washed her hair, and wore a full-length white dress of her own creation, platform heels, and red lipstick, prepared to move like an angel among the tourists enjoying their dinners, inquiring if everything was fine with their meals.

"You should have told us you were working tonight," Mia scolded her on the *microbús*. "We would have driven out here."

"It's nothing," Isabel explained.

On the ride back to Centro, the bus windows were down. The cloying late afternoon heat was blowing through, making it necessary to speak a little louder. Isabel said that she thought her mother would be accepting of the position that had been offered.

"Do you want to give this job a try then?" Mia asked.

Indeed she did.

7

It was still dark when Mia stole out of bed the next morning. She thoughtfully didn't flush, but I was awakened by the squeak of a louvered closet door as she got her robe. Just then a rooster crowed not far away.

"Where are you going?" I whispered.

"I can't sleep anymore. Stay in bed." She kissed the side of my head, then left.

I felt compelled to go down and join her in the Inferno, as we called the inner kitchen. This was going to be a difficult, momentous day for us. We took a French press of coffee and a basket of toast to the terrace. Mia brought a jar of her tart lime marmalade, made with tiny *limón agrio* and the barest minimum of sugar. It could pucker the lips of the dead.

We said little in the early going. Around us, every sound resonated in the silence: a knife edge on ceramic, a cup set down, waves cracking on the beach. The rich aroma of the coffee was welcome. A mildly sweet, floral air still lingered, soon to be banished by sunrise. The dozen or so sailing yachts moored off *Playa La Ropa* were ghostly gray on the uncolored surface of the calm bay, as there wasn't enough light to distinguish the greens, blues, and maroons of their sail cloths. The only thing black and white was our need for more patrons, what with Christmas almost here, and the high season on tap right after.

"I was up at three," Mia explained. "I couldn't get back to sleep."

"Have a lot of coffee," I said, like a general on invasion day. "Today we sell."

That brought a look that said she was going to try, but it wouldn't be easy. We'd talked through this business of commissions. Today we'd hit the hotels.

"Say it," I said. "Whatever it is, say it. I see it on your face."

"This is absolutely the most hated thing I can think of. Making sales calls."

"You fund-raised shamelessly for our kids' schools. You brought things back to Macy's without receipts and lied like a President. Why is it so hard to make a business sales call in your own interest? I don't understand that. This is a matter of survival."

She shrugged, unmoved by the question.

"We shouldn't be having to do this."

"But we do have to do this. You're being illogical. And you take rejection personally, even though it isn't."

"Everything is personal. If I'm standing there, talking to someone, and they say no to me, it's personal."

"We'll try a few places today," I said, "and see how it goes. If one or two end up referring people, we're ahead of the game."

Mia had her coffee in both hands, brooding.

"I never thought we'd have to do something like this when we were back home, planning to move here."

"Honey, *this* is home."

"Right now it doesn't feel like home. I'm sorry if you don't want to hear that."

"The cooking school is going to work." It was my duty to be the voice of determination. We alternated in that role.

"I know," she said unconvincingly. "Listen, I'm looking for you to take the lead with all your bullshit. I'm not going to be the one making the pitch."

"But you're coming in with me. You have to."

"I'm coming, but you're talking. That's your job."

Indeed. With my homes-for-sale magazine, I'd made calls every day on real estate agents. I also wrote ads, sales proposals, and slobbering features about supposedly wonderful communities that were an abomination, keeping my hand in with the writing even after our tiny staff grew to a dozen.

"Today is all about branding," I reminded Mia. "It's what we were doing when we designed the little cards about the cooking school. It's having those beautiful ceramic tiles saying 'Cooking School at Z' in the front wall. It's all branding."

"Don't patronize me."

"*You* are the brand. You -- not me. I'm a hand shaker and a food soldier."

"Please. It's too early to try to be funny." Irritated, she tried to cuff me, but I moved my head. At least she was smiling, albeit reluctantly.

"The Cooking School at Z is about Mia and about cooking. Be yourself, don't cower behind me. What you need to do -- don't hit me -- is make these calls wearing your apron. And we have to bake some of your lemon cakes to give out."

"You said that last night."

"And I'm saying it again. It's early. We have plenty of time."

"We'll be like the husband and wife team who did the termite inspections on our house in California. Is that it?"

"If the last two weeks taught us anything, it's that we have to be realistic. And we need to get Phil on our team. I should have thought of that before now."

"*You* want to involve Phil?"

"She has connections. It's one thing to cold call a hotel manager, it's another to have an introduction."

Mia obviously couldn't believe what she was hearing.

"Phil's an early riser," I said. "I'll get her over here for coffee. I

73

should have thought of this before." Actually, by contorting myself in the chair, I saw a window that was lit at Phil's place just next door. I went inside and called her. Phil agreed to come shortly.

Waiting for her at our door, I noticed a pickup truck beside the vacant property on our other side. A surveying team was already at work. Maybe we'd be getting some neighbors. That would be an improvement. People occasionally tossed trash there, and plastic bags often nested in the raggedy scrub brush and trees.

Phil finally arrived in fuchsia, head to toe, ready for an early doctor's appointment. It was just after eight. She believed she had ringworm, and pulled up her pant leg at the table to show us the symptom.

"There's a scab in the center of the ring," Mia noted. "It's something else, not ringworm."

"Perhaps I shouldn't go then," Phil said.

"When did you become a ringworm expert?" I asked Mia.

"I know because I raised three children. But you should go and have it checked."

With Phil pressed for time, and three sales calls lying ahead of us on this first effort, Mia got right to the point.

"Phil, we're going to do something today you originally suggested," Mia said.

Phil perked up. She began to fiddle with her Guatemalan necklace of pounded tin, whose provenance she had once explained.

"We're going to try offering a commission," Mia said, "to the owners and the managers and the concierges -- whoever's the key person on site."

"It's what I advised from the beginning."

"You offered to arrange some introductions, speak with people you know at the hotels."

"It's exactly the right thing," Phil said.

"Right now we have five reservations for this week, which is one less than we've been averaging. We can't keep operating at that level. It's already the week before Christmas."

"If you help us, Phil, you have to work with us closely. We had that experience with Harriet's guests, which we asked you not to do. We can't have you making deals on our behalf. I'm not trying to be rude."

Phil made a sly face. "I'm always controllable, Jeffy, if it's the right man." Her smile broadened. "I would never do anything to hurt you kids. I think it's just wonderful what you're trying to do here, and I tell that to *everybody.* And if you didn't have Pamela and Ned that day, you would have had no one, so don't be bitchy." She was pointing at me like a school marm.

Before leaving, Phil promised to place several calls on our behalf after her doctor's appointment. Mia and I pressed ahead with our plan for today, figuring we'd cut our teeth on several properties where Phil lacked connections to grease the way.

— • —

Even before Phil had arrived, Mia whipped up three of her Ligurian lemon cakes, baking them in ten-inch spring form pans. The olive oil, in lieu of butter, produces a surprisingly light texture, springy and moist, and a very different flavor. Fresh raspberries on top would have been authentic, but this wasn't Italy. After Phil departed and we pulled them from the oven, Mia enlisted me to help decorate each cake with an arrangement of very tiny basil leaves from our garden, set along a pencil-like tracing of raspberry jam. The design suggested vines with foliage.

We headed first to *Casa Nueva*, a small inn close to our home. Mia and I knew next to nothing about the reclusive owners. They drove what was possibly the only Buick LeSabre in Mexico, always in a stately manner, with the assumption that there were no other drivers on the road. More than once we'd braked suddenly to avert catastrophe as their green sedan, washed and shining, emerged from their blind driveway from up the hillside. Looking at each other through windshields, startled at near accidents, had been the sum total of our acquaintance. I set our minivan's transmission in first gear and climbed their steep drive. Mia put on an apron as we got out, muttering to me about it. She brought a cake.

We introduced ourselves to the husband, Harold Bradford. His wife Elizabeth was back in New Hampshire, it seemed, where they'd run the White Mountain Inn, which Elizabeth had inherited from her father. They'd sold it and come here two years earlier. The word on the street, in the gospel according to Phil, was that Elizabeth ran a tight ship.

"We're your neighbors, from Casa Blue right down the road. I think we invited you to our opening party last month, for the Cooking School at Z. It's something some of your guests would probably enjoy."

Harold informed me that they had a no-commissions, no-reference policy. Guests consulted the voluntary reviews written by prior guests in a big ledger.

"Perhaps we could leave our card next to the book. See how it goes."

"The Cooking School at Z isn't a restaurant."

"No, it isn't actually. But we would just leave cards," I said.

"That would imply endorsement," Harold said, clearly uncomfortable. I had the sense that Elizabeth had laid down the rules, and he wasn't going to screw with them.

"You should come yourselves some time," Mia said. "Just call. We'd love to have you both. And this is for you," Mia said, offering the cake.

"Elizabeth's the one who eats sweets. It's wasted with me." He sounded apologetic.

"You could put it out for your guests, with a card to indicate where it came from," I suggested with a winning smile.

He seemed to have problems with that as well, but kept quiet about it. He accepted the cake. I had the feeling he'd serve it to guests with coffee, or give it to staff.

"We'll come back," I said, "just to introduce ourselves to your wife."

"She'll be gone another two weeks," he said.

"We'll keep an eye out," I said pleasantly.

We returned to the minivan.

"That was a stellar beginning," Mia said as we got underway again.

"Part of sales," I said. "We'll try his wife when she gets here."

Then we swung by the Four Winds, the only lodgings near *Playa La Ropa* with a blatantly English name. It drew customers skittish about Mexico, trusting a name that sounded All-American. It had eight units, with blue trumpet vines scaling its walls, their yellow-throated flowers and large rough leaves rejoicing in the full sun. I hoped we too would soon have cause to rejoice. We often saw their clientele with distinctive red-and-white striped towels, walking to *Playa La Ropa*. Most were middle-aged or older. In fact, their guests invariably looked ill at ease in their Mexican environment, as if they were wondering why there wasn't jitney service in candy-striped carts.

Today Four Winds was being run by a prim Mexican woman with a pale complexion, hinting at Castilian blood lines. Her name was Señora Estevez. She said the owners were not there, but who knew? This was the State of Guerrero, in a nation with its fair share of kidnappings. Staff were trained to tell any Mexican strangers inquiring if the owner was home, *no se encuentra*, which translated as, "they don't find him," which was no answer at all. The wealthy owner of one tiny luxury hotel, with just four units high on a ridge, pretended to be his own hireling; several hotels were impenetrable without an electronic guest code, and wouldn't answer a buzzer from people not staying there.

"We'd be pleased if you'd recommend the Cooking School at Z

to some of your guests," I said to Señora Estevez.

"It's for people who enjoy cooking and good conversation," Mia added.

"There's a commission we give for referrals." I briefly explained how it would work. The words seemed to go right past her, although she understood English well enough.

Señora Estevez accepted the cake respectfully. Our cards were accepted, but received the same fate. She had little expression.

"I'll speak with the owners," she finally said.

"Or we're happy to work just with you," I said. If she interpreted that to mean commissions might accrue to her direct benefit, she was on the right track.

"We will see," she said. Sales call ended.

We turned heel. "We'll never see anything from her," I muttered as we returned to our vehicle. Why the frigid reception?

Phil later determined that we had overlooked Señora Estevez when inviting certain managers -- her peers by position, although some of the Mexican invitees had lesser blood lines -- to one of the pre-opening receptions. Word had gotten to her. We should expect payback for the rest of our lives.

"Three strikes and we go home?" Mia asked in the minivan.

"Those were aberrations. This is the one that counts."

We parked in the secured area at *Villa Real*, Zihuatenejo's largest hotel, with seventy-some rooms. A victory here would be everything. *Villa Real* sits at the midpoint of the *Playa La Ropa* beach, a collection of two-story, pricey suites that are well shaded, with spa and tennis courts, attracting wealthy international clientele seeking seclusion and luxury. The *VR* guests park themselves during the day on chaise lounges, in the shade of small *palapas* just within the roped-off property line. *Exclusivo*, said signs in the sand.

Standing by our mini-van, Mia removed her apron.

"What are you doing?," I asked.

"I'm not walking in there with that on."

We took a lemon cake and headed to the front desk like any two civilians.

"Good morning," I said to a scrubbed-looking young Mexican woman, a twenty-something who seemed to smell right off that we weren't guests or about to be. "Where would I find Heinrich?"

I'd reconfirmed his name on their web site, but in fact the general manager of the largest hotel in Zihuatenejo holds a position of such authority that his name is widely known. Heinrich Horsting had a reputation as a decent man and employer. I used his first name to imply that he and I were already acquainted.

"Yes. What is your business?" She was very pleasant.

"Actually it's a personal matter. It's a gift." That wily response often outmaneuvers the gatekeepers.

"I'm not sure if Señor Horsting is on the property. I can accept the gift for him here," she said.

I leaned in. "It needs to be delivered in person. There's a message with it."

She looked now at my wife, who should have provided supportive eye contact to my questioner. Instead she was pretending a great interest in a lion sculpture off to the side. And she was holding the Ligurian lemon cake as if it were a ticking thing that needed to be abandoned before it exploded.

"Maybe you shall see Josefina," the woman said neutrally, not wanting to get mixed up any further in this matter. She leaned forward slightly in her embroidered dress and indicated the concierge desk down the corridor of quarried tile.

"I hate this," Mia said as we went where we were sent. "Can't you just be honest?"

"I am being honest. It is personal, and you are carrying a gift." We fell silent, as we were already within earshot of Josefina, who was dressed like the other woman. She was wrapping up a call. Beside her station were two large pots, glazed yellow, which held a Mexican variety of poinsettia that has cascading small red blossoms.

She hung up soon enough.

"Josefina," I said, making a point of not looking at the brass nameplate pinned to her blouse, "we have a gift for Heinrich. Is he on the property? There seems to be confusion about that."

"Who shall I say is calling?" She looked at Mia, and the cake, and the two women acknowledged each other. I wondered if the game was up already.

"Jeff," I said. "And Mia." No last names.

"Señor Horsting will know you?"

"I certainly hope so." I smiled so broadly, she should have wondered if Heinrich and I went way back to school days together.

The logical next question would be *verboten* in the polite environs of Mexico -- exactly *how* did I know Señor Horsting? Now she faced a fork in the road. Josefina could summon Señor Horsting and ask us to have a seat, or she could try again to get us to leave the cake with a note, which would verge on rudeness, since she had already conceded that Heinrich might well be on site.

Josefina took a handheld radio unit from her desk -- the kind I'd seen on the waistbands of the other staff -- and asked for Señor Horsting in Spanish. There was a reason she'd been promoted to concierge. Riffling through her desk so she could justifiably have her face down, she spoke softly, quickly, to another woman, perhaps a secretary, so that her high-speed Spanish would be impossible for us to interpret.

"She says she does not know where Señor Horsting is," Josefina told us. "Maybe you leave your cake with a note, and I will see that he gets it." She looked from one to another of us, with the regret required by the occasion. I smelled evasion.

"We could wait a minute, if she wants to find out for sure."

Josefina picked up the radio intercom once again and spoke more quickly, with fewer words. I could feel Mia wanting to bolt.

"She thinks that maybe Señor Horsting is in a meeting."

But now, coming down the hall on some mission or other, was

a stocky, dapper fellow. He was wearing an open-necked shirt and a lightweight sport jacket that was perfectly tailored. His features suggested German lineage, especially the fleshiness around the mouth and neck. Josefina was pretending not to see him, but he was looking our way, ever vigilant.

On her own, Mia sidled over to that side of the wide corridor. The consummate professional, Heinrich of course paused courteously for a woman with a cake.

"Mr. Horsting?" Mia asked, even though he looked several years younger than us.

"Yes. Hello. How are you?" He smiled easily.

"I don't know how I am, to tell you the truth," Mia said. "I made this cake for you this morning. I was just about to think I wouldn't be able to give it to you, and you happened along. Call it good luck."

Heinrich glanced at Josefina for an intelligence report, but Josefina didn't chance it, with us looking on. I hung back, not to complicate the exchange.

"I'm sure there's a reason I'm lucky to get this cake," Heinrich said amiably.

"There is," Mia said.

I couldn't see my wife's expression from my angle, but I could imagine it. I'd seen her turn on the charm many times.

"Actually, my husband and I operate the Cooking School at Z, up on the hill."

"Certainly," he said. It would be his business to know about the cooking school.

"And I thought, how can I introduce myself to you and get a few minutes of your time? So I decided I would make you a cake and deliver it myself."

"Well, that is very nice," he said. Mia clearly didn't put him off. "Come, we can sit for a bit. I have a little something to do, but we let that wait." He and I shook hands as I hurried over and introduced myself as the husband.

Heinrich Horsting's office was surprisingly small, in a warren of even smaller offices behind the front desk area. It did afford him a broad window view of the beach, where he could check up on guests and observe the open-air bar under a broad *palapa* roof.

"Now you tell me," he said nicely, having pulled out a chair for Mia, and indicating one for me, and finally taking his own, "what is this wonderful cake?" He accepted the cake into his hands as Mia extended it across the desk.

"Ligurian lemon cake," Mia said.

"It's very nicely presented, yes." He set it down as if it had far greater value than its ingredients. "Our guests, you know, here in Mexico they look for a lighter dessert. So you come to tell me about your cooking school? How is it going for you?"

I was about to answer, but Mia cut in.

"Not so good, actually," said Mia. "Each day I wonder what we need to do differently so more people will discover us. The ones who seek us out have a wonderful experience. But the cooking school is new, and I thought everyone would flock to us. I know cooking better than how to build a business in Mexico."

"Well, I heard a good report from someone who knew one of your guests. You also had a young couple ... he was a chef I think? Maybe from Santa Fe?"

"They came last week."

"I should tell you that his girlfriend said she got a little sick in the stomach. She was saying to staff that it happened at your cooking school."

"What?" Mia and I blurted out at almost exactly the same moment.

"Actually, I think that is not the case," Heinrich said, "because they were out several nights in the town. She wanted an authentic experience, is what she told Josefina."

"So she was blaming it on us?" asked Mia.

Heinrich acknowledged this.

"Are they still here?"

"No. She is gone, and her boyfriend. I don't think they told so many people except here. She had to stay on the property."

"We use bottled water to wash everything. Even the limes. We're very particular."

"Here as well," Heinrich said. "I sometimes have guests who blame it on the hotel." But he didn't need to justify his hotel to us. *Villa Real* was known for its exquisite cuisine, with foreign chefs from around the world.

"We came to see you," Mia pressed ahead, "because we were hoping your concierge desk would refer people to us when they were looking for something a little different to do. We would offer a commission."

Heinrich's expression didn't give a clue to what he was thinking. I imagine he had seen and heard everything in a business where guests routinely demand discounts or free nights because a cat meowed outside their window after midnight and disturbed their sleep.

He said kindly, "It is hotel policy not to participate with commissions. But I tell Josefina to maybe say a little bit sometimes. You have a card for me?"

"Hundreds." Mia laughed.

"Give me a few dozen then. And I tell you someone who would be interested in what you offer, to go see. My friend at *Playa Madera* gets some discriminating guests."

Heinrich gave us the name of his friend, but said not to contact her for a day or two. First he would call ahead.

"You have to come some time," Mia said. "Please. We'd love to have you as our guest."

"Maybe sometime when we are not so busy, yes."

Mia and I both had a little spring in our step as we returned to our minivan. It seemed we'd finally won a champion.

8

"Last February, I never imagined things would be this way," my wife was saying. Mia has always been quick to tear up -- school plays, a reminiscence about her mother, anyone's wedding -- and her eyes were glistening now.

It was the Sunday after New Year's. We were having a late lunch on the terrace. Shortly we'd have to leave for the airport so Mia could catch her flight to New York. She was personally having to escort her father down here, a sudden turn of events. Daphne, our youngest, was sick.

"You can't know what's going to come in life," I said with a shrug.

"I know."

She tried to smile, with a tear coming down one cheek. She touched it away.

"Everything will work out. You look so sad."

"I'm not sad," she said, tucking her hair back from her face.

"Then what are you?"

"I'm just emotional today, that's all. There's just so many things to deal with. Thank you for putting up with me."

"You put up with me."

"I do, don't I." She covered my hand with hers, and I received a game smile. "You've been so good. Friday morning I felt like packing it in."

A threesome with a reservation had canceled. They called about twenty minutes before they were due. They'd decided to go bird-watching instead. Apparently they preferred the herons and pelicans at the *Barra de Potosi* to grilled quail. They didn't even apologize, according to Mia, who took the call and said she'd come within a hair of lashing out at them. Cancellations had become our nemesis. And I'd gone out of my way to spend for *langosta*, because these three were staying at a hotel we wanted to impress. That was the second time we'd had no one, and we were now in the first week of January, the official high season, when we had to make our money. Our spirits were flagging. Mia had even stopped studying Spanish. My own efforts to get better at the language were falling off.

On Christmas Eve we'd gone to the Rooster's Mass at midnight, *la misa de gallo*, in the old church near the waterfront. We are lapsed Catholics. But that night, listening to Mass and the congregation singing in Spanish, God seemed possible. I prayed. Yet what right did we have to ask any God for anything, given the financial struggles of the Mexican families in the pews around us? Nothing of earth-shattering importance was at stake, just the dreams of two people, two starry-eyed idiotic Americans, who already had it better than most people. Yet this was an absolute turning point in our lives.

"I prayed for the strength to just accept whatever happens," Mia said later.

Afterward we'd watched little children in blindfolds swing at a star-shaped pinada hung outside the church. It had seven tasseled prongs, which represented the seven deadly sins, according to a cruiser couple in the crowd who lived on their sailboat in nearby Ixtapa. Before going to bed in the wee hours, Mia and I shared memories of Christmases past, when our children were young.

— • —

Over the holidays we'd communicated with each of the children. Lauren certainly was the headliner, with a holiday saga from afar.

Our eldest had been in Europe through much of December, accompanying others from her company based in Chicago, which organized international furniture expositions. Straight out of college in the Bay Area, our first-born had secured a junior spot in the public relations department of an Italian bakery and restaurant chain expanding on the West Coast, and she'd gone forward from there, a smooth talker, a child not afflicted by shyness or lack of self confidence.

Lauren had seized an opportunity to experience Christmas with the Italian side of Mia's family in Bonassola, whom Lauren had only met once, as a young child. She said she had a spectacular time. Her fiancé, Steve, couldn't get there, or he would have flown over.

But Steve's mother was steaming that Lauren had been absent from the Christmas traditions at her house, given her coming entry into the family. Sensitive to that, Lauren and Steve had worked it out that our daughter would return just in time for the famous New Year's Eve party at the country club. But harsh weather delayed her flight, so Steve attended the party alone. Comments were made by the mother, who cut no slack. Why hadn't Lauren booked an earlier flight, as a precaution? Steve's defense of Lauren didn't cut it. When the mother later criticized Lauren to her face, sharp words were exchanged. Yesterday Lauren asked if we could indeed host a destination wedding in Zihuatanejo, because that was definitely what she wanted now.

"His mother was always trying to engineer the wedding plans, and now I absolutely don't want to deal with her," Lauren told us, very emotional. "Steven is okay with it. He's had to deal with her his whole life, and he tries to be accommodating, but this is crazy. What a mess. I think his mother can't stand me stealing her son. Steve and I talk about it that way. He's trying to move away from her, and from working for his father, without alienating his parents."

Our middle son Rowan, in his phone call, promised to come down and visit us in mid-January, so that was some good news. And Daphne, however sick, would be coming with Mia and her father. We'd never had a Christmas until now without at least one of the children, and usually all three, under our roof. We were happy to put Christmas and New Year's behind us. Even Phil was gone for the week, visiting old friends who had a home in Manzanillo far up the coast.

To decorate Casa Blue for our patrons, Phil had lent us her *nacimento*, an elaborate nativity scene which included *campesinos* with pack mules. Mia put out plates of *polvorones*, a Christmas cookie made with pecans, butter, vanilla and flour, rolled in confectioners' sugar. Each guest was given some in a sachet-like bag of Mexican lace tied with ribbon.

— • —

I checked my watch. It was almost time to go to the airport.

"Daphne and your dad will be very happy to see you," I said. "They do need you."

"How many times are you going to tell me that?"

"I'm just trying to make you feel better."

"The timing couldn't be worse." Now she checked her watch, then shoved back her chair.

"I'll clean up here. You get your things."

"Tell me there isn't some biblical torture going on here, to test me beyond my limits."

"I don't think you have any limits."

"I do," Mia said, "and I'm about there."

— • —

Ever since she was a little girl, our youngest child, Daphne, has managed to be bowled over by a flu bug or laid out by the plague at inopportune times. She has been called to account on this. And it does happen less often, now that Daphne is twenty-two. She can even joke about it with her mother.

But with her grandfather due to fly down with her on Thursday, this was not the weekend for Daphne to be so knocked out by a virus that she could hardly get out of bed, much less travel across Brooklyn to check on him and handle last-minute needs. There were still important things to do, involving medical records, disposition of some remaining furniture, and his bank account -- loose ends that should have been handled much sooner.

Just yesterday Mia spoke with Daphne on the phone about this sudden crisis, which precipitated Mia's flight out this morning, and I heard Mia's half of the conversation. "I know you're not trying to get out of anything. If you're having to crawl to the bathroom to vomit, you can't be leaving the house. I understand, sweetheart."

We knew our daughter was very close to her grandfather and certainly wanted to carry out her responsibilities. But the five-year-old Daphne, who could wreck Thanksgiving plans or neutralize a July Fourth family weekend with symptoms of cholera -- enough of those childhood cells were still alive in my daughter's body, and had gathered themselves in a rebel charge.

The Daphne Plan had seemed like common sense. Stanley's clothes would come with him in two large suitcases. The famous chair and table and a few other items were already shipped on a freighter. Other things were being gifted to people or left for the new tenant, who had reluctantly agreed to delay his move-in date a little. Daphne and Stanley had their airline tickets for Thursday. The new tenant was refusing to wait even longer.

And now that the moment was at hand, Stanley was again making sounds about not coming at all.

— • —

The ride to the airport takes less than twenty minutes. Once past the roundabouts and concrete roadbeds along the commercial outskirts of Zihuatanejo, it quickly turns rural. Cattle graze on coconut plantations that cover the hillsides. A vehicle or two might pass by -- rarely more. The broad highway, with two generous lanes plus a shoulder in each direction, separated by a wide median strip, could handle a summer Olympics. It had lain in disrepair until two years ago, a decaying feat of civil engineering.

"I'm surprised we never heard from the woman we sent the flowers to," Mia said about one of the week's guests.

"The one who cut off the tip of her finger?"

"She didn't cut off the tip of her finger," Mia objected. "She cut herself."

"She jumped around, squeezing that finger like she was going to bleed to death. Who cuts herself slicing a lime? And then she pulled an attitude, after you bandaged her up. Like it was somehow your fault, because you gave her tricky citrus."

"Stop." But I'd achieved my goal: I'd gotten her to laugh, and we'd both thought about something, if only for a moment, other than the business at hand.

The airport terminal had been spruced up a few years ago. I preferred the old terminal, without air conditioning, which smelled of jet exhaust and travelers' sweat, laced with the scent of nearby palms and underbrush. Now it was twice the size, a mausoleum of concrete and terrazzo and walls of glass. A copy of a mural by Diego Rivera or Marion Greenwood would have given it a sense of country, but not a peso had been spent to make it Mexican.

A half-man, half-boy in a security shirt and latex gloves opened Mia's suitcase on a TV snack table. He rifled through it while she paid for her ticket. The fare was exorbitant, because she'd gotten her ticket on such short notice, and this was the high season. It wasn't something we could afford at all. Our money seemed to siphon out of our lives.

We stood together on the long line for her flight, outside a glassed-in, secured waiting area.

"You have all the instructions," Mia said.

"Yes I do."

"I know you'll do a good job cooking on Tuesday."

"You'll hear the applause in New York."

"Maybe more reservations will come in."

"Everything will be fine."

Moments later, Mia's flight was announced in Spanish and again in English. We embraced, kissed and promised to e-mail. I lingered until Mia cleared the security machines. She waved at me and made a show-biz face, something like "Here I go, wish me luck," from the other side of the glass wall. I had a lump in my throat, to tell the truth, with all that she was being subjected to.

— • —

I went to the beach for the afternoon. I had drinks with the woman who'd come to the Cooking School at Z by herself on the day the Mormons had come, weeks ago. She was with her husband and was very complimentary, which was nice to hear. I didn't want to cook that evening, so I picked up a *torta* with spiced pork leg, grilled on a *comal* set up off the beach in a parking area that the locals used.

I read my book on the terrace as the sun set. It was an autobiography of a renowned chef with restaurants in New York, Paris, London and Tokyo. In contrast, the Cooking School at Z was such amateur folly. What had we been thinking?

Before long I closed my eyes. I was determined to think about something else for a change, or just go blank.

After a couple of margeritas, I drifted into a sexual fantasy back through time, and I tried to bring up the sensations. I remembered the ineffable softness of Mia's young breasts, often unfettered under a T-shirt during our brief time in college. Their swollen glory -- just what you always dreamed of, Mia liked to tease -- during pregnancy and nursing. Their encased firmness as the nation strapped down under Republicans, and we raised a family. Mia got into a workout regimen when our daughter Lauren was on the high school swim team, and later had her spinning classes. Hugging her in those years, she was mostly breastbone. And now Mia was back to the woman I thought of as her, only a little older, just like me. Wiser? This experience was certainly getting us there. If only we'd reflected on what we were setting out to do, instead of leaping into the purchase of Casa Blue with little financial reserves.

— • —

The next day, a Monday, we did have a reservation. It was an American couple from California, our first personal referral by Heinrich from *Villa Real*. I'd hoped in vain that other reservations would come in, but it would be just the two of them, and I'd have to do the program. It seemed like a bad move to cancel, even with a good excuse. Luckily they'd said they couldn't come until late morning, for a shortened program.

"This place is amazing," said Nancy Croft, once we descended to the terrace. Her husband, Andrew, seemed impressed as well. They were in their early forties, from Palo Alto, not too far up the peninsula from where Mia and I used to live. It came out later that he was a venture capitalist, with real estate holdings as well.

"There was an emergency in my wife's family, and she had to go New York on short notice," I explained. I assured them everyone was fine. "So it'll be just the three of us. You're simply my guests. I have all this wonderful food and we certainly don't want to waste it."

"We shouldn't impose on you then," said Nancy.

"It's quite the opposite. Having you is something I completely enjoy. I hope you'll stay, and today is complimentary."

What could they say? Ever shrewd, I figured they'd insist on paying.

"Go look around," I encouraged. "Make yourself at home."

Nancy went immediately to examine the colorful hibiscus blooms in their large clay pots. She had close-cropped strawberry blonde hair, and very fair, freckled skin. A tall woman, she was in mules and a two-piece linen outfit cinched by a beaded belt.

Andrew moved to the edge, where he seemed to study the eclectic structures immediately below: a three-story residence, with Tuscan colors and a clay tile roof, stood beside a single-story thatched cantina, which was a stone's throw from an old Volkswagen camper with a full wash line of clothes. It was as though God had decreed that no two things should be alike, or even similar, near *Playa La Ropa*.

"Some of this looks like it's pretty new," Andrew declared, his hands in his pockets. He had a shock of boyish hair, probably in the original brown, which he combed back with his hand as if he'd gone to an English boarding school. A soft belly bulge filled his golf shirt.

"All of this once was a coconut plantation."

"You probably got in at a good time," Andrew decided. "It's still developing. How'd it go, buying Mexican real estate? I've heard that can be an experience."

"It wasn't that bad, but let's hope we never have to leave here," I said.

I shared the story of Señor Echeverria, the *Notario Público* in Zihuatanejo who'd handled all our paperwork for the signing to acquire *Casa Rosalinda*. Our portly notary had been murdered, and his office burned down, back in the summer. He'd reportedly cheated some property owners, who took their revenge.

"Jesus," Andrew said.

"He seemed alright when we were dealing with him, but what did we know. I think our records were stored in his office. Some day we'll find out."

Nancy was moving our way, sporting a red hibiscus over one ear.

"The Cooking School at Z is new, isn't it? You weren't here last year."

"We just opened in early December."

"Things going according to plan?" Andrew asked.

"We're losing money more slowly at this point," I said, a fairly colossal understatement. Why I was even that honest, I'm not sure. Perhaps because he was an investor and I thought he would see right through a lie.

"Let's get to the important things," said his wife. "I want to watch you make the perfect margerita. I bet you're an expert."

"Hardly, but we'll do fine." It was too early for a margerita, really, but a little alcohol could help the morning flow.

I wet down the blue rims of three handblown stem glasses. I pressed each one into a bowl of coarse salt. Then ice, then a measure of tequila in each.

"Tequila's very in vogue," I said. "Apparently there's a shortage. Some of the lesser brands are blending in cheap mescal, which will give you a headache you wouldn't forget."

"Duly noted," Andrew said. "I'll only drink the best."

I added a soft purr of triple sec, followed by a healthy injection of fresh lime juice. A careful flourish of more *reposoda* tequila, the middle grade, to top it off. I fluffed the ice a half dozen times with a spoon. We each took a glass and toasted their vacation, even though it wasn't close to lunchtime. The drinks drew compliments.

I escorted them to the table and chairs where Mia and I eat breakfast. I brought appetizers from the Inferno. I'd raided our ceramics collection from Izzy. In one hand I held a cream-colored Michoacan platter, with hand-painted fish and fowl and foliage, all in a chocolate outline. The other had an intricately painted, majolica-type bowl from Dolores Hidalgo, set on a matching plate.

"These ceramics are gorgeous," Nancy said. "And what are we eating?"

"This one has manta ray ceviche, and that's guacamole of course. The red you see is tiny chunks of tomato. There's a bit of serrano pepper cut up. Onion, lime juice, nothing extraordinary. When you make guacamole, don't put it in a food processor. Mash it by hand. That's the only rule." I also had handmade chips from the market.

It turned out that Zihuatanejo was the first leg of a trip lasting several weeks. The Crofts explained it was to be like the summer they met in Europe, two young people just kicking around. Nancy spoke Spanish and seemed to be the one most in love with their plan. They were pretty much playing it by ear after Zihuatanejo, with plans to go through Central and South America.

"Andrew's afraid we'll be kidnapped," Nancy teased.

"It happens," he countered. "Seven hundred and fifty kidnappings for ransom in Mexico last year. I see where the state of Guerrero's federal deputy was kidnapped from his ranch by a band of men with automatic rifles. How far was that from here?"

"Hours. The kidnappings are primarily in Mexico City," I said.

"We're going through the Mexico City airport," he pointed out to Nancy.

"Just don't get in a gypsy cab," I said.

"Andrew packed his old clothes, so we won't stand out," said Nancy. "We're undercover."

— • —

I'd marinated quail in olive oil, garlic, and *papalo,* a cilantro alternative grown in parts of Mexico. While Andrew finished the quail on the grill, I reduced a sauce containing figs, sweet onions and sherry. I also brought to the table a fruit plate of brick-colored Mexican papaya, carefully washed grapes, and sour slices of star fruit. I could do a turn or two in the kitchen, after watching Mia for all these years.

"Where do you get quail down here?" Andrew asked. He had a Cuban cigar from my cabinet. We'd cleared, and Nancy had excused herself.

"There's a quail rancher north of Acapulco. He vacuum seals them. Mia and I drove down to see Acapulco in October, and someone had told us about him. We must have forty of them in the large freezer right now."

"He doesn't ship?"

"It's hit or miss on refrigeration. He offered to send them up on a bus, but you don't know what shape they'll be in when they get here. It's true with wine too. Sometimes it gets cooked in transit, which is why we don't order good wine."

"I hope this takes off for you," Andrew said when his wife returned. She stayed standing, because they had to go -- or simply wanted to leave, because it was kind of pathetic, with no other guests and only me, the second-stringer.

"Me too. You could come in on it," I said offhandedly. "A good tax write-off. I could organize this into a Mexican corporation, which we haven't done yet."

Nancy looked startled that I'd said this. I was startled too. Where had these embarrassing words come from?

But Andrew, the professional investor, was probably used to being cornered. He seemed nonplussed, and the easy-going smile never left his face as he said, "I'd never invest in Mexico."

I wasn't too proud to turn down his offer to pay.

Stanley emerged from the jet with his winter coat over his arm. Coming down the portable stairway, he seemed unconcerned that other passengers were stacked up behind him. He looked puzzled, like an exiled grand master in chess from an Eastern Europe who'd expected to see snow. He squinted at the palm trees. When he finally reached the tarmac, he waited for the family women. He was dressed in gray slacks, brown shoes with laces, and a long-sleeved shirt.

Our youngest, Daphne, slogged along beside him toward the terminal, lugging two bulky pieces of soft luggage. Daphne was wearing wrinkled, sand-colored linen pants that rode low on her hips, with a halter and strapped sandals. Her hair this month was wine red and short, the bed head look. The headset of her CD player hung around her neck.

Bringing up the rear was my wife. Mia was pulling her carry-on bag and toting a sizable Joe Namath lamp, featuring a replica helmet of the New York Jets quarterback as its base. The breeze blew her hair across her face, partially blotting her identity.

They disappeared into the terminal for a while, but finally emerged from immigration into the baggage area. We were separated by a wall of thick glass, so we could only wave. Even after they had their luggage our reunion was delayed, because one suitcase was missing. Mia filed a report. As they were finally leaving the baggage area, they encountered another problem: Mexican customs requires Americans to press a random inspection button with their luggage. Ninety-nine percent of the time it comes up green, but of course it came up red for Stanley. He was taken aside. While the customs officer rifled through his bags, Stanley complained about the stupidity of this. I prayed his behavior wouldn't get him in trouble; Mia profusely apologized for him in Spanish. Thankfully he wasn't put back on the plane.

"Welcome," I announced broadly as they came through. I clapped a hand on Stanley's sinewy shoulder. He was never one of my fans, but we tended toward civility in public. I'd given him three good grandchildren, which earned me points on his chart of accounts, but those points and more were lost when my investments went sour a few years ago, as he learned from Daphne's loose lips. I'd pledged to myself that I was going to be as welcoming as possible, because this certainly had to be a difficult day for him.

As for Daphne, I embraced her. She was weary, and just getting over her illness. She found the energy to say, "Hi dad."

Mia accepted my hug. "Thank God we're here," she confided.

"You had to bring the lamp?" I asked quietly as we all began walking.

"Don't ask, or I'll hit you with it. I could have killed him."

I escorted them through the clamoring taxi drivers. Stanley kept pace well enough on flat ground. Mia helped her father into the front seat of our minivan while I loaded the mountain of luggage.

"So how was your flight, Stan?" I asked as we got underway.

"Day like year," he said. This time-honored phrase originated with Stanley's father, a rough fellow who had come to America from Poland as a young boy and never spoke more than marginal English. He used it in his doddering days, waiting for the reaper. Stanley now muttered it too often.

"You started early this morning," I said.

"Flight like year," Daphne said from the back. Her talking produced a congested cough. We began discussing the flight down, the freezing weather they'd left behind -- safe subjects that took no energy.

Daphne asked, "Is this what it's like where you live?" Outside was the raw country of hills, coconut palms, and the occasional shabby billboard.

"Not really," I said. "We live by the water. How are you feeling?"

"Awful," she said. Mia put a hand on her in sympathy.

Stanley got his first glimpse of Zihuatanejo Bay as we neared *Playa La Ropa*. Daphne was asleep by that time, her head resting against the window. I eased onto the small, cobbled parking area at Casa Blue.

"I hate to wake her," Mia whispered.

Mia assisted Daphne to her room on the top floor. I escorted Stanley to the second-floor bedroom that would be his. Up and down three levels was going to be a problem for him, because he wasn't spry on the steps, but he'd have to deal with it.

"You live here in the open like this?" he asked, clearly surprised that his room lacked a wall on the western side overlooking the bay.

"It's always warm here. Check out your bathroom."

It had louvered swinging doors like a cantina. He stuck his head in and approved, announcing, "Nice john." Indeed it was: handsomely tiled, with two sinks, a large mirror, and a commode on one side, a spacious step-down shower on the other. It was four times the size of the cramped bathroom he'd left behind in Brooklyn.

"You have to change your thinking about the elements. Zihuatanejo's like being on permanent vacation," I said. "Wait until you see how nice the evenings are. You can watch the sunset from here."

"And what do I want with a permanent vacation? I've got a

permanent vacation coming my way, and so do you some day. I want life, not a tan."

I held my tongue.

He looked at the bay from the railing. "You two had the money for this? I'm impressed."

"Basically we traded out the equity from our house."

"That's what I thought. So you didn't have the money."

Stanley sat on the bed. He tested the firmness of the mattress. Next he removed his shoes and massaged his right foot, pulling on each toe while I pointed out a few room features -- the switch for the overhead fan, the available mosquito netting, the night light. He looked weary, but not overly so. Stanley's high metabolism kept his switch in the on position all the time. He could eat prodigiously without adding weight. His prominent nose lent him an air of intellectual curiosity. He still had some hair, which looked as it usually did, like he'd just figured out a physics' equation at a chalk board, after scratching his head a hundred times.

"You want to get a nap in?" I said. "We can get you up later."

"I'm alright. I just need the bathroom. My bladder's down to the size of a walnut." He left for a moment.

Mia came in with her shoulder bag, which contained some of her father's things -- a thick paperback biography of Churchill, tissues, a CD player with a headset we'd given him for Christmas. After he and his wife, Emma, had returned to Brooklyn two decades ago, he enjoyed playing coronet with a group of guys who performed swing, Rogers and Hart, and a bit of blues, at church and social club events.

"He's better now," Mia said quietly, so her father couldn't hear, "but last night was ugly. I didn't think I'd be able to coax him on the plane. Please get him changed out of those clothes. Give him some of your things. His shorts and shirts are in the suitcase that didn't get here."

I got replacement clothing from our room. I returned to find

Stanley taking in the view. Mia had gone.

"So you can't drink the water from the faucet," Stanley said. We'd taped a printed reminder on the mirror.

"Only on Tuesdays," I quipped.

"That's the day I don't drink water, so I'll be alright."

He changed his shirt. The scar that began by his navel, continued around his side, and ended high up his back had become white and puckish over the years. It came from field surgery during the Korean War -- a M.A.S.H. unit, like the television show, and he wasn't shy about telling people that they'd done great work, saving his life. Then I brought him down to the terrace.

"Is it this hot all the time?"

"It's in the eighties. It'll be the same until May. You'll acclimate in a day or two. You just came out of winter in Brooklyn. Don't try to tell me this isn't better."

He stood on the terrace, evaluating further. I stood by, like his valet. I sensed he approved of his new environment, even if he didn't want to say it. The pots of bougainvillea and hibiscus, the expanse of tile, the bamboo and the African tulip with all its flowers. He'd seen pictures. In person it impressed everyone the first time.

"My daughter thinks she can direct my life now," he said, pulling out a chair at the terrace table. "I don't appreciate the pushing. I got her, I got the doctors, all pushing. This is probationary, my being here." He looked at me very intently, to assure that I understood.

"I can understand your feelings. You want something to drink?" His first day was not the day for an argument.

I got cold water all around with lime. Mia soon came for hers, wearing a bathing suit. She nearly drained the glass, then headed straight to the infinity pool on the lower terrace. I heard the plunge, other sounds of contentment and gentle splashing, and in what seemed a matter of seconds, she was toweling off beside us.

"God, does that feel good," she said.

"You've put on some pounds since California," Stanley observed. "You look better, like you used to. You were too skinny from all the exercising. You have your figure back."

"Daphne's asleep," Mia told me, ignoring him. "I'm just going to let her go."

"You have a very good kid there," Stanley advised us, his tone implying that we didn't think so. She was his buddy from Brooklyn, and could do no wrong.

"Is that where you do your cooking class?" Stanley asked, indicating the cooking island.

"That's it. We have one tomorrow," I said.

"How many do we have signed up?" Mia asked.

I proudly held up a hand with all its fingers.

"We have five? You're kidding."

"There's another couple from the *Villa Real*, on a reference from the two that came Tuesday. And three women. One of them saw our name on the front tile and rang the bell. We spoke, and I gave her a card, and she called back. She's bringing her two friends. They're from Los Angeles."

"Thank you God," Mia said. "Finally, some people."

Mia must have hidden her darkest fears from her father, judging by his perplexed look.

"We wanted to start small," I explained. "We're still working through how to do this, getting all the routines down."

Something caught Stanley's attention. "What the hell is that?"

A solitary birdlike creature, which looked like a small pterodactyl, was coasting on the thermals far overhead.

"The locals call them *tijerillas*," Mia said, with a butchered effort at rolling the 'r,' but it was better than I could do. "They coast up there all day long." To me she said, "Here's some news I didn't tell you. Rowan is coming. He actually has his ticket. And he thinks he can stay more than a week."

"When did you hear this?" I asked.

"I talked to him yesterday, when he called dad to wish him a good trip. He's doing a treatment for a screen play, and he's getting tons of money for it. He can work anywhere, I guess, so he can stay longer. And Lauren called. She and Steve definitely want to do a destination wedding down here in March. I guess things really deteriorated with the future mother-in-law. They told her their decision, and now she's making a big stink. They dropped by Steve's family on New Year's for chili, and there was a big, big blowup. The mother threatened not to come if they get married here."

"You should get married where you have your family and friends," Stanley said authoritatively, "but I'm sure Lauren has her reasons." In his book, Lauren was almost as perfect as Daphne, but she held the number two spot because she didn't live in Brooklyn.

"This is bad news," I said.

"Steve's mother seems to be a very controlling woman who doesn't watch what comes out of her mouth," Mia said with a worried tone. "Her husband should put her in her place, but apparently no one does."

"Lauren won't put up with her mouthing off."

"She doesn't," Mia said, "which is part of the problem." She turned to Stanley to share information that she'd been withholding. "Dad, the bottom line is, the mother, Evelyn, is not thrilled about Steve marrying our daughter. She wants her son staying in Chicago, and working at the father's firm. Eventually he'd move up to take it over. That's the father's vision too. And the mother's afraid -- rightly so -- that Lauren will take him away from that."

"Which is one reason Steve is attracted to Lauren in the first place," I said.

"I like this Steve," said Stanley, using his index finger to drive home his point. "He came to see me with Lauren. I think he's a very good boy. They took me out to a fancy restaurant. I had a broiled lobster tail. They're good together. He pulled out her chair for her."

The three of us chatted further about the kids as I worked at the cooking island. We were eating early to accommodate Stanley's jet lag. I sliced several brined chicken breasts horizontally, doubling their number, then flashed them in olive oil with garlic and herbs. I whipped up a harmless sauce worthy of a hospital. I'd made potato salad earlier. A straightforward meal, Stanley's favorite. In his book, a sprig of parsley equaled a medley of herbs, and salt and pepper were an adventure in spices. Why Emma, with her background, had ever married Stanley was a mystery I didn't understand. Mia had her own ideas on that. Stanley was an army veteran, and a very good dancer, and certainly would take her away from her own domineering, immigrant parents into the fullness of America.

"It's a shame mom isn't alive to be here," Mia said.

"Your mother would have knocked your heads together if you'd told her you were going to try this in a foreign country," Stanley said.

"She'd love it," Mia said.

After we ate and watched the sunset, Stanley faded fast. Mia and I accompanied him up the steps to his room. Mia unpacked more of his things while he used the bathroom.

"How do I brush my teeth with this water?" he called out, his head sticking out from between the louvered doors. "Am I gonna get worms?"

"Use the bottled water in there to wet your toothbrush and rinse with," Mia said. "And stop being difficult. You know you won't get worms."

Mia reviewed the drill for the morning, even though we'd gone over everything at dinner. "We have cooking school at nine-thirty," she said. "Isabel will be here before that, at about eight, and you'll meet her after you have breakfast. Jeff runs out to the market early, and he comes right back. The roosters start sounding off at about four; don't get up if you hear them. Just turn over in bed. If you need anything, we're in the next room."

"I can manage," he said. "I get along just fine every day, despite what you and the doctors think."

Mia gave him a kiss, after wiping a blue smudge of toothpaste from his lip. "We're happy you're here," she said.

"You are," Stanley said. "He's not."

"I'm happy you're here," I corrected him. "You needed to get out of your situation and be with family. The doctor said that too."

He dismissed me with a wave of his hand, not wasting words.

"I want to point something out," I said. I intended to do some advance blocking and tackling for Mia. "You've been here three hours, and you haven't said anything positive about your new home, which is okay. But you haven't said one thing nice to Mia for going up to New York to help you. Whether or not you like it here is up to you. You have to open yourself to this. No one can do it for you. Together, we can make this work."

"I've been brought here against my will," Stanley said with passion. "This is my life, and I didn't want to come."

"It's what needed to happen."

"I need you to tell me this?"

"Just let it go, dad," Mia said.

We left him sitting on the bed. While I cleaned up the dinner dishes, Mia wrote a note for Daphne and placed it at the bottom of the stone staircase, in case she woke up when we were all sleeping and came searching for food.

"You had a long day," I said to Mia once we were in bed.

"Day like year. Day like century."

She turned onto her belly and exhaled loudly. She guided my hand to her lower back, under her light cotton nightgown. "Rub there," she said. She moaned in gratitude. We could hear Stanley hacking in the next room.

"That doesn't sound good," I said.

"He only coughs when he's lying flat. He still smokes

sometimes. He won't quit. He did lose his driving privileges, by the way. He never told us that."

"He doesn't have a car."

"But he'd kept up his license. The emergency room reported his second seizure to Motor Vehicles. They take away driving privileges for that. I found the notice when we were going through his things."

"He wanted me to know that this is a probationary period."

"Yeah, well, he can say anything he wants."

"I hope he gets along with Isabel."

"I talked to his doctor up there in person," Mia said.

"You told me."

"He said he'll do fine if he takes his anti-convulsant medication. We have to have his levels tested three or four times a year. Go higher. There, between my shoulder blades. Oh, that's it."

"Is this going to work with him here?"

"I don't know."

She sighed, sinking further into the mattress.

"It's going to be difficult having him in the house," I said.

"It will work out," she said. "Down lower."

I massaged where I'd been originally, at her waist. "Down more," she said, relaxing noticeably. "Further. Yes. O, I need to feel human again."

She sucked in her breath as I touched between her legs, her muscles clenching, her breathing getting deeper as I continued.

"Come on," she said, turning over. "I want you."

And I wanted her. We wasted no time. Mia held herself to a series of grunts as we climaxed, in deference to her father in his room. After a long kiss, she turned on her side to face the bay and fell soundly asleep. I spooned her, with my hand on her hip, my mind running through a particular memory from a long time ago.

Those first weeks of her sophomore year in college, Mia was sharing a room with another girl in a building near Hell's Kitchen.

One night we lay together in exactly this formation. Mia had been sleeping then, too, as I remembered it. Asleep and pregnant.

I was awake though, on that night nearly thirty years ago. I couldn't sleep. It wasn't just any night. I was looking past the radiator at the apartment windows across the street, where a couple was continually walking back and forth on the other side of sheer curtains. I decided that night keeping Mia in my life was more important than college, or anything else for that matter. Especially with the child she was carrying, which was something she -- we -- hadn't revealed to her parents, or to the two very Catholic aunts who'd raised me in an apartment tower in Fort Lee, New Jersey, ever since a Pan American flight carrying my parents went down in an Ohio farm field when I was four, an only child. Lying in that bed, with Mia asleep beside me, I realized I wanted to marry her.

Fools, both of us, for choosing that -- we were told as much in twenty different ways. Yet we'd stayed together through the years, so our track record said otherwise. Mia was very much a rebel at that age. She still wasn't sure for a few weeks more about whether she wanted to marry me. But I knew that night, in that bed, that she was the one. I was feeling so incredibly mature and insightful. I was twenty, Mia was twenty. Never before, and never again, did I experience such exuberant terror.

The truth is, my life to that point hadn't been much. And to be honest, becoming an early husband and father didn't hold me back from anything. I lacked drive, even then. I went on to a series of sales positions, God knows why -- in advertising; in meeting sales for a hotel chain, which brought the transfer to California; then in systems furniture, just before my little sideline real estate magazine grew into something.

Yet Mia could have been so much more, as I appreciated over the years. She'd worked hard, raising our family and bringing in extra money. But with another husband, in another circumstance, she could have been all that and so much more. She seemed destined for more, and others believed that too. She'd made her choice at a young age -- me, and a family -- and she made a life for herself and for us. She told me often enough that she had no regrets, and she wasn't one to look back, but still, there was this other dimension of success that had never come her way, because she'd never had the opportunity.

I wanted Mexico to work so badly.

10

The next morning, all five guests arrived almost simultaneously. We were one large, loud group descending to the terrace.

The marketer in me was flying high: one of the women attending the Cooking School at Z on this glorious morning was a face known 'round the globe.

Needing avocados for our Casa Blue starter martinis, I left everyone with Mia and slipped away to the Inferno. Daphne was there. She was nursing a mug of herbal tea with two hands, able to spy without being seen. She was in wrinkled hemp shorts and a T-shirt bearing the name of an obscure band.

"Do you recognize the woman with the turquoise jewelry?" I asked excitedly.

"I don't know. She looks familiar."

I named a couple of movies, and the roles this particular guest had played. I mentioned the second Oscar that should have been hers.

"Ohmigod," said Daphne.

Now a brunette, and several inches shorter than one would expect from seeing her on the big screen, Francine Longman was our first flesh-and-blood celebrity. She'd come with her older sister, Valerie -- same manufacturer, but a taller model, with a more pronounced nose and less of a front bumper. The third in their party was Jan, who'd booked the reservation in her name. She was a big, fast-talking woman, with hair held in one of those oversized clips in back, like the jaws of life. She seemed to be Francine's personal assistant and bodyguard, all wrapped in one. She quickly instructed me that no photos were to be taken.

The other patrons, Celeste and Rose from the *Villa Real,* were girl friends from Phoenix in their early forties. They'd gawked at Francine, wondering was-she-or-wasn't-she the celebrity, before introductions confirmed it. They knew they'd bagged a fabulous story to tell back home. And I now had a celebrity name for promotion, which would lend chic to the Cooking School at Z. Business was looking up!

"Go to my room," I told Daphne. "There's a camera in the second drawer. Bring it into the kitchen, but don't let anyone see it. Okay? Then join us."

Stars had visited Zihuatanejo before. John Wayne hunted jaguar and wild boar in the forties. Timothy Leary made a famous trip to Zihua to organize a group high, but authorities intervened. The Shawshank Redemption's hero escaped to paradise in Zihuatanejo, Richard Gere had rented a house last year, and hadn't Lauren Hutton just come? It was said that Barbra Streisand or her agent had built the five-level, white, modern home visible across the bay, and the Guggenheims had a place not too far away. And Bill Gates himself had visited on his yacht, tipping his caddy a hundred and fifty dollars at the golf course.

But this was the present. Francine Longman was actually in the Cooking School at Z, and would be ours for the next few hours. I needed to capitalize on this. I had to be shrewd.

— • —

While our guests had their dirty martinis on the terrace, the customary questions began about our house.

"Would you like a tour?" Mia offered. "We could do it now."

"Absolutely. Let's do it," said Francine, and the others echoed her.

Mia led them away. The tours of the house we'd been giving after lunch had sometimes stretched into midafternoon. Some guests then wouldn't leave -- and one couple had virtually invited themselves back, with bathing suits, so we could all continue having so much fun. In that case, I pretended we had a meeting with our accountant.

I went to tell Stanley about our celebrity guest. He'd risen early and spurned the sliced fresh fruit Mia set out for him. He'd requested a poached egg, and grumbled about the toast. Mia made sure he took his medicine. Now he was located in a chaise lounge on the lower terrace, largely hidden by the fronds of a potted palm. He was reading his Churchill biography with a second cup of coffee and a cigarette, using an empty beer bottle as an ashtray. Had he been born in our children's generation, Stanley might have attended college on a scholarship. He'd gone to war out of high school, then worked as a melon salesman in California right after discharge. A war buddy got him work back in the New York area, where he soon landed a union job as a linotype operator for the Newark Star Ledger. Once linotype machines became a thing of the past, he became a shoe salesman for Macy's. His sandals, beside him on the tile, looked top of the line. His footwear had always been strikingly superior to his clothes.

Without looking up, Stanley said, "Churchill wanted to use poison gas against the Iraqis in 1919, when he was Secretary of State in England's War Office. Lawrence of Arabia talked him out of it. What a world."

"Stanley, I came to tell you who's here today."

He knew who Francine Longman was, having seen her on the Sunday night movies on television. We could hear Francine's voice, very distinct from the other women on the house tour.

"Mia's not taking them in my room, is she?"

"I'm sure not. Do you want to meet her?"

"Maybe later."

We heard Mia bringing the group down the steps.

"Come up and join us in a little while," I said.

I hurried to the kitchen and pressured Daphne, who was eating fresh fruit and had the camera, to come join us.

"I don't know if I want to do this," she said. Earlier she'd agreed to be an aide during the cooking class. Why not have some fun? As a teenager she'd developed prowess with cutlery, from too-fast-for-the-eye mincing to high-speed cucumber slicing, as precise as a Vegematic sold on TV. Growing up, her older sister Lauren was already established as mom's auxiliary cook, and worked dinner parties with Mia right through college. Since that slot was taken, Daphne used knife work to stand out.

"Either way is good," I assured Daphne. I'd been a parent long enough to know not to encourage. As for Daphne, she'd been on antibiotics long enough not to be infectious, and wasn't coughing this morning. Although she still didn't look a hundred percent, her short hair and her wan complexion from New York living would make it difficult for anyone to know sickly from normal.

"I don't know," Daphne said. "I have to see."

"Whatever," I added, copying her vocabulary. "Or you can just hang out with your grandfather by the pool, or you can just watch. So, do you think her breasts are real?"

Daphne shook her head in exasperation, both with a celebrity who would have the surgery and a father who would comment on it, which I knew would needle her.

— • —

As the show began, Francine Longman seemed a bit tentative. This would bear monitoring. Her sister, Valerie, and the other couple were definitely interested. The assistant, Jan, was on duty, and not a true participant.

Mia determined after several minutes of queries that none of our guests were proficient in the kitchen. She opted for a new twist we had discussed -- providing a primer in some skill that patrons could use back home.

"We're going to start with a very important basic that many people have trouble with. Of course, they don't always *know* they have trouble with it. And that's garlic."

Mia brought out a basket of the stuff, and tipped a generous number of bulbs across the prep surface.

"Garlic and olive oil. If you didn't know how to handle these in my grandmother's restaurant, she'd scold you with one of those witch's fingers I hope I never get when I'm on her age."

Everyone laughed, including Francine. She propped her sunglasses up on her head, carefully tucking her hair behind her ears, engaged now. I noticed our daughter coming over.

"And before we begin, this is our daughter Daphne," Mia said, opening a place at her side. The women murmured a welcome as Daphne took her spot. "She might be willing to help us with this. She just came down from New York last night to stay for a few days."

Mia demonstrated how to slice across the top of the bulb to make it easier to separate the cloves. "What you don't want to do is spend ten minutes peeling and dicing. If it takes you that long, you'll never do it. So...."

Daphne pressed the flat of her chef's knife on several cloves and smacked it theatrically with her hand, mashing the cloves just so. That made it easy to remove the skin.

Once it was the guests' turn, Francine's sister turned squeamish. "I'll hit the knife and it'll pop up and stab me," Valerie said.

"It's safe," said Daphne. "Just put the heel of your hand on the blade and lean your weight on it if you're scared."

"The key is to have the blade flat," Mia said. "The edge can be down just a little."

Mia coached Celeste and Rose. Daphne assisted Francine and her sister, who seemed worried about their nails.

"Sometimes we want garlic minced in a dish we're making ... other times little slices work, little chips, if you want the garlic to be noticed ... and there are times you only want that wonderful infusion of aroma. In that case we don't crush it too hard" -- she demonstrated -- "and we just put the bruised cloves in the hot oil for a few seconds. In that case, as soon as your nose tells you that you've coaxed out the flavor, remove the garlic from the oil. It doesn't take long. Garlic should never be allowed to turn brown."

Daphne then demonstrated the safe way to mince, with fingertips curled in, wowing the women with her speed. The knife was a blur moving across the cloves. The guests tried. Daphne then demonstrated another trick: how to convert cloves into paste with the flat of a heavy cleaver. The loud whack of the cleaver brought startled whoops. Francine was the first to try to emulate our daughter, despite her assistant's cautioning. Our guests praised each other's successes and yelped in fun. Next, each woman solemnly cut the top off a fresh bulb and drizzled it with olive oil. Mia stuck the bulbs in the oven. Their inviting aroma was soon wafting through the air, making everyone salivate.

"So we have our garlic," Mia said. "Now, how do we cook with it?"

Mia put out a number of skillets and set different levels of flame beneath them.

"Francine," she said to our celebrity, "I need your forgiveness in advance. I'm going to ruin your garlic."

"No," Francine objected, mostly for fun, but not entirely. "I never do the garlic correctly, that's what I'm learning."

"You haven't opened a yogurt in five years," her sister scoffed. "What garlic? What cooking do you do?"

"Shut up. I'm going to start cooking when I get back to Los

Angeles."

"Oh yeah," said Valerie. "I can see that."

"Pay no attention to her," Francine announced. "Our dad wouldn't have garlic in the house. So this is a special moment. I can't give mine up." She had her hands prayerfully together, seeking and of course knowing in advance that the world would acquiesce.

"What do you mean, 'Our father wouldn't have it in the house?'" asked Valerie. "He left us when I was four, the bastard."

"Take her garlic," Francine said, moving her sister's forward as if placing her bet.

"Get your hands off my stuff," Valerie said, feinting a chop at her sister's fingers with her chef's knife, a move that alarmed everyone.

"You can have mine," Jan quickly volunteered. She'd done some garlic, just to be part of the group."Let's everyone be careful."

Under Mia's guidance, Jan added her garlic with a spatula to a pan set over high heat. The oil was smoking, a no-no with olive oil. The garlic turned brown in seconds, and the oil quickly broke down.

"You can detect the burnt, bitterish smell?" Mia asked. "Olive oil doesn't go above medium heat, not by itself."

The class experimented with different flames. Mia had them slice some stale bread into croutons, which they worked up in the skillets. They sampled like food critics. I went to the kitchen and fetched a pan of roasted bulbs we'd made first thing in the morning. They discovered how easily the cooled, roasted garlic surrendered each clove with a little pinch.

"Now smush a few of the roasted cloves with the flat of your knife, scrape some on a crouton, and see what you think of that."

"One thing about garlic," said Celeste from *Villa Real*, "is if your boyfriend is going to have it, you should have it. Otherwise...."

"It's like if he smokes," said Celeste's companion, making a face.

"You want to drive the guy away," Mia said, "add minced raw garlic to the dish at the very end. You can clean out a convention center with your breath."

That prompted Francine to volunteer a story about a leading man she'd had to kiss. "The guy had the breath of a dying dinosaur," she said, "and I told him that. He got revenge by grinding his mouth on me in a kissing scene. He actually cut my lip on the inside. I cursed him out right on the set. It was the most unprofessional thing I've ever been part of."

"That was everywhere on the entertainment news," said Jan.

"I thought about cutting his balls off," said Francine. She hefted her chef's knife, then sliced through the air.

At that juncture, when they least expected it and with everyone relaxed, I raised the digital camera and squeezed off a snapshot. I'd slipped into the kitchen to get it. Mia just happened to be next to Francine in the photo, and they were sharing something amusing.

"We can't have that," Francine interrupted. "We can arrange a picture later."

"I thought you'd all like a few candids. This is digital, I can forward them to you."

"No candids," Jan insisted. "Rules of the road. A certain expression comes up, something a little off, next month it shows up in print."

"Believe me, I had nothing...."

Jan cut me off and said privately, "People send the snapshot to their friend, who makes a print for someone else. We're not doing photos." She was trying to be matter of fact about it, but she wanted to kill me. She smelled what I was up to.

But no one demanded the disk, that was the key. I had my snapshot for marketing! I could include it in a limited-run brochure here in Mexico, well beyond the reach of Francine Longman's intellectual property attorney. I might even post it on our website, which Steve, our daughter's fiancé, had built for us.

— • —

Mia progressed to shrimp scampi, emphasizing how important it was to keep the heat low so the shrimp would braise. "You want these marvelous juices to develop and linger in the pan. You can savor it over rice or swab it up with bread, depending on how you want to serve it.

"We have fresh wonderful shrimp in Mexico, which Jeff just got for us at the market this morning" -- she nodded my way, and applause followed as I took a little bow -- "but we need to talk about which shrimp you should buy at home. Personally, I think tiger shrimp tastes like tiger. So I don't buy it. Let's talk about the other options...."

Things couldn't be going better. I'd handled the snapshot issue deftly. Stories were told and laughter rang out as they shifted to the tricks of roasting vegetables successfully and the preparation of an eggplant caviar they wouldn't find anywhere else. The group landed on a new subject: just how sexy was a man who could cook. They ate as they went, and ordered mimosas and wine.

"This is my favorite vegetable," said Valerie, salaciously wielding a crooked zucchini as if that joke had never been thought of before. Guffawing and laughter ensued.

"Shhh, we have a young girl here," Rose teased, pretending to cover Daphne's ears. Our daughter backed away from being touched, but she was enjoying the moment.

"You need to leave, dad," said Daphne.

"You need to leave," I countered.

"No," said Francine, "Daphne stays with us. She's ours."

"Get me a beer, honey, would you?" Mia said. "If I drink white wine at this hour, I'll have a roaring headache. Anybody else want one?"

I brought the beer from inside, then moved on. Daphne was tutoring at Francine's elbow. I took up a station where I could watch and listen. It seemed that the actress had appropriated our daughter for herself.

"I have to get you on screen," Francine said, "the way you can do this." Daphne was crafting Chinese rosettes, spirals, and chrysanthemums as everyone marveled. Valerie was absorbed in her own artistry. She was carefully fashioning the squash into a realistic penis, in between sips of wine.

The lunch hour was drawing near. The women were having a great time, although I couldn't hear everything they were saying -- I only knew the talk was about men. Mia had the shrimp scampi underway. She summoned me with a wave.

"Everybody wants to meet dad," she said. "I was telling them his story, and how he just got here, and he's not excited about it. They want to cheer him up. See if you can get him to come up here."

I went to the lower terrace and discovered Stanley asleep in the chaise lounge. Slack-jawed, his breathing was raspy. He hadn't taken off his faded madras shirt with its frayed collar. It bore damp spots of sweat. His book lay where it had fallen.

I wrestled with the question of whether or not to wake him. I decided not to, given all he'd been through within the past twenty-four hours. I quietly rolled over a large patio umbrella to provide more shade. On the upper terrace there was the clatter of ceramic and the clink of silver, as the table was being set for lunch. It was by far our best day yet.

I settled on the chaise next to Stanley to savor the moment. Listening to the activities on the upper terrace, I felt so happy for Mia. A moment like this -- her contralto laughter sometimes separated itself from the ruckus and gales of laughter over whatever stories they were telling -- was so sweet after the months we had been through. I closed my eyes too.

117

I somehow sensed Jan blocking my sun.

"You joining us?" she asked.

"Certainly. Thank you."

We were very much alone, with Stanley still fast asleep.

"She's enjoying your wife," Jan said to me about Francine, as if I had asked. "It's good for her."

"I'm glad to hear it."

Without missing a beat she said, "Pictures aren't allowed," she said.

I sat there as though I had no idea what she was talking about.

"No audio, no video, that's the rule behind closed doors. We're paying customers. We sue people over it. I'll set up a snapshot of Francine with you and your wife before we leave, something you can show guests. I'll have her autograph it. Let me have that disk, and put a new one in."

"This is Mexico," I reminded my officious opponent. "Don't threaten me."

"*You're* in Mexico. But I can have your daughter sued. She lives in the States."

"My daughter was just standing there," I shot back.

"Our lawyers will say she was complicit in a scheme to defame. Or whatever they come up with. She'll need an attorney, poor kid. You get the bills. Don't think I'm kidding. Where's the camera?"

"It's not here. I left it somewhere."

"Find it."

She sneered, turned and left. Had that really happened? I glanced to see what Stanley might have heard. His eyes were just opening; he was disoriented.

"You want to come up and eat now?" I asked Stanley.

He shook his head, rubbing his whiskered face.

"I need to join them," I said.

"Go ahead."

I mounted the steps to the upper terrace and was suddenly in demand.

"Have you got your camera?" Francine asked me.

"Not right here." I was taken aback by the question. She didn't seem upset.

"Get it then."

Mia and Daphne looked very happy, just like Francine. I stole a look at Jan, who was moving on the outside of the group with a stony expression, clearly displeased at this new direction.

"What did you say 'Zihuatanejo' means?" Francine asked Mia. "The women's hideout?"

"'A place for women.'"

"Same thing. We want pictures."

I got my camera from the ledge behind a potted plant. Francine had the group pose as a whole for the first shot, knotting up like relatives at an annual family reunion. Then Francine and Mia and Daphne hooked arms around each other and I obediently took that photo, followed by several more of other configurations. In the final one, Francine put her cheek to Mia's so I could take a tight shot of their two faces beaming at me. I noticed that the pitcher of mimosas I'd resupplied once already was empty, because only drops came out when Celeste tried for a final refill.

"Put that on your website," Francine said, "and say that Francine Longman described the Cooking School at Z as the highlight of her trip."

11

Francine could not bring herself to leave, she was having so much fun. She'd come to Zihuatanejo to flop and restore herself, having just finished seven exhausting weeks shooting a film in Africa (confidentially, she said, she hated the director). But being locked away in a rented hilltop mansion in Zihuatanejo -- I knew the property, which had bizarre Grecian columns -- lost its magic after the first forty-eight hours, even with an infinity pool "that absolutely overlooks the entire galaxy." She liked kicking back with regular people for a change. And if she wasn't leaving Casa Blue, neither was anyone else, which was fine with us.

"This is exactly what I needed," Francine said, not for the first time.

It got to be two-thirty, the heat of the day. Francine sprawled theatrically in her chair, and let her tongue hang out to everyone's amusement. In any pose, Francine Longman was simply beautiful. Her languid companions were nibbling on the fruit plate and cold iced tea I'd just brought out. Mia looked absolutely buoyant.

"Would I like going to the market in town?" Francine asked Mia. They were all in the shade of the terrace umbrella, below the greater shade of the African tulip tree. "I understand it's an incredible experience for the senses."

"You should go. I'll take you."

"We'll do that," Francine said, although this would never

materialize during her remaining time. Once she left the property, we could never reach her again.

Mia floated one out there for the ladies. "Do you know why the Spanish conquerors banned the cultivation of amaranth in Mexico?"

"Is this a trivia question?" asked Celeste, who was partial to thick slices of papaya.

"It wasn't trivial at all," Mia said. "It seems the established Indian civilizations were given to lopping off the heads of their fairest maidens to appease the gods. They'd collect the warm female blood..."

"Oh God, do I want to know this?" asked Valerie. "I'm just getting my period." This I could hear from where I stood, observing like a waiter, a non-person.

"...And they'd mix it with amaranth into little patties that they cooked and shared as part of the ceremonies. Amaranth was the indigenous people's main source of protein. Once it was prohibited by the Spanish, malnutrition spread. Thousands died after it was banned."

"Of course men probably dreamed up sacrificing the women," said our daughter. "It's never the other way around."

"You say it sister," Valerie said.

"Until a few years ago, right here in Zihuatanejo, a young man who wanted to marry a particular girl could kidnap her for a few days and force himself on her," Mia said. "It still happens, although it's illegal now. Sometimes family members conspire, even the girl's."

"You're kidding."

"I'm not kidding. Go down the coast below Acapulco, to Costa Chica. A big part of the wedding celebration used to be checking the sheets to see that the girl was a virgin. This is fairly recent. If she wasn't, she was sent packing with her family. The groom's mother hung a clay pot out in front with a hole in the bottom, to advertise the reason."

"I'll tell you when women will be equal," said Valerie. "It's the day men start cleaning the porcelain in the house."

Righteous condemnations of women's misfortunes around the globe, and in American marriages, continued until three, when Francine had to leave, according to Jan, who would brook no argument. Our celebrity had a five o'clock appointment with a producer who'd apparently flown down from Los Angeles at her request.

Francine had instructed Jan to pay the tariff for the whole group, which included several bottles of wine and Cuban cigars they all sampled after lunch, plus a considerable tip. A good-sized credit-card payment headed for our bank account.

— • —

"I have an idea before we clean anything up," Mia said enthusiastically. "Daphne and dad haven't seen the beach yet. Let's leave everything and have a walk and a swim."

Ten minutes later, the four of us were in the mini-van and in our bathing suits. Mia was completely energized.

"I think today was the breakthrough," she said. "We're going to have momentum."

I could see in the rearview mirror that our two passengers in the back seat didn't quite understand. They'd thought the Cooking School at Z was doing reasonably okay.

"We had a slow start," I told them over my shoulder. "We thought we'd get more people right away."

"So are you losing money?" Stanley asked.

"We haven't sat down and figured it out. We'd have to break out a lot of startup costs." We weren't bringing in enough to pay our bills, but that didn't need to be shared.

At the south end of the *Playa La Ropa*, I drove down a rutted track used by the locals. This brought us to some cracked concrete surfaces close to the beach.

"Don't park under a coconut tree," Mia reminded me.

"I wasn't going to."

Mia turned to the back seat. "Four days after he drove us down from California without getting a scratch, a coconut fell on the right front fender. Three weeks to get it repaired."

"The paint still doesn't look right."

Daphne found that hilarious. "Dad, even I know you don't park under a coconut tree."

We took a few towels. The Mexicans belonging to other vehicles were either sitting in lawn chairs, listening to their car radios and talking, or they were down at the waves with their families, some in swimsuits, others enjoying the bay's warm waters in regular clothing. The men returned acknowledgments.

"The water's a perfect temperature," Daphne announced, standing in water up to her knees. She shielded her eyes as she looked across the bay. Seeing her from the back, I remembered her in that pose as a little girl, minus the butterfly tattoo, its upper half visible above her suit bottom.

"Were you ever in the Pacific Ocean, dad?" asked Mia.

"About fifty years ago, in Hawaii. I had to keep my bandages dry. I could only get my feet wet. Me and Jerry Fagan from Staten Island. The poor guy died from head injuries in an Amtrak crash about ten years ago. I never went to the beach when I was selling melons in California after the war."

Stanley loved the ocean. He regularly fished years ago in Long Island Sound or out in the ocean for blues. He'd like it here, the ability to come down to the water every day. He peeled off his T-shirt, which advertised a knish wholesaler on Houston Street by Second Avenue -- just in case anyone on *Playa La Ropa* happened to need some for a fiesta, I suppose. Mia took his T-shirt, and in he went. Eventually we all were in, ducking under waves and laughing.

Stanley's mobility improved in the water. He actually went for a long swim, with his slow, quirky stroke. Mia inherited his love of swimming, but didn't join him. She went for a walk down the beach with Daphne while I kept an eye on her dad.

Standing there, very much in the moment, still basking in the celebrity visit, it felt like a new beginning. I had renewed faith that the Cooking School at Z would succeed.

— • —

After Stanley dried off, we went walking in the direction the women had taken. The sun was getting lower on the horizon.

"You better today with being here?" I asked.

"I feel like a fish out of water, you want to know." A man who refused to own sunglasses, Stanley kept squinting at the sunny zipper that held the surface of the bay together.

"You'll adjust," I assured him.

We halted as a dead, puffed-up blowfish rolled past, covered with spines. "That's me. I'm like that fish. I don't belong here," Stanley said.

"You couldn't stay where you were. You'll come down here and swim every day."

"Listen to what I'm saying." He looked to see that he had my complete attention. "I have a certificate of deposit and my Social Security check. I'm leaving if this doesn't work out. Let's get that straight. Now that I'm here, I'm wondering how I let Mia bamboozle me into this. That girl's got an iron will, just like her mother."

"And you would leave to go where?"

"Back to New York. I can rent a room with friends. And what kind of life is this here for you two? I don't understand why you're not in the States."

I could see our women far in the distance, coming our way.

"I can tell you who would have liked it here," Stanley said, transitioning seamlessly. "Beatrice." A woman friend, come and gone, the only female relationship he'd had since his wife died.

"Beatrice," I repeated, with great gravity. "She would have been thrilled to have you bring her down for a month, all expenses paid."

"I don't hold that against her," Stanley said. "I've moved on."

He may have moved on, but Mia hadn't, not on the subject of Beatrice. Several years after my mother-in-law died, this woman latched onto her father. Ten years younger, she was an alcoholic bottle blonde, memorable for her aged, pale yellow Cadillac and her love of Atlantic City's blackjack tables. She seduced Stanley into underwriting her good times, and left the scene soon after a scathing confrontation with Mia. Afterward, we conjectured that Beatrice would have left him soon anyway. He was running out of cash.

"I left behind the people I knew," Stanley said. "I had a life with them."

"But you'll make new friends down here. You have to give it time."

His glance said I was a patronizing idiot.

"Ok, then," I said, running out of patience. "You're in a new country. You're walking on a beach that rich people pay a lot of money to visit. We think it's wonderful. No more cold, no more icy sidewalks. You can't miss the cold. It fell to sixteen degrees in New York last night. And you have your daughter and me, and your grandkids will visit."

"You think Mia loves this?" he asked.

"Yes."

He opened his hands as if it were hopeless, talking to someone with so little insight.

"You see yourselves being here forever?" he continued.

"This cooking school is Mia's dream. Whether we're here five years from now ... we'll see. What in this life is certain?"

"Well, you could leave me behind in five years, with all the new friends I'm going to make, right? What is that man doing?"

A middle-aged Mexican was crouching in very shallow water. It was low tide. In one hand he held a plastic bag containing some sand crabs. With his free hand he was plowing in the sand, feeling for more. I explained this to Stanley.

"That's his dinner, huh?"

"Probably." Then I said, "Do you have any idea what you sound like, with all this complaining?"

"Half of it, I like to hear myself talk. You live alone, you get like that. But you, what are you doing here? You never had a career. Now you're on the downside?"

"The Cooking School at Z is a business. It takes two of us. Mia's the one out in front. I join in when there's a man in the group, otherwise I stay in the wings and do the work back stage."

He shook his head, displeased. Sometimes there was no reasoning with Stanley. Deal with it, was how Mia and I felt. We'd gone out of our way for him, and he had to meet us in the middle. We believed Stanley appreciated that at some level.

"Dad," Daphne snickered as she approached with Mia. "That bathing suit. I can't believe we gave that to you."

I was wearing the blue Speedo that our three kids had sent down for my birthday, along with a funny card.

"Speedos are acceptable on *Playa La Ropa*," I said.

"I saw one on the beach, on a young guy," Daphne said.

"He wears it because you kids gave it to him," said Mia. "All you men look like you're carrying a little baggy of mushrooms if you need to reach for a snack."

"Thanks."

"I took Daphne down to show her Eloi's, where I'm thinking of having Lauren's wedding." She pointed it out to her father. A few people were sitting outside the beachside one-story cantina, which had a large open area and bar inside, besides the resin tables and chairs on the sand under beach umbrellas. At night they turned on white Christmas lights, regardless of the time of year.

"This is a beach wedding she's having?" Stanley asked.

"They do them beautifully," Mia said.

Nearing our towels, Daphne bailed out and headed for her beach towel. The three of us continued toward the southern end of the *playa*.

"Dad says he's going to fly home if he's not happy here," I informed Mia.

"I see. Well, you should wait at least until that chair monstrosity we're shipping down here arrives, so you can take it back on the plane after I chop it into pieces."

Unaffected by his daughter's sarcasm, Stanley gave me an accusing look. "You two wouldn't be here if you hadn't lost all your money, and you wouldn't have dragged me down here either."

"I didn't 'lose' all our money. Investments didn't work out, the same way it was for a lot of people. Multimillionaires lost everything. People a lot smarter than me."

"Where money's concerned, that's almost everyone. Forgive me for saying."

"Dad's right," Mia said. "You lost it, it's gone, and I forgive you." Her smile took on another dimension. "Now that we're here, I forgive you," and she put her arm around my waist.

"That's twice you lost it," Stanley said.

We all knew what he was referring to. Fifteen years earlier, there was an opportunity to invest in cattle on an Oregon ranch, which was sold as a marvelous, perfectly legal tax shelter. The IRS decided otherwise, and charged back interest that almost killed us. We managed to keep the house.

"Both of you are talking about money that I earned for this family, which has not exactly been suffering over the years. I don't want to hear about it."

"Now you're being sensitive," Stanley said. "I'm sorry for

bringing it up."

"If some day I get as difficult as you're being right now, I'll swim out as far as I can on a moonlit night."

"Jeff," Mia said sharply.

"Just hope you never get old," Stanley said.

"And how would I avoid that? No thanks."

"Stop already, both of you," Mia said.

We'd actually reached the treed peninsula at the southern end of the *playa*. A palapa-roofed cantina was on our left, its sandwich board listing its overpriced choices in English and in Spanish. A Nahuatl Indian girl, cute in a calico dress, came over from a spot where she had been sitting with her mother beneath a tree. She extended her little arms with an array of bead necklaces on each.

I politely declined.

"You want to feel sorry for yourself," I told my father-in-law on the way back, "tell it to that little girl and her mother. They have problems. You have no problems, compared to their lives. None of us do. Tell it to Isabel who'll be with you after Daphne goes back."

"So you think I should be quiet and happy? All these changes, with my daughter and the doctor dictating my life, and I should accept that?" He licked his dry lips, searching for words. He was upset. "Three times I had those seizures. You wake up from it and you don't know what happened, you don't know anything, except you soiled yourself and you terrified the people around you and there you are in a hospital bed and it's hours later or the fucking next day."

"That's why you're with us," Mia said, locking arms with her dad. "You take your medicine, and it won't happen again. You could asphyxiate or hit your head and die from that. Now you'll be fine. And we want you here."

"We do," I said, "if you want to be with us."

Loved, if only for the moment, Stanley changed personalities again. "I wish your mother was here to see you with the cooking. And that Daphne. She's a swimmer, like you."

12

Timing it perfectly, Phil dropped in just as the shrimp were coming off the grill. We were having soft tacos tonight after the beach -- nothing fancy, just a mild mango salsa without peppers. Mia was being ever so careful with her dad's stomach, so he wouldn't be erupting in the toilet and going off about "Montezuma's Revenge." He'd broadcast his concern quite graphically.

Phil was decked out in a muumuu of sorts, printed with toucans on a yellow background. She descended the stone stairs on my arm. Her plump neck was encircled by a necklace of hand-painted, small wooden parrots. Her thin-strapped sandals seemed far too dainty for the pressure on her fat feet, but the straps didn't explode as she regally approached my father-in-law.

"So you are the famous *Señor Stanley*," said Phil, closing in on dad, who was at the table by himself. "Sit, sit, sit. Don't get up. I'm Philomena Drisopolous, the neighbor next door."

"I was going to introduce you properly, Phil," I said.

Stanley struggled to his feet anyway, because that was the way you respected a lady, as well as certain younger women who met his standards. Phil purred when an additional place setting magically appeared. Dinner began.

Mia volunteered to Phil that today had been our best day ever. "Five people, and a good group. They had so much fun."

"That's won-der-ful," Phil pronounced.

"One was a celebrity."

"I *know*," said Phil, happy for us.

That she knew would have startled us at one time, but no longer. I asked anyway. Her half-day housekeeper had spotted Francine Longman out front.

"And it was so much fun," Mia said, "having Daphne teach the class with me. That was a treat." She glanced fondly at our daughter.

"Pop," said Daphne, to get her granddad's attention. She brushed the corner of her mouth to show him; he took the cue and brushed away the offending food particle. Daphne had finally stopped sniffling, perhaps from swimming in the salt water.

"So you cook as well as your mother?" Phil said. "My God, you're so young."

"No. I don't really cook."

Phil held forth with unbridled enthusiasm about the unavoidable success of the Cooking School at Z, directing her comments primarily at Stanley.

"So you must be a broken-hearted Brooklyn Dodger fan," Phil said. "I know about baseball. It always surprises people that I do." She laughed with great merriment.

"We have the Mets."

"My Angelo doesn't know anything about baseball. He's Greek. Occasionally he follows basketball. The one time we went as a family to see the San Francisco Giants -- we had our son, he was very young -- and Angelo couldn't explain the game. Our son had to explain it to him. So how do you like Zihuatanejo so far? Isn't it magnificent?"

Mia and I continued eating, but we were all ears.

"Magnificent," he said.

"When we first came here," Phil continued, "I thought it was just the most special place. And it still is. I understand you do

130

beautiful paintings."

Dad looked accusingly at Mia. How else could Phil have learned that he liked to paint. Mia averted her eyes, finding this the ideal moment to pick up my Negra Modelo and replenish my glass.

"I do some painting," he admitted.

Daphne said, "Beauty is in the eye of the beholder. Never tell pop a painting is beautiful. Tell him you *think* something is beautiful, in your eyes. Tell him your personal experience of the work."

Phil looked befuddled, so Daphne launched into a monologue about the nature of beauty. Dad weighed in now and again; Mia agreed or disagreed as she saw fit. For this heated, academic discussion to suddenly arise on a terrace in Zihuatanejo? Phil's mouth hung open. Mine would have too, if I hadn't witnessed it before. This subject had first arisen when Daphne chose "The Nature of Beauty" for her science project in tenth grade. It earned her a D. She sent photos of the exhibit to her grandfather, who wrote an excoriating letter to the teacher without consulting anyone beforehand, and that hadn't turned out well for his grand-daughter. Daphne's project had nothing quantifiable about beauty, that was the problem for a science experiment. To this day, the two of them would occasionally go on a rant over this subject, mixed in with a bit of theater.

"Why is a skinny little bitch in a magazine ad supposed to be beautiful?" Daphne was asking. "Your basic woman could knock her down with one slap. How is it beautiful to be weak?"

Mia said, "Daphne and a bunch of her girlfriends took boxing one quarter during her freshman year."

"I'll tell you about beauty," Stanley said, leaning closer to Phil than he had all evening. "When my wife Emma died, Daphne went to the funeral home and did a charcoal portrait of her grandmother in the casket, propped up. This was something artists did in medieval times."

"They made death masks too," said Daphne.

"Yes, and I still remember Daphne making us ask the funeral director for permission. On the back of the painting she wrote, 'With love to Grandpa.' I still have it," he reminded Daphne. "Did you know that?"

"No," Daphne said, embarrassed. "I didn't know where it went."

"I brought it here. I'm going to hang it when I get a nail."

Mia's eyes filled up. A silence descended on the group.

"A cup of coffee would be lovely right now," Phil suggested.

I went to make some. Mia cleared the dishes. Daphne helped her mother. That left Phil alone with Stanley. On this dead-quiet evening, the way sound carried, the three of us decided to eavesdrop from the Inferno, just like a Shakespearean comedy.

— • —

"I'm here to die," Stanley was soon saying.

"We're all here to die," Phil chastised. "All over the earth. I find the Mexicans have a better compact with death than we do."

Clever, but Stanley wasn't buying.

"Two years ago," Phil continued, "I had heart trouble. I could hardly move. I became terribly overweight." This allowed an inference that she viewed her current self as normal, which I found startling. "Finally my doctor changed my prescription, and it made all the difference. You're lucky to be here with family. Jeff and Mia are the nicest couple I know, and they're so talented. You and your wife did a wonderful job with Mia. What a child."

Daphne whispered to her mom, "You're so perfect." Mia shushed her.

But moments later Stanley and Phil dropped their voices. We could no longer hear their words. They were disagreeing, judging by the body language, but Stanley grinned several times, which meant it wasn't serious.

I poured boiling water into two large French presses for coffee. Mia carried one, I carried the other, and Daphne brought a tray with the cups, a pint carton of *leche*, and the sugar substitute that Phil preferred.

"Did you convince dad this place isn't so bad?" Mia inquired as we rejoined them.

"It's not just about the place," Stanley said.

"It's about growing old," said Phil. "We're in agreement. What is everyone doing tomorrow afternoon?"

"I don't know what I'm doing an hour from now," Stanley said.

"An hour from now you're sleeping," Mia said.

"It's Sunday tomorrow," I answered. "No one has any plans."

"Then I'll come by for you at two o'clock," Phil announced.

I helped Phil to her feet, as she chose this moment to get up. "I have some friends going sailing on that lovely yacht with the green sail that you probably saw out in the bay today."

"I don't go sailing," Stanley said.

"Nonsense. You're here to have fun. We'll pick you up. Some people are coming you'll love to meet. The Wilmeyers. He used to own a chain of bakeries in Columbus, Ohio. And a physician and his wife, they'll be coming. They're a sweet, sweet couple who just started coming last winter."

"I'm not going," Stanley objected again.

"I'll have him ready," said Mia. "He used to sail all over Sheepshead Bay with his friend."

"What are you people doing, ignoring my wishes?"

Daphne stepped in. "Mom, let grandpa do what he wants."

"Am I in charge of my own life?" Stanley asked angrily. He rose from his chair, glared at everyone, and stormed off to his room.

"No, not when you act like you are, with this dark personality," Mia said to herself, and anyone who cared to listen. In the campground below, someone was playing a squeezebox: "Besame

Mucho," or "Kiss Me A Lot," a Mexican standard. "People somewhere are having a good time," she said.

I helped Phil climb to the upper landing, where she paused to gather her breath. She regrouped the moment we stepped outside the house.

"We'll cheer him up," she said gamely. "Such a lovely man. Some of you should come."

"All of us will probably come. I'll let you know in the morning."

13

All five of us set out in the minivan to meet the cutter, which was at the small pier along the north side of Zihuatanejo's harbor. Forced to go, Stanley wouldn't. Allowed to choose, he would. He lectured Mia about the distinction.

I skirted the downtown via *J.M. Morelos*, taking the *Paseo de las Salinas*, eventually turning left onto a steep cobbled roadway. I slowly negotiated the enormous potholes and Sunday's considerable parade of pedestrians, including many children. Vendors or vehicles occupied every cranny. *Prohibido* was hand-painted on bare wood signs by the narrowest of turnoffs.

I started backing into a precarious spot.

"What are you doing?" Mia asked. "You can't park here!"

A boulder-strewn waterline was forty feet below the road's edge. The rusted pipe railing had been broken off long ago. An old Morris Minor, one of several that sneak around town, had the front portion of this little spot where the roadway swelled, leaving just enough space in back for our mini-van. Other vehicles would need room to inch by. I needed to have the wheels on the driver's side very close to the edge. I rolled down my window so I could monitor the situation.

"Dad!" Daphne exclaimed, after she looked back. Too far, and we'd slip over.

"It'll work."

"You're too close to the edge," Mia said. "Jesus!"

Phil had her hand anxiously at her throat. Stanley maintained the silence of the damned.

"Dad, don't go here," Daphne insisted.

"Jeff, you're gonna kill us," Mia shouted.

"It's under control," I said, my head out the window. "It's this or I have to go all the way back into town. Phil and Stanley can't handle that walk." Already we were thirty minutes late. Phil, who was chronically tardy, had kept us waiting. I feathered the brake hydraulics, inching back as I craned my head farther out.

"Mother of God," Phil chimed in, a frog in her throat.

A pair of young European trekkers with big backpacks, and an increasing number of Mexicans, were pausing to watch and discuss. They looked to be divided into two camps about our fate.

"I'm getting out," said Daphne, who went for the door handle.

"We're all getting out," said Mia. "Stop."

Everyone exited the passenger side while I held my ground. Several Mexican men and boys had moved to the edge and were instructing me in Spanish as they watched the tires. Mia was showing me the available space with her hands. Girls were shrieking each time I released the brakes, while their mothers watched stoically. One made the sign of the cross. Looking straight down, my front wheel was nine inches from the edge. Plenty of room. When I finally turned off the motor, relieved applause broke out. I clambered over the console to exit on the passenger side.

"'Is good," said a Mexican fellow, much impressed.

"Dad," said Daphne, "you're insane."

Mia asked, "How are you going to get out if that little car in front leaves and there's something bigger in its place? You can't back up."

"We'll take a taxi," I said blithely.

I folded the sideview mirror against the minivan to give a few more centimeters for cars to inch past. Mia put her arm around my waist, but it was a ruse. As we headed for the pier, she pinched my side hard enough to hurt.

— • —

Five Seasons, a cutter over sixty feet in length, was perpendicular to the end of the pier. We'd seen it in the bay before. It was a sleek, white-hulled craft that had raced competitively in Australia back in the Fifties.

"*Bon jour, Madame Drisopolous*," said the captain, a graying Frenchman. With all the gallantry, his captain's cap should have sported a white plume.

"Phil, you look lovely," said his much younger wife, Sue, who had a Kiwi-sounding accent.

They greeted each one in our party. Advised ahead of time by Phil, they gave Stanley an especially warm welcome. Salsa music was playing.

Phil had given us the lowdown on the captain and his wife during the drive over. For each it was their second marriage. They had retrieved the cutter from slow decay in a dockyard. They spent two years restoring her. Sue was a New Zealander, and she was far superior at sea to her husband. Phil had heard that she had once soloed from New Zealand to Acapulco in a much smaller craft. In inclement weather, Sue reputedly took the helm of the *Five Seasons*, but her French-born husband was loathe to give over control when guests were aboard for little cruises out of the bay. They hired out for informal excursions along the Mexican coast, coming and going like gypsies, sometimes venturing to U.S. destinations as far north as Los Angeles. There were rumors that they shuttled "magic mint," a hallucinogenic plant grown by Indians outside of Oaxaca, but Phil didn't believe it. While magic mint was still completely legal in the U.S. and Mexico, transporting it was surely a delicate matter.

"Phil, you made it!" someone cried out.

About a dozen passengers, ranging in age from their early thirties to twice that, saluted with their plastic tumblers of strawberry margeritas. Phil raised her arms and danced toward her fans. Introductions followed. Stanley tried to hang back, but Phil dragged him forward. Several passengers seemed well along in their drinking. Mia and I had met only one of the couples previously. These were some of Phil's high-season buddies from California, a hard-drinking set down to *par-tay* from San Francisco, San Clemente, Santa Barbara and other sainted and expensive home ports.

"Hi," said the Frenchman's son, his voice from another latitude. He surprised us, seeming to come out of nowhere. He was a handsome, tanned lad in his mid-twenties, with dark hair and a ready smile. He shook our hands, giving his name, Guy. He moved past us, undoing lines, securing whatever bags the passengers had brought aboard. His smile seemed particularly bright for Daphne, who responded in kind.

Some of us sat on the running bench that had been installed along both sides of the cabin. Others stood in small groups as we motored into the bay, picking up speed. A refreshing breeze sprang up. Rum punches found their way into our hands. Sue fetched a *cerveza* for Stanley from the galley below decks. On her next run she brought up a platter of spicy tuna tartar on rounds of cucumber, and crostini spread with an onion and liver pate dotted with capers.

Camera in hand, I sidled near Mia and Stanley. They were discussing Mia's remembrance of a summer vacation when he'd taken her out in a sailboat on Lake Ontario. The light and shadows were just right on their faces. Judging by their expressions, yesterday's bickering had never happened.

At the click of the camera, they looked at me -- surprised, but with no objection or comment. They resumed their conversation. Checking the digital display, it was the perfect shot, the best I would ever take of my wife and her father.

— • —

Soon the captain and his son ratcheted the mainsail up the mast. Under sail, the cutter sliced mightily through the broad ocean swells, gently rising and falling as we left the headlands behind.

"I'm tasting bile," Mia confided. She covered her mouth to burp. For this trip she was trying wristbands that pressed certain nerve endings. Nothing ever worked, but she was determined to overcome seasickness, not wanting to be the sort of person who stayed behind -- or made others decline an invitation because of her.

A couple approached. They were perfectly balanced in height and shape, and wore pressed shorts. She sported a floppy red hat. Sunscreen gave a ghostly hue to both their complexions. Claude and Rene Fabricant.

"Aren't you the couple with the cooking school? How is that going?"

"It's going fine," said Mia.

"Phil was telling us you're having a bit of a challenge getting enough people to come."

"In the beginning." Mia burped again, covering her mouth. "Excuse me."

"You should come sometime," I said. Phil was going to hear from me about this. A little spin control was in order.

"I don't cook anymore," Rene said brightly.

"The cooking thing's going away," her husband declared. He wore amber prescription sunglasses, and seemed to be peering at us from within a personal aquarium. "No one has time to cook for themselves. People go to restaurants more. Our two kids, I don't think either of them keeps anything in the refrigerator." We all steadied ourselves as the cutter took a pronounced swell.

"Is that good or bad?" I asked. "Maybe we need to teach the pleasures of preparing good food."

"I doubt these kids are teachable," he said.

"Are the cooking classes over at the Madrid hurting you?" the wife inquired.

Mia and I looked at each other. Time froze. We'd eaten at the Madrid, a restaurant on a large outdoor terrace right along *Playa La Madera*, the next beach over from Centro. Its aging hotels, with ten or twelve units apiece, had been constructed long ago. Madrid's chef was good -- Marco something from Europe, formerly sous chef at the *Villa Real*. He drew discriminating customers, people who could appreciate his beets with mango salad, or his tower of lobster, fashioned architecturally of spiny *langosta* tails, *chayote* shafts, and julienned vegetables in an accomplished light chile sauce. Marco had an outside grill area, which included a set-up where a Mexican woman made fresh tortillas in front of the guests. A perfect theater.

I said, with the most even tone I could summon, "I wasn't aware the Madrid was offering classes."

"When did this start?" Mia asked.

"We only came down last week," said Claude. "I don't think he had the sandwich board out on the road at that time."

"I know he didn't," his wife said. "But there was a little slip of paper about it that came with our check, and he came around and explained. That was what ... three nights ago?"

"Two nights ago," Claude said. "You don't remember?"

"Why would I? You were no company. You were half asleep through the meal."

"When are the classes?" I asked.

"I think it said Mondays and Thursdays. Late morning. There's a demonstration, then you have lunch. It sounds like great fun. He's such a character." Rene shared with us the price, which was much less than a morning with lunch in the Cooking School at Z.

They moved on. Mia and I looked at each other without saying a word. We could have leapt overboard right then and drowned ourselves. No one would have noticed.

"I can't believe it," Mia said. "He's open the days we're closed?"

She was looking a little weak-kneed. Her color was bad. She steadied herself against me as we rode up a slightly larger swell. A big belch came forth.

"You don't look so good," I said. "Did you eat the spicy tuna?"

"Are you kidding? I haven't eaten a thing."

Suddenly she crouched and stuck her head over the side, leaning as far out as she could, all the while holding onto the steel cable railing for dear life. I held the waistband of Mia's shorts, just in case. She dry-heaved her heart out.

— • —

As the *Five Seasons* came about, Sue pointed out a pair of very large turtles copulating on the surface of the turquoise waters.

"Go for it," yelled a drunk near the captain. A crony stood and lewdly pumped his arm, milking the moment for laughs.

"Don't give it away, honey," countered one of the women.

Having vomited, Mia felt better. We worked through the crowd, promoting the Cooking School at Z whenever I could slip it in with a measure of grace. Stanley was engrossed in conversation.

I told Mia, "I think Daphne's having the best time of anyone."

When he wasn't fulfilling duties, the shirtless and fatless young Frenchman, Guy, was glued to our daughter. She was in her two-piece bathing suit, the T-shirt long gone, with the cocoa-colored *pareo* snugly defining her hips. Daphne was deploying a sort of deep laughter her mother and I hadn't heard before. Mexico was already having its effect. Earlier that day she'd broached the idea that maybe she would skip a semester and stay with us. She'd said her life was so grueling.

"Absolutely not," Mia had argued. "You have a degree to

finish."

"And we already paid for this semester," I'd said.

"And you have an apartment...."

"...Which is full of your stuff," I said.

"Okay. Stop." Daphne had raised her hands, not wanting to be shot. "Jeez."

"You can come back in June."

"Can I say something?"

We ceded the floor. This conversation had taken place in the great room, where I'd been reading the New York Times online to see what was going on in the world, as I did once a week. Mia had been working on menus.

"It's like I have no life in New York. All I do is work, and school. I'm on the subway all the time. It's crazy. This is so real here. And I'd like to spend time with grandpa."

"Cut out clubbing until dawn," Mia had said, "and New York will become very real. You'll be amazed what it looks like when you're awake for a change."

— • —

Once we were back inside the Bay of Zihuatanejo, and under motor once more, our captain brought his human cargo over to *Playa Las Gatas*, a sandy cove just inside the southern headland. He weighed anchor. Sue offered snorkeling gear all around. Four accepted. Daphne and her admirer soon went over the side, along with two of Phil's friends.

"The story goes," Sue explained loudly, "that the reef you see was constructed by Calzontzin, the king of the Tarascan Indians. A hot little princess of his supposedly liked this spot. I've no idea if it's true, but it's a lovely story. But I do know how *Playa Las Gatas* got its name. Can anyone tell me?" She paused, looking over the group. "This used to be a gathering place for little cat sharks. *Las Gatas.*"

"You're making that up," someone challenged.

"Not at all. They're harmless little things, or they were. The locals fished them out. I believe they sold them to the Chinese for shark's fin soup."

"You enjoying yourself, Stanley?" I asked Stanley, who'd come to my side.

"Was Mia sick?"

"She's over it."

"These people like to drink."

"Mia wasn't drinking." Mia was nearby, speaking with the couple who'd advised us about the Madrid.

Sue told the rest of us about the endangered sea turtles that laid eggs on the *playas* of Zihuatanejo Bay, between June and October. Volunteers with the *Viva La Bahia* effort had collected 53,000 eggs last summer and relocated them to protected, remote beaches, in case any of us wanted to join the effort. "The leatherbacks eat jellyfish, and they die from mistakenly eating plastic bags, so never let one get in the water," Sue said. Her husband blew a policeman's whistle with great panache, summoning the snorkelers.

The sun sat low in the sky by the time the *Five Seasons* very slowly edged up to its mooring buoys. Lines were secured. Other boats had taken all the spots along the pier. The *Five Seasons'* passengers took turns, three at a time, going down the ladder into a gray Zodiac and being motored to the dock, where the inebriates had to climb up another ladder, an adventure that included a lot of whooping, laughter, and near spills. All the passengers made the short journey, save one. Daphne was going to stay aboard with her young Frenchman.

"We'll be at home," I said. "Call later for a ride if you need one."

— • —

Alcohol affects Philomena D. in an unusual way. She could sit and imbibe for hours and could seem her normal, extroverted self above the waist, which includes her hands, speaking ability, and facial expressions. But she would lose the ability to walk. Her legs become jelly. Getting up from her bench, then in and out of the Zodiac, had been quite the challenge. She'd struggled into our minivan. Fortunately I had room to back out safely. Once home, Mia and I each took an arm and maneuvered Phil into her house. We'd given Stanley the key to our place.

"You're both so wonderful," Phil said as we assisted her in the direction of her bedroom. "I so enjoyed Stanley. I hope you had a good time."

"Everything was great," Mia replied, almost collapsing to the floor as Phil suddenly lurched her way.

"It was wonderful of you to arrange for all of us to go," I said. "I need to give you a check."

"It was all taken care of, darling."

At the bedroom I pushed the door open with my free hand. Mia said, "I've got it from here."

"I hope I'm not too much of a bother," Phil said.

I leaned toward Phil to kiss her cheek and wish her good night. She looked my way, a bit bleary-eyed. "Your breath is stinky," she confided. "Yours too," she told Mia.

I returned to Casa Blue and found Stanley in his room.

"Phil was three sheets to the wind," Stanley said.

"She likes to party. And I imagine Daphne's at a party right now." With music on Sunday evenings, Ivelisse's restaurant next to the pier was quite the gathering spot, drawing all ages.

"Daphne needs a boyfriend," Stanley announced.

Our daughter didn't discuss her love life with us. Somehow we had raised three children who kept their relationships, or lack thereof, as state secrets. Until a relationship was firmly established, the most we ever extracted was that one or another of them was 'hanging out' with a member of the opposite sex. Stanley, who had been living in the same city as Daphne, had the best inside intelligence.

"Why do you say that?" I asked.

"She comes over sometimes. She takes a long bubble bath because she doesn't have a tub. I feed her and we talk."

"About boys?"

"Whatever she wants," he said. "Sometimes boys. Usually I make her pot roast. I give her the leftover to take for sandwiches. I usually get a small cobbler at the bakery for dessert. I wish we still had Ebinger's."

He was phrasing this in the present tense, as if Brooklyn were still his home. I knew that Daphne would put the leftover pot roast in her refrigerator until it had visible slime or a detectable odor, at which time she still hesitated to toss it in the garbage. She was almost a vegetarian, except with her grandfather. She didn't want to hurt his feelings. He believed his pot roast, sweetened with dried apricots, was irresistible.

— • —

When the phone rang later that evening, Mia got it. I also got it at the same moment on the extension.

"Mom."

It was Daphne.

"Yes honey. How are you doing?"

"I'm fine. I'm going to stay over on the boat. They all invited me."

A plural, familial invitation.

"I just wanted to call so you wouldn't worry. I know how you and dad are. Okay, so I'll talk to you tomorrow."

"Call us in the morning and we'll pick you up."

"That's okay. Bye." As fast as a hummingbird, she was gone.

145

Our daughter may have lived on her own in New York for several years now, but here she was within our sphere of influence. My old paternal juices were flowing by the time I joined Mia.

"The parents are on the boat," I said. "I'm sure she's safe." Beyond "safe," I did not let my imagination run.

"This is why it's good for her to live in another city," Mia said.

"She's a young woman now," I noted.

"She's a girl who thinks she's a woman. Just the way I was when I was twenty-two."

"We were already married, and had a baby."

Mia shook her head, apparently trying to dislodge the memory of being a parent that young. "So on Monday, I say we go to the Madrid and check his program."

"We'll see what he's got."

Mia moved closer. It had been a long, eventful day. We considered each other.

"Is the Cooking School at Z going to make it?" Mia asked. "What do you really think?"

"I think we need it to."

14

The next morning Mia looked like she'd experienced a hard night at sea. We were going to view our competition at Madrid, but her greater worry was Daphne. Things always happened to her. Random things.

"She's still my baby," Mia said during breakfast, explaining why she hadn't slept well. "If I'm not being cool enough for everybody, it's too damn bad."

"You were her age once," I said.

"That's why I worry about her."

"This is just a spontaneous little romance that came along...and it's probably something she'll always remember. A summer love."

"I'm not calling it that."

I believe everything was weighing heavily on Mia at this point -- her dad, the Madrid, our cooking school. She sighed, letting out her exasperation.

"Mia, our daughter's twenty-two."

"And this is Mexico, and this is Daphne. I liked them all better when they were in diapers."

Isabel arrived punctually at nine, packed into jeans, a white T-shirt, and new running shoes, with her hair clipped back and ready for action on this, her first day. We spoke about her family, reminding her how much we had appreciated the lunch prepared by her mother. Isabel had come with a large plastic bag of Cooking

School at Z aprons and side towels -- more, perhaps, than we had ordered. Her mother had apparently gotten carried away.

Mia devoted the first twenty minutes to breaking the ice between Isabel and Stanley. He did know how to be extraordinarily gracious with individuals from outside the family, from his days selling shoes. Then Mia toured Isabel through Casa Blue and some of the tasks that would be her responsibility. Privately, *sotto voce*, she reviewed in some detail the particulars of her father's illness and how to care for him, in the very unlikely event of a seizure. I contributed a few cautionary notes. Basically, when neither Mia nor I were home, Isabel should definitely be with him or in immediate proximity. We'd encouraged Isabel to bring a book, and she had -- a biography of Sonja Henie, the ice queen, in English. If Stanley wanted to go out, she should accompany him, first telling us where they were going. We were discouraging anything other than a trip to *Playa La Ropa* for this first week or so. Mia and I crossed our fingers that this would work.

Daphne called shortly before we were due to leave for the Madrid. Mia was relieved to hear her voice, but the call was short and sweet.

"She's fine," Mia said, hanging up. "She was just checking in, so we wouldn't worry about her."

"What else did she say?"

"She's fine, everything's fine. Fine, fine, fine. That's what she considers to be information."

"Is she coming back soon?"

"She doesn't know what they're doing. Of course not. Why should she know anything about anything?"

— • —

A tiny cluster of aging little hotels and apartment buildings -- none more than four stories high, sprouting small balconies and tiny terraces over a stretch of a few hundred yards -- overlook *La Madera* beach in the hotel zone just outside Centro. In Europe, it would seem like housing for pensioners, packed cheek to jowl.

Mia and I parked by an empty residential lot where craftsmen were fashioning rattan furniture out of drying bamboo. A large sandwich board was propped on the shady road, hand-lettered with "La Madrid Cooking Shool" in English -- a letter missing -- and *Escuela Cocina Madrid* in Spanish right beneath it, with the hours and complimentary adjectives filling the remaining space. An arrow aimed down a cobbled alley to the restaurant's shabby tiled veranda, right at the beach, front and center.

"You're sure he won't know us?" I asked Mia.

"We ate here that one time, long ago. I just don't think he knows who we are. You said you've passed him in the market some mornings, and he just nods because you see each other there. He never talks to you, right?"

"If we have to introduce ourselves, we give our names and let it go at that."

Two eager Mexican lads ushered us to the outdoor grill, where white caterer's canvas was draped overhead for shade. Beneath it were nine or ten guests assembled around their flamboyant host, Marco. He welcomed us with a hand wave without missing a beat as he completed his tale about a kitchen fire on a cruise ship. We'd missed most of it, but people whooped and clapped at the story's conclusion. Marco bowed. Physically small, he had an outsized head, with lush, curly hair that was partially orange, held back in a simple pony tail. He wore a white chef's tunic with his name on it. His long fingers helped him articulate.

Frozen margeritas were brought to us.

"Not exactly Casa Blue martinis," Mia whispered. "I'm not drinking this thing." She set it down on the nearest table.

Marco held forth once again in his mysterious accent. He'd grown up somewhere between the Camargue in southern France and Basque country, or in Italy near the Albanian border -- it depended on who you asked.

"Peoples make too much out of food these days," Marco began. "It is only the egg, it is only the fruit, it is only the bread. It is only that."

Personally, I thought that was an odd thing to tell people who had come for a cooking experience.

"We don't need so many foods. You know?" He rubbed his snuffly nose.

"I tell you a story, from when I was in Brazil. I met this man was a yogi. A great yogi. This man taught at the university. He had very few students, maybe no students, because the Brazilians...." Marco made a gesture, suggesting we should understand without his saying more. "The Brazilians, they love life too much for the yoga."

Marco took a few steps closer to his audience and dropped his voice. "For two years this man when he was young lived in the mountains in India. He was a great ascetic. He tells us how he ate only potatoes, nothing but potatoes, and that was enough. Maybe something green that he grew, some tiny teeny plants, but no more than that. Water to drink."

He finger-waved at three more guests who came in, making it twelve. The Cooking School at Z had yet to draw this many patrons in a week.

"This man, to me, was the smartest man when he talked. He talked about the silly things that we do, yes? You know these silly things? 'I'm not happy'..." -- Marco made an exaggerated long face, which brought a ripple of laughter as he rubbed imaginary tears -- "...and I must have this, and I must have that. The sex is not so good. The work is too hard. What is it you say? Yadayadayada," and his hand made rolling motions.

"What were you doing in his class?" a guest interrupted.

Marco shrugged. "A lover," he confided with facial contortions and raising his eyes toward heaven, drawing laughs. "So why are we here, my friends, if this is true? If food is nothing to this great man the yogi?"

Marco looked around for answers. More margeritas were being carried around. Several people took a fresh one. This audience was on its way to becoming very appreciative, I thought, and might soon need chairs.

"Because we're not great yogis, or yoginis, or whatever it is," answered a woman in a straw hat.

"No, this is not true," Marco said with great drama. "It's because food is so unimportant, there is room for love. We can put love into the food. There is not already something else there that amounts to much. With food you have nothing. There is only the egg" -- now a magician, he opened his fist and there was an egg -- "and there is only the fruit" -- a large strawberry materialized suddenly in his other hand -- "and there is only the loaf of bread, but you know...." His hands full, he slowly looked down at his crotch, which produced great hilarity.

He even had me smiling

Mia consulted her watch. "It's all show. He hasn't cooked anything," clearly a check mark against our host.

After donning a white kitchen apron, and tucking in a side towel with great flair, Marco instructed each of us to take an egg from the bowl his assistant was bringing around.

"Each of you," he began, "you have an egg with no love. No little chickey-dickey inside. But we will put the love in when we make one of my favorites which is Frittata Marco. I name this after me because each person should have a dish named for them, there is no question of that. So you change this a little and you call it Frittata Fred ... or Frittata Helen."

More laughing.

"We each contribute our egg," he said, moving about like a priest with the bowl, until everyone had cracked and contributed their egg's

151

contents, save one gentleman, whose egg fell to the ground.

"Someone now will make this whippy," he said, seeking a volunteer to take the whisk to the bowl, "while I show this man to crack an egg."

Another egg magically appeared in Marco's right hand. He helped the man crack it one-handed, into a glass. Marco encouraged applause.

"You drink that," said Marco, "I give you free dinner tonight."

"It might have salmonella, Lloyd," his wife cautioned.

"Salmonella is on the shell of the egg if there is salmonella, it is not inside the egg. Because we cracked the egg beautifully, there is no salmonella. He is safe."

Still, the man refused. Marco shrugged. Everyone was having a great time, and even Mia was starting to warm to him. His charm was irresistible.

Marco picked up another egg from his work surface and abruptly tossed it in my direction. I missed catching it. It fell on my shoe. The eggshell showed cracking, but nothing leaked out.

"It's hard boiled," someone said.

People hooted. Marco apologized, not wanting to humiliate. He had me chop the roasted peppers, garlic, and potatoes, mince herbs roughly, and fold the mixture into the bowl of eggs, along with crumbled *queso* cheese. All the while he was talking to the audience. Salt and pepper he personally threw in with a great flourish.

"You see how skilled this man is," he told everyone, meaning me. "He and his beautiful wife have a cooking school at *Playa La Ropa*. You want to learn better cooking, you go there too. I only have fun. The food is not important. This is Señor Jeff" -- he did a slide step to the side, then gestured my way as though I were playing bass and it was my time to be acknowledged -- "and Señora Farrell is here, whose food is said to be sublime."

Once Mia had been applauded -- she looked sheepish, and I

could understand why -- Marco instructed us all to watch carefully. We would see a miracle.

Marco studiously added two tablespoons of olive oil to a hot skillet. He swirled quickly and returned it to the burner. He supervised as a fresh volunteer poured in the egg mixture with great reverence, not wanting to spill a drop. Then Marco had one of his young staff dash off with the skillet to the restaurant's interior kitchen.

"We cook only the time it takes for a fish to make love. Very quick. It is my wish that love is not so quick for any of you. Please now, we do this together: *uno ... dos ... tres.* It is finished. Manuel!"

Manuel high-stepped it back with a frittata that had been made ahead of time in an identical skillet, a ploy that fooled two gullible guests who had no idea how long it took to cook anything. Some Mexican children had come over from the beach and enjoyed the gag as well. Marco positioned a platter above the skillet that Manuel was holding. With great drama, on the count of three, the two men flipped the golden frittata, lightly browned, only the plate. Applause broke out. He had another volunteer brush it quickly with an emulsion of roasted peppers, a bit of lime juice, and some balsamic vinegar.

Waving a chef's knife, Marco swiftly counted off his guests. In the wink of an eye, he created thirteen equally sized slices, no mean feat given the odd number. Two volunteers took spatulas and served it up on individual plates. Frittata Marco was delicious. We ate as Marco demonstrated a twice-cooked pork recipe -- already braised, it would now be quickly finished on the grill, the aroma of the cumin, oregano, and cilantro from the marinade taking on grand proportions over the hot embers. This would be available only during lunch.

"The guy's a kick," said the egg-dropper, who seemed to consider me his kin.

What could I say? "Absolutely."

— • —

Just before noon, Madrid's opening time, Marco also introduced his audience to conch empanadas with salsa. He had everyone in stitches as he illustrated how it was necessary to hammer the tough meat of the conch to render it digestible, overdoing it with an array of instruments from a tool chest, even feigning a mighty blow with a ball peen hammer. Meanwhile, Manuel brought around empanadas from the kitchen.

"Tastes like chicken," someone cracked.

"It is chicken," Marco said. That broke up the place. He bowed deeply, and gestured toward his kitchen staff, who'd come out. Real conch empanadas appeared for sampling.

"Now you are to stay for lunch as part of the program, and tonight you must come for dinner," Marco said to all. "If not tonight, tomorrow, but at least three times while you are in Mexico. This, I make no money. I become poor, we charge so little. My friends here, Señor and Señora Farrell, they charge too much -- no, no, no, I am kidding only -- but they know how it costs. You pay but it is not much and it is only to introduce you to La Madrid. And I am able to practice my magic that I teach myself when the restaurant is empty. A chef must do something with his hands."

Everyone thanked Marco personally for the wonderful time. Several pairs moved off to tables for lunch.

"So you see what I do," Marco said to us. Apparently mind-reading was another of his talents. "It is nothing."

"No, it's not nothing," Mia said. "You're just ... you. This was fun."

"I hear you are so wonderful. Truly. I do this crazy thing to make business. But you give me your little cards and I will send people -- after they eat here once. Once they must eat here."

"We're giving commissions."

He shook his head violently. "Maybe send people to me too. Yes?"

True to his word, clients began appearing at our door that very week because Marco put in a word, and we reciprocated whenever we could.

— • —

"I felt about six inches high when he gave us a compliment," Mia said on the way home.

"He's right, we really are doing something else."

A propane tanker was lumbering up the grade, impossible to pass, but eventually we were home. Stanley was in his favorite spot by the pool, reading. Isabel came over to Mia, bearing an envelope.

"This was delivered for you," Isabel told us.

Mia took the standard business envelope, thick with several pages. In the upper-left corner three Mexican surnames in a very Old World script were engraved, with an address in Mexico City. Presumably a law firm.

The subject matter was headlined in bold, underlined type, above a thicket of single-spaced Spanish. Three pages of prose, followed by two more pages of what looked like a civil engineer's or surveyor's report, with lines and calibrations.

"What is this?" Mia asked.

"Isabel, can you help us?" I felt immediately concerned, even though we didn't yet know what it was saying.

Isabel read it to herself for a very long time. So long that an American would have felt compelled to say something, anything. Finally she said, very quietly, "I'm not sure."

"What do you think it says?" I asked.

"Your land here" -- she gestured downwards -- "is in a problem with the land there." She gestured toward the undeveloped property to our north, which was all scrub trees and brush clinging precariously to the steep slope, unchanged since we'd first visited Zihuatanejo years ago. We'd walked this road many times. "I am not so sure. Is maybe where properties are."

"Where properties are...," I repeated, hoping she could clarify.

"I don't know how you say," she said. She could go no further.

"That's okay then," said Mia. "You've given us the heart of it."

Isabel looked embarrassed.

"You helped us a lot," Mia assured her.

"Thank you, Isabel."

We moved to our room to change out of our clothes. I sat on the bed and tried to decipher the document using my meager Spanish. I couldn't.

"Who are we going to talk to about this?" I asked.

"The accountant," Mia suggested. "Maybe go see him."

"I think I will. I need to know what this is. Do you want to come with me?"

"This is Isabel's first day, and I don't want to leave them again." She didn't seem as worried about the document as I was. "The neighbors may need us to sign off on something so they can build. Who knows. I'll probably work in the garden. Go ahead, I'll be here when you get back. We'll go for a dip then."

I drove to town without lunch, telling myself not to panic. But there was no way this hand-delivered notice from a law firm in Mexico City could be anything but trouble. Driving slowly, hunting for a place to park, my stomach was clenched. I scraped the back bumper against a high curb on *Altamirano* and cursed.

Americans are required to pay both U.S. and Mexican personal taxes if they reside in Mexico. Also, there are business taxes to be paid, licenses to be purchased. Señor Felipe Rodriguez was the name that kept coming up when we'd asked around about a local accountant who could handle the Mexican side of things, and he'd been doing just that. He was widely endorsed as an honest, sage individual. We'd spoken on the phone just last week about the *predial*, our annual tax bill.

I passed through an ornate ironwork gate, then turned up the concrete steps to my left. The ochre walls were mildewed. This narrow stairwell never saw the sun, and a dank smell pervaded the air. At the head of the stairs I knocked on the door. Eventually I heard footsteps.

"*Hola*," Señor Rodriquez said in his subdued, dignified way. In his fifties, he was wearing royal blue slacks, a pale blue guyabera open at the neck and brown lace-up shoes. We exchanged a few pleasantries. I asked if he would translate an official document that had come.

Señor Rodriquez indicated the wooden armchair in front of his desk, which was nothing fancy, nor were the cabinets, books and shelving in this small office overlooking the street. A new laptop did sit open on a old work table. The window was open, letting in the noises. A ceiling fan stirred the air lazily. Behind him on a shelf were family photos. His pride and joy, I knew, was the son in a graduation photo, Diego, who had studied accounting at a college in New Mexico. The young man, in his mid-twenties and full of hope, looked exactly like his father.

"I received this today," I said. I handed it to him. "I don't know what it says. I don't think I want to know either."

Señor Rodriguez solemnly extracted black-framed reading glasses from his eyeglass case. He put them on with one hand, all the while holding my letter in the other. Like Isabel, he read without comment for a long time. I sat patiently, then impatiently. As he finished a page, he carefully put it behind the other pages in his hands.

"What does it say?" I finally interrupted.

"You must have an attorney," he said, inclining his head so he could look at me over his reading glasses. His lips pursed, conveying that this was big.

"What do I need the attorney for?"

"Your house is built on land that is not yours." His English was slow but clear.

"That's impossible." Every muscle in my body was tensed up. My breathing was shallow.

He put the letter down. "The line of your property is here," he said, slowly extending his arm. "This letter says the walls of your casa come too far." He used his other arm to indicate, crossing it over the first arm. Surely I had to understand. It was only part of our land that was the problem.

But this couldn't be. "By how much?" I asked. "Does it say?"

"Ten meters approximately."

The clock stopped moving. I ceased breathing altogether, and may have become invisible for just a few moments. When I was a little boy, I apparently ran from the monstrous news of my parents' simultaneous deaths and crouched in the corner, covering my ears. This was a version of that feeling, not unknown to me during the worst moments of my life. I suspect all the blood drained out of my face, because Señor Rodriguez was regarding me very closely, with great concern. He was also holding his head in a way that said, yes, this was a considerable problem.

I could hardly get the next words out. "What do they want, assuming this is true?" I cleared my throat.

"These attorneys for the property owners wish for your attorney to speak with them. In seven days, is what they are saying. And that this is very serious."

"'Very serious' how?"

"You must remove the offending part of your building."

"I can't do that," I protested, as if he, Señor Rodriguez, were the one making the demand.

He raised his hand just enough to remind me of his allegiance. "They are asking for money as an option," he said, double-checking the appropriate page as he spoke. "No amount is here. I believe it is for the money, in my opinion."

"How could this happen?" I said aloud.

With a sympathetic look, he handed the letter back. He was not an attorney, so it was not for him. I was not a citizen, didn't have money, didn't speak Spanish worth a fig, didn't know the ways of the legal system -- so it was not for me either. Only it was.

"So I need to talk with someone."

"Perhaps you should first speak with your *notario*."

"Our *notario* was Señor Echeverria."

He took in air through his teeth, and his look became even more sympathetic. I didn't have to explain that our *notario* had been assassinated and his office burned, destroying all documents. The fate of that scoundrel was widely known.

"The bank is responsible," I remembered. We had a *fideicomiso*, a trust with a Mexican bank, not a deed.

"Yes, but no. To be candid, in this matter there is not the kind of liability you have in the States. There is arbitration, and the courts, but...." He did not look hopeful. "The blame will be the *notario*, and no records would exist outside the bank. You would be wasting your time in my opinion."

"I need an attorney," I said.

Señor Rodriguez folded his hands on his desk and spoke very confidentially. "For this matter, I would not use an attorney from Zihuatanejo. This family that owns the property, they are very wealthy people, very important people. They are very influential in Mexico City and the business of our country. Everyone in Mexico knows this name."

I must have looked unconvinced, because he went further.

"Zihuatanejo is a very small town," he reminded me.

We locked eyes. I finally understood. I should draw my own conclusion, because he was not going to utter the words, which might be repeated somewhere to his detriment. No attorney from here would have clout in Mexico City with what had to be a leading law firm, representing people of such power and influence.

"You have maybe the American title insurance?" he inquired.

It killed me to shake my head, no. Title insurance is not available to Mexicans, who rely on a *notario's* title search and a bank's sign-off and the opinion of a Mexican attorney at times. But Americans can buy title insurance from a few sources in the States, and in the greatest of ironies -- it was beyond irony, really -- I had been the one to cleverly inform Señor Rodriguez that rock-solid title insurance was now available to his American clients. He hadn't known.

Ken, our California attorney, had put us on to an insurance specialist in Houston who would write such a a policy. Mia was sold on the idea, but I didn't want to spend the money. Why couldn't we could ride the coattails of Señor Izzy, a shrewd and wealthy businessman? Izzy wasn't the type to leave himself exposed to anything. Why, Izzy had even personally introduced us to his *notario*. And I kept emphasizing the cost to Mia. Five thousand U.S. dollars just for the application and the title search. Eight thousand or more for the premium. That was money we needed. For the better part of a month, Mia hammered away that we should obtain title insurance for our peace of mind, bringing up the stories that people were telling us about catastrophes in Mexican real estate.

"Did you read that article in the Times that I put on your desk, about the whole community of Americans in Baja who lost their homes?" she said one morning when we were still in California.

"This isn't Baja," I'd argued. "It's a single piece of property, it's already been developed and lived in. It's like blowing thirteen thousand dollars."

That very morning we were conceptualizing the cooking island for the terrace of Casa Blue. It needed to be a grand affair, with a high-end stove, fine tile work -- something patrons would ooh and aah about. Rough costs were taking shape. Mia finally relented, and I never gave the brochures and other papers about the title insurance another thought.

— • —

I'm sure the walk to the execution chamber is never long enough, and neither was the drive home from the accountant's office. Stanley and Isabel seemed to be gone somewhere. The house was deathly still. It no longer felt like a place I owned as I moved through it.

I found Mia in our garden, a series of three tiered planting areas with concrete borders. She'd had this constructed along the southern extremity of our property against the terrace support wall, where it would catch the sun all day. Partially hidden under her broad straw hat, Mia was crouching to tend her newer tomato plants, which had reached the blossoming stage. She was in a two-piece bathing suit. Her upper body and her face showed smears of dirt as she stood to greet me.

"What'd you find out?" she asked. Her expression grew more serious as I approached.

"It's not so good."

"Tell me."

"The other side of this house encroaches onto our neighbor's property."

"What!" She dropped the snippers and squeezed my arm. Something like a wail came from her -- a yowl, a guttural sound of agony and disbelief.

"They want money."

"No. No, this isn't true. Tell me this is not true."

"It's a very well-connected family, an old family, in Mexico City."

Mia let out what could have been the last breath of a dying person. She covered her mouth with a dirty garden glove as the full realization took root.

She asked, "And we don't have title insurance?" Was there the slimmest of possibilities that I'd gone ahead and arranged for it, but had neglected to mention it to her?

"No. We don't," I acknowledged. "We should have."

Her eyes filled with tears. I deserved to be strangled. Or shot by a firing squad.

"So we might lose everything," she said, removing her gloves and letting them drop to the ground. She removed her hat too, discarding it without a thought. Her hair was a gnarly mess underneath.

"You're jumping ahead," I said. "We need to see what they want."

"Oh Jeff," she said.

"I know. I wish I could go back and do things over."

It was too much for words, really. She looked away. At some point she said, "We should have gotten the title insurance. It didn't matter what it cost."

"I know. I'm sorry."

"Every time you touch money, it goes bad. Every time."

"I have no words for this." I touched her elbow. She didn't withdraw; she didn't accept it as an apologetic gesture either. It was as though I wasn't even there.

"Why is all this happening to us?" she said to any passing souls, who might have knowledge of the spirit world.

— • —

I reached Ken Hewitt, our attorney friend in California, at four o'clock our time, two o'clock in his world. Mia stood by with one arm pressed protectively across her chest and a hand covering her mouth, listening to my half of the conversation only. She couldn't bear to actually be on the extension. The call lasted seven minutes. Then I put down the phone.

"Okay," I said. "You heard what I was saying."

"He knows someone?"

"Somebody he went to law school with at Boalt Hall, who lives in Mexico City now. He's Mexican American, in international law, or trade. Something like that. He's personally not the right lawyer for us, but he knows people. Ken thinks the friend can hook us up with a lawyer who's got some juice."

"Juice. Now we need juice in Mexico City in order to survive?" This was beyond comprehension.

Two agonizing days later we finally heard from Ken Hewitt's friend in Mexico City and old classmate, Max Cisneros. Max was cordial but a man of few words. He listened to us. He said he would get back to us shortly. He didn't exactly emote sympathy, but neither was he uncaring.

The next day we received Max's e-mail with the name of an attorney and the contact information. Someone who would be right for this situation, perhaps, to the extent that any attorney would want to represent us against this other distinguished firm and their clients. We called right away, but were unable to speak with him. We were advised to call the following day.

The following day this recommended attorney, Señor Juan Serna Lozano, was in court and unavailable. We were asked to call again.

The day after that, Señor Lozano's secretary asked us to fax the notice that triggered this land dispute.

Two days later we followed up with the secretary because we hadn't heard anything. We discovered that the fax hadn't gone through. It was Friday. We sent it again.

The following Tuesday we finally spoke with Señor Lozano. Next week he would be in touch with the attorney who wrote the threatening letter. We confirmed that yes, we wished to engage his services, which we asked him to bill through Ken Hewitt in California, who was overseeing all our legal affairs.

"It said on the notice to respond within seven days," I noted.

"We're already past that."

"It is important to move slowly," he said, and he excused himself.

15

Three weeks later I was drinking a Negra Modelo at the terrace table, earnestly reading the maintenance section of an instruction booklet. My hands were filthy, and left vengeful fingerprints on the pages. Dusk was approaching on this final Sunday of January, the heart of the high season, and I was tired and frustrated. We'd been running the cooking school from Monday through Saturday. I hadn't wanted to spend two hours on this particular project during our one day off.

I also hadn't noticed that Mia had crept up beside me, drink in hand.

"You got it working," Mia said, referring to our infinity pool. Jets were again forcing the water.

"I'm trying to figure out why I have this part left over." I held it up for her to see.

"But you got it up. Good boy." She was barefoot in a cotton pullover dress. Mia began idly pulling my sweaty, grimy hair into points, just to amuse herself or to annoy me. I ignored her until I couldn't.

"What are you doing?" I snapped.

"Look at me." She canted her head to examine the new look. "You're still not cool, even though I like a man who's good with tools." She kissed my head with condolences.

"Thank you for that." I messed it again and returned to the

manual.

To be frank, this was one of our better days, with a bit of humor in it. We'd been soldiering ahead, waiting anxiously for their attorney to respond with a specific demand. Not a word as yet. I'd been hounding my attorneys to do something, to the point where Señor Lozano had stopped taking any calls, and Ken was tired of having to repeat, in response to my badgering phone queries, that there was no news.

What did they want? There were times when Mia and I felt confident that something reasonable could be worked out with the neighboring landowner, with a payment schedule. Yet there were nights when one or both of us got depressed to the marrow. And there were very dark times beyond depression, when we figured all was lost, we just hadn't discovered it yet.

"It's nice to be able to do something and have it work right," I said.

"You saved us a lot of money. We didn't have to hire somebody. You're my hero."

"That I am."

Mia and I were economizing. This business with the pool pump was the sort of thing that gobbled up our cash. The new water pump had arrived yesterday via DHL express from Mexico City. It was crucial to have the pool up and running again without further delay, so I'd driven into Zihuatanejo to pick it up. After five days without water circulation, the pool's crystalline waters had turned murky. The pool had begun to look like a petri dish for bacteria -- not good at a cooking school in Mexico.

I'd devoted the afternoon to the pump's installation, assuming various yoga positions amid wrenches, wires and dirt in a cramped crawl space. Lizards and spiders had box seats. At times I muttered curses with the Maglite between my teeth, trying to illumine a dropped machine screw. A handier man would have been done in an hour. A rich man would have called someone. A man with a skilled son would have enlisted his services, but Rowan, visiting from Los Angeles, had no talent in the fix-it category. He'd gone to *Playa La Ropa* with Stanley.

Repairing anything that used electricity could cost princely sums in Zihuatanejo, once taxes and shipping were figured in -- and the commercial dishwasher we'd splurged on, now inoperable, testified to that. A replacement computer chip was under warranty. Labor was not. It would require a trained serviceman to fly down from Guadalajara to install the part, at an estimated cost for the total job exceeding six hundred dollars.

Welcome to the Cooking School at Z, where dishes are washed by hand, in the old way. Was there a marketing spin we could put on that?

— • —

Actually, Mia had joined me on the terrace about business, not to discuss the pool.

Starting much earlier that day, she had meticulously reviewed our invoices, receipts, printed bills, and my handwritten records of market purchases. We'd been stuffing these scraps of paper into an accordion file. It had swelled as the weeks went by, like a dead steer in the sun. So she'd made piles of papers all around herself on our bed and on the floor, to see what she could decipher about our operating finances.

"Do you want to know where we are with money?" She'd pulled out a chair for herself, set down her Campari and soda, and tucked her hair behind her ears.

"Probably not," I said.

"Well, you'll be surprised. We're actually making a small profit."

The breath rushed out of my body.

"You're kidding."

"I'm not kidding." Mia made a big grin I hadn't seen in a while.

We leaned awkwardly in our chairs to kiss and threw an arm over each other's shoulders, like a swim team after a victory.

"Think about it," Mia went on. "This past week we had seventeen people. That's averaging almost three a day. The hotel referrals, especially from *Villa Real*, are helping. Marco at Madrid has sent couples. The little quote from Francine Longman on our website has helped. We're profitable after thirteen people a week." She shared more details. Yes indeed, the Cooking School at Z was at least temporarily in the black.

"Now we have to ramp up further if we're going to put money in the bank to cover the slow season," I said. The number of visitors would diminish sharply in late April, and wouldn't pick up until mid-November at the earliest. Fewer visitors to Zihuatanejo, and rainy days to contend with.

"We could handle three times the number of reservations we're getting," said Mia. "So that's the next step."

"You figured in everything?"

"The cost of being here, keeping this place going, all pro-rated. Food, phone bills, Isabel, restaurants, taxes." She ticked them off on her fingers, and moved to the other hand. "Keeping up health insurance back in the States. The minivan needed tires. The new pool pump. I'm figuring in a monthly allowance for that sort of thing."

"How does that compare to what we thought it would cost?"

"It's about double. I even found the old piece of paper with the original estimate. Do you remember? We did that on the plane. God, we were so naive, not to mention half potted."

I remembered cavalierly jotting down figures for our expected lifestyle and the Cooking School at Z, influenced by those miniature bottles of Grand Marnier and a belief that everything in Mexico would be really, really cheap. We never did an actual business plan. Too many variables, not enough experience with Mexico.

"I have some other news." Mia was crunching ice with her teeth.

"Daphne?" I guessed.

"Very good." She audibly crunched a big cube.

"You're going to break a tooth doing that," I cautioned. "Do you want to visit that street off *Benito Juarez* with all the dental consultants? I don't think so."

"Our daughter's now in Mazatlan."

"She e-mailed?"

"They'll be taking people out on the *Five Seasons* for about a week, she thinks. Then they're heading back south toward us, depending on the ocean and the winds."

"So you have two good things to be happy about."

"At least they'll be coming in the right direction."

Just to taunt me, Mia put another big piece of ice in her mouth and resume crunching. I moved her glass away. She stood, seized my *cerveza*, and poured it over my head. I made a lunge, but she jumped back and laughed at me. She fled at a lover's pace down the steps to the pool, with me high-stepping in pursuit. Mia dove in clothed and I jumped in after her.

"So maybe the Cooking School at Z could make it after all," I said. I was standing in the pool, and she was in my arms.

"There's a chance."

— • —

Soon we were sitting at the pool's edge, in a spot where the bamboo didn't block the last of the sun. We'd just been kissing and groping in the water -- more than that, really -- but Stanley and Rowan were due back any minute. I was anticipating a lovely evening in bed.

"Did Daphne say anything about when they're coming back to Zihuatanejo?" I asked Mia, my hand caressing her thigh.

169

"Not a clue. Just the usual Daphne e-mail. She writes like they're telegrams and she's paying for every word."

What came every few days, via satellite e-mail, were a fact or two, doing okay, whereabouts, bye. From her life in New York, we'd grown accustomed to brevity in her communications -- she always said she so busy. But how busy could she be, couped up on the *Five Seasons*?

Some day this might qualify as a romantic lark Daphne would always talk about, a fling with a young Frenchman -- that's the tolerant interpretation, assuming this escapade ended safely. I held onto that broad-minded thought. Mia would have none of it, however. She was still stewing over the way Daphne sailed off with Guy and the parents, not even coming home for more clothes, clearly avoiding us. Mia brought this out to Daphne via e-mail; our daughter responded that there would have been a giant fight if she'd come home to tell us what she'd made up her mind to do anyway, so she hadn't. She noted that Guy had spent a year studying electrical engineering in Paris, and had thoughts about enlisting in the Australian Navy some day, as if that element of seriousness should make all her parents' concerns go away.

Our talk swung back to business, but first Mia felt compelled to kiss me one last time.

"I think we can cut food costs," Mia said, removing my hand.

"We'll take a shot."

"I'm going to work on it."

The sun was now below the horizon. In the cooler air, Mia's nipples became pronounced in her wet dress.

"I don't think we can charge more," I said, reaching to touch.

"I agree." She pressed my hand against her breast and kissed me tenderly.

We then stared in unison at the sunset. It was one of those moments of extraordinary calm. The fallen angels assigned to screw up our lives were hiding behind the low, hazy cloud line, the pastel of their colored wings showing through as they took a break.

"I wish we could come up with a backstop," Mia said. "Some other way to make money, because...." She paused. "I think I hear them."

I'd also heard sounds. We scanned the rooms above us. I quickly dropped my hand.

"Let my people go!" a male voice boomed.

It was Rowan, our son, speaking with gravitas as he stood shirtless at the railing in his room, arms upraised like Charleton Heston. He started laughing at himself, the kind of crazed laugh that makes you laugh along, and we certainly did. Yesterday he'd been a farcical Romeo from his stage. When some prank or concept seizes Rowan, he brings it back again and again. He'd been this way since the age of ten. Thank God he was finding an outlet for it in Hollywood. All through college he'd been a slacker, and hadn't finished his degree, and God knows what else he could possibly have done to make his way in the world.

"What kind of child did I raise?" Mia said to me. She called out, "Rowan, how's dad?"

"I'm fine." Stanley's disembodied voice was coming from his room. "I'm gonna take a shower, get all the sand off."

"Rowan, check the e-mails before you come down," Mia called. "There might be something from Daphne. I just replied to her. She might have replied to me."

"Did you tell her to piss off?"

"That's not your business."

"What did you say?" I asked Mia.

"I told her to get her butt back here. I'm going to shower. Why don't you get the potatoes going before you come up?" Her hand brushed my crotch, and to hell with it if anyone was watching.

— • —

For dinner, Mia was preparing quail -- boning it first, then a brushing of light garlic butter, with sprigs of *papalo* worked in, an herb used in parts of Mexico where coriander won't grow. We'd roast some vegetables from the garden and drizzle them with a balsamic vinegar reduction sauce, leaving some vegetables plain for dad.

When Rowan had come from Los Angeles nearly a week ago, he'd brought with him the duty-free limit of four bottles of wine as a carry-on. One of the remaining two -- a zinfandel from Amador County in the Sierra foothills, with a massive, jammy taste -- was getting just a slight chill in the refrigerator.

"Something will work out," I said, picking up our new optimism.

"Check the potatoes," Mia answered.

I opened the oven door. I drew out the baking pan and probed the small, quartered potatoes for doneness. They were being slow roasted with several heads of garlic and cut-up red bell peppers, all of it rubbed with olive oil from the outset.

"Still a while," I announced. I set about mixing olive oil, mustard and a liberal quantity of chopped fresh tarragon for the potato salad.

"You could be a personal chef in the evenings for the people who rent some of those big places closer to town," I said.

"I don't know how much of that kind of work there is."

"Probably not a lot in the low season."

"Phil says a few bring their own chef, but some ask for an American cook when they rent. We'd have to work it through the rental agents and the owners."

"What else then?" I asked.

"Or we could serve dinners here. We could handle private parties of what, eight or ten?"

"I was thinking of that too. But then we'd be competing with the restaurants. That might be a bad thing."

"When is our real estate problem going to get taken care of?"

"The ball's in their court. I'm concerned they're going to want too much. We don't exactly have a lot of financial flexibility here."

"We're not giving up this house. We are not dropping the cooking school. Don't even think that for a second."

These were things we'd been saying again and again, but how could we stop talking about it?

"I'll call Ken again in the morning."

— • —

When Rowan finally joined us, he was wearing the same clothes he'd had on earlier in the day -- wrinkled cargo shorts, a street-vendor's knockoff of an expensive Tommy Bahama shirt, and a fake Rolex. His wet dark hair looked combed only until it dried, at which point it became a Chia pet, a look firmly established at this moment. He had his mother's striking brown eyes. His eyes alone should have landed him a girl by now, in Mia's view, but Rowan said he had no time for relationships. And he'd put on so much weight, he was getting blubbery, a fact he blatantly advertised with his unbuttoned shirt. His freshman year of high school, he'd joined the football team partly to please me, partly because a coach pestered him into trying out. He'd rarely been inserted into a game, which brought to an end his athletic career, leaving just his skill at poker and his fondness for the ponies.

"Was there something from Daphne?" Mia asked.

"The brat's fine," Rowan said, although he and Daphne were in fact very close. "Your favorite child is here. What more could you want?"

Rowan stretched, successively cracking his knuckles, his lower back, and his neck, before he surprised his mother with a hug, actually hoisting her off the ground.

"Stop!" Mia protested, holding her knife aloft.

He put her down.

"Did she tell you they're thinking about sailing to Hawaii?" Rowan asked with a straight face. But he was only joking.

"This is not humorous," Mia said.

When I took the potatoes out of the oven, Rowan plucked a roasted wedge from the pan, juggled it, then popped it in his mouth. "Aaaaah!" he cried, quickly spitting the thing back into his hand.

"God that's hot," he said. "Shit. I think I burned my tongue." He hurled the roasted bit of potato from the terrace as far as he could, with no regard for where it might land.

"Don't do that," his mother said.

"What, I might kill someone with a roasted potato?" He twisted the top off the *cerveza* I'd brought out for him earlier.

"What I want to know," Rowan began, "is how Daphne gets away with ditching school, blowing college tuition, you're paying her share for rent -- and I had to push in college and work the whole time, or you were on me. If I knew I could have done this, I would have gone to fucking Europe, or quit college even sooner."

"She's my baby," Mia said, just to taunt him.

"She's spoiled rotten," Rowan said.

"This trip of hers is not something we endorse," I said. "And for the record, no tuition was lost."

"How'd she weasel out of that?"

I explained how Dr. Edmonds, Stanley's local physician and our friend, had agreed to write a note stating that our daughter could not return to New York at this time for medical reasons. How was her school to check? So the bursar's office had issued notification to Daphne's e-mail address of a tuition credit for the next semester. As for Daphne's apartment, a friend had needed a place for a while. It had been sublet by our daughter, using e-mail from the high seas.

Rowan moved off to assemble the ingredients for a margerita to chase his beer. His version included a slice of salted orange on the rim and some grenadine. Now that the last light of the day was almost gone, he deemed it appropriate to put on his sunglasses, with their tiny ovoid lenses and wire frame.

"You need to get some real sunglasses," Mia said.

"I like these."

"They look stupid, and they don't block out enough of the ultraviolet rays."

"All of which begs the question of why you're putting them on now," I said, "when there's very little light."

"Both of you, ssssh," said Mia.

Rowan sipped his drink. "So the cooking school's not exactly doing that well," he said with concern.

I must have looked surprised. When he'd asked about our venture, we hadn't shared our deepest anxieties. We mentioned the real estate thing in a way that made it sound more like an annoyance than a threat to our very survival.

Rowan explained, "I could hear you from up in my room, mom, talking about not giving up the cooking school. Sound carries here. I hear grandpa when he farts. Do you know how much he's farting? What are you giving him to eat?"

"Believe me, nothing exotic."

"I'm worried for you guys."

"Things will work out," I said.

"I hope so. This is paradise. I plan on visiting six months out of the year when I'm rich. Good food. Beach. Someone to make the bed for me."

Stanley finally appeared, freshly showered. Mia made him a lime and tonic.

"So you're afraid you're going to lose the house?" Stanley asked us both.

Mia and I looked at each other.

"Even I could hear you upstairs a little while ago, Mia, and my hearing's shot."

"What else is everybody hearing?" I cried out.

"More than we want," Rowan said gravely, leaving it at that. "At night? I'll say no more."

I explained, "Mom went through all the bills this afternoon and the revenue figures. It's something we'd been putting off. We're making a few dollars."

"If just making money was the object, we wouldn't be here," Mia said. "We want to have a life and not be worrying about money. But we don't need to get rich."

Our prescient son asked, "Are you going to keep Isabel?"

Now it was Stanley's turn to be startled.

"Just an innocent question," said Rowan, raising both hands in his own defense.

Stanley and Isabel, after an awkward start, had hit it off. They had their little routine for going to *Playa La Ropa* every day -- he walking in front with his case for paints, she bringing up the rear with his folded-up wooden easel. On the beach she read, he painted. Isabel listened to his stories and they discussed all manner of subjects, each working on their second language. The young woman filled a need for Stanley, whose inner chemistry required him to address fifty thousand words a day to someone.

"Isabel won't make or break us," I said.

"What are you paying her?" Stanley asked.

Mia told him.

"That's all you're paying the poor girl? Christ."

"That's double what the other young women are getting in the bed and breakfasts and the private houses," I said.

"You're in Mexico, dad," Mia said. "Those men building the new wing at *Villa Real*, they earn twelve dollars a day. And those are the good construction jobs."

"It's a pact with the devil, being an American here," I said. "You're kidding yourself if you pat yourself on the back for being a little generous. But you're also introducing money they can't earn anywhere else. Tourism is the best thing going in Guerrero, other than drugs."

"Don't tell this to Daphne," Rowan warned.

Our daughter was an unrelenting critic of capitalism, and had protested at the United Nations more than once. She was nauseated by luxury goods and SUVs. Somehow this rabid viewpoint could coexist in her young brain alongside the reality of her parents' support for her student life, provided by the fruits of commerce. Mia and I wrestled with a similar dichotomy. We exhorted guests to use just the right temperature on boned quail in the oven, while thousands of nearby Mexican families scratched for food money.

"From now on, I'll pay Isabel myself," Stanley announced. "I get my Social Security check, I don't need to be saving any of it."

"You need supplies now that you're painting," said Mia. "You should go out on the fishing boats and enjoy yourself. You know how you used to love that. And you need money for the flights up to Houston. We'll have to be going there for your check-ups sometimes, and staying overnight."

"I don't need you telling me what to do with my money. My whole life I've been handling it. And better than you."

That last comment was aimed my way.

"Dad, this isn't Jeff's fault."

"He lost money he should have put under the mattress, or you wouldn't be like this, so worried. I hear you down here talking. I know what's going on. A parent knows everything when you get to my age."

And so it went through dinner. Rowan knew before today that his parents once had money and lost it, and it was one of the few things he dared not joke about. Even though he was no longer living at home at the time when it happened, he'd picked up on the turmoil and how angry his mother was for months afterward. We told him eventually, with the thought that it was an important life lesson.

"I should be paying rent while I'm living under your roof," Stanley volunteered between forkfuls. "And how much is this meal? I can pay board."

"Shut up," said Mia. "All of you."

16

The next day was a Monday, and my wife was a woman on a mission.

While I ran the cooking program by myself -- we had two easy-to-please guests from a Southern state known for deep-frying everything -- Mia sequestered herself in Casa Blue's great room with a thermos of coffee, intent on tuning up the recipes and crafting other program changes. Sophie Blackwell, the travel writer from New York, would be coming to review us in twenty-four hours. News of this unexpected blessing -- or curse -- arrived during breakfast when we received a call from Heinrich, our new best friend. Apparently he'd suggested us to his famous guest at the *Villa Real*. She'd been intrigued by the name, the Cooking School at Z, and had juggled her schedule.

"She needs to see the new look I've been thinking about," Mia said.

"This might not be smart, initiating big changes tomorrow."

"We can do it."

I was very concerned. "Living on the edge," was all I could say.

"And you love it." She patted my cheek.

Several well-used cookbooks, sets of notes, her collection of handed-down family recipes, notes on the costs of ingredients -- Mia set it all around her in piles on the floor, along with our recipe cards from the program. She settled cross-legged on a pillow, ready to write in the large spiral bound notebook at her side.

Rowan and I peeked in. "Shades of high school, mom," Rowan quipped.

Mia scowled at us.

"This reminds me of you planning the high school sports banquets in the gym," he continued. "Remember the lasagna and the iceberg lettuce with bottles of blue-cheese dressing?"

She gave her two men the finger. "Go," she insisted, pointing to the door.

Early in the afternoon Mia summoned all of us. Her pencil was tucked behind her ear to great effect. She listed the program improvements she wanted. A broader sensory experience, extending beyond food. Less emphasis on dishes and techniques people might replicate at home, although we should stay sensitive to our guests' wishes. More offerings that would be new tastes for people.

Rowan was instructed to put aside his scriptwriting and create special recipe cards for tomorrow. Stanley accepted his marching orders concerning his paintings. Isabel was to clean our best ceramics for serving. On the phone Mia finalized an arrangement with a cooperative in Mexico City, something she'd been working on for weeks. I made a shopping run to the *Mercado Centro*. Upon my return, I was assigned to make a dish that needed to sit overnight. Others bustled around me. Over a late dinner, Mia ran through the choreography.

"Are you sure people are going to want all this?" Rowan asked.

"It will work. We need more than just the food."

"Maybe the people will be very happy," Isabel said, siding with my wife. Isabel was part of the team. I'd be driving her home later that night.

"You're introducing too many distractions, but I'll do what you want," said Stanley.

"Just be yourself," Isabel told him. "Cranky and funny. People will like that."

Everyone laughed.

"Okay, now we need to run through it again so there are no mistakes," Mia insisted.

— • —

"Sophie's World" on TrueTravel's website was garnering praise from every quarter, landing its author media appearances and interviews in recent months, many of them available for replay on her website. Sophie's prose was wickedly clever as she wrote up restaurants, hotels, and the local scene in her destination reviews. She was the daughter of a renowned chef and an English theater impresario, and had traveled extensively, a woman of the world though only in her late twenties. The *Playa La Ropa* crowd had been buzzing about her arrival for weeks.

Sophie's *schtick* was articulating the unfiltered thoughts people have but don't say in polite company. She could be devastatingly candid. Her wealthy tech-boom boyfriend, Kurt, sometimes accompanied her on the road, and his printed quips added further spice. But they'd been quarreling -- also chronicled in the column -- so Kurt wasn't on this trip, according to Heinrich. He also confided that last night she had hooked up with a young man at the hotel bar, who had stayed the night in her room.

Isabel answered the bell and escorted Sophie to the great room, where Mia and I and our four other guests were already socializing. Assembling there introduced a second venue to the experience, instead of spending the entire time on the terrace. Patrons could enjoy our ceramics and other artifacts, plus the view of Zihuatanejo Bay, while anticipation built for what would happen on the terrace below.

Sophie Blackwell gave our hands a firm shake. She was a full-figured young woman, a fact not apparent from the website. She was a natural blonde with blunt-cut, shoulder-length hair. She had a disarming, Wisconsin sort of face, but her quick, clever smile was urban, not from the land of cheese. A clipped accent documented her time in England. She was wearing a loose-fitting khaki dress of synthetic fabric, with a scoop neck -- the sort of outfit a traveler could roll up in a suitcase, and eminently practical for her work. Stanley would tell us later that Sophie also had taste in shoes. She certainly had the best nails in the room.

"Thank you," Sophie said, accepting her Casa Blue martini. She set it aside after a taste. Mia also noticed the disinterest. Uh-oh.

"We were all talking about questions we wanted to ask you," said Kristi, wife of Ted. They were Phil's friends, dressed in matching white shirts, silk-screened in green with a palm frond pattern, as if they worked at the same resort. We'd recruited them yesterday because we had only one other pair, Lorna and Happy, from the *Villa Real*.

"Were you a writer before this?" asked Lorna. She and Happy were wealthy sisters in their early forties from Highland Park outside Chicago. Heinrich had nudged them into switching their reservation to this Monday.

"In seventh grade, I started a diary. But I stopped after three weeks. At that age, life was better than writing about it. I still don't write. Someone said I download, and I think that's closer to what I do."

"You must want to be a chef one day," said Happy, "the way you love food. You're so indignant when something isn't right." I'd shared downloaded examples of the Sophie's World column, which our guests had scanned in the moments before Sophie arrived.

"I had my phase of thinking I'd be a chef," Sophie said, "which ended in about thirty seconds. I don't think it's necessary to be able to cook in order to appreciate excellent food, do you? I love your pendant."

A gracious turn, that was. Happy blushed and touched her choker with its dangling amber.

Sophie told a story about working during one summer break in college at her uncle's restaurant on Cape Cod, rated highly by Zagat's. "I enjoyed being the blowtorch girl for the creme brulee, but the rest of it had no appeal."

"Your writing style has such a unique voice," I said. "It's fresh, and you have a great ear for phrases. You put down what people say to their partner back in the room, or think to themselves. We've followed your column." We had first read Sophie's World back in California, when planning a trip to a city she'd written about.

"Thank you." Sophie regally inclined her head. She had an extraordinary presence for her age, but seemed to welcome homage.

Mia asked the sisters, "Have you been to Zihuatanejo before?"

Happy and Lorna explained how every winter they took a trip somewhere new, the two of them without husbands, and they gave their first-time impressions of Zihuatanejo. Kristi then asked about a large pot from Mata Ortiz, which was on the shelves -- brick red with black etching, highly intricate. I told the story about the potters of Chihuahua while everyone carefully passed around two bowls, marveling at how light they were. Sophie seemed impressed, or was she just being gracious? She was mysterious, and not haughty, but certainly had a confident reserve.

"Well, let's head down to the terrace," Mia announced.

"I want to see what he's doing," said Happy, glancing below at our artist in residence, who was working at his easel.

— • —

Stanley was in rumpled khaki shorts, weathered boaters, and a favorite orange shirt that had smears of paint colors. His sweat-stained baseball cap looked like something he'd had in childhood.

Lorna, whose shell of hair was lacquered in place, examined Stanley's painting in progress up close, narrowing her eyes as if looking for disguised references to the devil. "I love what you're doing," cooed Happy, who seemed less discriminating. "I don't like photorealism in watercolors."

Stanley was using tropical parrot hues and suggestive washes with a lot of white space, a new style for Mexico. His talent with painting had always seemed a major incongruence given the other facts of his life, like a flower growing from a sidewalk crack, but it was indisputably real. My mother-in-law said more than once that she wished he had found a way to make a living as an artist. But Stanley was content to paint, with little interest in the commercial aspects. He avoided being cutesy or sentimental. He loved conversing with people who sidled up as he was painting on location, when he was no longer a shoe salesman. On this morning he was halfway through a signature view of Zihuatanejo Bay, painted from a pencil sketch he'd done on *Playa La Ropa*.

"Do you sell your work?" Ted asked.

"I'm not trying to build a home collection," Stanley said, completely deadpan. Sophie laughed. Her teeth were perfect.

"Do you have other paintings we could see?" asked Lorna.

I asked Isabel to get the nine paintings we'd arranged inside. Isabel delayed bringing them out, so it would seem she'd gone hunting for them. None were priced or framed. The impression we wanted was that no one had asked to see these paintings until this moment, so they had to be gathered.

"We're supposed to get some of these framed for sale in the guest shop at *Villa Real*," I noted, which was true.

As our other four guests looked through Stanley's work, Mia struck up a conversation with Sophie about New York City, and establishments they both knew. Rowan then happened along, unscripted, in an unbuttoned shirt and baggy surfer trunks. We introduced him all around.

"Rowan's down here to get a script treatment together," I said. "I'm introducing two writers with deadlines to each other."

I detected interest on Sophie's part.

"Welcome to the hardest place in the world to get anything done," Rowan said.

Ted and Kristi, who were attending gratis, committed to buying a conventional scene of fishermen on the *Playa Municipal*, featuring colorful beached *pangas* on the sand. I'd find out later whether they were just being shills. Happy declared that she wanted the painting Stanley was presently working on.

"It's yours then," he said.

"I'll come back another time. We're not leaving until Thursday."

"It'll be finished and dry for you to take today. I even have cardboard. *Muchas gracias*. I'm learning the language."

Stanley insisted on kissing her hand. His silliness charmed the sisters.

— • —

We assembled our guests at the shaded cooking island on the terrace. Jamaica flowers floated in a black pottery basin, along with pink blossoms Rowan heisted from a nearby *clavellino* tree, with its smooth, thick branches reminiscent of elephant trunks. The wafting aroma of garlic bulbs and *epazote*, roasting at low heat in the oven, could get skeletons to sit up in their coffins.

Mia set out a small platter of roasted, skinned chilies rolled up around a filling of *albahaca*, caramelized onion, and dorado, spritzed with lime. The four guests oohed and licked their fingers. Sophie sampled and seemed impressed.

"We're going to have some tastes from different countries," Mia began. "Some of these dishes you might want to make at home for special occasions, so we have recipe cards for you. But the Cooking School at Z is about learning only if you want it to be. Jeff describes what we're doing as a 'participatory restaurant.'"

'Jeff' had come up with that phrase exactly two hours ago, over breakfast. Mia made my momentary inspiration sound like the touchstone of a deep personal philosophy.

Isabel then presented *tiritas* -- raw strips of fish drizzled with lime, blessed with sliced onion, and celebrated with a very fine confetti of cilantro and steamed red pepper. Matchsticks of jicama were arranged beside it on the small black plates. She graciously accepted compliments.

"This is just to demonstrate how incredibly fresh the seafood is that we're able to get in Zihuatanejo," Mia said.

"It is always very fresh," Isabel said to Sophie.

Right on cue, I described going to the *Paseo del Pescador* each morning, or to the fishmongers at the central market. Sophie put mysterious jottings in her little notebook, with its austere cover of brushed aluminum. She left it open at her side for access. What was she writing?

Rowan made another unscheduled appearance, popping a chile in his mouth. He ignored my look of displeasure. "Don't think we ate like this when we were kids," he said, after surveying the food.

"Sometimes the kids got hotdogs," Mia admitted.

"So you didn't grow up with wonderful food?" Sophie asked.

"We ate a lot of leftovers from things mom catered. Sometimes for days. You ever hear how indentured servants had it in their contracts that their masters in New England couldn't serve them salmon more than three times a week? We tried to unionize, the three of us sibs. Mom wouldn't feed us."

"You know that's not true," said Mia.

"'Italian mom' showed up on Sunday. Now *that* was a meal. The family gathered around the table for dinner, the three of us kids snapping at each other, dad yelling and trying to referee."

"Family album stuff," Sophie said.

"Exactly. I'm off. I just wanted to see what everyone was having."

Unscripted, but did the moment play well with Sophie? It was hard to tell. She glanced after Rowan as he walked away.

I began to make papaya granita with vodka, which would go in the freezer and have to be stirred gently once in a while so it would be slushy for dessert.

Sophie asked Mia, "Do you ever ask your guests what they'd like to make?"

"I used to," Mia said. "Now I'm of the mind that people would rather I just decide, and they're happy to be surprised."

More notes were taken as I took orders for *cervezas*. Earlier I'd served a light, scarcely sweetened limeade to cleanse the palate as we went along.

"What did you grow up wanting to do?" Sophie asked Mia.

"As a kid I wanted to have a restaurant," Mia explained, "but I didn't know that I wanted that. Does that make sense?"

Sophie waited.

"I thought I wanted to go into fashion. What I did do was get pregnant. I did a little catering for people out of the house when Jeff and I were first married, and we had two more children. Somewhere in those years I realized where all my cooking could have been focused."

"Do you now wish you'd done it?"

"I don't look back and worry about what might have been. But it's unfortunate each of us doesn't break into triplets and lead three different lives." She reached for Happy's plate, adding it to the dirty ones Isabel was collecting. "I come from a family that's been in the restaurant business since the 1800s. The genes must be inside. And I grew up around my mother's little restaurant in New Jersey...."

"What town?" Sophie asked.

"Leonia, outside Manhattan. But the restaurant's not there anymore. It didn't do that well. She never wanted me to follow her footsteps. But I find the Cooking School at Z very satisfying. I can teach people and see the gratification, and when women cook side by side, they open up. We have wonderful conversations here about things people wouldn't tell their best friends back home."

"You don't have actual line experience in a restaurant?"

"No."

That question didn't faze Mia, but it got my hackles up. Where was Sophie headed? Was that a precursor to a line in her upcoming column, trashing Mia for lacking the proper credentials?

Mia explained our first real course, Pig on the Moon -- pork triangles in a circle of emerald sauce, a visually appealing dinner-party dish she hadn't made since our California days.

Isabel brought out the brined pork loin. Mia demonstrated how by cutting an end on an angle, and then in a reverse direction, it produced a large triangle of raw meat. Two further cuts produced three smaller triangles, the desired size. Ted and Kristi began replicating that.

"Sophie, would you do the emerald sauce?"

"I'd prefer not to," she said.

"Well we need you to join the spirit of things. This is Zihuatanejo, and you're at a cooking school."

Before Sophie could think about it further, Isabel produced an apron that went over Sophie's head. The others, who were already wearing aprons, voiced encouragement. Sophie relented.

"Emerald sauce is very, very easy," Mia began. "In the States we use baby spinach leaves. Spinach is not so easy to find here, so we're using young swiss chard from my garden." She instructed Sophie to load the leaves into our ten-quart pot on the stove. A steam rack was already inside, along with two inches of lightly boiling water that Isabel had arranged.

"We'll have you" -- she indicated the Chicago sisters, who made no claims of culinary talent -- "grill the pork for us on a hot, hot flame. It's brined for tenderness. There's no marinade, just give it a little perfume of oil" -- I showed how -- "which will make it char. The emerald sauce can be made with cilantro instead of garlic, and Jeff and I sometimes have it with our favorite seafood instead of pork. Whichever you prefer."

Once the chard was steamed, Sophie placed it in the food processor, followed by chives, garlic, and basil as instructed. She reduced it to a fine texture, then added chicken stock and processed further. A little cream and salt, another whirl, and the result was a vivid green emulsion that cried out with freshness. Sophie clearly knew what she was doing each step of the way, and stopped at exactly the right consistency.

"It's that simple," said Mia, "and look how beautiful." She put it in a sauce pan over low heat.

Sophie took notes.

— • —

When the pork was ready, Mia flipped up the heat on the emerald sauce and thickened it with cornstarch in water. I brought over a set of the El Fortin ceramic plates and a pitcher that Mia had purchased when we first moved down, crafted in the ancient way by ceramists from Tixtla, in the Guerrero interior. It was very inexpensive, unlike the pieces Izzy sold us with the house. All the guests were struck by their very dark, simple beauty.

"I think the pitcher has the curves of a woman," Mia suggested.

"I think I met her when I was young," said Ted.

"And was I that person?" Kristi challenged him.

"We were all that person, darling, at one time," said Lorna. "For some of us it lasted only about twenty minutes, before our hips turned into chili rellenos."

The pitcher's curves indeed seemed derived from the female figure, most charmingly evident in the generous hips at the base, narrowing upwards to a waist, then widening again to the top opening and spout. The sturdy handle resembled a mighty arm, its fist braced against the hip.

"Where did you get this?" Kristi asked admiringly.

"I'll tell you the whole story in just a few moments. First, each plate gets a full moon of sauce."

Sophie handled that. Without being told, she used her side towel to wipe away any errant drops. The emerald color was vivid on the charcoal black of the ceramic plate. Happy and Kristi placed three pork triangles in a pattern within the moon of sauce on each plate. Mia garnished one with hyphens of chive, and Kristi did the rest.

Isabel brought out strips of crunchy, barely blanched red bell pepper to swab up the excess sauce. People swooned as they sampled this dish, Sophie included. While that was going on, Mia asked Isabel and me to bring out some larger, more striking pieces from her *El Fortin* collection, in answer to Kristi's earlier question.

"There's a cooperative of women who make these," Mia explained. "They're trying to preserve a culture that's disappearing. Mexicans are moving on to modern things in their kitchens just like Americans. The clay comes from a special mine, and it's brought out on donkeys and put it in a furnace. Then it's purified and reduced to a fine dust. The original designs are pre-Hispanic. The artisans make figurines for nativity scenes, large pots, drinking cups, a lot of other things. We're about to use something called an *apaxtlis*, a big casserole dish."

"I love how simple it is," Happy said.

Sophie examined a bowl. She seemed completely engaged by it.

Mia continued, "Some people in the rural areas, in Guerrero and outside Oaxaca, still buy these for local festivals. But the cooperative's future is uncertain right now. It's hard work, and the women don't make more than about forty pesos a day. That's four dollars. So it's a labor of love."

"Can you buy these?" asked Happy.

"They'd be happy to sell them. I can arrange to have whatever you want shipped to you. It takes four to six weeks." That was the arrangement Mia had finalized yesterday. She'd been corresponding with a woman in Mexico City, the agent and advisor from whom Mia had purchased our pieces, and who had once arranged a shipment to friends of ours in California. The idea of selling them through our cooking school had been in gestation since Christmas.

"How much of this do you sell?" Sophie asked me on the side.

"Actually, we're just starting to offer it," I said. "It's not anything we make money on. Mia just believes in what these women are trying to preserve."

"This is one I have to have," said Happy, fawning over a *jarro*.

"We'll get you something on it before you leave," Mia said.

"I need the contact information," Sophie said. "And tell me about the blossoms in this tree overhead. Are they orchids?"

— • —

Next was a tomato soup recipe, incorporating the roasted garlic that had been in the oven when they'd arrived. A touch of cloves, a carrot for sweetness, several other ingredients -- in all probability, none of our guests would ever make such an elaborate tomato soup again, but Mia was betting that guests also wanted to have a hand in making memorable dishes they'd never had before. The conversation had shifted to Mia's roots, beginning with the full Bonassola story. Wine had loosened everyone. Sophie jumped in with hilarious tales of a working assignment for "Sophie's World" in Umbria, where everything went awry.

I slipped away to see Stanley and how his painting was progressing. It was nearly complete.

"I hear them laughing sometimes," he said. "Call me crazy, but I think that's a good sign."

"They're happy so far," I said.

"Good. The blonde, she's gonna write something nice?"

"I think so."

"So how much do I ask for this painting? I'm asking myself

that question and I'm not coming up with an answer."

We kicked it around until he stated a price.

"Go lower," I said. "You've got the woman from Chicago already wanting it. If she thinks it's too expensive, it'll be embarrassing all around. We want everything ending on an up note."

— • —

"Now we'll make something really special," Mia continued. "The taste is magnificent, it's unusual, and it's better the next day. For a dinner party for eight people or thirty-eight people, make this ahead of time. It's a chicken recipe from northern India. Our kids used to call it marigold chicken, because of the color."

I brought out breasts and thighs I'd purchased in the *mercado*. We'd prepped and refrigerated them yesterday, and Mia now dusted them in flour. Ted and Lorna did the browning in butter in a large cast iron skillet, putting the breasts aside as they were finished.

Once Sophie softened the chopped onion and garlic in a little oil, Mia introduced a long list of spices, ranging from caraway seeds to turmeric. The wafting, pungent scents embraced the cooking island. Mia and Sophie went on to add chicken broth, hand-mashed tomatoes and still more spices, and Ted reintroduced the chicken breasts and ladled in some sour cream. Meanwhile, the others were having their tete-a-tetes.

"I can't imagine ever having children," I overheard Sophie telling Mia. How they'd progressed to such an intimate topic was a mystery to me.

"It's so different now," Mia was agreeing. "I look at our children and I'm not sure any of them will have babies. But we do have a wedding coming. Our oldest daughter is getting married here in March."

"Here at Casa Blue?"

"She's having it at a place called Eloi's on the beach. We'll have a big party here the night before." Then they swerved into wedding talk. They seemed like old pals.

Mia soon had me transfer all of the ingredients into the *apaxtlis*, and we stuck it in the oven. Then we all took a break with a little limeade.

"When we grew up," said Lorna, "our father had a summer cabin on a lake in Michigan. The Upper Peninsula. Do you know how we cooked lake trout? Just like the Indians."

"Which Indians?" asked Kristi.

"The people who were there first. You wrap the fish in wet leaves, and then you slather mud on it, and then you put it in the campfire. When it's cooked, the dried mud comes right off, with the leaves and the fish skin. You never tasted fish like that."

Other childhood memories about food came to the fore. Later someone asked, Where did those years go? Kristi revealed that she had had a bout with ovarian cancer. Life, death, appreciating the days one had -- the talk continued unabated as the party shifted to the table. We sat everyone, and Isabel brought out jasmine tea and basmati rice from the Inferno. Several people asked for beer. Then I brought out marigold chicken that I'd made the day before and had just reheated inside, as theirs would take hours to finish. The yellow contrasted beautifully with the black *El Fortin* bowl, and the serving ladle was Mexican pewter.

"The sauce should look a little curdled like this," Mia noted. "The mouth feel should be melted silk on your tongue."

Happy served sliced cucumbers sprinkled with minced serrano chilies, and a dish of mildly vinegared carrots, both of which she'd made under Mia's tutelage. Rowan reappeared with his shirt buttoned and took a chair. The noise level rose as several conversations took flight.

Sophie was opening up to Mia about Kurt, and how it affected him, having their relationship chronicled in print.

"You're asking too much of him to go along with that," I overheard Mia say. The two women were sitting side by side, directly across from me. The others were having a separate conversation.

"He's okay with it. The notoriety thing."

"Is he the one?" Mia asked pointedly.

Sophie didn't know what to do with that -- how else to explain the laugh, the widened eyes, followed by coughing. She patted her upper chest until her throat cleared.

"Excuse me," Sophie said.

"Just an experienced woman to a younger one," Mia said.

"He might be." Sophie sipped her beer.

"May I comment, since you write about your relationship so openly?"

"Everyone does."

"Once you give yourself to the other person, and make an irreversible commitment, and stop worrying about Sophie, and analyzing Sophie, you'll be happier. Life isn't about fulfilling our needs. It's about fulfilling others. Although you're still young enough to take self-discovery seriously, so don't be in a rush."

"You're very old school."

"If I wasn't, do you think I'd still be married to Jeff, who's sitting across from us trying to hear everything we say?"

Four eyes looked my way. I put on my best smile. "It's the most interesting topic at the table."

"So you think I should listen to Kurt," Sophie asked Mia, "when he says to stop traveling and writing my column?"

"I'm not that old school. I also think you love playing the naughty girl to an audience, but at some point you'll want something else. You're very talented."

Our guests had a full view of Zihuatanejo Bay from our new, more forward table position, and they kept commenting on it. When they returned home, they could describe it as a scene right out of a foreign movie -- even more so, after Phil barged in. She raved extravagantly about Mia and me and our Cooking School at Z, to the point that it made me uncomfortable.

I could read Sophie's lips as she whispered to Rowan across the table, "Is this woman on your payroll?"

He shook his head. "My parents provide her with drugs."

"It's hard to believe that it was just a month ago," Phil was saying, "that Jeff and Mia thought they might have to close the Cooking School at Z. And now look what they've done with it. There were some days when nobody came. Can you imagine? All this wonderful food and no one to eat it, which I always say is more fun than the cooking. They do such a good job."

Sophie clearly had heard.

"The ultimate flattery," Phil was telling the Chicago sisters, "is that their program spawned a competitor, and *their* food's not as good, and *he's* a professional chef who used to work at *Villa Real.*"

"And what would his name be?" Sophie asked, all business now.

Phil listed the failings of Madrid's program after identifying the restaurant. Why was she bringing this up at all? I couldn't catch her eye. I gave up and brought out the granita, which was quickly consumed in the growing heat of the day. Mia soon led our guests on a tour of Casa Blue. The sisters left with dad's painting, but not before they placed an order for *El Fortin* pottery. I gave Sophie one of our new flyers, with the reference from Francine Longman.

"I had a wonderful time," Sophie said, hugging Mia as she left.

"Get some time in the sun," I said. "You're returning to New York in winter."

"You're welcome here tomorrow," Mia said, "if you want to slip in."

"I've got hotels to visit all day."

Sophie waved ta-ta with her fingers and got into a waiting taxi, making final eye contact with us in a reassuring way, and then with our son in his buttoned-up shirt, conveying something quite different.

But in the final analysis, Sophie being Sophie, Mia and I weren't at all confident about what would be shared with her legion of readers.

17

"How many of you are Catholic?" Mia asked the eight guests standing around our cooking island. She had a large slab of ahi at hand. More than two weeks had passed since Sophie's visit.

A woman from San Francisco spoke up. "Born Catholic. Educated by real nuns. Still recovering. I think I should count double."

"Do you have to be a practicing Catholic?" another asked.

"The question is whether you remember the prayers," said Mia. Four indicated yes.

Mia lifted the shimmering tuna, caught twenty miles from shore this time of year. I'd purchased the best part of the loin, the *filete de atún*, just hours ago. It glistened, nearly pulsating with life.

"First, I rub it very lightly with sesame oil," which she did with her hands. "Your pan's at medium heat. There's no need to splatter your stove. Put the tuna on" -- Mia did so, creating an immediate sizzle -- "and say a Hail Mary to yourself."

Mia waited the requisite amount of time, praying to herself.

"Now do it again on the other side."

Some quietly laughed this time.

"Now all the edges. You're searing it for good hygiene and a complementary mouth feel, to counter the cool flesh inside. Banish the idea of actually cooking it."

"That was twelve seconds," said a non-Catholic, who'd timed

her prayer.

Mia finished the edges and it was done. "Two Hail Marys, and a heavenly taste. Or use the pledge of allegiance. Either way, it's spectacular."

On the cutting surface, Mia quickly scythed through the lustrous inner flesh. Like a card trick, she fanned the translucent slices on a colorful Talavera platter. She added green sprigs of mint for further color. Each guest received a tiny blue cup of dipping sauce I'd prepared earlier -- fresh lime juice, a bit of sauvignon blanc, and Chinese rice wine vinegar from our Asian supplier in Mexico City, with minced cilantro and a touch of salt. The guests passed the platter around, picking up tuna with their fingers, dipping, then putting it in their mouths as if participating in a religious experience. The compliments flowed.

"In the States, use champagne vinegar if you can find it," Mia said. "That I can't get in Mexico, unless you return next year and bring me some."

"Oh, we'll be back," two said at once.

— • —

Success was finally coming our way. We were reaching the maximum number of eight patrons on some days, and a few times we'd had to tell callers, "I'm sorry, but we don't have any openings that day. We'd be pleased to have you on...." A more pleasant pair of sentences does not exist in the English language.

It wasn't one thing going right with the Cooking School at Z, it was everything. Sophie's critique on TrueTravel's website had helped (we forwarded copies to our supporters). Three days after she visited us, Sophie had posted the review. She had indeed written about Madrid, but ruthlessly positioned it as a poor relation, good only for the vaudeville aspect. That seemed harsh, although it helped our cause. As for the Cooking School at Z:

"It was like prepping for a dinner party with the mother you wish you had -- dry sense of humor, fatter than you, concerned about your life. Most importantly, Mia Farrell's got the touch. Pig on the Moon gets the Blackwell full-body hug for creative, and if Marigold Chicken isn't included during your visit, hijack the recipe at gunpoint and try it at home. Think Nobu, Chez Panisse, highest Hong Kong, not a metro fusion bingo. And leave your man; it's a place for women. We girls got all chatty and true. Mia whispered that I'm the problem, not K, in The Relationship. And yet I sing her praises (magnanimous of me, yes?)."

Unfortunately, not every aspect of the Cooking School at Z experience won uniform praise.

"Somebody's father in rags actually wielded a brush at an easel, reminding me of a plein air face painter at a school fair. Eureka, TT'ers, if you collect sentimental watercolors from Ole Cape Cod and Montauk."

Sophie ended with the compliment we promptly marketed far and wide, minus the first two words.

"Pricey, but ten years from now you'll remember every detail. Righteous Kurt would have liked that Mia buys everything from Mercado Centro's local producers including the ambulantes, the Indians on the sidewalk. Bring your camera for the view and the group hug ending; it might even be the real thing."

— • —

Heinrich was recommending more guests. We'd taken full advantage of Francine Longman's endorsement, distributing a fresh set of handbills to supportive hotels, which included her cheek-to-cheek photo with Mia. And now we incorporated the endorsement from "Sophie's World" on the flyer. A few new hotels had begun referring their guests as well. Expenses were on a better track, with the daily tuna our costliest item.

Orders to the *Tixla* clay works were being generated on most days, as sympathetic patrons placed orders for shipments to their homes in the States. We were helping the cooperative, and it provided a charitable aspect that our program needed, given our price point. Despite Sophie's disparaging comments, Stanley was selling two or three paintings a week, contributing his proceeds to the house and cursing her daily. And Isabel and her mother had finally come in with some pieces to sell. The clothing items were slow movers, but the embroidered tablecloths and napkins were being snapped up.

After the high season, business would fall off. We hoped we wouldn't have to shut down altogether. But cooking outside in the humid swelter of summer, with rains interrupting and mosquitoes on the rampage, wouldn't be possible. We'd have to play it by ear.

Mia was helping Lauren plan for the destination wedding coming at the end of March, which gave mother and daughter something exciting to anticipate, amid all the stress and uncertainty about our future. After so many weeks without a peep about the title problem, we were almost able to tuck it in the back of our minds. Almost, but not quite.

— • —

Stanley no longer spoke of returning to New York. When Rowan had to fly back to Los Angeles, Stanley even came with us to the airport and didn't make a crack about needing to leave with his grandson.

Stanley had his routine. After chatting with guests early in the program and finishing that day's painting, he would troop off to the beach with Isabel. He'd take a long swim. She'd sit in the sand, her knees drawn up demurely in her dress. Then they'd walk the length of the beach together, still teaching each other their languages, talking about their lives, in this casual relationship across class lines that was quite uncommon in Zihuatanejo. Stanley, of course, talked nonstop -- he didn't need someone to listen, merely someone within listening distance. With all his swimming and a good diet, not to mention his tan, Stanley looked fitter than he'd been in years.

Well after the noon hour the two of them would trudge back up the hill. Stanley would usually stop for a late lunch at Phil's. Isabel would continue on to our house, to assist us with the cleanup.

Phil was showing a newfound interest in food. She had a man to cook for. Here was a guy from the old school who expected to sit down and be served, and she was just the woman to do it.

She learned some lunch basics from Mia. Stanley hated salads, but Phil learned how to put a potato in the oven for an hour at four hundred, and how to cook a protein source in olive oil on medium heat, ending up with something Stanley would swallow. He didn't notice food. Spices to him were salt and pepper; his herb was parsley on a potato, Irish style. He liked its mintlike, breath-improving properties.

"So what do you two talk about?" Mia asked Stanley one day when he returned from lunch with Phil. The three of us were in the pool.

"And how is that your business?" he snapped.

"I thought family talked to each other, or did the rule change."

"We discuss life. You. This place. Singers we used to like. It breaks up the day." He changed the topic at this point, having said as much as he cared to on that subject.

But Phil opened up without much prodding. Señor Stanley, her occasional nickname for him, filled a void in her life. We all knew she didn't care if she ever saw her husband again, although she wasn't one to say a bad word about him. As for Isabel, she withdrew if she heard Mia and me criticizing Phil's husband. Her tolerance for men was on the low side, and it disturbed her to hear such talk.

Angelo happened to blow in for a few days, so we had him and Phil over for dinner. He was all-business -- a tight-fisted Greek in Phil's words. He was a garrulous man who was doubly certain about the truth of everything that came from his mouth. He was half the size of his wife. When he and Philomena disagreed about something -- major, minor, it didn't matter -- he would inevitably become angry with Phil. Mia believed that Phil deliberately baited her husband during the dinner so we all could see what she had to live with. It was a strange two hours. How that relationship had come to be, Mia and I couldn't imagine. Stanley's fingers or his feet were going nervously the entire evening. It was all he could do to sit through it.

One day, as Mia moved our guests along from the ahi appetizer to the sweet *atolfo* mangos that were coming available -- "Take the section of mango that you cut off and invert the skin...that's right. Now crosshatch the fruit with a knife like so...now do this... and you end up with little cubes" -- I went to the lower terrace for additional bottled water. We were running behind on this day. It was a single group of eight that had prepaid -- our requirement for a large reservation -- but they'd required a ten-thirty start time.

A certain spot near our pool provides a discreet view of Phil's concrete patio, which juts out from her second floor. Getting the water, I noted Stan and Phil at the outdoor table, enjoying their customary lunch. Angelo had left Mexico again. An animated conversation was underway. Phil's voice sometimes carried when she was excited. I moved to where I could eavesdrop.

"...No, you're wrong about that, Stan. It's absolutely not your place to hand over your savings. You're paying a little something for room and board, and that's enough."

I couldn't make out his response.

"Well," Phil continued, "that's one more reason not to. If Jeffy doesn't know how to handle money, how are you going to sleep at night if he has yours? And I always thought he had common sense.

That's a heartbreaker."

Apparently he had told her how I'd lost our money on bad investments several years ago, which he would have carved on my tombstone as well. Then Stanley uttered another short, unintelligible burst.

"Listen," Phil responded, "suppose you go to Houston for a checkup or some tests. Do you want to be asking Mia and Jeff to help pay for it? You need your financial independence. Trust me, I know about this, you foolish man. Finish what's on your plate. I followed your daughter's instructions to the letter."

I hadn't asked Stanley for money. To my knowledge, Mia hadn't brought it up. I found it touching, really, that he wanted to make such a gesture. When he raised the topic that evening, we were ready for him.

"Dad, to be honest," Mia said, "if Casa Blue doesn't work out and we have to go back to the States, you'll need it to get started here on your own if you don't come with us at first. Money gives you the option. Keep it."

— • —

Rowan plays his cards close. Apparently there was a new queen of hearts in his hand, although we didn't learn this right away.

Apparently it began the day that Sophie reviewed the Cooking School at Z. That evening she also reviewed two restaurants. Afterwards, Rowan hooked up with her -- or she'd hooked up with him -- and they taxied to Ixtapa, just up the coast, where MTV Latin America happened to be shooting some of its Top Latin Lists. They insinuated themselves into the late-night rave party. When Rowan returned to Casa Blue late the next morning, we knew that he'd been in Ixtapa, and he mentioned that Sophie had been there as well, but what we took from this acknowledgment was that he'd simply hosted her.

Once he was back in the States, we resumed our routine of speaking with him by phone on Sundays. It was during one of these calls that Sophie's name arose.

"Sophie will be out here in Santa Barbara at the end of the week," Rowan said. "Something with a new hotel, a yoga restaurant -- what is that? -- and she'll be down in Santa Monica afterwards, crashing with her girlfriend. We might hang out together."

I immediately marched around the corner, into the great room, where Mia was listening on the extension. We exchanged a meaningful glance.

"Did she call you?" asked Mia.

"I don't know. One of us mentioned it. Whatever."

"So the two of you are going out?" Mia asked.

"Oh God," he said. "Why did I even mention it. A complete brain fart. She's just in town, that's all."

I had read Sophie's latest destination review, of San Paolo, and knew the relationship with Kurt was still on a downhill path. Sophie laid it all right out there as a stream-of-consciousness rag on the two of them, fueled by too much *coqueiro*.

"I don't see our son and Sophie together," Mia said after the call. "They're Macy's and Gimbel's. Did you think they had a relationship?"

"I don't think he knows what Gimbel's is. Or was. And I don't think you know your son as well as you think."

"He shouldn't go anywhere near her," Mia continued. "She has to work through all this business with Kurt that she writes about."

— • —

Two days later, Mia and I and Isabel were cleaning up after the day's program.

"Hi," called Daphne in a singsongy way.

She'd appeared on the terrace without any of us hearing her

arrive. And there was Guy, standing beside her.

"Oh my God," Mia shrieked. "You're here!"

Mia rushed to embrace her child. Then I gave Daphne a hug. Both of us acknowledged Guy, who shook hands. His calloused grip was surprisingly gentle, given his strong forearms from working on the *Five Seasons*.

"You look so healthy," Mia said to her daughter.

That was an understatement. Daphne was in an unbuttoned, gauzy lemon shirt over her bikini, with a salt-stained *pareo* wrapped around her waist. There was less of her -- that was the first thing I noticed. Her matted hair, casually tied back, looked salty and sun-bleached and almost Rastafarian. She had a deep tan that was excessive across her upper chest, where her skin was peeling and reddened. Daphne's eyes sparkled at us with love and all her secrets -- all those experiences we would never know, but knew from our own lives.

"Hi grandpa," she said, moving to give him a kiss and a squeeze once he got to his feet. We introduced our daughter to Isabel. I wondered what Isabel was thinking at that moment, contrasting her life with that of this other young woman, our daughter. All of us moved into the shade of our African tulip tree.

"When did you get in?" Mia asked, still excited.

"This morning," Daphne said. "We waited to come, because we didn't want to walk in on your class."

"I can't believe it," Mia said. "Yesterday I had this presentiment you might be coming. Then dad said he thought he'd caught a glimpse of the *Five Seasons* going over to the docks."

"I wanted to surprise you."

"The wind is not so good," Guy explained. "Very calm. It took us a long time coming south."

"And where are your parents?" I asked him.

"In the town I think."

"They're certainly welcome to come by," I said.

Mia asked, "Do you want something to drink? Are you hungry?"

The lovers -- that was certainly clear -- looked at each other. "I'd have something," Daphne asked. "All I had was some instant oatmeal for breakfast."

"Instant oatmeal?" Mia said.

"It's what I like," Guy said bashfully. "Maybe a little strange."

"Do you want something?" Mia asked him.

"Sure."

"I'll get something together," I volunteered. "Everybody sit down."

We'd put all the food away. In the Inferno I assembled some leftover roast pork from the refrigerator, *mojo* sauce we'd saved for our own dinner, pieces of roasted chicken from two days ago, tortillas, salsa, and the pitcher of hibiscus sun tea that Mia had made, along with some sodas and beer. They were all seated around the terrace table as I brought in the food.

"Dad, we saw four humpback whales yesterday," Daphne said.

"They're early this year," I said. "Usually they don't come until the first part of March. That must have been awesome."

"So is the cooking school going okay?" Daphne asked.

"We've been getting people," Mia said. "It's been great this month. We were able to use the article that Sophie wrote to promote ourselves. Did you look at it on-line?"

"That was so cruel of her, calling you fat. You're not fat."

"She didn't say I was fat. Actually, she's a big girl herself."

"Everything's just been coming together," I said.

"Awesome," Daphne said.

"Heinrich's been wonderful at the hotel. He's sending so many people here, and we have a few other new referrals working. And dad paints every day. People like seeing that. They're buying his work."

"Oooo," Daphne teased her grandpa. "Mister Gauguin."

"That would be me," said Stanley, hoisting his beer before drinking.

I looked around for Isabel, to ask her to get a tomato for me, but she'd retreated from sight. I sliced the pork thinly at the cooking island, warmed the tortillas and sauce, and soon we had a late lunch for the two returnees.

Mia hung on every word our daughter said, but I know my wife. She was also scrutinizing Daphne. She and Guy clearly were very comfortable together. Daphne's hand rested on his forearm now and again. He seemed too polite to touch her in front of us, which in its own way was endearing. He was a good-looking young man, at ease in his own skin even in this situation, and he clearly was the quiet one in this relationship. As for the way our daughter had simply run off with him on the *Five Seasons* ... seeing her now, safe and in love, I could forgive that.

Guy and Daphne ate heartily, and Mia kept replenishing their glasses of tea. The kids told funny stories about people they'd taken out on the evening cruises.

Eventually Mia asked Daphne, "So what's next for you?"

"I'm going back to New York," she said definitively. "I can register for the spring quarter, and line up a job again. Maybe they'll take me back where I used to work."

"Which job was that?" I asked. We could never keep them straight. Daphne had had a succession of part-time jobs, all of them paying her under the table.

"Working for that dress shop on Ludlow," she said. "She liked me, and she was really cool about my schedule. So I'm gonna see if I can do that. I'm getting back into my room on the first."

"That's just a few days from now," Mia said. "Does this girl who's subletting your room know you're coming."

"Not really, but like she knows it's just temporary. And she's being a bitch. Nobody wants her there. She works nights, and she's always yelling about everybody being quiet so she can sleep during the day."

"So you're going to leave right away?" Mia asked, as surprised as I was.

"I know, it's so soon. Sorry, mom. I can get a ticket for the day after tomorrow. I checked on the airline website. Then I'll come back for Lauren's wedding."

So she was leaving Guy, I thought to myself, and going back to finish her degree. He seemed nonplussed.

"Guy's gonna come back here for the wedding," Daphne went on. "I invited him."

"That's fine," Mia assured them both.

"The week after, Susan and the captain are going back to New Zealand for the rest of the year."

And Daphne would be in school. No longer did we have to worry about her sailing into oblivion.

"After the wedding, Guy's going to come to New York when I'm back there, after he sees some friends in Sao Paolo," Daphne continued. "He wants to try living in the city for a while. My friend has this connection to a French restaurant that his uncle owns in the West Village. We're thinking he can probably get a job there."

Mia and I were stunned.

"Have you been to New York before?" I asked Guy.

"I've only heard about it now," he said. "I think it will be interesting."

"He can stay with me and my roommates," Daphne said.

"It should be very good fun," said Guy.

— • —

With Daphne, though, it's never over, as we found out later than night. Mia and I were reading on our comfy sofa in the great room, grateful for the quiet time and an opportunity to digest all the changes. Daphne made an entrance wearing a robe. She leaned back against the railing, a position of strength for addressing the two people who had brought her into the world. I saw her as a young Lauren Bacall, lacking only the cigarette.

"Okay," she said. "I didn't want to say this with Guy there, because he didn't need to be involved. But after the wedding, when his parents sail to New Zealand, I might go with them. Instead of being in New York."

My mouth hung open. No one spoke for several seconds.

"Okay, I knew you'd be shocked, and you'd make a big deal, but it's something we're going to think about. We decided I'm going to move back into my old life in New York, and he'll plan to come out, just like we told you. But we're both thinking about this too."

"Let me get this straight," I said, clearing my throat.

"There's not anything you need to get straight."

"Wait just a moment. You're going to leave everything for this young man? What do his parents think of this?"

"What difference does that make? Although they're fine with it."

"So you've discussed your Plan B with his parents."

"Yes. And we're not calling it 'Plan B.'"

"What's waiting for you in New Zealand?" Mia asked, visibly struggling to play the listening parent, lest Daphne roll her eyes and leave.

"I don't know. Whatever's there."

"And school?"

"I can take classes some day, if I want to finish my degree."

Daphne could be a cool customer. She'd clearly thought this through and braced herself for this confrontation, and she looked from one to the other of her parents.

"Daphne," I said, but I didn't know what else to say. The two women who were dearest to me in this world were both looking my way for what was to follow, but all I could do was throw up my hands.

"Your father and I need to talk about this," Mia said. "This is a complete surprise. I don't want any of us to say something we'll regret later."

"You need to understand, this is my life. It's not like I would be the first person in the world to do something like this. You both moved down here on an impulse. You risked everything. And great-grandma Anna left Italy and didn't know what she'd find in America, from what you've told me."

She'd done her homework.

"This is different," I said.

"See, you always say it's different. But it's not. It's the same."

18

In the days immediately following, Guy did set sail with his parents up the Mexican coast. Daphne did go to New York. Mia and I could once again exhale, our standard physiological experience after being with Daphne for any amount of time in this phase of her life.

Guests were now coming in numbers to the Cooking School at Z, creating our best week ever. It was incredibly gratifying. Mia and I greedily kept reviewing our daily revenues and expenses, counting profits. The cooking school was getting on track!

It seemed even more cruel, then, that the title problem was still hanging over our heads. Each unexpected ring of the doorbell, every time the phone rang, I had this inner twinge: here was their attorney's response, making demands that would squash us financially and put the Cooking School at Z out of business.

Mia has the ability to block out certain things while she deals with life by the glass. She'd adopted a working proposition that the title settlement would be something we could manage. Maybe we'd never even hear from our rich neighbor again. To me, her faith seemed without foundation, on a par with the Mexican widows who believed Our Lady of Guadalupe would create a miracle in their lives.

Whatever, there was no point in two of us being miserable. I stopped mentioning the title problem. But I couldn't relax. It preyed on me. I had nightmares about how this could turn out.

Our high-powered attorney, Juan Serna Lozano, had made the last move. Why was the land owner not responding?

"*Ni modo,*" said our accountant, Señor Rodriguez, unable to shed light on the issue when I turned to him. There was nothing to be done. Whatever happened, accept it as fate.

"Are they delaying?" I asked Ken in one of our phone calls, when I was completely exasperated. "Do they have investigators trying to determine the most Mia and I can afford? What the fuck are they doing? I'm going crazy down here, Ken. Find out if they've got some move going in the Mexican court system to steal Casa Blue. I don't see how you're helping us here." I was stalking around the great room with the phone to my ear, too worked up to sit down.

"You're getting way, way ahead of yourself," Ken counseled me.

I was phoning Ken every three or four days because our Mexican lawyer, Señor Lozano, was no longer returning my calls for updates. Ken did obtain the back story on that. It seemed that Señor Lozano "had other more pressing matters" than dealing with persistent American ex-pats like us. Señor Lozano now regretted that he had been so foolish as to take on this case as a favor to Ken's friend Max Cisneros.

"Lozano's having to expend too much political capital on your behalf," Ken said, "but I'll deal with that. Just keep your focus on the Cooking School at Z. When they respond, we make our move. In the end, I have confidence in Lozano because of Max."

"You have confidence in my lawyer who won't talk to me?" I wanted him to hear how stupid that sounded.

"He's got his airs, but Max did you a big one getting this guy aboard."

"What's his bill going to be?"

A copy of The News, an English-language paper out of Mexico City which would soon go out of business, was on a table top. The headline of a story I'd read before caught my eye. Struggling shrimp fishermen out of Chiapas, Mazatlan had protested mightily against the central government's plan to end their diesel subsidy, so it was being reinstated. It was an inspiring victory. The little guy could prevail.

"Whatever it is, it'll be worth it. Max says the guy's got a lot of juice. I told you that in the beginning. You don't want a Mexican attorney who's grateful for the work and returns your calls in five minutes."

"Tell him to get a dollar figure. We need the damn number."

"He knows that."

"Tell him again."

"It's not in our interests to seem eager."

"Find a way that is in our interests. And I've been doing research on the Internet. I think we can sue the bank. There's this commission called CONDUSEF for short. It's a channel for binding arbitration with a bank, and they clearly...."

"Jeff," he interrupted.

"What?" I'd picked up a small ceramic figurine that was a deep ultramarine, *azul anil*, the color that was supposed to ward off evil spirits.

"That's all been looked into. Under the administrative rules, there's no binding arbitration unless the bank agrees in the first place that it's binding. The bank won't do that. The commission you're talking about has no enforcement powers. You're in Mexico. So you could take it into the Mexican courts, but you won't get anywhere against plaintiffs of this stature. And you couldn't afford the legal bills."

"So I have nowhere to turn?" My pacing brought me to the railing, where jumping was an easy option.

"Actually, no, you don't. In court, at the very best everything would get pinned on your *notario*, and there's no estate there to recover from. This is very complicated. You're telling me Izzy's in Portugal or Peru, so we can't pursue him. Let the plaintiffs respond to us in their own sweet time. Or maybe never. Maybe Mia's right, they'll just let it slide."

"There's a pint-sized Caterpillar in operation on their site, which I could actually see from where I'm standing right now if it wasn't for a tree that's in the way. He's doing some clearing and moving dirt. We have not been forgotten, trust me."

— • —

"What's bothering you?" Mia asked me during dinner that evening. We were by ourselves, as Stanley had gone to Phil's.

Envision a seagull on a piling, with the wind ruffling its feathers, motionless. That was me.

"I was just thinking," I said.

Mia had opened a noteworthy pinot gris. I took another big swallow. A guest at our cooking school had sent the bottle down from Oregon as a thank-you, in the arms of a friend she'd referred. "Still tasting that day, can't wait until next year," read the gift card.

"Thinking about what?" Mia was sitting forward, irritated that I was distracted. She rapped the back of my hand with her butter knife to get my attention.

"I was just wondering if the reservations will keep coming in like they have been," I said.

"That's not what you were thinking, but the reservations do look good into the first half of March," said Mia. "I did a count this afternoon."

"Six weeks ago, we'd never have imagined this." I smiled wanly.

Mia adjusted her light shawl. Certain evenings, it gets a little cool. She seemed bemused. She was tapping her index finger against her lips, her eyes sparkling from the newfound success of the cooking school.

"You look lovely," I said. "Do you know that?"

"You'd look handsome if you'd cut your hair," she said. "You're getting scruffy. Are you thinking you're going to let it grow into a ponytail like these dissolute characters I see in town?" They were hippies from long ago, the drug days when Timothy Leary famously came to Zihuatanejo and tried to launch a new kingdom of expanded consciousness.

I returned to my theme. "You, right now. You look lovely."

She put her hand across the table, and I took it. We both understood. The two parents with one brain thing was working. We'd agreed to stop talking about our title problem, but she knew I was obsessed.

"When you married me, did you ever expect to be in a place like this?" I asked.

"It wasn't out of the question."

That surprised me. "Because?"

"Because it seemed like we'd always do something big."

"Speaking of which, is sex out of the question?" I asked.

She shrugged coyly, not showing any cards.

"What are you thinking?" I asked.

She squeezed my hand. "You really want to know?"

"Right now, what are you thinking?" I pressed. "Tell me."

"I'm thinking I don't want to have to cook pork again, ever. I'm tired of it. Maybe next year, but I'm sick of looking at it, sick of handling it, sick of the taste. I was running through the menu in my head."

"You're holding my hand and you're thinking of raw pork, after what I just said about sex?"

She considered that for a moment. "Pork loin," she clarified. "Thick, meaty. I made the association. But we can talk about the title problem, if you need to."

"There's nothing new to say. It just hangs out there, completely beyond our control. It's wearing me out."

"Let's go up to bed," Mia suggested.

"I promised your father we'd play Scrabble tonight."

215

"When did you promise?"

"After lunch."

"I think he and Phil went out to meet up with some of her crowd."

"Then I'm free tonight."

"No, you're not free. You're a man obsessed with legal matters, which is not attractive to a woman. But come on anyway." She winked, to take the edge off.

Sex that night was mostly an act of kindness on her part, and not to be prolonged. I undressed and got into bed and waited for her to finish brushing her teeth. No talking. She kissed me hard and moved things along. Afterward she bestowed on me a long, lingering kiss of a different caliber, to reconfirm that she loved me and understood, and then she fell sound asleep.

— • —

Late in the morning on a Friday, not long after, Mia and seven patrons, all women, gathered around the cooking island. They began dicing, laughing and doing spontaneous little dances to a Motown CD one of them had brought -- word had gotten out that we'd accommodate music requests, as long as all patrons that day went along. I called Ken yet again. This Friday request for an update was our ritual. Other calls during the week hinges on my level of anxiety. I was outdoors, in the chair by Mia's garden.

"Ken's not in the office now," said his secretary, "but I know he wants to speak with you. Let me see if I can reach him."

He wanted to speak with me? That was a change.

"I'm sitting in traffic," Ken said. He sounded a little staticky.

"I'm not hearing you too clearly," I answered. "Speak loudly."

"There's a big storm. You're probably hearing the rain on my car. It's like kids are drumming on the roof. We're going up skiing in the Sierra for the weekend if we can get there. The interstate may close, so I don't know. I've got the family with me. Listen, I had a conversation with Señor Lozano last night. I was going to call you. He has the number."

I stationed myself by the wet bar near the pool, a premium spot for phone reception. I eased myself onto a stool. My eyes locked on our painting of two sensuous Cuban women smoking cigars. I could imagine Señor Lozano smoking a cigar, conferring with the attorney who represented our super-rich, reclusive neighbors.

"It could be worse," Ken said, "but they're not taking it lightly. That's unfortunate. Apparently there's some history, involving the guy who sold you your house and his *notario*. So it's good that that's finally out on the table."

"What history?"

"There had been a previous survey by this family that's threatening you. Then your guy -- what was his name again?"

"Izzy."

"Then Izzy contested it on some basis or other, and he was spreading money around in the right places. It was just people talking at that stage, but Izzy ticked them off. Then the family in Mexico City that's behind this suffered a tragedy. The grandmother and a daughter were killed in a light plane crash. This thing with your property went on the shelf for a while. And in the meantime, Izzy sold to you."

I remembered aloud, "He never advertised the house."

"You're talking about Izzy?"

"Yes. Supposedly he was giving us an inside track on *Casa Rosalinda*, the old name of this place, before he advertised. But he never wanted it out that he planned to sell. And remember how he rushed to get the deal done?"

"After he squeezed you on price."

"Fuck," I said angrily. I plunked my forehead into my hand.

"'Fuck' is right, Jeff. Which I would only say to a friend, and I wouldn't say it if my two children in the back seat didn't hear it every day at school. You've been fucked. My heart goes out to you and Mia. I mean that."

"You reviewed the papers before the sale," I pointed out. Desperate, I could almost believe that he shared some liability. "You didn't see something to tip us off?"

"I reviewed the short preliminary sales agreement. You were agreeing to buy if everything could be lined up. The *notario* handled the sale documents."

"And the *notario's* dead." I took a half-finished small bottle of tomato juice from the refrigerator, my mouth was so dry.

"He had to know," Ken said. "The rain's letting up. Are you hearing me better?"

"Izzy, that little cockroach."

"It does make you want to sue."

"How?" I said, even though we'd been down this road before. Ken had in fact educated me. "He's not even in Mexico anymore. And he's wealthy. Do you know how many courts that would involve, and in how many countries?" I took a drink.

"You'd never see a cent," said Ken.

Then I remembered something. "You haven't told me how much they want."

"First, let's just put the lawsuit idea to bed."

"I could hire somebody to wring his shriveled dick of a neck. How much is a hit man in Portugal?"

"That's not something you should be saying, even though I know you're not serious. You're on an international line. I have to advise you of that."

"The little Peruvian bastard."

"Jeff," Ken said sharply.

"You still haven't told me how much they want."

"It could be worse, but it could be better. Señor Lozano says he talked the family down considerably. And I believe him. Mostly they had revenge in mind when they opened the discussions -- their attorney admitted this -- and the family is still bitter from their tragedy. I'm also told that they own businesses in the *maquiladora* areas near the border, and the people in Washington pretty much screwed them last fall with some of these new policies. You're American. People emotionally connect one thing with the other. "

"Ken, just give me the number."

There was a silence. My tone was too harsh, and I knew it immediately.

"Jeff," he said in a new voice, "I don't consider you a client. I consider you a friend. Because in the end here, I wasn't planning on sending you a bill. With my clients I get to the point right away, because the meter's running. Most of them are in construction, that's what they want."

"I'm sorry. I shouldn't have used that tone."

"I hear from people who were at your place in the fall that you and Mia have an unbelievably wonderful situation right now. We're all happy for you. I want to help you keep it."

"You and the family have to come down," I said lamely. An ill-timed invitation, I realized too late. Gaffe number two. Another silence ensued.

"You haven't told me the number," I repeated shamefully, submissive now.

"A hundred and ten thousand. That includes twenty thousand for Señor Lozano. "

"Pesos?"

"Dollars."

— • —

I was speechless. I'd been thinking maybe thirty thousand, on the bleak side. Ten thousand if we were lucky. It was only an eight-meter-wide slice of their property, which covered two acres in its entirety.

219

"Because they've come down from what they'd originally had in mind, due to your attorney's influence, they want all of it in ninety days. Señor Lozano won you that much time. They were saying sixty days to start with. They're paid and you're home free forever, or they take it to the courts. And you won't win there, as we discussed. Also, I should add that Señor Lozano made it clear to me that he wouldn't represent you in court. He's a qualified attorney, according to Max, but I get the sense that he doesn't really practice. He's more a lobbyist, something on that order. I'm sorry to tell you all of this at once."

"He's expecting twenty thousand dollars for what he did?"

"Please hold on one second." He spoke to his wife, then his children, and then came back on the line. "We got two kids arguing in the back seat about whose leg is over the line. It all starts at a young age. Later they want representation.

"Okay," Ken continued, "Lozano says he saved you a lot more than that. The whole amount goes in one payment, to him, when we do the documents. He'll forward the payment to the family. All of this gets done at some proper signing of papers, not in a back alley, and the papers will be recorded. I'm not sure the money will ever be reported, but that doesn't concern us. In effect, you'll be paying for the eight meters plus five more meters they insist upon since you're already built on it, to have a proper buffer."

"For a hundred and ten thousand dollars?"

"That's the number. I'm not billing you, as I said."

"I'm sorry, Ken. I didn't mean any of what I said before. I was upset. But Mia and I don't have that kind of money. We didn't have that much cash when we moved down here, and we've spent a lot. We're just now turning a profit. In the summer we'll have to start drawing down our account to pay the bills and scrounge by."

"Congratulations again on turning the Cooking School at Z around. We are going to come down there, incidentally, for your daughter's wedding. We've been able to clear the calendar. It's not that far off."

"There's no way to borrow it, Ken. They don't do mortgages in Mexico. We don't have any rich relatives."

"If you don't have some big collateral back here," he affirmed, "you won't get any money from a U.S. bank. They don't want Mexican property with a rotten title. Hell, especially not if it's just a trust."

"So let's counter their offer."

"They're not accepting a counter. That was made clear. And Señor Lozano isn't negotiable on his part either. It's bundled up in one payment."

"This is on the up and up?"

"According to Max, yes. I hunted him down in Japan and ran it all by him, for his impressions. That's why I didn't call you right away."

"So, do you have an idea for us?"

"I'm sorry. Max didn't have any suggestions either."

"Where does this figure come from?"

"In absolute terms, they're selling you forty feet of road frontage of high-dollar view property. It's the equivalent of a very narrow building lot, really, if you just look at it that way."

"But I'm not building anything else."

"Which is not their concern. And don't forget, standard procedure by a judge in Mexico is to double the appraised value because of the intrusion. Which is irrelevant here, because these landowners have the juice to influence the outcome. It's not as outrageous as it seems. They could be demanding double that amount, and nothing would get in their way."

"I have to think."

"I know you do. And I'm sorry to be the one telling you, Jeff. I'm doing everything I can."

"I'll get back to you," I said. "And thank you."

"The rain's letting up here. I'll take that as a good sign."

221

— • —

Mia and I went to dinner that evening at Orlando's, which sits atop a very high hill. The tables are outside and overlook all of Zihuatanejo Bay and Centro. It's owned by a rich absentee American as a tax write-off, and a place to bring his rich buddies. The caretaker's inept Yugoslavian wife is the cook. However, customers are rare at Orlando's, even on a Friday night, so we were able to speak privately.

"I think we should tell dad," Mia said as we finished margeritas.

"What does that accomplish?"

"I don't want to tiptoe around him every day. Making up stories when he asks me why I'm not happily smiling away." Mia hadn't bothered with any makeup after showering. Having lulled herself into thinking we'd get off somehow, this news from Ken was truly crushing.

"Does he really need to know all this may come to an end?" I said. "When has he been as happy as he is now since your mother died? He complains, but that's part of being him."

"He still should know," Mia insisted.

Our dinners came. For me an insipid mush of *pargo*, a spongy fish to begin with, which had been fried badly. Mia had ordered the ahi, and asked for it rare, mistakenly believing it couldn't be ruined.

"Okay, so we have two choices with your father," I said. "We tell him, or we don't tell him."

"Of course we have two choices," Mia said. She took a mouthful, then put her fork down, disinterested in what was on her plate.

"Let's list the reasons for and against and reach a decision."

"Get the check and let's get out of here," Mia decided. "If dad is still up, I'm going to have a talk with him. I don't want to be in this shitty place."

"My opinion on this doesn't count?"

"I don't want to live a lie. And do you want to be the one to break the news to him some time in the future, and explain why we didn't tell him sooner, when it's his life that's on the line here too?"

"I'd tell him there was no point in him worrying about it, because he couldn't do anything."

"And would you like me to not tell you important things for that reason?"

Point taken, after some squirming.

"You're sure you want to do this?"

"I'm sure."

I had to go find the cook, who was also the waiter.

"All of this...," Mia said, taking in the panoramic view of Zihuatanejo one last time as we stood by our seats, waiting for the cook to run our credit card and bring the receipt for signature. She kept shaking her head back and forth.

"We have to give up all of this? I'm not doing it, Jeff. I'm not leaving. They'll have to come with soldiers to evict me."

19

The figure, a hundred and ten thousand U.S. dollars, was never out of mind as the days moved by. There was no way we could come up with that amount. Yet we had to try.

Mia put on her game face each morning and soldiered ahead with the Cooking School at Z. I devoted myself to gold panning on the Internet. I also called virtually everyone we'd ever known with ties to the financial industry. I investigated mortgages and credit cards and creative insurance policies. It was all to no avail.

"I want you to have my two certificates of deposit," Stanley said at dinner one night. "One you know about. The other I keep in a different bank."

He'd taken the news fairly well when Mia first told him.

"Dad," Mia said, extremely touched.

"Of course if you hadn't squandered the family nest egg in the stock market," he said to me, "we wouldn't be talking now. Or if you'd followed my daughter's advice to spend for the title insurance."

What could I say? "We do what we do in life. Shoot me. I can't undo it."

"How much money are you talking about, dad?" Mia asked.

His mouth was stuffed with eggplant that he first had to swallow. We waited.

"Ten thousand dollars. A little more." He said it as if it were ten times that amount. Still, it was a nice gesture. In return, Mia and I didn't interrupt his monologue about how we'd uprooted him, dragged him to Mexico, and now were going to leave. He could have stayed in Brooklyn, he pointed out.

"Dad," Mia said firmly. "Everything you're saying is correct, in hindsight. But that's the last time I want to hear you bring that up again. Because we acted out of love."

To her credit, Mia also racked her brain for ways to raise money. She contacted two physicians who'd once offered to bankroll her in a restaurant in California; some couples for whom she'd been a personal chef in San Jose; and a venture capitalist who'd regularly hired her to put on dinner parties. Times were hard, the mood had changed drastically in Silicon Valley. The relationships had grown stale, and being countries apart didn't help. Mia described our plight to these people in such graphic, candid terms, it made me wince, because who would want to throw their money away? But Mia said she didn't want to mislead anybody.

Fraud seemed to be our best chance.

"We've never done anything dishonest," I reminded Mia over a second cup of coffee one morning, before my run to the market. "Not intentionally we haven't. I think we're entitled this once to skirt the system, and we'll pay the money back. It's not fraud, really, if you pay it back." I hadn't unveiled my scheme yet, but my thought was to somehow establish an address in the U.S. and acquire a raft of credit cards.

"Look at me, Jeff. You are the least slick person there is," Mia said. "Every time you have tried something slick, it's blown back in our faces. Spitting into the wind comes to mind. So we are not going there. Cross it off your list of possibilities."

"Then I'm out of ideas."

"That doesn't mean we're giving up." She checked the time. "You need to get me some fish."

"The fish aren't going anywhere. They're dead, like the Cooking

225

School at Z before too long. What's your solution? I'm serious. Hope isn't a strategy."

"My solution is to see what comes along. They gave us ninety days." She was dead serious. "Sometimes you can't tackle life head on. You just have to trust."

"And if something doesn't come along?"

"I am choosing to believe that something will." She opened her hands, a gesture that asked what could be wrong with that?

"Why do we have to play by the rules?" I asked. "Look around. You see a million people who'll do anything to survive. Our neighbors who own that land are screwing us, and so is their attorney, and so is our Mexican attorney. Do we let them dictate to us? We lose Casa Blue if we don't do something."

"Go buy the fish." Mia would have no more of it.

I was pissed when I left. I drove aggressively to Centro. An unusual wind was rattling the palm trees along the *Paseo del Pescador*. The fishmonger's wife, Ivelisse, examined both sides of the bills and coins that I paid for my fish, as she always did, and I tried to smile. Our joke, the one about the expired money I'd once given her -- once, only once! -- brought sadness to me. Everything in Mexico would soon be history. Ivelisse smiled warmly as she provided change. I saw that she'd lost an incisor. For some weird reason, I wanted to take that as an astrological sign. When the fishmonger's wife loses a tooth, the Americans are cooked.

"*Gracias, Señor Jeff*," Ivelisse said in closing.

"Goodbye, Señora Martinez," I said with great formality. My return to English came from my suspicion, at a level where destiny and failure held hands and were about to leap off the cliff, that Mexico would never work for us.

Our minivan, parked by the *Sector Naval*, would not start. The red light for engine service laughed at me when I turned the key in the ignition. This had happened one other time, just for a few turns. I had to try a number a times before the engine finally turned over.

Turning in my seat to back out, I found a flatbed truck was now blocking my way. Where had that come from? Boys were clambering on and off, unloading cases of paint. I waited impatiently.

And then I was struck by an awful insight. In fact, I shuddered, as if struck by an arrow to the heart.

Why was I blithely assuming that we would at least be allowed to sell Casa Blue for a reasonable price, if that was our only option? Would they let us pay off the hundred and ten thousand, pocket our remaining, shrunken equity, and return shame-faced to the States? Our litigious neighbors had the upper hand. They could block any sale, and insist that we sell to them at whatever price they wished. They could crush Mia and me. Who would buy Casa Blue without a clear title?

We were in fact at their mercy -- and so far they'd shown none, because what was being presented to us as a good deal negotiated by our attorney in Mexico City certainly didn't qualify.

— • —

Stanley had set up his easel on the terrace for his regular morning performance by the time I returned. He was just starting to apply a white background wash. Garlic bulbs were roasting aromatically. Mia had spread an array of our garden vegetables and some produce bought yesterday at the *mercado* -- eggplants, peppers, three kinds of tomatoes, onions, jicama -- around the cooking island, along with colorful vases of fragrant basil, rosemary, and flat-leaf Italian parsley. A carafe held olive oil. Today was Mia's traditional Italian theme, except for julienned jicama.

Isabel was helping with the set-up, and also with some of the prep work. Mia was teaching her to cook. Perhaps some day Isabel could make it on her own in the tourist restaurants, although her

skills with English would probably bring the highest dollar on
the market. The young woman had aptitude and desire, but if the
cooking school folded, any job would pay far less. With a heavy,
guilty heart I watched Isabel set out a matching pair of Michoacan
work bowls, painted with dreamy horses and rabbits being chased
by children: one held semolina for its firm texture, the other a white
all-purpose flour to blend. She used the vice to fix the hand-cranked
pasta maker on the counter's edge. Two cauldrons of hot water were
simmering on the range. How could this stop happening?

"What can I do here?" I asked Mia.

"Not a thing. Isabel and I have everything under control."

Mia glided past me, with things to do before we went upstairs
to the great room to receive the morning's guests. Mia was
wearing an embroidered cotton top and a long blue skirt, giving
her an indigenous flavor. Today Isabel was dressed completely in
fashionable white, including white jeans she had poured herself
into. She had an apron tightly wrapped around her.

"Isabel," I said, "give it another year, and I think you could run
a class. Maybe we'll have a Mexican theme each week."

Isabel smiled gamely. "That would be good," she said politely,
but she knew the truth. Stanley had spoken with her, introducing it
gently. Only with her did he display a tenderness granted to no one
else, not even Phil.

Mia returned and said, out of the blue, "Maybe we should
write a letter to these people wanting our money. Let's see if they'll
lower the price."

It had been like that. Talking to ourselves, then blurting out
rescue plans.

"We talked about that yesterday."

"And this is today."

"You know as well as I do that their attorney expressly told Ken
that the principals absolutely do not wish to be contacted." Ken
had gotten our neighbors' illustrious attorney on the phone once,

only once, for a conversation that lasted less than two minutes. "They believe they already made a major concession, as a gesture to Señor Lozano. And they're not even in the country. We're supposed to be grateful."

"'The principals have an estate in Spain, and that's where they are now,'" Mia mimicked. "I've heard all that. They have to come back."

"And how would we know if they did?"

"Don't talk to me with that tone of voice, Jeff." Mia had a fork in her hand, and she pointed it my way. Then she returned to work.

"You see how the rich people live in seclusion, even in Zihuatanejo," I continued. "Ken and Señor Lozano both say it's absolutely the wrong thing to do to seek anything further. I agree. This is Mexico. We've gotten what we're going to get."

"What have we got to lose?"

"We still need their good will to let us sell the property and walk out of here with some money."

"'The kindness of strangers.'"

"What?"

"Blanche Dubois. That line from 'Streetcar Named Desire.' My mother always used it."

Stanley came over, a little jar in hand, to get water from the tap. "It's not a good thing," he said, "painting the same scene over and over. When I was in Brooklyn, I always painted for myself. Not that I'm unhappy to do it, given your situation. I'm just saying."

"People buy the vista of *Playa La Ropa*," I said.

"I could do it in my sleep," Stanley said.

"How did the minivan drive?" Mia asked.

"Acting up again. The service light came on."

"Why don't you get it fixed today?" Mia asked me. "I need it tomorrow, and I don't want to get stuck somewhere. I don't need you this morning. Isabel and I can handle the women."

Isabel heard. She was just bringing knives she'd washed and

polished in the Inferno. Her white sneakers featured gold laces, a new twist. Her hair was pulled back tightly in a tortoise barrette. She bore a look of great industriousness. Excusing herself, she slipped between us to the sink. Her body language, sometimes sullen, sometimes frightened, seemed to say, Will I have a job? I knew the truth. Isabel was angry with us for jeopardizing her future and her family, for giving her opportunity and now this.

— • —

I stayed to welcome the day's guests. Once they descended to the terrace, I slipped away.

I drove the minivan to Centro. Isabel had an uncle who worked on cars in a vacant dirt lot with an aluminized shed roof. He brought in electricity on an orange extension cord from the adjacent auto parts store. I'd expected to leave the vehicle and taxi home, but he said the job he was doing could be put aside, and he'd work on our minivan.

I decided to stick around. I ended up having a couple of beers at a popular hangout along the *Paseo del Pescador*. I chatted with Julio, who ran the bar and had his own views about Mexico's chances in soccer's World Cup this time around. I sat there watching a match on TV, making small talk sometimes.

I was completely unaware that people were trying desperately to find me.

20

When I returned home with the minivan, I immediately noticed that no music was playing. For Mia's Italian program, the patrons seemed to enjoy Andrea Bocelli, Puccini, or string quartets, and it usually could be heard when you walked in.

On the terrace, two of the day's couples, all in their thirties, were sitting at the table, which was odd. I could see they were on a second bottle of wine. Mia was nowhere in evidence. Neither were the other three people I'd met earlier. These remaining individuals rose one at a time, each taking a cue from the other, their chairs scraping noisily on the tile. One of the men, in mirror sunglasses and a Tommy Bahama shirt, stepped to the fore.

"Hey, it's good you're back," he said. His partner, a redhead with a bare, flat midriff and tight capri pants, came to his side.

Something was up.

"Mia asked us to stay until you got here. Her dad had a problem on the beach, like a stroke or a heart attack."

"Your wife didn't know," the redhead said sympathetically.

"So Mia had to run down there," he continued. "She asked us to stay and tell you so you'd know."

This couldn't be true. "Is he okay? What else did she say? "

"Actually, we haven't heard from her."

"How long ago was this?"

"Half an hour," said the woman. "Probably under that."

"It was definitely less," said the other young woman, stepping closer. She was wearing a pink BeBe T-shirt.

"Do you know where this happened?" I asked.

"I guess on the beach, is what she said. They'd taken him into the hotel down there. I hope he's alright."

Almost certainly the *Villa Real*.

"Thank you for staying," said a voice that could have been mine. I had already exited, although I hadn't left yet. Just hours ago, at breakfast, Stanley had been his usual self, criticizing an historian's book for having his facts wrong about post-war England.

The couples had already assembled their things. I thanked them again. They went up the steps and let themselves out. A minute later I was out the door too, after verifying that there were no phone messages and that the stoves were off.

The engine of the minivan wouldn't turn over.

"Goddam it," I yelled. I pounded the steering wheel.

At first I half-ran, half-walked on the way to *Playa La Ropa*, like a man rushing to catch a plane. I quickly broke into a sweat. At the dolphin fountain, where I turned down the steep grade, I nearly ran into an Indian woman in a calico apron and flipflops. Then I went all out, running only in the sense that it was the fastest I could go. I felt bitter that we were cursed in Mexico, where it was one thing after the other. I veered left where the drivers assemble with their white taxis. They stopped their conversations, watching without expression as I ran down the side street toward the *Villa Real*.

The clerk at the desk had been on the lookout for me, and summoned Josefina, the concierge. She'd become a true friend of the cooking school. It was Josefina who called us with the guest referrals.

"How is he?" I asked, not needing to say who.

She didn't know, but we hurried together to a *casita* unit close to the beach. The door stood open. A Mexican woman who might have been the hotel nurse came out just as I went in. Mia,

Heinrich, and Dr. Edmonds were standing inside and talking. Isabel was across the room at Stanley's bedside, tending to him. He looked dead to the world, with the sheet to his waist, naked above. His prominent hooked nose stood up like a shark's fin from his pallid face.

Mia and I moved to each other. She'd clearly been crying, and tears now welled up again in her eyes. After we hugged, she looked very grim.

"What happened?" I asked. "How is he?"

"He had a seizure on the beach," Mia explained, "like the ones he had in Brooklyn. It happened when he was coming out of the water after a swim. Isabel rushed in to get him."

"Your father-in-law had a grand mal seizure," Dr. Edmonds said. He was in shorts, battered sandals, and a faded shirt. As tan as he was, his bald dome was peeling in spots. "Stanley took some water into his lungs" -- his tone was troubling -- "but you can thank Isabel that it wasn't worse."

Isabel, the hero of the moment, was delicately cleaning the sand from Stanley's head with a damp washcloth, as if he were a loved one in her family. She must have heard us talking, but wasn't acknowledging it. Stanley's long white zipper of a war scar showed on his chest. Isabel looked to be whispering to him in Spanish or praying.

"It's linked to his episodic cardiac arrhythmia," Dr. Edmonds explained further. "We'll run some tests, but I think it's like the episodes he had in Brooklyn. This is what's called 'postictal sleep.' It's very deep and should last a while. He'll wake up eventually and he won't remember anything that happened. As long as someone stays with him, I think that's all we need. Heinrich can send the nurse over if there are any little changes. I'm just three minutes away if you have to call. I'd rather have him here than at the hospital."

A grand mal seizure. I'd seen one as a boy, when a friend's

father suffering from brain cancer had suddenly collapsed to the floor. His entire body shook, like a cartoon character getting an electric jolt. I'd run terrified from my friend's apartment. I tried to block a vision of that happening to Stanley and him sliding underwater.

Mia went over and sat beside Isabel. She ran her fingers over her father's shoulder and chest as she assessed him close up. Then she touched Isabel's knee appreciatively. The young woman accepted the gesture with great seriousness.

"We've been dealing with some stressful events recently," I told Dr. Edmonds.

"That wouldn't have made a difference," Dr. Edmonds replied. "He looks very fit, compared to when I first saw him."

"Señor Stanley swims every day," said Isabel, speaking up proudly on his behalf. "I watch him. *El es fuerte.*"

"I suspect he's metabolizing his medication more efficiently, and his levels haven't been checked. He hasn't been looked at since I came by your house after New Year's?"

"Nobody said we needed to." If I sounded accusing, so be it.

But Dr. Edmonds wasn't taking any responsibility. "Call me when he's awake. I'll come by. We can also arrange a flight to Houston for an MRI and get a full examination."

Mia thanked Dr. Edmonds before he left. Soon after, Josefina arrived with two staff, who carried large vases containing flowers to cheer up the place -- bird of paradise, red grenade heads of ginger, an assemblage of colorful lilies. From Heinrich, it was clear. He'd been standing by through all of this, occasionally speaking into his handheld unit.

"Heinrich," Mia said, "you've been a friend. I don't know what else to say, the way you've treated dad since he came here."

"He's a very nice man, your father." Heinrich then accepted Mia's grateful embrace, patting her nonstop on the shoulder. "Is there anything I can do? Maybe some food. Are you hungry?"

"We're fine," we both said.

"Okay, so I check back in later."

"Jeff, maybe you can run Isabel home. She has a family that needs her."

"The minivan isn't working. It died."

"Didn't you just go to have it fixed?"

"Yes."

"I take care of that," Heinrich said, turning to Isabel. "We get you home."

Mia then convinced a reluctant Isabel that it was alright to leave.

"Isabel," I said, "we don't have words to thank you."

"It's okay," she said. Her clothes had salt stains, her legs were sandy from the calves down. Her pristine white sneakers were a thing of the past.

"Thank you so, so much," said Mia. "Dad might not be alive if you hadn't saved him."

"Maybe I come here tomorrow," she said.

"Please, you should," said Mia. "Have a taxi get you. Come by the house, and if we're not there, come down here. Whether we move him depends on how much he sleeps. We're going to cancel tomorrow's program."

Isabel and Josefina left, with Heinrich right behind them. Mia and I were now alone with her dad. We went to the bed. She sat and took his hand tenderly.

"Come back," she said softly.

"I came home," I told her, pulling up a chair at the bedside, "and four of the guests were waiting for me."

"I wasn't sure they would."

"What do you want to do? He's not going to wake up maybe until tomorrow, if it's like what happened in Brooklyn those times. And that's what Dr. Edmonds said."

"Maybe you could go home and get me some clothes."

"And I'll call to cancel tomorrow's reservations. You know, I'm a little pissed right now. Dr. Edmonds could have said something about a check-up."

"He did. I remember. He wanted to see dad in three months, and it hasn't even been that long."

Back home, the raw dorado left in the sun all this time was starting to stink, so I tossed it, along with the wilted produce. I rinsed and stacked dishes so we wouldn't have insects everywhere. A serious cleanup could wait. I did notice that four little hand-painted, antique ceramic spoons, from our set of eight, were missing. Guests always asked about where they could get them. Evidently some of today's guests had solved that problem.

— • —

Midnight found me sitting in a teak chair on the *casita's* outside patio, contemplating my world beneath a sky full of stars. The rhythmic slap of the waves was calming. Mia was inside, asleep beside her father, right there in case he needed anything.

I started picking again on the quesadilla that room service had brought an hour ago, and I heard Mia's bare feet coming on the tile. She'd wrapped herself in one of the hotel's white robes. She left the door open so she could hear.

"I don't know what woke me," my wife said, taking the other chair. "Dad seems to be okay. His breathing sounds normal."

"Can I get you something from room service?"

"I don't think I can eat." She did accept my beer to finish.

"We were lucky this afternoon," I said.

"I know. And we have to do something for Isabel. Let me have a piece of what you're eating."

"Let me order you one."

"I just want a taste of yours." Throughout our marriage, it tasted better if it came from my plate.

Mia ran her hand through her hair, trying to wake up further. She'd slept hard. But in the shadows and at this hour, she was young again in my eyes. The marks of age were gone in the moonlight, and the young woman I'd married was here with me again.

"I'm not going to accept that it's over for us here," Mia said.

"It's not over," I said. But I felt that it was. The days were ticking by, and money wasn't going to come our way. We'd end up selling and leaving. It now felt ordained. Stanley's misfortune seemed to seal it.

"Something good can happen," Mia said, voicing hope.

"I hope it does."

The minutes passed as we entertained our own thoughts.

"And I want Lauren's wedding to be spectacular," Mia said, completing a thought that had apparently been working in her head. "If it ends up that we're not going to be here, at least I want a party everyone will remember. I'm not cutting corners on our first child's wedding. We're going out with style, if this is coming to an end." She looked to see if I wanted to argue. She seemed very emotional and fragile.

"We also have to help Lauren deal with the mother-in-law somehow," I said. "This woman's having far too much to say about a destination wedding." Lauren's frustration had been evident in all her communications.

I saw a man, who looked like security, watching from the path by the next *casita*. He noted that I was looking his way. He moved on into the shadows.

We were left to ourselves again.

— • —

"Do you remember our wedding?" I said to Mia.

It was past twelve-thirty. She'd been up and down several

times to check on her father. I'd ordered some boiled shrimp from the kitchen, ostensibly for me, but I knew it was a way to get something in her stomach. She'd take them from my plate.

Mia had nothing left to say, so I brought up this memory to get her out of the moment, and perhaps smiling once or twice.

We'd had a priest from the Newman Center at N.Y.U. marry us. My aunts who raised me came from Fort Lee in pillbox hats -- my only living relatives, seated right in front, straight from the Eisenhower era. Mia's mother wore a pale blue mother-of-the-bride dress, and held a handkerchief in her hand throughout the ceremony. Stanley came, but he wasn't a happy man. He glared when our eyes met. I was marrying his only child before she had time to develop into the educated, successful person he'd imagined, and I'd gotten her pregnant to boot.

"Looking back," I said, "at the time I felt so like Benjamin in "The Graduate," just violating every rule. I'm guessing Lauren's feeling some of that, and we can help her through it."

Five months along, Mia had worn a simple white silk wedding dress made by a friend from the Fashion Institute. My aunts were very gracious. They surprised me by staying late at the small, informal reception we'd arranged, with pizza and lasagna in the back room of an inexpensive Italian restaurant, separated from the main room by a curtain of red plastic beads. Mia's parents left early. Our choice of this crummy restaurant -- plus refusing any financial help from them -- plus the pregnancy, and both of us dropping out of college, and now getting married -- it was too much to ask them to overlook. These were people from a generation that wanted their children to do better than they did, and she was saddling herself with me.

"It's important to do Lauren's wedding right," Mia said.

"I feel that way too."

"Lauren has only a few things she's insisting on. Other than that, she doesn't care as long as it's nice."

"We'll work on that tomorrow. Let's figure out how we're going to sleep."

"I don't think I can now."

"Then let's go down to the water. I brought your bathing suit. I think it will be calming, and maybe we'll sleep better."

— • —

I finally convinced Mia that her father could be left alone for fifteen minutes. The small night waves, luminescent in the moonlight, fizzed around our ankles as we stood there. I held her hand. The water was the same temperature as the air. Lines were slapping idly against the metal masts of the sailboats moored off shore.

"Two years ago," Mia said, "when we were back to having no money, I was thinking about where my life might have gone if I hadn't met you."

"The money reference," I said. "Are you ever going to let that go?"

"Probably not," she said. She eased her arm around my waist to convey that she loved me.

"....Or what if we hadn't met until years later -- and we didn't have children until we were older. Or we didn't have children at all."

Waves came and went.

"And...?" I finally said.

"And I can't imagine being happier than I am right here, with the children, which is a life I never would have imagined then. You just can't know."

She turned to look in the direction of Casa Blue on the hillside. I did too. Given the full moon, we could see the shape of things and make out its outline.

"Ready to go in the water?" I asked.

"I don't really want to, Jeff. You go in if you want to."

In one motion, I stooped and slipped an arm under her knees, so I could pick her up like a girl at a swim party. Her initial protest shifted into a vehement warning against dropping her as I carried her in.

"Jesus," I said. "You're not as light as you used to be."

She twisted my nose until it hurt.

"Maybe you're not the man you once were."

"I'm not. You've worn me out."

I staggered in the deeper water. We bantered and laughed, braving the small surf. A wave finally took us down. Then we continued farther out, but briefly, so we could get back to her dad.

— • —

Stanley did come out of his recovery sleep just as Dr. Edmonds had foretold, and with no recollection of the incident. We had to describe it.

"So my sweetie here saved my life," he was saying twenty-four hours later, his arm affectionately around Isabel's shoulder as he shuffled on the terrace. His mouth had fully recovered, but he seemed shaken that his chronic condition had pursued him into Mexico.

A week after his seizure, we finally got him back on *Playa La Ropa*. The regulars would have to be dealt with, all the prying questions about how he was. By now he knew how his slack body had been carried by a helpful assemblage of Mexican men and tourists up to the *casita*, after a skilled, unknown tourist worked him over in the sand to make him cough up water. The indiscreet glances and well-meaning probing into his health dwindled after his first two visits to the beach. Isabel became fiercely protective according to Phil, who joined them at the beach most days. Phil taxied down, as the walk was too much for her. She stayed in the shade of a *palapa* at all times, drinking and holding court in her armchair with passing acquaintances, but always with one eye on Stanley, just like Isabel. She cut quite a figure in her silk-screened beach caftan in swirling ocher and chocolate tones, always with perfectly red toenails on her large feet.

— • —

Stanley had gone to a clinic in Zihuatanejo for blood work, on Dr. Edmonds' recommendation. Samples had been sent for analysis to one of the two good hospitals in Mexico City. Mia then flew up to Houston with her father for an MRI and other tests, staying over two nights. Stanley insisted on paying for the tickets and their two nights in an economy hotel, and Mia didn't argue. He also insisted that they eat at Denny's. He wanted some "real food," he said, uncaring if that offended anyone.

I conducted the Cooking School at Z both days, with Isabel's help. While it was a far cry from cooking with Mia, we needed the money, and it was a passable experience, especially since I started them drinking very early in the program. Besides, I thought darkly, we'd never see these people again, even if it wasn't that great with me. We wouldn't be here next year.

Stanley simply needed to adjust his dosage, as Dr. Edmonds suspected. With all his exercise, he had indeed been metabolizing his anti-convulsant differently. The radical change from his Brooklyn life to his workout swims at *Playa La Ropa* had been his undoing.

After the seizure, we kept Stanley more abreast of our struggles to retain Casa Blue. He deserved to know. We got him to promise that he would keep all this to himself. It was particularly important not to tell Phil, lest the news spread from her lips to the entire population of the Americas, hurting business.

I was still fishing around for money, but some days I didn't bother.

241

— • —

"You have to think about whether you're going to come back to the States with us," Mia said, broaching the topic one night as the three of us played Scrabble in the great room. Stanley almost always won. Mia was sitting in tonight expressly to have this conversation in a casual setting.

"The three of us in an apartment somewhere?" Stanley said, laying down six letters for thirty-two points.

"We'd probably rent a house."

"In the Bay area," he said, as if it were a foregone conclusion.

"That's where we can pick up with our old connections," I said. Mia and I were leaning that way, although we hadn't decided. We could hardly bring ourselves to think about it, even now.

"I don't know anybody there. And you California people are different."

"Not that different," I said.

"You're all optimists, like you two. You expect good things. People from Brooklyn are like the Irish. We know not to expect too much."

"You have your Social Security checks and your two certificates of deposit," Mia pointed out. "And you made friends here. You'll make more friends." Mia put down six letters, tapping into a red, triple-value square, and taking the lead.

— • —

Mia and I decided privately that we would give Stanley a lump sum from whatever we could rescue from the inevitable sale of Casa Blue. It would encourage him to stay on for a while in Zihuatanejo.

It would be easier all around, starting over in the States, if it were just the two of us at first. We agreed that he would be happier here, with Phil and Isabel and all the beach regulars who played cards under the sea grape trees, until we had the right situation put together to bring him.

Fortunately we had the wedding coming up in the second half of March. It was a welcome diversion every time Lauren called and something more needed planning. We'd been entrusted with most of the details. Lauren wouldn't be coming down until several days before the wedding, in order to conserve vacation time for the honeymoon.

"I just find it so uplifting to be dealing with young people excited about starting a new life together," Mia told an elderly patron at our cooking island. The guest's hands were arthritic, but she was cutting vegetables as best she could. Others chimed in. Wedding talk was fun for everyone.

Mia and I had decided that we would not detract from the wedding by telling anyone else -- even our children -- about the likely end game for Casa Blue. The focus needed to be on the wedding couple.

It would be difficult faking our way through the weekend when wedding guests would talk of visiting next year. Guests would inevitably ask questions about our success with the new Cooking School at Z, but to disclose the truth, and to listen to everyone discussing our fate and overshadowing the wedding itself, wasn't something we could allow to happen.

We were so eager for the day to come, and Lauren's arrival.

21

"Actually," Lauren was saying, "right now I'm not sure that Steve and I should go through with this wedding."

These startling words were uttered by our eldest child on a Wednesday night, at the conclusion of dinner on our terrace.

The marriage was set for Saturday, three days away.

Lauren had just reached Zihuatanejo that afternoon, after hooking up with her younger sister at Houston's airport. Daphne, still red-haired, but with new pink strands for the wedding, was coming off two all-nighters. She was getting some sleep. We were down to Mia and me, our other two children, and Stanley.

We all fell silent at Lauren's words. Rowan was carrying so much weight, he was breathing with his mouth agape, which was the only sound. The full moon, so close, seemed to pull up a chair for this one. Somewhere down the hill, I could hear Mexicans having a party and their squeezebox music.

Mia and I glanced at each other to see who would speak first.

"I think a lot of brides have misgivings right before the wedding," I said.

"What brings this about?" Mia asked.

"I've had this uneasy feeling for the last few weeks," Lauren said.

"Christ," said Stanley, cracking his forehead. "Women and feelings."

"Dad," Mia said sharply.

"Can you get your money back for the dress?" Rowan asked, sipping his *anejo* tequila.

Lauren gave Rowan the finger. "This isn't meant to be something for your jokes."

"You don't expect us to take you seriously, do you?" he said.

"It's what I'm feeling right now. Shut up."

Lauren and Rowan: they were close, but relentless with each other. When they were in high school, the girl next door, a star on Lauren's swim team, had died a difficult death from leukemia. Susan had practically grown up at our house, entering through our kitchen door at will. Living through Susan's experience had pushed Rowan and Lauren beyond the standard razzing of siblings, into discussions of life and death and the sharing of profound emotions. I would always remember Lauren and Rowan outside the church, embracing after their friend's funeral.

"Are you serious about this?" I asked.

"I am, yes."

"You sent me that card and said how happy you were together," Stanley pointed out.

"Pass the tequila," Mia told Rowan. "There isn't enough alcohol in Mexico for tonight."

"This feels like one of your trial balloons," I said to Lauren. I extended my hand in a way that said, Don't take offense.

On matters of business, Lauren exuded confidence. Clients loved her, with her short, efficient hair in its original chestnut color, her no-nonsense black-framed glasses, her trim physique, and her decisive ways. She'd run two marathons this past year. She also knew her mind on matters of business. On matters of the heart, however, she could be tentative, and sometimes became a drama queen just to hear the family's views.

"It sort of is a balloon," she confessed. "But I'm serious."

"Give us your reason why," Mia said.

A giant cry arose from the Mexican party, celebrating something.

"Go ahead," Rowan interrupted. "I want to hear this. Because Steve's an okay guy. He makes you happy. And he's working his ass off to save money so you two can drop out and open your little restaurant on the Jersey shore. What else could you want from a guy?" And then his eyes widened theatrically, as if struck with The Great Insight. "Oh, *that*," he said.

"You know, sometimes you're really, really not funny," Lauren said, narrowing her eyes.

"Rowan," Mia said curtly. "You're over the line."

Mia refilled her own glass, then poured one for Lauren.

"Steve is better than an 'okay guy,'" I said.

"Do you love him?" Mia asked.

"Yes." She tossed back half of her tequila. "It's his relationship with his mother that's the problem. His mother can't stand me."

"You're not marrying the mother," Rowan said.

"Maybe I am. That's the issue. Steve and I had all of this worked out between us, with the restaurant next year. Now I feel him hesitating."

"Why? What happened?" Mia asked.

"You're going to be living five states away from his parents," I reminded our daughter.

"Six," said Stanley.

"Evelyn has always wanted to control this whole wedding," Lauren said. "You know that."

"Which is why you and Steve changed it to a destination wedding," said Mia.

"She wanted it at some country club with too many people, and all her friends, but Steve and I shut her down. That was a huge deal. She also hasn't gotten over the big blowup we had during the holidays. I missed the parties where I was supposed to be paraded in front of all their friends, even though she doesn't like me. Her

246

new crusade is to insist that we stay around Chicago, near her, and she's been working on Steve. And I feel him starting to shift, even though he says he isn't. He may be caving in. The woman is relentless. I do not want to have crises involving his mother for the rest of my life, and I definitely am not living nearby."

"It sounds like you're exaggerating a little," I said.

"I'm not. Believe me. Wait until you meet this woman. She is something else."

"Inaccessible by Greyhound should be the rule," said Rowan. "What else is there to eat? I need fuel." He left the table to look.

"She wants us under her wing," Lauren continued, "having grandchildren, me raising kids, Steve staying in his father's firm and taking over the business. He's the only boy. She's got the two older daughters who are basically stay-at-home moms, right there in the same town. That's not going to happen."

"It's good that you see all this now," I said.

"I'm not going to marry Steve and live near that woman, but we need to talk. I just feel something going on inside him."

Rowan returned to the table. He'd found Mia's homemade chocolate macaroons, dusted with cocoa.

"Those are not for today," Mia said sternly.

"Holding out on me, are you?" he accused, popping one in his mouth and taking a second. He moved the plate of them around the table. This situation called for a lot of chocolate. Mia threw up her hands.

"He's not coming down until tomorrow afternoon with his family," Mia said. "I thought that was maybe a little strange. He could have come with you. I had to make some special arrangements so you two could get the blood test Friday and turn it around right away."

"I wanted him to come down today," Lauren said. "He thought he should come with them, kind of a unity thing that would help smooth the way. He couldn't get them to come a day earlier."

247

Was that significant? Mia pursed her lips as she mulled this question, aiding the process with more tequila. Rowan slowly rotated his spoon to help his analytic skills, looking serious for a change.

"Plus," Lauren continued in her fiancé's defense, "he's been crashing to wrap up his project so he can do the Costa Rica honeymoon for ten days."

"He works for his father, but he's worried about getting the time?" Stanley asked.

"So what's your plan?" I asked.

"I'm going to talk to Steve tomorrow night after he gets here. I'm sure everything will be fine."

"Which is why you told us everything isn't fine," I had to say.

— • —

It took forever to get everyone organized the next morning. Daphne and Lauren ran off very early to the beach, then farted around over breakfast and in the bathroom. Daphne had an email from Guy, who was under sail to Zihuatanejo, expecting to arrive for the wedding. Rowan got up late and held court with Stanley on national affairs. Isabel had the day off. There were things to accomplish for the wedding, which would entail running around Zihuatanejo. We were temporarily closing the Cooking School at Z through Sunday.

It was almost eleven when a taxi spit out Mia, me and our two daughters in front of Donna's Dress Shop in Centro.

"This is our daughter Lauren, who's getting married," Mia said, presenting her to Donna Cabaldon, a stylish Mexican woman with a pale complexion and the highly coveted blue eyes that distinguish high class. Her hair was drawn tight, sealed in back with a carved turtle clip. Donna catered to Americans and the wealthy from Mexico City.

After introductions, and compliments directed Lauren's way

about being such a beautiful bride, Donna brought forth a white-on-white shawl. It had cross-stitched, creamy white flowers created with a heavy silk thread that had a fine sheen. The women all touched it, then Lauren wrapped her shoulders before a mirror.

"Jalisco?" Mia asked.

"Yes," said Donna, it had been made there.

"I thought for tomorrow night at the dinner," Mia suggested to Lauren. "Or, at the beach if it gets a little cool later in the evening when you're in your wedding dress at the reception."

"Definitely," said Lauren.

But both women looked to Daphne for a final opinion. She gave it thumbs up.

— • —

As the four of us walked to our second destination, Mia and I couldn't find the right moment to speak with Lauren. Centro's streets fill with vehicles, parked and moving, making it difficult to walk together. The narrow sidewalks are raised a good eighteen inches, requiring care, and are crowded with displays, little sandwich boards, people with bulky packages, families from stores sitting out front, runners with deliveries. Not until we were in a promenade near *Juan Alvarez* did Mia ask her question.

"Lauren, how excited is Steve about starting a restaurant with you?" After too much tequila last night, Mia was wearing her darker sunglasses. "Is the restaurant mainly your idea?"

"He's definitely for it. Evelyn is against it. Now she's saying we should do it near Chicago, where we'll have family support, and he could keep his job."

"And you're afraid he's starting to listen to his mother?"

"She's making it sound like some wise compromise. And I can feel Steve starting to sway that way."

"What about his father?" We split around a very thin woman

with three young children, one in her arms. The oldest child, a boy, was waving around a plastic bag with a roosterfish, which is eaten by the poor.

"His dad's a big weenie. He always chimes right in with Evelyn. He and Steve go deer hunting every year in Wisconsin. 'What if you were in New Jersey?' he says. 'We couldn't run off hunting for a few days.' Last week Steve said maybe his mother and I could kind of work things out 'if we gave it time.'"

"Tell me again why you're so locked in on New Jersey," I said.

"Dad, it's going to work," said Lauren. "Relax."

"He wants to give it his dad seal of approval," Daphne said. While Mia and Lauren were in sleeveless dresses, she was in a short skirt, a halter top, and short, black lace-up boots, a great outfit for Williamsburg, Brooklyn.

"Let's go down here, and I'll show you where the fishermen come in," Mia said.

She led the way across an open basketball court. We congregated at the wall facing the bay, all four of us resting on our elbows.

"There's a place in Cape May that's exactly like what we want to do," Lauren began, facing the water. "A young couple started it. They open Memorial Day, close on Labor Day, except they stay open weekends up to Thanksgiving. They have three soups to choose from and three entrees. That's it. It's all homemade, usually Italian or French. They have a clam soup with anise, potatoes and leeks that's to die for. Their fish stew is unbelievable. People get takeout for their hotel rooms and the rentals. People are on line out the door! They told us everything. They go to France sometimes in the off season and write off the trip. What a great life! And they grow a lot of their own herbs and vegetables."

Lauren was incredibly enthused. I listened carefully, biding my time.

"Okay, so my friend's parents have a successful little restaurant on Long Beach Island, off the coast of New Jersey. They're retiring to Florida. They'll lease us their space, and Steve and I want to do something like the couple in Cape Map to start with. I'll locate there next January to supervise the improvements. Then Steve will move in with his parents to save rent, and he'll keep working. That's only for sixty days, then he'll join me. We'll be living on top of the restaurant. It's this old frame building, like a house. We'll open in late May for the beach season. I already have the names of some great places in the Bowery for used kitchen equipment."

"It sounds wonderful," I said, "but is it your dream more than his? We sort of talked about this last night."

"You need to really talk and see where he is with this," said Mia. "You're right."

"We all know where your dream comes from," I said. "You have your mother, your grandmother, women going way back. It's probably in your DNA. But I don't necessarily see it as his dream."

"For him, it's the idea of having his own business," Lauren said. "And then we'll grow from this."

"Why don't you just work like a year or two and save everything," Daphne said. "Then quit and travel around the world. Why would you want to be serving people every day? People suck."

"Let's go on on the beach," Mia said.

We squirreled away our shoes and headed onto the sand.

"Steve seems like the kind of person who might want to appease everyone," Mia said, "the way your father does, which might be why you like him. You grew up with that kind of man around."

"Why are you talking about me in the third person?" I objected.

"That can be okay," Mia continued to our daughter, while touching my arm in a conciliatory way, "as long as he'll make a hard decision when he needs to."

"Now you're trying to direct things," Lauren objected.

"Every parent wants something for a child. My parents wanted me to take a whole different direction with my life. Be sure Steve's heart is in this a hundred percent. And whatever the answer, you don't get married because of this one answer. It's a much bigger commitment, because there will be other issues like this in the future. I think you know that."

We moved among the *pangas* with their white, blue and blue-green hulls bearing names like *Rosalia* and *El Aquila*. Brown pelicans were congregated in the shallows, waiting for discard from land or sea. Some fishermen were still around, sitting or working under the short palms up the beach.

"I'm never getting married," Daphne announced. "Who can bear all of this discussion?" At that moment she locked arms with her sister in a show of solidarity.

— • —

To prepare further for the wedding that might or might not be happening in two days, we all went to the *Mercado De Artesanias*, along *Cinquo de Mayo*.

"Basically this has kitsch ceramics for tourists," I explained to the girls, "but there's a woman here who makes something."

Mia said, "Your father wants you to consider something for bridesmaids' gifts, which I think is crazy, but he wants to show you. Please, humor him."

The artisan's market consisted of canvas and frame stalls one after the other, exploding with bright painted bowls and figures, bead and shell necklaces and bracelets, painted coconut wall hangings, every kind of cheap thing. Except, that is, for the work of Señora Gutierrez, who spoke no English. She labored in the stifling heat at the back of a stall run by her daughter.

I introduced us in Spanish to the adult daughter, who was tiny. She spoke rapid-fire in a shy, birdlike register. Señora Gutierrez was hand-painting bowls about six inches in diameter with exquisitely realistic faces of young women, each one different, rendered in pleasing shades of red, yellow and brown. The surrounding decorations on the bowl made it seem like they were enjoying themselves at a celebration. There were seven or eight finished ones.

"They're great," Lauren said.

"In my view, these are better gifts for the wedding party than the silver bracelet sample your mother showed you back at the house. If one of the girls had this, there'd be no question twenty years from now where it came from. It's a permanent memory of your wedding. "

"Dad, this isn't what a bride gives," said Lauren.

"Daphne?" I asked.

"A little weird. I don't know if Steve's sisters would exactly want these." Both his sisters were in the wedding party.

Lauren made a thumbs down, so we went to the silver store and purchased the bracelets Mia had set aside.

— • —

"You didn't tell Steve about our problems with the cooking school, did you?" Mia asked Lauren.

We were having lunch outside at the cantina where I'd been on the day that Stanley had his seizure. We'd ordered already.

"Actually, I did," she said, wincing. "I'm sorry. But he's not going to tell anyone."

"This concerns me," I said.

"He'll keep it to himself, dad."

Wonderful. Without consulting us, Stanley had shared our secret with Daphne, his soulmate from Brooklyn. She'd been the one who told Lauren during their flight down from Houston. Then Lauren let us know last evening that she knew. That being the case, Mia and I had taken Rowan aside and told him last night. He was stunned. He'd come to think of Casa Blue as his private retreat and workplace, as he'd visited twice already this winter. Now the whole family knew, plus Steve. It was outside the blood.

"You specifically told him not to tell anyone," Mia checked.

"I did. He knows not to do that."

"Tell him again," Mia said. "I don't want this getting out and overshadowing your wedding. I certainly don't want it being a campfire topic for everybody who comes to our party tomorrow night."

— • —

When we left the cantina, the shops were closing for the siesta break.

"What else did you want me to see?" asked Lauren. She'd commandeered her mother's straw hat, so she wouldn't burn.

"We need to go back to Eloi's on *Playa La Ropa* to show you what I have in mind for the reception, and how it will set up for the wedding," Mia said. "I'd like to do that this afternoon."

While the Friday evening gathering at Casa Blue would have class, Saturday's reception had a cantina theme. Everyone would drink, dance and just have fun. Eloi's was basically a higher class beach bar, with a palapa roof, a large resident parrot that cursed in Spanish, and two iguanas. The owner was being paid to give the inside space over exclusively to our private party. Mia had cooked up decorations that included hanging coconuts and big hands of bananas.

"Let's go home first," Lauren said. "I'm so sweaty. I need to jump in the pool."

On the taxi ride, the three women sat in the back. "So what are we thinking, ladies?" I asked.

"We're all thinking, with one mind I might add, that this is going to be a spectacular wedding," Mia announced.

"If it actually happens," Daphne said.

22

I had so much shopping to do on Thursday for the big party the next night, I asked Isabel to meet me early at Cafe Glob on *Benito Juarez*. It was nine-thirty by the time the two of us finished buying at the *Mercado Centro* across the street.

Something had to be said to Isabel before we went to Casa Blue.

"Isabel," I said in the minivan, once we were both belted in. I held back from starting the engine. "I feel you are angry with us because of what might happen with the cooking school. Is that how you feel?" Stanley, of course, was keeping her abreast of our problems, and I'd learned last night that he had given her another despairing installment. And Isabel hadn't been herself all morning. Her usual pep was missing.

Now, at my question, she bowed her head and just shook no, no problem. She avoided eye contact. I imagine she felt it was not her place to acknowledge such a thing to her employer.

"We're angry too," I said. "You know that, don't you? And we're doing everything we can to keep the cooking school going."

"I worry for my children and my mother," Isabel said, locking eyes bravely. Her hair was up and she was in a worn Polo T-shirt, because of the unusual work we had ahead of us today. She was in the sneakers she'd bleached after she rescued Stanley, because stains would not matter so much. We'd bought her a new pair she was saving.

"What will happen?" Isabel asked.

"We don't know what will happen. You'll be with us as long as we're here, and we hope we're here next year and forever." Perhaps that needed restating.

"Okay."

"Is it okay? Is there something else?"

"The wedding reminds me of my husband."

She brought her hand to her mouth and she looked out her window, with her back to me. We knew she had no desire to have Carlos back. In fact, a woman had moved in with Carlos in Los Angeles -- this Mia had discovered. Her world was lived on a wholly different plane, and there were times, like now, when it tore at my heart. I wanted to touch her shoulder reassuringly, but dared not.

"We should go," I said, turning the key in the ignition.

She nodded, wiping one eye, then the other.

— • —

Back at Casa Blue, as everyone helped with the unloading, Lauren was about to join Steve and his family for a day of sun, sand, and touring Zihuatanejo. They were staying at *Villa Real*.

I pulled her aside. "Did you and Steve have a talk last night?"

"Everything's fine."

I scrutinized her eyes for truthfulness, but after a quarter century of being grilled by her parents, plus her business experience, she could be inscrutable.

"There's something you're not telling me," I insisted, stepping aside so Rowan could pass with boxes of produce. He was singing about a chain gang.

"There's nothing," Lauren said, trying not to lose her temper. "Mom already put me on the witness stand. Steve and I are fine.

We talked last night about his mother, and all our plans, and we're fine. Gotta go. Love you." She kissed me and left with her tote, leaving a light perfume and a palpable vitality in her wake.

I was unconvinced. Not that they didn't love each other, but something else. And if we were being intrusive, well, she'd brought it up, and everyone was putting out enormous effort to make this weekend memorable.

— • —

We'd gotten to know and like Steve, but we'd be meeting his family for the first time. Everyone else coming down from the States for the wedding would also be coming to our house. So Mia was determined to mount the mother of all parties, a five-star wonder in the categories of food, color and hospitality.

"I want to show these people we know what the hell we were doing," were her exact words that Friday morning. We were grabbing a quick breakfast in the dark. She was ready to work in thick-soled sandals, a sleeveless cotton top, and knaki shorts.

"This'll be enough food to feed all of Guerrero for a week," I told her as we reviewed everything.

"His family are Midwesterners. I'm sure they can pack it in." And since they favored steak and potatoes, according to our daughter, Mia had worked into the menu some fairly straightforward dishes, like *papas rellenos*, a Baja specialty using baked potato and cheese. They could be enhanced, according to individual taste, with salsas, moles, and other spicy flavors.

"I'm wondering if it will look like we're trying to upstage the reception tomorrow, which his parents happen to be paying for."

Mia said, "That is something I'm definitely not worried about."

— • —

"How much of this are we making?" groaned Daphne, who'd been stationed at the cooking island. It was mid-morning. A rousing Beethoven symphony was playing through Casa Blue. The place looked like a staging area for a royal banquet.

"Just keep chopping," I said, putting two more green papayas in front of her. Her job was to convert them into tiny green dice, for mixing with lime, mustard, chilies and cilantro. Next, Daphne prepped for a toasted coconut salsa. I had my own work nearby, assembling oregano, cumin, onion, white vinegar and other ingredients to bathe a pork roast. Reducing the fresh coconut into thin flakes seemed to be tough going, even for Daphne.

"Shit!" Daphne yelled, after burning her first batch in the oven.

But there was no stopping, and no mercy from Mia. Daphne rendered more coconut and let her mother toast it this time, while she went on to the fresh jalapenos, green peppers and onions from our garden that needed mincing, and the thick halves of succulent *atolfo* mangoes that had to be flipped inside out and cubed.

Still ahead on her list were chayote with carrots; a salpicon, or cold meat salad, of tomatoes, onions and vinaigrette steeped with *cecina*, flayed strips of salted beef that hung like broad, long belts in the market; and julienned pick-up sticks of raw jicama, for dipping into the three options on the *mole* sauces.

"I'm not getting married," Daphne announced loudly to all. "Never, ever. And if I do, it's on a beach where none of you can find me. And my husband and I will fast on our wedding night."

— • —

Stanley was enlisted at noon to fashion fish cakes from the raw dorado and other ingredients which I'd diced to Mia's specifications. When Phil popped in to check the action, Stanley conscripted her to peel some tomatoes that Mia had black-roasted and cooled. Phil donned a Cooking School at Z apron, planted her bulk on a stool, and merrily joined in.

"The tomatoes have to be mixed with minced garlic and onion, and some *epazote*," Mia explained. "It marinates, then we smear it on large tongues of lightly grilled squash and eggplant just before serving."

"'Large tongues of lightly grilled squash,'" Daphne called over. "Mom, you're starting to sound like your cooking class. You're losing it."

"Have you got just a plain steak for me tonight?" Stanley asked.

"No. If I do one for you, I have to do it for anyone."

An argument could have ensued, but Phil stepped in.

"Angelo and I were married at a Greek Orthodox church," she recalled dreamily, dabbing profuse sweat from her forehead with a side towel. She rarely spoke of him anymore. "I never touched a thing at our reception, just a forkful of the wedding cake. I only drank champagne. I was a slender girl in those days, Stanley."

Mia, Daphne, and I exchanged discreet glances, to see what we were thinking. Word had come from Angelo recently that business required his presence in Europe for another two months. Stanley was becoming ever more central to Phil's life. Phil had been in Oaxaca at the time of Stanley's seizure, and learned of it only on her return. Mia suspected that Phil told Stanley, in their initial private conversation after his seizure, how much he now meant to her. If we left Mexico -- when we left Mexico -- we were wondering if Phil would talk of getting a divorce, and if Stanley would live with her. People of their generation were very close-mouthed in front of their children about something like this. They weren't talking, either of them.

"So Lauren is still getting married tomorrow?" I overheard Phil ask Mia.

Mia gave Stanley a frosty look. He'd obviously told Phil.

"Oh, I know everything," Phil told my wife. "I'm part of the family. I'll never tell a soul. But I hope all this work isn't in vain."

"I'm sure they're getting married," Mia said confidently. But she too felt there was something going on, from the way Lauren was denying it, and saying everything was fine. Lauren had clearly decided she'd had enough of everyone's questioning and opinions on what, at the end of the day, was a private decision.

— • —

"How did I get this job?" Rowan protested. He was stuck at the end of the cooking island, sentenced to cleaning eight pounds of fresh shrimp.

"I want the little black veins out," Mia said, examining his handiwork.

"What black veins?"

"Right there," Mia said, pointing.

"Is that shrimp shit? Oh my God, I'm not touching that."

"You're doing it," Mia insisted. "Stop trying to be funny." She then went to the Inferno, where she whipped up a big salad we workers could have. Phil made two plates. I was busy assembling a lime granita, infused with vodka, which would harden into a slurry by late afternoon.

"Are we having fun yet?" I asked from my side of the cooking island. Someone had put Andean flute music on. Rowan was trying to whistle along, dancing in place like an idiot, waving two knives above his head.

"How much more of this is there?" Rowan asked. "Is it time to kill myself?"

"We've got *carnitas* with avocado salsa, chicken with *pipian verde* -- pumpkin seeds and serrano chile sauce -- *ceviche*...."

"I'm going to make Mexican bread pudding. This is Lent," said Isabel, who'd taken a station next to Stanley. Most recently she'd been busy setting out the candles on the large candelabras which Izzy had left, readying dishes, and setting out flower arrangements.

"And you have some cookies you want to make too," Mia reminded her.

"*Sí.*"

"Rowan, we're having orange lime margaritas tonight," Mia said. "You need to prepare the citrus?"

"Yesss, Queen Mia. Your every wish."

As the afternoon moved along, the day grew warmer. The group's energies were flagging. Weary or not, Mia drove us forward.

Finally tables were covered with embroidered Mexican cloth from Isabel's mother, dishes and cutlery were set out, and we put on ice one of the two cases of Chilean white wine I'd procured. The Negra Modelo, Sol and Superior were already in an ice chest.

"Hurry, people," said Mia. "Time is becoming an issue. And you have to shower and change."

I brought my Cuban cigars to an accessible place, resigned to the fact that our male guests would slip extras into their pockets until I was cleaned out.

— • —

Sophie made a grand entrance very late in the afternoon. Rowan had invited her, and to our amazement -- forcing us to recalibrate our sense of their relationship -- she'd accepted. The young woman certainly had presence. She came down the steps wearing a long white linen skirt, a companion white top with an elegant touch of vined embroidery, and brick-red backless sandals with half heels. Still a big girl, Sophie had shed some pounds since she'd come weeks ago, and she was dazzling. But in the very first minute Rowan in his food-stained T-shirt forced on her a thoughtless hug, leaving a faint tomato juice stain right beneath her heart.

"You moron," said Daphne.

"Rowan," Sophie said, so disappointed.

"God, I'm sorry. I don't do this kind of work. I never thought."

Mia applied club soda with a napkin as Rowan continued apologizing.

"Thank you for that wonderful review," Mia told Sophie during the commotion. "So many people complimented us on it."

"It brought in a lot of guests," I added. I had a clean towel for the effort.

"I felt this gravitational pull to be here," Sophie said, trying to be herself again. "I need to be in Rio by Tuesday, so this is on the way, isn't it?"

Love has its own geography. Rowan and Sophie were soon lost to us, as they retreated to the grand room.

— • —

Lauren returned just before five. Mia and I left the activity downstairs and paraded into her room. She immediately showed off a silver necklace Steve had bought her while they and his family were seeing the town.

"How is everybody on his side?" Mia asked. We were hungry for an update.

"They're themselves. One of the little girls got up to go to the bathroom in the middle of the night, and saw a lizard on the wall. I guess she shrieked and startled everyone, and she wouldn't calm down or go back to sleep." Lauren was straightening a few things in the room, which had been left a mess. "Other than that, everything's under control so far. Except that Steve's mother was concerned about her hair, and she didn't want to do this, and she didn't want to do that. Naturally she brought up the restaurant in New Jersey, and she slipped in how nice it would be if we were all near each other. Steve handled it pretty well."

"Good," Mia said.

Things were looking up.

"I need to talk to you guys about something," Lauren said, "but first I have to jump in the shower. I am so sweaty. Give me two minutes. Just stay here." Lauren pushed through the cantina doors to her bathroom, already pulling her shift over her head. I caught a glimpse of red panties, possibly a good sign in the circumstances.

"Uh-oh," Mia said. "What kind of news requires a shower first."

Lauren soon emerged in a robe, vigorously rubbing her hair with a towel. This was a girl who'd been a swimmer in college, and would shower, brush out her hair, and jump in the team van in a matter of seconds. Even now, in her late twenties, she looked great with a scrubbed look. Her basic vitality came through. Fifteen minutes for hair and a little makeup and she'd be ready to party.

"Sit down and tell us what's happening," I said. "Is the wedding on, or is something still undecided?" Mia was sitting on the bed, and I was standing a short distance away, my arms folded like her guardian.

Lauren sat by her mother.

"Everything's fine," Lauren said. "I just couldn't tell you what I have to say, sitting here like a dirtball."

"Please answer my question," I said. "'Everything's fine' is not an answer."

"Yes. Absolutely we are getting married." Lauren seemed amused. She crossed one leg over the other and arranged the robe on her thigh.

"Okay, here it is. Mom and dad, Steve and I had a great talk last night. He's committed to leaving Chicago. I needed to hear that one more time. Steve's great. I was just kind of spooked."

"That's wonderful," Mia said.

"But there's more to it." Lauren's eyes had a devilish sparkle.

Suddenly grasping our daughter's forearm, Mia said, "Tell me you're not pregnant."

"No, it's not that," Lauren said. "I brought up a trial balloon last night with Steve, and we talked about it. Then we decided to sleep on it and talk again today, which we did. We made some time for ourselves when his people were at the beach."

Lauren seemed to be enjoying the suspense.

"And...," I said.

"Steve and I want you to think about coming in with us on the restaurant we want to start. And maybe not in New Jersey. We could find something in California. I mean, that's if it doesn't work out here with the money and the title problem."

I wonder if I looked as stunned as Mia did. Probably more so.

"We could do our concept in Morrow Bay, San Luis Obispo, maybe Capitola," Lauren continued. "It would have to be year round, so Steve and I wouldn't want to do it all ourselves anyway."

Mia instantly teared up. I had an immediate lump in my throat. I felt blessed to be this girl's father.

"Or we could tweak it just a little, to be a family restaurant," she said, because neither of her parents had spoken up. "Steve's good with it. He likes California, and it puts less pressure on him because he could probably do some consulting out here. He'd stay with that and bring in some extra money. And the two of us would still be able to get away whenever we needed."

"Lauren," Mia began, "you and Steve need to do your own restaurant. It shouldn't be with us."

"Dad?" asked Lauren. She was used to her mother not consulting me.

"I don't know what to say. Basically, I think you and Steve need to go on your own to establish your marriage. So I think your mother's right, although I'm completely taken off guard. If you'd been married for a few years, or if you had children, I might feel differently."

"We'd be fine with you guys. I have this idea that it'd be like the *trattoria* in Italy with all the family involved," she said to Mia. "It just seems perfect, and if we have babies, we have built-in sitters."

"You're getting way, way ahead of yourself."

"I'm just talking. We're not even thinking about a family."

"Did he tell his family you're thinking this?"

"No."

Enough talking. Mia hugged our eldest child. I sat on Lauren's other side and joined in. But while I held my girl, I did wonder again if Steve knew what he really wanted.

23

The *mariachis* lined up by the pool, looking very serious in their sombreros, tight black pants with silver buttons, ruffled white shirts, and their short-waisted, ornate black jackets. Our guests quieted down on both terraces. Bright music leapt from the trumpets, backed by thrumming on scarred guitars and a standup bass that had survived a *Revolucion* or two. Some people clapped. I moved about, taking photos.

Sophie, Rowan, and Daphne stood watching from the grand room upstairs, like a box at the opera. Some of Lauren's friends mingled near the musicians -- two from her high-school swim team, a handful from her college days, a pair from her firm, all staying at an inexpensive hotel at *Playa La Madera*. Steve had an equal contingent of his pals. All of these young people were making moves, having their own great time.

Phil and Stanley observed from their table in the corner. Our attorney, Ken, and his blond, bejeweled wife, Donna, had surprised us by actually coming down for the wedding. I moved among them, conversing and taking more photos, my assignment for the evening. A professional photographer would do tomorrow's wedding.

No one looked happier than Mia. Standing beside Isabel, her two children, and Reyna, my wife was beaming. I snagged a great candid. Mia then wanted a picture of Isabel's youngest, who was dabbing a stick in the pool, trying to attract one of the twinkling votive candles, which were floating in green boats that Reyna had made from banana leaves. Señor Rodriguez, our accountant, had come with all his family, and I'd noticed his eldest, Diego, striking up a conversation with Isabel earlier, and now he was sidling in again.

Finally I rejoined Mia. We'd expected a better deal than the four hundred and fifty U.S. dollars that the *mariachis* demanded in advance, more than quoted. But right now, what was money?

Mia was beyond caring about the cost of things. She nudged me to check out the engaged couple. "Look at the two of them."

Steve and Lauren were front and center, arms around each other's waists. The *mariachis* shifted into a slow, romantic rendition of *"Besame Mucho."* He brought his hands together several times, until the bridal couple obliged him and smooched. Everyone applauded. Rowan hooted raucously. Steve and our daughter then went into a full-on kiss worthy of a romance novel, which set off the crowd, except for Steve's family. Their expressions of enthusiasm were more modest, but they were having a great time among themselves. They held to the upper terrace by the food.

"I hope they're enjoying themselves," I whispered to Mia.

"I think they're having a great time," said Mia, who couldn't take her eyes off Steve and Lauren.

"I meant Steve's family."

Mia's expression changed to concern as she looked their way. "We've done everything we can to make them feel at home. If they want to be standoffish, I can't be worried about it."

— • —

An hour earlier, when Steve's clan arrived for the party -- Evelyn and Harold, plus two daughters in their early thirties with their husbands, plus their three grandchildren -- Steve introduced

267

them to us. We discussed their flight down. Evelyn and Harold stayed on the safe subject of how lovely the terrace looked, and the nice aspects of their hotel. There were star turns by various members of their clan, and we paraded our children through as well. Eventually, though, it was just us with Harold and Evelyn.

"There were so many people who would have liked to share this with them," Evelyn said, a sly criticism of the destination wedding.

"They should have come," Mia said pleasantly. "We have plenty of room here and at the reception tomorrow."

Evelyn was silent in a way that suggested Mia had missed her point, which of course wasn't the case at all. A tall, big-boned woman, Evelyn had platinum frosted hair. Her fleshy face held rumors of a once-attractive woman. She was wearing a black, patterned cocktail dress with long sleeves and a jewel-encrusted neckline, with heels. Perfect for the country club. Her sole concession to the Mexican venue was an ornate silver and coral pin she'd bought in town. We'd seen her in Steve's family photos, which hadn't conveyed the reality that her head was somehow too large, or it was the hair creating this illusion.

"So tell me, what do you think of this New Jersey idea of theirs?" asked Harold. "Personally, I think they're making a mistake."

Storklike, with sparse hair, he was wearing an open-necked Polo dress shirt, an unbuttoned seersucker jacket, khakis, and bucks. He was enjoying one of my Cubans.

"I think they'll be fine, whatever they decide. They're both very capable."

Evelyn said, "Steve's got a good opportunity ahead of him in Harold's firm. He shouldn't be letting it go."

Harold jammed the cigar in his mouth so he could join everyone applauding a song. Then he said, "We'd like them to stick around Chicago, if they're going to do this restaurant thing. They'd have support from family. Steve has all his friends. It's the sensible thing."

"It'd be good if they were getting this message from your side too," Evelyn said, greasing it with, "I know how much they both respect you."

"We're nobody to talk," Mia said. "We got married very young and struck out on our own."

"It was different then," said Evelyn. "You probably didn't have all the benefits these children have."

"That's certainly true," I said. I was amazed they were bringing up all of this.

Mia plucked a fresh glass of champagne from a passing tray. She immediately took a big swallow.

"Mia and I think Jersey's a great idea," I said. "They'll have a chance to find themselves. Test their entrepreneurial wings. Although I don't imagine they'd stay there forever. So tell me specifically where you went in Centro."

"I think your home is so lovely," Evelyn said, "but I think the little town is dirty. Which is all of Mexico, in my view. I'm not a fan of dirt. We came back to the hotel for lunch, although Steven wanted us to have an experience eating real Mexican food." She shuddered.

Harold button-holed a server to ask for another scotch.

"To be so young," Evelyn reminisced. "You think you're so clever and you know everything. Nothing matters when you're in love."

"I wish I had those days back," I said.

"We already had three children, with two of them in school, when I was the age Lauren is right now," Mia said.

"Steven's the baby in the family," Evelyn said. "His sisters are five and seven years older. He was our little surprise."

"And he's still surprising us," Harold said.

"I find the Jersey notion very disappointing," Evelyn said. "Steven is not someone to be working half a year at the beach. I don't know where this idea originated exactly...."

"It came from my daughter," Mia said.

"He says it's also his. Don't just blame her." She ran a disapproving finger inside her filigreed necklace of gold sea shells.

"We weren't blaming anyone," Mia said.

"They'll want children," Evelyn continued as if she hadn't heard that last remark, "and they'll want to own a house. What kind of life is there at the beach in the winter time?"

"It's an adventure," I said. "And I know Lauren's not thinking about having children yet."

"Have your career, make your money, and do this restaurant kind of thing when you're older," Harold said. "The way you and your lovely wife have done it." He raised his scotch in salute, then drank a good portion of it. Then Evelyn and Harold excused themselves.

"Is she a real person?" I asked. "Why would she keep bringing all of that up?"

"And she hasn't had anything to drink yet," said Mia.

— • —

Soon the *mariachis* took a break.

"Steve's going to be good for her," Mia said, watching Steve and Lauren circulate among the groups.

"She gives him some chops," I said. "He's very accommodating otherwise. Which is probably what Lauren requires. They go together."

Mia extended her glass toward one of the *Villa Real* catering crew. Heinrich himself, in an expensive sport shirt and black slacks, was orchestrating service even as he mingled with guests.

"You look very glamorous tonight, Mrs. Farrell," Heinrich said. Mia planted a big kiss on his cheek.

"Everything is very nice," Heinrich said. "All very nice. I can

270

smell the flowers. I love that we smell the flowers." He moved on.

Mia took my arm. "I can't believe this day is here. I think Steve and Lauren are having a good time, don't you?"

"Stop worrying about whether everybody's happy," I said. "And I need to go up there and get a few shots of Steve's family."

— • —

Steve's two older sisters were tall like their mother. One of their husbands, a big man himself, was loading up at the long food table. In the center was an ice sculpture by Heinrich's chef, amid an artful display of lily spears, green bamboo shafts, and what looked like enormous green grapefruits, which actually came from a *cirian* tree. Our food offerings from a day of cooking were set out in our most valuable, colorful ceramic platters and bowls, none of them heaped high any longer. Under the table, two little nephews of Steve were hounding a small lizard.

"Good food," said the brother-in-law, who'd artfully mounded his plate. His hair was flat on top, and he had a beefy neck. His wife, Beatrice, came over and asked that I take a photo of their little family. She held their two-year-old, who was dressed for the Grand Old Opry. The husband carefully put down his plate and joined the frame. Just as I snapped the picture, the little girl shrieked and turned away. She'd spotted a small bat veering by.

"They only eat insects," I assured the child, but she wouldn't pose for another try.

"Lauren is very nice," Beatrice said, shifting the child to her other hip. The compliment was empty, without any eye contact. Perhaps the sister was distracted by having this child to deal with... or, I thought, she just couldn't pretend very well. Who knew what conversations had taken place in Chicago about Steve's choice of this very independent California girl. Evelyn had initially said she wouldn't attend a destination wedding, and we'd heard that Steve's sisters weren't thrilled about it.

"And our family likes Steve a great deal," I replied. "They're a good couple."

She nodded and asked me, with greater interest, how we grew such beautiful hibiscus in the confines of a pot.

— • —

Never had Casa Blue looked so festive. The orange and magenta bougainvillea looked like confetti suspended in the outer rim of darkness. The raceways of white lights on the African tulip tree, coupled with the heavy white blossoms of the vines, made both terraces more partylike. The evening's humidity lent a tropical note. The reflections in the bottom-lit pool, the glint of wine glasses, the flash of smiles -- something magical seemed imminent as the *mariachis* eased into a slow, nostalgic tune without the horn section. Sophie and others made a point of telling us how nice everything was.

"Did you meet Steve's people?" I asked Stanley, still at his little table with Philomena. I'd made them join heads for a picture.

"We did," he said.

"You should spend a little time with them," I said. "You'll probably never see them again after this weekend."

"I'll talk to them tomorrow after the wedding."

"Are you having a good time?"

"I wish Emma had lived to see this. You know how she loved weddings."

Phil gazed sympathetically at Stanley. She touched his shoulder in a consoling way. "Be grateful you're here, Stanley," said Phil. "It's much better than being fondly remembered."

— • —

A spoon clinking on crystal silenced everyone at about nine-thirty. Night had us in its grip. The *mariachis* were on the upper terrace, having a smoke before a brief, final round of songs.

Rowan and some of the bridesmaids and pals launched into toasts, some touching, others raunchy. Steve and Lauren were required to stand in the open, near the pool, to hear all of this. They fired retorts as best they could.

Next came Steve's sisters, with cloying wishes for a happy suburban future, and their memories of little Stevie. Many in the crowd had had enough to drink. From the way Mia was laughing, she was certainly in high gear. I moved toward her. She was in ecstasy about the entire evening, under a full Mexican moon. I offered a simple, affectionate toast to Steve and Lauren, and Harold did the same. Then it was Mia's turn.

"To life and everything it holds," she began, moving near the couple. "Blaze your own path. Do it while you're young, and never look back."

"Yes yes," Heinrich said. Many others applauded. Daphne whooed and pumped her fist as if blowing a train whistle. She'd certainly had a few drinks. Steve's family clapped briefly, which irked me. Mia deserved better, as a matter of protocol.

"When you're older, you want to be able to say you followed your heart. You took the challenge. If you do, you'll never regret it, wherever it may take you."

I saw several sets of eyes checking out Steve's mother. Her expression gave nothing away.

"So here's to your restaurant at the Shore, if that's what you want." She raised her glass. "Here's to your every wish for a spectacular life, whatever it may hold. We love you both so much."

Applause broke out in earnest. Lauren kissed her mom. Steve kissed Mia as well. I took several photos, then hugged them both.

"Well," Evelyn said, stepping forward for her turn, "I have a toast from Harold and me. And I truly don't know where to begin.

I remember when you were just this big" -- facing Steven, she framed a length with her hands -- "and now here we are. Where does time go?"

Evelyn looked around, at ease in the spotlight.

"We know the two of you will find happiness," she said, nodding at the couple. "And we all want to share that happiness with you. Remember that family is everything. Never neglect the people who love you, because we're the support you can count on in tough times."

Somewhere in her tone there were hints of problems to come.

"Of course, to be with family you have to stay near us," Evelyn added, an attempt at humor, "and we love you both so much." She laughed, and Harold did. "But that's our little ongoing discussion.

"And we can't let this night end without thanking our hosts, the Farrells." Evelyn turned in our direction. "This house, this feast tonight -- you're so very gracious." She beckoned applause from people.

Mia and I acknowledged everyone's appreciation.

"We're so impressed that you went to all this trouble during your busy season with the cooking school. We were wanting to have this reception in Chicago so you wouldn't have this burden, but you have gone all out."

Lauren's smile seemed to be stuck in place. Steven shifted his weight. I felt it was time for Evelyn to stop.

"It's so unjust for your dream to have just this one season -- I can't find words for how shocked I was when I learned that, and I speak for my entire family. I can't imagine how I would feel if I had to part with this house, with this wonderful view, and this weather." She gestured to Mia. "So we all toast your courage, your talent, and your accomplishments this evening. This lovely party is something you deserve to remember for the rest of your lives, the way we will."

Her family applauded politely, but it was otherwise a scene of confusion. People outside our immediate family looked at each other and whispered.

"Thank you," I said, hurrying to closure. How had she learned? At my side, Mia looked stunned.

But Evelyn wasn't ready to surrender the floor. To Lauren and Steve: "You have such a bright future. I've seen it in you, Steven, since you were little. I know you both have your dreams, as all of us have at a young age. I'm so...." She brought her fist to her mouth, finally overcome. "That's all I can say. I wish you the love from all of the people who couldn't be here tonight." Never mind that Evelyn spurned the young couple's suggestion of a country club reception several weeks out for those who hadn't made the journey down.

Around the terrace and up in the great room, I could see our family members explaining to little groups.

"What was she talking about?" I heard from one of Steve's pals.

Reyna looked lost, as she received a translation from Isabel. Heinrich was stunned. Others too. Had they heard right? The Cooking School at Z was closing? We were leaving? I felt as if we'd broken trust with so many people, for them to hear it this way.

"Why did you say that?" Mia asked Evelyn, stepping up to her.

"Say what?" she responded innocently.

"About us closing."

"Isn't it common knowledge? Oh dear. It was meant only as a compliment for what you've done."

I felt sure she was lying. Something about her eyes, and the jutting, challenging chin, had no connection to her insincere apology.

"That was a secret," Mia said. "What would make you say that to everyone during a party at my house? This is their night. Your son's night, and our daughter's."

Steve moved in. "I asked you not to say anything," he told his mother in a sharp tone. "And you promised me." Upset, he turned to our daughter. "Lauren, I told mom because I thought it would help everything."

"I can't believe you did that to my parents," Lauren said to Evelyn. As for Steve, she gave him a hard look, for he'd broken his promise not to tell anyone.

The whole terrace fell still. Our voices had been raised. The *mariachis'* eyes widened. On the upper terrace, the musicians had stopped chewing, their mouths full. Rowan was nervously flicking his fingers, waiting to see where this would go.

"Now just everyone settle down," Harry blustered. Evelyn herself was swelling up with righteousness, as if she'd never been criticized so boldly.

"These people are jealous," Evelyn told her son. "They don't want you living near us. Let's just say that, if we're being honest."

"That's not how we feel at all," I said.

"Let's just watch what we say here," Harry advised.

"'Watch what we say?'" Mia replied. "It's already been said."

Suddenly a *mariachi* cried out on the upper terrace. He'd been leaning to hear, trying to grasp exactly what these crazy Americans were saying to each other, but he'd lost his balance and fell, shattering a glass and tackling a potted hibiscus tree, but fortunately not coming over the edge. He quickly struggled back to his feet.

Lauren told Evelyn, "Today Steve and I invited my parents to launch a restaurant with us in California. That's right. All four of us, instead of our New Jersey plan. But they won't do it. They want us to find our own happiness. So you can't say what you said, because it isn't true."

"I can say whatever I damn well please, young lady," said Evelyn.

"Don't talk to me that way," Lauren shot right back. "I've been bending over backwards to build a relationship that you don't want. You don't want me in your family."

Isabel held her girls against her legs. Harold finally seemed at a loss for words. Daphne stepped closer, to defend her sister if necessary.

"This is crazy," Steve said. "We need to stop this."

"I'm not the one creating the problem," Evelyn said. She looked around for agreement, but everyone was holding their breath, waiting for whatever was next.

Then Evelyn turned to her husband and said in a different voice, "What are we doing here? Come on. We need to leave. All of us," she said, indicating the rest of her brood.

"Mom, what are you doing?" Steve asked.

"Just shut up, Steven," Beatrice told him. The oldest child, Beatrice was also the one, we'd been told, who was the mother's principal sidekick and knew everything.

"You're being stupid," Steven said, sibling to sibling.

"Watch your mouth," said Beatrice's husband, the one who'd loaded up on food. He certainly consumed the calories for a prolonged struggle.

"Watch yours," said Rowan, who'd had more than a few beers. He stepped forward.

"This is what I get," Evelyn said in her son's direction, which sounded like a phrase she'd used before. "After all I've done, and all the effort we've made for you."

"I think everyone needs to calm down," I said.

"Yeah right," said Beatrice's husband.

"Please," Mia said to all, stepping more into the center.

"It's time to go," Evelyn said. "Right now. You might want to come with us, Steven, because we have some things we should talk about." She glared at Lauren, then at Mia and me.

When Steven didn't move, Evelyn shrugged as if it was only to be expected. Spurned, she squared her shoulders and moved toward the stairs, but then turned back dramatically to await her entourage.

"Steven," said Beatrice, "you just have no idea."

"C'mon, we're leaving right now," Harold said. He called individual names as needed.

"You want to step outside?" the aggressive son-in-law asked

Rowan. They'd been staring each other down.

"Stop this," I insisted, stepping between the two young men. I put a hand on the chests of both as they moved close, but the son-in-law pushed my arm aside. "You're in Mexico," I told him to his face. "Dealing with the police would not be good. People go to jail and aren't heard from for months."

I made that up, but it gave him pause.

"We are all leaving," Evelyn announced one last time. She turned and went up the steps, leaving our sight, with her family members, young and old, arrayed behind her on the climb.

I decided to follow them up, to see them out the door. Rowan and Daphne started to join me, but I put an end to that.

Steve's family was already well up the stairs. On the landing between the floors, I saw the angry brother-in-law elbow an antique Talavera vase off its pedestal. The large blue ceramic piece, intricately painted, shattered on the stone steps with a tremendous noise. We normally didn't have it there; Mia had set it out for the special occasion. Even his family, waiting for him by the front door, looked startled.

"What the hell do you think you're doing?" I yelled, coming up, but I was a good distance below.

He cursed me and continued on, surprisingly nimble on his feet. He and Beatrice were the last ones out the door, closing it behind them.

— • —

Mia and I had to acknowledge the truth. Yes, we were being forced to close down the Cooking School at Z and sell Casa Blue.

"We have no choice," Mia announced. "It's financial." People had gathered around us. As the *mariachis* eased through with their instruments, I gave the leader a nice tip.

"This is so awful," said Sophie, giving Mia a hug, then me.

"And that horrible woman. I've never seen a display like that at something like this unless a person was drinking heavily."

"Was that urn like an antique or something?" asked a member of Lauren's swim team. "I saw it when I came in. It was so beautiful."

"I don't want to be criticizing Steve's family," I said, wanting others to hear. "Everyone will apologize before the wedding tomorrow, and we can all move forward from this."

"It's just something that happened," Mia added, also wanting to salvage something for the engaged couple. Steve and Lauren were only now rejoining the group. They'd been talking privately.

Everyone listened as Mia shared the short version of our title dilemma. We ventured our opinion that Izzy, who'd sold us the house, had concealed the problem. Ken corroborated that to our shocked listeners, in a way that made us not look like idiots.

"The cooking school is such an asset," Heinrich said. He kept shaking his head at the shame of it. "My guests love to come."

In my wildest dreams, when Lauren had described the bad chemistry with Steve's family, I had never imagined that the animosity from Evelyn ran so deep, or that she would be so public with it.

"We need to go," Steve told Lauren, not caring who heard.

"Why?" Lauren asked.

"We need to go, we need to be alone. I need to go. I'm sorry. I don't mean to offend anyone. I apologize for all of this."

Lauren looked torn. With an eye movement, Mia encouraged our daughter to go with her man. She took his hand, and off they went, sucking any remaining joy from the terrace. Señor Rodriguez and his family quickly excused themselves as well, after heartfelt goodbyes.

The remaining guests were still incredulous about the fate of Casa Blue. Ken, of course, knew everything, and conveyed the admiration we still enjoyed from all our old friends in California.

"Isabel, Reyna, I'm so sorry," Mia said to them.

Isabel looked completely crushed, as if she were hearing all this for the first time, even though she'd learned it from Stanley. Now it was real. Reyna was sitting in a chair that had been brought for her. Lucy, her youngest granddaughter, was asleep in her lap. Renya's expression spoke of the consequences coming to her and her family, another trial to bear in a difficult life. I felt awful.

Stanley assured Isabel that she would stay on with him. "I'm keeping you with me, kiddo," were his exact words. Isabel still looked miserable.

Phil was teary-eyed, but didn't look that surprised. She may have known, or at least suspected. If so, she had probably kept a secret for the first time in her adult life. But the truth had been outed. The Cooking School at Z would reopen on Monday, but word would quickly get around Zihuatanejo that we were a dying enterprise.

As for tomorrow, did we have a wedding?

— • —

All the remaining troops volunteered to help with the cleanup. Surfaces were wiped with a vengeance, food was discarded, empty bottles were put in a pile.

"I want nothing saved," Mia declared, for no evidence should remain of this night. "Take it with you, or throw it out."

Even Heinrich pitched in, along with a server he'd kept on. Rowan went around snuffing out the candles with spit on his fingers. Donna was actually loading the dishwasher in her good dress before we stopped her. We wrapped desserts for the young people to take back to their hotel. For them, the night had just begun. I unplugged the strings of white lights.

At Mia's request, Heinrich called *Villa Real* to speak with security. We got word that Steve's people were in their suites, but

Steve and Lauren seemed not to be on the premises. We thanked Heinrich profusely before letting him leave. When Steve and Lauren hadn't returned after a decent interval, Rowan, Daphne, Sophie and the last remaining friends went looking for them in the beachside cantinas. Our three returned forty-five minutes later without finding them. The hour was getting late. All the friends and schoolmates who'd come down had returned to their hotels.

Sophie, Daphne and Rowan then headed out once more, to see if Steve and Lauren had gone into Centro.

Stanley hugged Mia before he turned in.

"Lauren's got your spunk," he told her. "She'll be just fine. You get to bed too."

Mia and I were finally alone.

— • —

There was nothing left to say. I cleaned up a few things, just to busy myself. Mia stood at the edge of our terrace, her arms folded tightly, lost in thought. She was facing the bay. Somewhere in that general direction, our daughter and her fiancé might be deep in conversation. Who knew what they were deciding.

I finally joined her.

"What those two young people are going through right now...," Mia said. Fresh tears coursed down her face.

"Yesterday," she continued, "they were looking forward to this weekend as the happiest time in their lives." She shuddered, then tried to take a deep breath. "Somehow all this should have been avoided. I started it. I made the toast about them doing what they wanted, and the restaurant. I had too much champagne. I should never have said that."

"You were speaking from your heart."

"Lauren was completely out of line with what she said to Evelyn. I know she's our daughter, but what got into her?"

"Maybe it's better that everything came out."

"It's not better. It's terrible. Listen, I'm staying up," Mia decided. "I need to talk to her. I hope she doesn't do anything foolish."

"They're adults, Mia. They'll work it out. This is not Romeo and Juliet."

She regarded me. "Sometimes you have just the worst timing."

And so we stood there, and time passed, and the night seemed extra quiet.

"I don't regret that we tried Mexico," Mia said. "I would always have wondered, if we'd walked through this house and flown home and hadn't made an offer."

"I remember the toast with Irma, our one guest at the grand opening, like it was ten minutes ago. Remember her? And how happy you were the day Francine Longman came. We had to try. And we'll try something else."

— • —

At first light, bleary-eyed, I walked to *Playa La Ropa*. Everyone else was still asleep back home.

Dreadful possibilities were running through my head. Perhaps Lauren and Steve had obtained a car and driven off into the Mexican night, unaware that the drug business and the hard ways of Guerrero made that unsafe. Were they camped out at the airport, awaiting a flight? Had they holed up in a rented room in Ixtapa or Troncones?

I checked at the front desk at *Villa Real*, confirming that they weren't there with Heinrich's security people. Thankfully none of Steve's family were up yet. I left a sealed, handwritten, conciliatory note written by Mia to Evelyn late last night, asking for a meeting -- just the two of them -- to try to talk this through, as soon as possible, to rescue the day.

282

The first staff were just beginning their work at the cantinas along *Playa La Ropa*. Noisy, hungry birds were everywhere. A pelican cruised along the wave line. A pair of Mexican men were throwing their hand nets, the droplets sparkling as the gossamer webbing exploded open in the first silvery sun.

Walking back from the southern end of the beach, no longer expecting to find my daughter and her fiancé, I did.

They were behind a coconut tree in an unimproved area. Steve was on his back, sleeping in a casual sprawl. Our daughter lay against his side, her arm draped across him, her head on his chest. They were still in their good clothes from the party. There was every indication that they'd sequestered themselves in this spot all night, perhaps talking intensely until they'd fallen asleep.

And what had they decided?

I noticed, as I moved to awaken them, that they were no more than fifty yards from the unfenced crocodile preserve. I'd spare Mia that little detail until some day when we could all laugh about this, centuries into the future.

24

On that Saturday of the wedding, the women of Eloi's, in their embroidered blouses and long red skirts, congregated at a large metal arch on the beach. With the sun edging into the horizon, their fingers wove vines of trumpet flowers into place for the ceremony. Nearby, two men in black trousers raked the sand. Others had set out thirty or so white folding chairs, enough for the expected guests.

That aspect of the arrangements went smoothly.

Lauren's missing wedding dress had finally been delivered by the airline on Friday in a smashed cardboard box . We had kept the truth of its condition from our daughter. Isabel slipped the wrinkled mess to a trusted dressmaker, who had labored into the night. She had returned it this Saturday morning -- a breath-taking gown once again, with seed pearls and lace.

"You look incredible," I said to Lauren. We were inside Eloi's, ready to go. However, the judge hadn't arrived. Through potted plants I could see the assembled guests on the beach, waiting.

"I just love this dress," Lauren agreed.

Keeping with American custom, Steve had not yet seen her in it. He had, unfortunately, seen his bride-to-be arguing with his mother last night. Working through that triangle relationship would be a challenge. According to Lauren, Steve was one hundred percent in her camp, wanting to establish their own life together.

Last night they'd reaffirmed their commitment to each other under the palm tree, before falling off to sleep.

"You're so beautiful," chimed in Mia, fixing our daughter's veil. Daphne, meanwhile, was fussing with her sister's flowers, to get the ribbons to hang evenly from the handheld bouquet. Tuxes and beautiful dresses were the order of the day, but Lauren and Steve had discouraged shoes. I was barefoot, like the bride.

Finally the *Juez Civil*, the marrying judge, showed up, fresh from another wedding. He pressured us to hurry, as a third ceremony lay ahead on this lucrative evening. His fee, prepaid, was exorbitant and required.

"It's actually happening," Mia said to me, so excited.

"From here on, it'll be fine," I said. "Put everything else out of your mind. Our oldest child is getting married. That's all that matters."

"We raised a great kid," Mia said.

"We absolutely did."

The judge hurriedly reviewed a few points with us, then took his position on the beach. Mia hooked Rowan's arm. It was time. She grinned, raised her eyes half-seriously -- could this be happening, finally? -- and off they went, stepping out of the cantina's shadows and proceeding down the aisle of raked sand.

The Wedding Song soon began playing on the beach, which was our signal.

"Ready?" I asked Lauren. Two of the Mexican women smiled approvingly at the bride, and gestured for her to go.

And so Lauren and I strode into the sunlight, with Daphne, the maid of honor, leading the way in a ruby, off-the-shoulder dress of raw silk. Two matching dresses were packed in the luggage of Steve's sisters, or perhaps those gowns had been left behind in the trash. I never wanted to know. Evelyn had responded to Mia's note, saying simply that she deemed it best to leave. Their entourage had actually flown home earlier in the day. It had a stunning effect on all of us.

As we marched in, Steve was waiting under the arch with the best man, a longtime friend who'd flown in from Amsterdam. With the sisters not participating, Rowan and another groomsman had backed out of the wedding party. Isabel and her family were sitting with Stanley, Phil, and the Rodriguez clan. They and everyone else were turned to watch the entry of the bride.

"Tell me I can do this," Lauren whispered. She was tearing up, perhaps a delayed reaction to all the trauma. She squeezed my hand.

"You can," I whispered. "It's what you want."

"I hope we're as good as you and mom."

"You'll be marvelous together."

The wedding would take place where the stretch of dry, soft sand ended, just before the beach hardened and sloped down to the water. Mexicans had spontaneously convened in their bathing suits, along with a smattering of tourists -- perhaps a hundred in all, arrayed in a crescent, keeping a respectful distance. Daphne read from the Song of Solomon; Steven's best man read a poem about the true nature of love. Three musicians played stringed instruments, and sang in English and Spanish.

The judge asked if anyone had reason why this man and this woman should not be joined in holy matrimony. An awkward silence and a few coughs ensued.

"The reasons should be touching down at Houston's airport about now," I whispered to Mia beside me.

"Shush."

I thought it tragic that Harry, Evelyn and their family had turned their backs on this day. Steve and Lauren had reaffirmed to themselves, and to us, their decision not to be deterred, but the absence of his family couldn't be overlooked. The months ahead would require some difficult conversations, once they were back in Chicago.

286

After the vows, and after rings were exchanged, the assembled crowd began chanting, "*Be-so, be-so*," demanding a kiss. Lauren and Steve obliged, to much laughter and applause, not once but twice.

Just then the whir of an outboard motor caught everyone's attention. It was Guy, who'd promised to make it. He pulled his Zodiac up on the sand. Daphne, who was standing by the bride, looked overjoyed as her young man gave her a conspiratorial wave and slipped into the seating. The Five Seasons had been expected in port yesterday, in time for our Friday night party, but contrary winds had helped us on that one.

— • —

Why should the arrangements for Eloi's have been any different than our other dealings with property owners in Mexico?

Weeks ago, on behalf of Steve's parents, Mia had paid the patriarch, Eloi, a "location fee" that far exceeded the receipts from his regular Saturday night patronage. In return, he'd agreed to restrict the cantina to only our party for this night.

But Eloi had died three weeks ago. Eloi's wife, daughter and two sons all had equal say in the business now, and couldn't agree whether to honor the original contract with us -- but they were in unison about keeping the location fee. As we all moved inside for the reception, after posing for photos, the bar was filled with sandy, boisterous cantina patrons, who applauded the bride and groom. The music started, the dancing began.

I was telling a couple from the bar that it was a private party, that the dancing was only for our guests, when Lauren took my elbow. "Dad, let it go," she said.

"You're sure?"

She nodded.

"Come join us," she told the twosome I'd intercepted. He was in a Señor Frog T-shirt and surfer shorts, she was in a two-piece with a gauzy blouse knotted at the waist, and here was Lauren in her wedding gown waving them in. Steve and Lauren actually had moves. People formed a circle and cheered them. In all, about a dozen people drifted over from the bar, and we ended up with a packed, motley crowd that jammed the dance floor as a DJ played old rock favorites. The party grew raucous, and people cheered wildly when the cake was cut. A tape blasted *Querida Esposa*, a song about everlasting love. Our daughter's instincts had been right, I came to realize, because the bar crowd brought added enthusiasm to offset Steve's missing family.

Later, as the music began to wind down, Mia found me and said, "We should tell all our people to come up to the house." She was sweaty from dancing, with tendrils of dark hair matted on her forehead. She looked lovely beyond words.

"Let's check with Steve and Lauren," I suggested.

"I just did. They said they'd come up in a little while. Actually, maybe we could just walk along the beach first."

I looked around one final time. Phil was on the dance floor again, her arms upraised, hips moving and knees flexing, in the midst of the bar crowd. Ken and Donna were mixing it up with the bride and groom's young friends, working on a Texas two-step now blaring. Isabel was dancing with her girls, and Diego was part of that. I sensed something beginning between the two of them.

Mia collared Stanley and the three of us went down to the water, where we ran into Rowan, the tip of his cigarette aglow in the dark. Sophie was with him, playing that child's game of trying to stay just out of the water's reach, holding her dress up to her knees as she scurried in bare feet. They were in love, I realized.

As the five of us made our way down the beach, the night provided a warm, briny stillness, with an astringent note from the palms.

"Aren't they great together?" Mia said of the newlyweds.

"Good kids," said Stanley. "A good marriage. The hell with

288

what his mother says."

He and I were still in our tuxedo shirts. My bowtie hung loose; his hung out of his pocket. Rowan had his sleeves un-cuffed, so they extended well beyond his hands, like a little kid in oversized jammies. Sophie had an arm around his waist.

"That's a problem they need to deal with right away," Mia said. "His family shouldn't have left. I'm sure Evelyn was the instigator when they got back to their rooms, but who ever heard of that kind of behavior? I wonder if she never wanted to be here. She was so against the destination wedding in the first place."

We exchanged pleasantries with a passing German couple with their dog on a tight leash, so it wouldn't slobber on the dresses.

"Which house is Casa Blue?" Rowan asked.

I picked it out for him amid the constellation of lights on the hillside.

"That place can't leave the family," our son said. "I like telling people in L.A. I have a place in Mexico with house staff. And you guys are so happy down here."

"This is not the night to talk about that," Mia said, but she took his free arm appreciatively. Rowan now had a woman on either side.

"We had this experience," Mia continued. "We pursued a dream. Now we'll move on. Your father and I have come to grips with that."

I think everyone understood how untrue that was.

— • —

We spread the word about our family gathering back at Casa Blue. Taxis were summoned. Daphne and Guy chose to walk back, and Sophie and Rowan went with them. Heinrich, Ken, his wife, and others said good night, thanking us profusely. Isabel and her family had left earlier in a car we'd arranged for them. Only the young friends of the couple were staying on, to party with the bar crowd probably into the wee hours.

Gradually our core group assembled around the terrace table. Mia brought out wraps for the women, as people were cooling down after all the action. Stanley and Phil sat together. I made coffee and brought wine, beer and hard liquor to the table, as well as some leftover chocolate macaroons. We kept pulling up chairs as people arrived.

Eventually Lauren and Steve joined us. Our daughter had changed into casual clothes, but she kept the wedding veil on her head.

Steve was actually next to me. We made eye contact, and I said something reassuring while others were critiquing the wedding. No one was bringing up the subject of his family. In truth, the pall of the morning gradually passed once the wedding began, as everyone closed ranks in their hearts, determined to make it a fine day for the bridal couple. Steve seemed strong, and surprisingly at peace.

"Mom, you're crying," Lauren said at one point.

"I'm not crying," Mia said. "I just have a little wedding cake in my eye."

It was so ridiculous, people had to laugh.

"I can't believe how much you did to make this a great wedding," Lauren said to Mia, loud enough for all to hear.

"And your father," Mia said. "Don't leave him out."

"It was a wonderful party," said Guy, which was surprising to hear from him.

Mia and I were given a toast and a round of applause.

"I just wish it had worked out with your family," Mia told her new son, for all to hear. She choked back tears.

"We're going to see them as soon as we get back from the honeymoon," Steve said. "We can make something happen. This needs to be addressed, and aired out, and we all move on like a family."

"We're going to do an intervention," Lauren said.

"I thought your mother hardly drinks," I said to Steve.

"But we do. We'll drink before we go there."

Lauren's wry humor lightened everyone's mood. I was proud of Steve, and Lauren, for their decision, for not avoiding the situation. Mia regarded Steve fondly, and even touched his cheek.

"But that's all in the future," Lauren said, popping up from her chair. "Right now, there's a little gift that needs to be presented."

Taking his cue, Steve stood too. The couple disappeared up the steps. To the extent that I'd been reserving judgment, I appreciated at that moment what a good young man our daughter had married. Together they were strong.

A lot of stage murmuring began about what they'd gone for. I sensed that most everyone seemed to know. I could tell by the look on Phil's face that she definitely was in on the conspiracy. She winked at me.

Steve came back down carrying a heavy box more than two feet square, beautifully gift-wrapped, with a bow of gold-laced ribbon that I recognized. Mia and I had used that ribbon for the Cooking School at Z's grand opening, the day when Irma was our only guest, back in what seemed like another lifetime.

Lauren joined Steve in placing the heavy gift in front of Mia.

"Open it," she said.

"What did you do?" Mia protested.

"Open and find out," Steve insisted.

Mia had to stand, because the box was so big. She slowly loosened the ribbon. She cleared away the wrapping, doing it reverentially, and wondering aloud several times what it could possibly be.

Steve helped her bring forth a very large Talavera-style water bowl, rich in the polychrome blue tone that in Mexico portends good luck. It featured a painted banner with a lemon yellow background. On it in plain script, *The Cooking School at Z* had been lettered by an artisan. Beneath the banner was a rendering of women preparing and cooking food, amid fruit and flowers that continued all the way around the bowl.

"I ordered it a long time ago," Lauren said, emotional now, touching her mother's hair. "It's a long involved story...."

"Everything in Mexico is a long involved story," said Mia.

"...But the artist is a wonderful potter who Phil put me onto."

"We hope you like it," Steve said, kissing Mia, hugging her.

"And whatever happens," said Lauren, "wherever you go, it'll always be yours. It's from Steve and me, for you and dad."

"Well," said Stanley, having the last word, "whatever happens now, you'll always have a pot to pee in."

25

But what happened to the Cooking School at Z?

We had a pot to pee in, and we had the indelible memory of that post-wedding celebration on our terrace, surrounded by bright stars and swooping bats, with the slap of the waves in the background as our children ultimately stirred up another round of drinking and dancing. Rowan stumbled hard on the dance floor, and the next day his toe was swollen, but fortunately not broken.

The story, of course, does not end there.

Mia and I reopened for business two days after the wedding. Patrons flowed into the Cooking School at Z all that week. Mia and I found it so affirming, and unbearably sad.

We couldn't bear to put Casa Blue up for sale until the following weekend, even though the deadline was fast approaching. Mia and I needed a week of normalcy for ourselves after the wedding, after all the trips to the airport and the goodbyes, before we could once again face the inevitable.

"Let me tell you my secret to preparing tuna," Mia told our aproned guests every morning. "Twelve seconds a side. Or you say a Hail Mary, turn it, then say another. The tuna comes out heavenly." And every time, people laughed and clapped.

The women wanted to know every detail of our daughter's destination wedding in Zihuatanejo, which Mia was delighted to share (leaving out the in-laws entirely). She had photos as well.

The men's eyes glazed over after the first few minutes, but they were ignored. The relative merits of destination versus traditional weddings were hotly debated.

The hotel managers were discreetly inquiring whether we were still open. Individuals with reservations started contacting us to see what the story was. The word was quickly spreading.

"The phones aren't ringing as often," Mia said during the second week after the wedding. We were walking the shoreline at Troncones, north of Zihuatanejo, having felt a need to get away from Zihuatanejo, if only for a Sunday afternoon. A number of surfers were working the waves, some Mexican, most of them foreigners.

"We just keep going," I said with a shrug.

"Look at that little boy," Mia noted.

A naked Mexican child was enjoying himself in a big hole in the sand that his doting father had dug for him, at a point just barely reached by the waves. The little boy waved his arms enthusiastically and laughed whenever water gently flowed in, sharing his mirth with his dad, then with us as we drew near.

"Why isn't life that simple?" Mia asked, squeezing my hand as we passed.

— • —

Our local real estate agent, an ex-pat New Zealander named Irene Fergus, had listed Casa Blue on two community websites that post Zihuatanejo properties up for sale. My digital pictures of Casa Blue didn't do justice to our home -- no still shots could capture its magic -- but my flowery prose waxed on about the view, the terrace, the architecture and the brief walk to *Playa La Ropa*. Mia couldn't bring herself to look at any of our advertising.

The initial inquiries came from local people. What a shame! Did we have plans for the pottery collection? How firm was the price? Were we showing the property? But no serious offers materialized. The word spread quickly about our title dispute with the very powerful aristocratic family from Mexico City, known to be people politically connected at the highest levels.

"The title issue scares everyone off," said Mrs. Fergus, who didn't color her short, steely gray hair. She was always dressed impeccably, and had a favorite pearl necklace -- the freshwater kind, with a lavender sheen. She tended to fiddle with her pearls, out of compassion, when she had to tell us something that wasn't uplifting. She was a breast cancer survivor, and Mia and I agreed we would have become staunch friends if we'd had a future in Zihuatanejo.

"You don't have all the legal protections here that you enjoy in the States," she reminded us. "And your house has a history. People, I'm afraid, do factor all that in. Two owners with bad luck, and no one wants to be the third, with this title dispute looming over everything."

We'd listed Casa Blue at a very attractive price -- less than we'd paid, which was humiliating. If there was no serious offer after two weeks -- so little time! -- our plan was to lower the asking price sharply, to a level that was dreadful to even think about. We simply had to have a buyer lined up by the deadline, so we could pay off our neighbor, sell the property, and salvage some of our investment to help us start over in the States. Otherwise, our neighbor could take us to court, where their political influence would spell doom, and we couldn't afford attorneys anyway ... or, we could choose to sell Casa Blue to them for a pittance, as our only alternative.

Who knew what they would do if we missed the deadline? The bulldozer was gone from our neighbor's property, without finishing its work. Large piles of excavated dirt and rock gave no hint to what they were planning. That too could be a deterrent to a potential buyer of our house. People would want to know what was coming next door.

"The truth is," I told Ken on the phone, "they have all the cards." I was idly picking dead blossoms from the a potted yellow hibiscus on the terrace.

"The offer we negotiated is still out there. That's what you paid Señor Juan Serna Lozano for, to get an offer on the table." He said each syllable of the name with mock reverence. "Don't fade to black yet."

"How about your builder clients? Why wouldn't one of them give me a loan? We could boost the interest rate to whatever's needed." A lizard skittered up to my bare foot, then reversed direction.

"It's not something people I deal with would want to do. You're in Mexico."

"How about you?" I had the audacity to ask. "You understand this whole thing. Just a loan we could pay back. You know we would."

"Jeff," he said.

"I'm serious."

"I know you are. I feel your desperation. I'm your attorney, not your banker. Let's stay focused."

Through all of this, Mia insisted that I keep her posted on every detail of the offers, no matter how small. After the title insurance debacle, and given my history in making money decisions, she was staying close to the deal.

— • —

Making a bad situation worse, The New York Times published a big story in early April about a fresh outbreak of kidnappings in Mexico City.

Then four days later, delivering a one-two punch to the country's image, the worldwide media put out news accounts of the Mexican army dealing too harshly with a drug ring in the interior of Guerrero, with a number of indigenous people killed, many of them innocent according to locals. I remembered Reyna's story about *El Arracadas*, and could only wonder.

Regardless, these headlines were having a chilling effect on the real estate market, according to our Mrs. Fergus.

— • —

I called Ken one afternoon when Mia was out. I didn't want her hearing this.

"I have something new to put in the equation," I said. "I'm prepared to go back to the States and work in the off season to help generate money to pay back a loan."

He laughed, which surprised me. "You're a true Mexican, Jeff. You'll come north of the border to feed your family."

"Whatever it takes, I'll do it. I can put a job together. Or two jobs."

"May I ask what Mia's take is on that?"

"I'm not telling her for now."

That brought silence. I was in the grand room, amid all the marvelous ceramics and pottery we'd be leaving behind, my gaze fixed on the hazy Pacific far away.

"Jeff, from me you want honesty. No builder or anybody else I know is going to make you a loan on property that's in a trust in Mexico. I'm sorry to have to tell you that. Whether you work here part of the year is immaterial. But maybe it will make a difference with some of the other people you've been reaching out to."

"It hasn't yet," I said.

— • —

Phil's network discovered a one-room efficiency that could be available to Stanley the first of June. It was on the ground floor of an old two-story stucco complex with six units, toward the largely undeveloped south end of *Playa La Ropa*.

"Dad, I think it's perfect for you," Mia said as we all performed an inspection. Twin beds. A small, decent bathroom. "You step right outside to this little terrace here. You have this outdoor cooking area that's protected, and this tile counter, and the table and chairs to eat your meals."

"And look," said Phil, who'd come along. "You step right onto the beach. What do you think?"

"I wish it was twice the size."

"It's the same space you had in Brooklyn," Mia noted. "You're spoiled at Casa Blue. To have *Playa La Ropa* at your front door, this is reality."

Arguments were made for and against. Some retirees from Commonwealth countries were playing horseshoes and jabbering in a nearby grove of sea grape trees, as they did every day. Stanley could insinuate himself, and they'd no doubt argue politics, which would force blood to his brain. The month-to-month rent was affordable now that high season was over. Before the end of the year he could move to the States to join us.

He and Mia had wrangled about that strategy. Finally lines were drawn in the sand: Stanley could stay on temporarily in Mexico as he wished, tended by Isabel, befriended by Phil, until our situation clarified back in the States. Once Mia and I found work and suitable housing, he'd come north. Still, it was hard for Mia to think of leaving her father. Stanley's swimming regimen had brought him back to his old self, however, and everyone was committed to monitoring his meds. Stanley was happy, he had a life here and people around him. And of course he'd insisted that he might decide in the end to stay on in Mexico. Mia couldn't foreclose his options. God forbid.

"Take this place, Stanley, before it goes," said Phil, whose ankle was in an Ace bandage from a recent stumble. "If you don't like it after a month, we'll find something else."

"Isabel can get here on the bus," Stanley conceded. He'd made clear -- more often than needed -- his sense of obligation to the young woman who had rescued him. Isabel was enshrined in the hall of fame, next to the MASH doctors and nurses who had saved his life in Korea. Stanley also remained adamant that Isabel would make him fluent in Spanish, and he was still teaching her English.

"I think it's a great deal," I said of the unit.

"It's what you want," Phil assured him.

She and Stanley saw each other every day now. Where that relationship would go was another question. They were clearly beyond friends in their caring for each other, but Phil still had a husband. It was a subject no one was prepared to bring up. We half expected that in several months, when we were ready for Stanley to come north, they'd present a united front about his staying on in Mexico. Truth be told, they were a couple in most senses of the word, but their values were from another generation.

As for where Mia and I would go to start life over, we had a hard time even talking about that. We hadn't cut the cords attaching us to Casa Blue. Probably back to the San Jose area, if we could afford a tiny apartment in an outlying community.

But many times a day now -- this we did talk about -- we'd each have our moments.

"I was arranging things with Isabel this morning at the cooking island," Mia said. "And it just came over me that pretty soon it will all be over. We won't be arranging flowers in the morning. And Isabel caught my eye, while I was sort of frozen with this thought, and I know she knew exactly what I was thinking. She had this embarrassed, emotional look for just a fraction of a second, and then she went inside so I could cry in privacy."

"I was watering your garden for you a little while ago," I said. "The next owner's not going to keep a vegetable garden, whoever it is. I felt goofy standing there with the hose, because some of those new plants won't come in in time. I felt like I should have pissed on it all."

— • —

The day before our plan called for drastically lowering the asking price -- late on a Sunday morning, still our only day off -- Mia and I returned from an errand to find a message that Ken had phoned.

Stanley had taken the call. He'd left a written note in his scribble, which only Mia could decipher. His sevens looked like ones. At first I thought it read that Ken had died, not called.

Mia and I weren't eager to call Ken right back. The phone conversations with him were always emotional downers, in part because he'd taken it upon himself to keep reminding us of the looming deadline. Frankly, I wanted a day off from him.

As we headed to our room to change, Mia said, "So dad must have gone. I'm glad Phil made him do it."

Stanley had said he wouldn't go sailing again with Phil and her friends on the Five Seasons, which was back in Zihuatanejo, because he didn't want to field everyone's questions about his future and that of Casa Blue. Nor did he want to discuss Guy and our Daphne with the captain and his wife. Guy had in fact gone to New York, where he'd secured a job at a French bistro in Park Slope. Technically he roomed with two of Daphne's friends, but from what we could tell, Guy was spending plenty of time at our daughter's place.

A decision was imminent from the two of them about whether they were going to sail to New Zealand when the Five Seasons undertook that journey -- soon now, before the season for tropical storms. We'd asked Rowan to lobby against it with Daphne. He was flying to New York during the coming week, for a job interview with a late-night talk show and to spend a few days with Sophie.

— • —

We changed into other clothes; I made bloody marys. Mia settled into one of the slingback chairs on our terrace, overlooking Zihuatanejo Bay. I also prepared some tuna, and presented it on one of our small, tan, Michoacan platters. For dipping, I'd put together some minced jalapenos and onion, cilantro, oil, and a touch of balsamic vinegar. Today was the chef's day off. My turn to serve, I insisted, not letting her get up.

Not two minutes after I sat with Mia, the phone rang inside. I grumbled as I went to answer it. It was a couple registering for the Cooking School at Z. I took the registration, then brought the phone and the reservation book outside with me.

During breakfast Mia had said she wanted to talk about anything but Casa Blue today, so we discussed the newly weds. They were now back in Chicago, where it had been cold and rainy all week according to the Internet. Lauren and Steve had bravely gone to his parents' house, uninvited. Mia had been pressing our daughter to apologize for her angry words at the Friday night party, regardless of whether Evelyn apologized or even thought she'd done anything wrong. See what happens, Mia advised. It's a first step. Don't go near Evelyn's decision to fly home before the wedding.

"That was about the most difficult thing I have ever done," Lauren had said in a three-way phone conversation yesterday. "I almost couldn't get the words out."

"You took responsibility for your part," Mia reassured her. "You stepped up. You cleared the air and opened the door to a relationship. How was Steve?"

"He apologized too, for not emphasizing enough that it was a secret about your problem with Casa Blue. But she knew it was. We were just play acting as if she hadn't understood, so she could save face."

"And...."

"And Steve's father privately thanked him in the kitchen for saying that. He was very appreciative. I think he's on our side. And I guess there was a big argument in Mexico about leaving, because one of the sisters was adamantly against it, and Harold was on the fence. Anyway, Steve and I were very concise. We didn't apologize like we were responsible for everything that happened. We said it all needed to be talked about some day."

"How did Evelyn take that?"

"She started to be her righteous self, but Harold shut her down, thank God. That's progress. We gave Harold the snapshots you sent, the ones with their family in them. I had them in my purse, so I could call an audible. It felt like I should."

"Now it's entirely Evelyn's turn," Mia said. "And if you have any contact with her, you're clear now. You can act normal."

"We're going to cut her off if she starts a rant about us and our restaurant plan. But politely."

"Perfect," I said.

Mia and I then discussed whether the dishwasher -- it had to be working perfectly if we were going to sell the house -- was cleaning the dishes properly. And so we were talking about Casa Blue once again. There was no escaping it.

— • —

Before we got around to phoning Ken, he called again. I took it on the terrace.

"I have a proposal for you," he said straight off.

I was completely surprised.

"Really?"

"I've been speaking with Max," Ken said. "You know we're getting short on time here."

"What's the proposal?"

Mia was washing the tuna platter, even though she wasn't supposed to touch a dish today. She turned off the faucet so she could listen. I urgently jacked my thumb toward the house -- she should get on the extension -- but Mia didn't budge. She found it too excruciating to participate in these calls, but would milk every detail from me afterward.

"I want you to think about what I'm going to say," Ken cautioned.

"Did you get us an extension?" I held my breath, afraid to hope.

"I assume you were serious when you said you would return to the States to work."

"I was." I also was glad Mia wasn't on the extension, hearing this for the first time from someone else.

"Here's the deal," Ken said. "Max and I are willing to put in the hundred and ten thousand. It's mainly Max."

"You and Max?"

"Under two conditions. First, we change the ownership into a Mexican business corporation. This can be done, it's not hard. Then Max and I can fully secure our interest against the property. It's just good business."

I was back on his words about putting in the money.

"Are you there?" he asked.

"Yes, I'm here," I managed to say.

Mia silently mouthed, "What?" I raised a finger for her to wait.

"You're surprised, I know. We're really not interested in owning Casa Blue, okay? Neither one of us. Hawaii's my place, and Max has a second home in Florida. So don't feel threatened. It's just a way of creating a little mortgage because you can't get a sane mortgage down there."

"I understand."

"But, you have to pay it back over a few years with an attractive rate of interest. Max is a businessman. He's providing most of the money, and he's doing this as an investment, not because you're a swell couple. If you can't make payments, you'll have to sell. You with me?"

"I think so."

"Condition two, and I have to be blunt. You have to work in the States, Jeff, starting soon, to earn some money for six, seven, eight months out of the year during your off season. And you have to keep doing that to create the cash flow, unless the Cooking School at Z makes you rich, which I don't think either of us anticipates, but crazier things have happened. That way it's reasonable to think you might make the payments, not just a prayer."

"Okay."

I looked at Mia, to communicate that this call was something major. My eyes were probably popping out of my head like a poached fish.

"So you and Max would put the money up?" I said it so Mia could know what was happening.

Mia screamed something.

"Say hi to Mia. I heard her reaction. Now you tell me," Ken continued, "why you think you could come back to the Bay Area and find decent work on a half-year basis."

"What I've done for twenty years is sell. If you can sell, there are always opportunities."

"Then my suggestion is you get on a plane and spend the next month looking around up here, so you feel confident you can find work. I want to hear that from your lips. That's key to the deal. You need to express confidence. I don't want you backing into this and it blows up."

"I'm there."

"We'll draw the documents and take care of all the other crap in time for the deadline, which is fast approaching, my friend. Mia's going to have to do without you part of the year. I'm sorry to have to say that."

"What would we be paying, and for how long?"

Ken cited a term of several years, and a rate of interest that certainly wasn't my dream rate.

"If we don't generate enough money to pay you back, Mia and I could lose Casa Blue. That's what you're saying."

"Don't think of Max as a rich uncle. He's a good man, with a wife and and a lot of kids. This is strictly an investment on his part, as if you were investing in -- I don't know -- British Columbia. He's not Scrooge, but he's not Santa Claus. He's no different than a bank would be. By the way, I do have a client who keeps a flat in North Beach, and he doesn't use the place very often. Maybe you and he could work something out for a rental if you find work in San Francisco. I'm just talking out loud here."

"I don't know what to say, except yes."

"Thank Donna. My wife's been kicking me to make something happen for you two, after seeing your place at the wedding. You're the only couple in all the crowd to go do something like this. And it feels right for you down there."

Mia was holding on to me. My excitement had become hers, even though she didn't know the particulars. Now she moved off, squeezing her eyes in ecstasy that the impossible had happened. She made fists of victory.

"You two discuss it," Ken said. "Call me after eight tonight, that's when Donna's sister should be gone. I got kids underfoot in every room."

"Ken, this can happen? You're sure?"

"The deal can happen with Max involved, and it helps that he's Mexican. Call me. And think about what you're committing to before you do."

"I don't know what to say."

"You're repeating yourself." He laughed. "Call me later."

Ken hung up.

"Tell me," Mia insisted.

"Ken's friend Max, the attorney, is going to make the loan, and Ken will be a small part of it too."

"You're kidding me," she said.

"It's real. You heard me ask him."

Mia whooped, her arms extended like a soccer star who'd just made the winning goal. We both acted silly, strutting around. I lifted Mia off her feet and spun her.

"There's one other thing," I said, with Mia in my arms.

"What?" Her mood instantly changed to wariness. Something in my expression must have given me away. She stepped back.

"I have to agree to go to the States for six to eight months out of the year, to work, until this is paid off. I'd be here at Casa Blue for four or five months, when the cooking school is busy."

"That's part of the agreement?" Mia asked. She was shocked.

"I suggested this privately to a few people, Ken included, thinking it might help us get financing. I just never dreamed Ken would take the initiative himself."

"I can't imagine you not being here and doing this, and neither can you," I said. "The cooking school is catching on. We know it's going to work. We just need this one loan."

"And what would you do, living up there?"

"Work. I'd deal with it. Seven days a week. You're looking at a motivated person. And who knows, maybe I'd get a dozen credit cards and do a juggling act. Somehow, I'll make it work. We'll need that money in the off season."

Mia stood there, processing this. Our future was on the table. This was a huge decision.

— • —

Thirty minutes after we received the offer, Mia and I were walking along the tide line on *Playa La Ropa*. Mia was wearing her big straw gardening hat. She'd been getting too much sun lately. She had a *pareo* wrapped around the waist of her bathing suit. We felt we had to get away from the house for this discussion.

"I could fly down sometimes," I said. "You'd be alright here with your father."

"How happy would you be, living like that?"

I patted a mongrel that came up to sniff my crotch. It was straining on one of those blue nylon leashes that stretches out of a canister. The dog's owner, an embarrassed young woman, apologized, but I smiled and waved her off.

"I could manage."

"We've dealt with other things. I guess we could deal with it. I just wasn't expecting anything like this."

I took her hand as we maneuvered around Mexican teenagers playing soccer on the hard sand. Girls, boys, showing off, laughing, calling out for the ball.

"We came here so we could be together and start a new life," Mia said. "And now we're going to live apart?"

"It's not forever. I can't imagine it would last more than two years. Three on the outside."

"And what do you see yourself doing?"

I launched into a spiel about advertising sales, or exploiting my old real estate and shopping center contacts for work, or maybe selling online for another income source as a second or third job. I'd have a better idea after I went up there, I told her.

"It's my responsibility to do this."

"Because you lost all our money?" Mia asked. "You're back on that again."

"Yes."

"Well, you also made all that money, which was pretty impressive."

"Whatever," I said. "We belong here. This is home now. And there is no other way for the moment."

Mia stopped in the shallows, as a wave rushed past our ankles. I joined my hands around her neck. She gave me The Big Look.

"Sometimes I'm amazed at us," Mia said with a great deal of love. "There's a part of me that feels like I should say no, but I'm not going to do that. We will make this work. We'll make the Cooking School at Z succeed. I'll try to find private catering, I'll host parties, I'll do anything we can think of, to get this separation over with. I'll take in boarders. Whatever we need to do, until you're here full time again."

"Our luck's turning," I said.

And at that moment, we had our decision. The Cooking School at Z would live to see another year.

I moved in for a kiss, clumsily bumping her straw hat as I ducked my head. Mia grabbed the hat before it fell in the water. After a long kiss, like a couple of newlyweds, we held each other tightly.

It was an embrace for the ages, but it only lasted until a soccer ball bounced off my head. At first the Mexican boys and girl were totally silent. Then we all broke into relieved laughter.